PRAISE FOR *THE LESSER DEAD*

"Buehlman offers up a colony of fierce, brazenly unscrupulous vampires who reclaim the genre from angsty goths and return it to its fearsome and ferocious origins . . . The sharply witty tone and graphic style mine the darker facets of vampirism, while Joey's complex relationship with Margaret and the poignant, prickly camaraderie he shares with Cvetko, an older vampire, add heft and humanity to Buehlman's distinctive, twisty entry into a crowded genre."
——*Publishers Weekly* (starred review)

"Surprising, scary, and, ultimately, heartbreaking . . . I've read a number of good horror novels this year, but Buehlman leaves them all in the dust. His last two books were terrific, and this one is sheerly amazing. If your idea of fun includes being seriously discomfited, grab up *The Lesser Dead* as soon as you can."
——Tor.com

PRAISE FOR *TH~~E~~*

"[An] eruption of characters ~~...~~ ~~...~~ ~~...~~ range from the merely unusual to the bizarrely imag~~...~~ of enthralling fantasy. [A] vibrant, bracing atmosphere."
——*Publishers Weekly* (starred review)

"You find yourself believing the unbelievable and fearing what you thought belonged only in those old-world, pre-sanitized fairy tales."
——Andrew Pyper, author of *The Demonologist*

PRAISE FOR *BETWEEN TWO FIRES*

"Cormac McCarthy's *The Road* meets Chaucer's *The Canterbury Tales* in this frightful medieval epic . . . [Buehlman] doesn't scrimp on earthy humor and lyrical writing in the face of unspeakable horrors . . . An author to watch."
——*Kirkus Reviews*

"Fans of historical fantasy and horror will find this epic darkly rewarding."
——*Publishers Weekly*

continued . . .

PRAISE FOR *THOSE ACROSS THE RIVER*
One of *Publishers Weekly*'s Top-Ten SF, Fantasy & Horror Novels
A World Fantasy Award Nominee for Best Novel

"One of the best first novels I've ever read."
—Charlaine Harris, #1 *New York Times* bestselling author

"What a treat. As much F. Scott Fitzgerald as Dean Koontz. A graceful, horrific read." —Patricia Briggs, #1 *New York Times* bestselling author

"Beautifully written . . . with a cast of Southern characters so real you can almost see the sweat roll down the page. The ending is exceedingly clever."
—*Boston Herald*

"An unsettling brew of growing menace spiked with flashes of genuine terror—do not miss this chilling debut. Christopher Buehlman is a writer to watch. I look forward to hearing from him again. And soon."
—F. Paul Wilson, *New York Times* bestselling author of *Fear City*

"Buehlman's lyrical prose vividly captures a landscape made familiar by William Faulkner and Flannery O'Connor. A delightfully genre-bending juxtaposition of supernatural horror and gothic drama."
—*California Literary Review*

"A horror story that manages just the right balance between building dread and suspense and delivering action." —*The A.V. Club*

"Sublimely crafted . . . It is clear that Mr. Buehlman brings his poetic background to bear in creating the rhythm and meter of the story . . . A well-crafted novel that is a pleasure to read." —*New York Journal of Books*

"In its unnerving depiction of small-town creepiness and heathen savagery, this surefooted debut resembles nothing more than Thomas Tryon's *Harvest Home* . . . Viscerally upsetting . . . This is lusty, snappy writing, and horror fans will eat it up (or vice versa)." —*Booklist*

"Buehlman packs suspense and secrets into his debut novel . . . Keep[s] readers on their toes right up until the big reveal." —*Publishers Weekly*

"Fans of novels like *'Salem's Lot* or classic radio dramas will find this story impossible to put down . . . [It] feels completely fantastical by our rational minds but believable by our deepest fears." —*Suspense Magazine*

Books by Christopher Buehlman

THE LESSER DEAD

CHRISTOPHER BUEHLMAN

BERKLEY BOOKS
NEW YORK

BERKLEY

An Imprint of Penguin Random House LLC
375 Hudson Street, New York, New York 10014

Copyright © 2014 by Christopher Buehlman.
Penguin supports copyright. Copyright fuels creativity, encourages diverse voices,
promotes free speech, and creates a vibrant culture. Thank you for buying an authorized
edition of this book and for complying with copyright laws by not reproducing, scanning, or
distributing any part of it in any form without permission. You are supporting writers and
allowing Penguin to continue to publish books for every reader.

BERKLEY® and the "B" design are registered trademarks of Penguin Random House LLC.
For more information, visit penguin.com.

Berkley trade paperback ISBN: 978-0-425-27262-6

The Library of Congress has cataloged the Berkley hardcover edition as follows:

Buehlman, Christopher.
The lesser dead / Christopher Buehlman. — Berkley hardcover edition.
pages cm
ISBN 978-0-425-27261-9 (hardcover)
1. Vampires—Fiction.   2. Nineteen seventies—Fiction.   3. New York (N.Y.)—Fiction.
I. Title.
PS3602.U3395L47 2014
813'.6—dc22
2014016672

PUBLISHING HISTORY
Berkley hardcover edition / October 2014
Berkley trade paperback edition / October 2015

PRINTED IN THE UNITED STATES OF AMERICA

Cover photographs: woman © Joanna Jankowski / Arcangel Images;
texture © Ensuper/Shutterstock.
Cover design by Judith Lagerman.
Interior text design by Tiffany Estreicher.
Title page image © sorsillo/iStock.

Penguin
Random
House

For Terry White

(That's my aunt. She was a stewardess and model in the seventies. There's a reasonable chance she did cocaine at Studio 54.)

(Don't put that part in the dedication.)

PART 1

FOR STARTERS

I'm going to tell you about a year. This year. 1978. A lot of shit is happening and I think somebody had better write it down before we all forget.

New York City is the place.

If you're looking for a story about nice people doing nice things, this isn't for you. You will be burdened with an unreliable narrator who will disappoint and repel you at every turn.

Still with me?

Too bad for you.

I can't wait to break your heart.

I'm going to take you someplace dark and damp where good people don't go. I'm going to introduce you to monsters. Real ones. I'm going to tell you stories about hurting people, and if you like those stories, it means you're bad.

Shall we go on?

Good. I hate people who pretend they're something they're not.

We're going into the tunnels.

We'll start up here in Chelsea; there's a bricked-up ground-level window with half the bricks out, not a big space but big enough, then we'll go deeper, down where I stay.

Where *we* stay.

I hope bad smells don't bother you.

I hope you brought your own light; I don't need one.

I hope you're not fat.

Here's a little taste of what you're in for, out of sequence, but I told you how unreliable I am. It's not all this nasty, but this is probably rough if you're not used to it. If you can get through this, we can hang out.

We heard them before we saw them. Hunchers. That's what we called people who hunched in the tunnels. We stayed in the tunnels too of course, the deeper tunnels where no sunlight came at all, but we weren't Hunchers.

We weren't even people anymore.

When Margaret saw that her home had been broken into, she didn't hesitate. She tossed off her flip-flops and marched right for the open trapdoor with me behind her, not caring whether I followed, not caring how many of them there were, and there had to be at least two to pull the chain and get that trapdoor up—it was a big heavy bastard of a door made from part of an old subway car and broken-up seats. She walked with one hand balled on her hip, her stained bathrobe open enough to see her tit if you cared to. She was pissed. It was her place, after all. She was our duly elected mayor.

"Goddamn it," she whispered, kicking a peeping shower of rats out of her way. She picked up and threw down a shred of a hamburger wrapper in disgust. Whoever they were, they had brought food. You *don't* bring food into the loops.

They had tied belts together to lower themselves into the hole. A weak light danced down there, a flashlight, and I heard the sound of a lighter. Somebody sneezed a wet one. Somebody else laughed.

She didn't bother with the belts. Just dropped down. I stayed up and watched. This was really a job for one vampire. Normally Old Boy or Ruth would have handled this. Old Boy was like her part-time bodyguard, lived in an abandoned train car just down the tracks past Purgatory, but he was a secretive fucker and you never knew where he was. Ruth was out hunting. She was always hungry.

Turns out there were four of them, the intruders, I mean; black guy and three whites, but with Hunchers the race thing gets less important because they're always dirty and dirt has one color. These guys looked hard, prison tattoos, prison muscles, probably came from the tracks under the Bowery. Guys under the Bowery are mostly wanted men and ex-cons, hunching down there in the piss-smelling dark rather than going back to Attica, which doesn't say much for Attica. They weren't from the tracks above our tunnels. We had a few Hunchers above us, but not many and they knew better; our guys would sooner take a whiz on the third rail than walk into our loops.

"Whoa!" the black guy said when the fast-moving woman-thing in the bathrobe landed near where he lay back on the couch, Margaret's prized antique couch, and he jumped and dropped his flashlight.

One of the white guys said, "Shit!"

Margaret snatched up the flashlight. Shone it at them each in turn. Not that she needed it, just wanted to make sure they were good and night-blind.

Two of them spoke at once.

"Get that out of my face!"

"Bitch, you'd best get out of here if you know what's good for you."

"Don't talk like that to my mom," I said in my high, little-boy voice. I have a great little-boy voice, but I had barely gotten *mom* out before she started. She started by breaking the flashlight on the black guy's head—Margaret's a little racist, but it's not her fault, she's Irish. Or maybe he got it first because he was on her couch. Either way, you know how these things go, everything happens in a hurry. The hurt guy yelled, everybody stood up or tried to, there was a sick *thump* as somebody's head got stove in, then another one, but I admit the gunshots surprised me. I saw it all from the trapdoor, but what did it look like for the poor bastard with the gun?

His muzzle flashes, and there were two, lit up a dead woman with shining eyes and big dirty canines that belonged on a panther. He yelled before she even touched him. One bullet hit her, the second ricocheted madly in the vaulted brick room. And then she touched him plenty.

The last guy tripped over the coffee table trying to find the belt to climb up. She was on top of him then, putting her knee in his back and pulling his head by the hair at his temples while he went, "Gah! Gah!" until she rocked back like she meant it, his spine popped, and he yelled. She pulled his snotrag from where it tongued out of his back pocket and stuffed it into his mouth, this to shut him up, but he lost consciousness anyway.

She stood up then, a little wobbly, and said something garbled. She spat out a rope of blood.

I leapt down, landed on one of the dead guys, pocketed the dropped Zippo, and sat on the wooden chair. Not the couch.

"What was that?" I said.

She spat again, bloody with a tooth in it.

She put up one wait-a-minute finger and I realized what had happened. She was in pain. He had shot her in the mouth and her busted mouth was forming up again. That didn't take long. Eyes take longer. You don't want to get your eye hurt in a fight.

"I said," she said, slurring just a little on top of her thick-as-bread Conny-whatsis accent, "never call me your mother again."

A DOOR INTO NIGHT

I like the taste of sweat.

How it runs from the head, through the hair, like water filtering down through earth and tree roots into a spring; only instead of getting purer, sweat gets filthier, picks up grit, maybe tobacco, a hint of shampoo, but under and through all of that is salt. Almost too much salt, like honey was almost too sweet, what I remember of honey. They say the tongue's cut up into little provinces, salty, sour, bitter, sweet. I don't know if that's true, but I do know that salt is about the only taste I enjoy now. Salt in blood is the best, of course, and blood is a feast: iron-coppery and personal and as good in the stomach as ever was a steak. Sweat can't satisfy, not by itself, but it does hint at what's next. Sweat is to blood as dirty talk is to sex. It's an offer. It's a tease.

If I can, if I'm not too hungry, if I have time, I lick before I bite, with the flat of the tongue like a dog. Maybe your eyes are half-closed because this is sexual for you, or maybe you're good and scared and making that ripe, rotten fear sweat I shouldn't love but do. Maybe my hands are tangled in your hair so you can't run, or maybe you're so charmed you're smiling like an idiot and leaning down to me so if anyone sees, they think I'm telling you a secret. In a way, I am.

The secret is *vampires are real and I am one and no cop is coming and no doctor can help you and your own mother won't believe you if you tell her.* The secret is *I look like a high school freshman but I'm pushing sixty.* And the secret is *I'm stealing from you what is most truly yours and I'm not sorry.*

My name is Joey Peacock. I live in the tunnels under the subways. And don't go thinking the underground is so bad for us. It would be for you, if you're still warm, but things change when you're turned. Darkness isn't so dark anymore. Everything seems candlelit, even the blackest black, so that what looks to you like black dirt and a wall covered with black mold takes on a kind of warm glow for us, full of layer and detail like modern art, not that Guggenheim shit, but the pretty stonework-type stuff. Or like Rothko. You know Rothko? He's at the Guggenheim, but he's different. First time I saw one, I thought, *What's the big deal, squares of color, so what?* But there was something about it. A foxy European chick with a scarf and high boots was staring at it and I said, "What do you see?" and she said, "Just keep looking," so I did. I think she was French. But she was right. The edges of the square of color started waving and then the painting glowed, like it was full of radiation. She said, "Did a door open for you?" and I said, "Yeah."

Night's like that now. It's always been there, full of radiation or whatever, and maybe that's what cats stare at when they look off into nothing but now I see it, too. When I first changed, I used to spend hours under bridges and down under manholes just trying to count the different kinds of black. Only none of it was exactly black anymore. I know I can't make you see it, but it's like *The Wizard of*

Oz, only flipped. Above the tunnels in the neon and lightbulbs, that's like black-and-white, boring-old-uncles Kansas. Down in the tunnels isn't exactly exploding with Munchkinland colors, but it is . . . incandescent. That's a pretty word. That's a five-dollar word, but it works. The tunnels are gently, subtly incandescent. They breathe. They are most certainly not ugly.

Know what's ugly? Sunlight. Even looking at it indirectly is like staring into the jet of a welder's torch, all that light bouncing off the sidewalk and off the chrome of cars. Even peeking at it from the shadow of a manhole cover hurts. Overcast days make us queasy, unless we wear sunglasses. We all have sunglasses.

And don't go thinking that because I live underground I let myself go. I'm a good-looking kid, kind of young Frank Sinatra–ish, and I'm not going to spoil all that by letting myself get ratty-looking. The Hunchers, they don't care, they're here because they're running away or sinking or already sunk. They live on flattened-out pieces of cardboard because they're too lazy to steal rugs and they camp out in Grand Central or Penn Station where people can see how dirty and sad they are and they beg. They let their hair knot up and their fingernails have quarter moons of muck under them; they run around covered in grease and filth and they crawl under their sleeping bags with rats peeping at them and drink brake fluid or sniff glue or cut themselves with broken glass or whatever, but the point is they're nasty. They eat rats, call them track-rabbits. Not all of them are so bad, but most of them. There's one black woman living up above us, mostly on the streets, some-times at Union Square station, I don't know how she keeps the weight on, but she's like an island. Won't look at any of us directly, I think she knows what we are, everyone calls her Mama. Mama has two shopping carts full of stuff, all organized though, like neat. Shoes in one bag, shirts in another. But filthy.

I don't have anything to do with Hunchers, except to feed on them sometimes. Just sometimes. They're mostly full of booze, and booze hurts on the way out, or drugs, which give me a headache. We're much cleaner. Like cats. That's it, they're rats and we're cats. None of them have nice clothes, but that's maybe not their fault. They're poor.

Me, I got money. I charm people out of it all the time, and I use most of it to keep myself looking sharp. I have three mirrors, and don't go believing that baloney about us not reflecting. We reflect. We just don't show up so good in photographs. We blur. You know that guy who never takes a good picture? Ask yourself if you only see that guy at night. If the answer is yes, maybe don't spend any time alone with him, you know what I'm saying? Maybe only hang out in big groups.

Nice clothes are important to me, even if they're hard to keep clean down here. There's a big trough or basin not far from my room; everybody uses that to wash clothes and bathe. Fill it up and you could only just keep your chin above water sitting down, not that we fill it all the way because the spigot's not hooked up and it takes so long to get water from the busted pipe we use. Somebody sunk a big hook in the roof above the basin, a long time ago; it's rusty now, and there used to be a pulley and a rotten old rope hanging from it, but it was in the way so Margaret got rid of it. There's like twenty bars of soap around the tub we use and share, plus a couple of boxes of detergent and an oldey-timey washboard. Me, I hate doing laundry by hand. I keep a jar of quarters for the Laundromat and I use a dry cleaner on 3rd Avenue who doesn't ask questions. I like the mod look: tight coats, paisley, zipper boots. I know I look a little dated when I walk into the disco, and like a throwback when I hit the punk club. Sometimes I wear a fedora, which looks funny on a young guy, but I remember when you'd sooner leave your house without your nuts than without a good hat. I remember when you used to have to take your hat off in elevators and houses and when you spoke to a woman; some people still do that. I don't bother.

We get water from a pipe that's probably been busted fifty years. Just enough water gets out of it to run down the wall and somebody chiseled out a kind of groove near the bottom, like a niche just big enough to fit a bucket into. It takes about a minute and a half to fill a bucket. We have a cheap fold-up table for folding laundry and whatnot, we keep it near that big concrete trough; I think this place, our common place, used to be some kind of a cleaning station. Anyway, there's mold and dirt all caked on the wall except where the water runs out of its rusty pipe, but the wall is clean where the water washes down in a footlong track. The pipe is really rusty, that's how you can tell it's old. Some joker even wrote **RUST** where the water runs, chiseled it into the wall and there's still flecks of white paint in the letters, but the water washed most of it away. People must have been using this for a long time. It's kind of beautiful there, the way we see, though you would probably think it was just a wet wall with crap all around it and a busted pipe. You'd probably rather have a milk shake than a quart of blood, too, so we'll have to agree to disagree. Anyway, I'm glad I have a way to wash my hair. Having clean hair is maybe the most important part of looking attractive.

I love long hair, if it's clean. I don't have long hair myself because it makes it too hard to pass as a kid, and little-lost-soccer-boy is my favorite disguise. Just after sunset I dress out down in the subway, slip my little plastic shin guards under my knee socks, carry cleats in my free hand, and then it's *I got separated from my mom and dad, help me find their hotel across the park.* Works like a charm. I could pass as a little girl, but damned if I'm wearing a dress.

I'm open-minded, but not gay.

ROBERT PLANT AND THE MEXICAN CHICK

Except I am a little gay for Robert Plant.

I saw Led Zeppelin at Madison Square Garden a year or so ago, maybe four or five years, it goes so quick now. Anyway, I was really close to the stage, and there he was. Robert Plant. Long and lean, golden-curled like a woman but wolfy, his hairy belly snug in his jeans, the bacony smell of marijuana warm and close around me (when I remembered to breathe—I forgot for a good half an hour; I know I didn't breathe at all during "No Quarter," and that song went on so long three pearl divers in a row would have died). Plant was right at the peak, as good as he was ever going to get, nowhere to go but gray and fat, and that happens fast. I thought about turning him just to preserve that, the *that* that was Robert fucking Plant in 1970-whatever, but of course vampirism would kill his career, turn him into a talented bum like Billy Bang. More about him later. The undead don't care about careers. Vampires are all retirees, happy enough to bend your ear about what they used to do, but their only passion is for a dark, warm liquid, and the only thing that satisfies them to the bones is getting more. It's worse than heroin, believe me, and I've seen plenty of junkies.

But just thinking about sticking my nose in that big, honey-colored shag of hair on Robert Plant made me pop a boner. A really hard, uncomfortable one, and in my tight jeans, too. I tried to pretend it was for the foxy, spaced-out Mexican girl hip-grinding near me in her midriff shirt and turquoise rings, slinky and stinking of patchouli, but no dice. My dead pecker was hard for Robert Plant. I thought about leaving because I don't think of myself that way, nothing against the gays, but Joseph Hiram Peacock is all about the trim. No way could I leave that concert. It was too good. I love the *shit* out of Robert Plant.

I wanted to try to get backstage, but even if I did, what was I going to do? Bite him? Wave my boner at him? Get him to sign it? When the music was finally done and everyone heaved for the exits, I saw the Mexican girl shouldering her way through the crowd with her friend, a helplessly ordinary brown-haired waitress type with glow-in-the-dark blue eye shadow. That was where *my* night was going. I followed them out.

Down into the subway, which I think of as my front porch (yes, the whole thing) and all the way to the East Village via Union Square. Blue eye shadow lived there, above a rock-and-roll bar, and I was afraid my new girlfriend would go up with her, but she didn't. She kept going, past Tompkins Park, all the way to grimey, crimey Alphabet City, and I followed her, thinking, *Don't take a cab don't take a cab don't take a cab, I'll protect you.*

I saw her go into a moldy-looking brownstone with a big blood-shot eye spray-painted on the side along with a jungle of names and letters in all colors. Bottles in paper sacks in the alley, an egg carton, a warped shopping cart turned over and shot through with weeds. Third-floor light came on, backlighting a *balconeta* with a little garden of potted plants. I skinnied up the brick wall and tapped on the glass. She let me in. They always let me in. It helps that I was turned when I was fourteen, baby face, big blue eyes, thank God I was mostly through puberty. My voice can go either way, which is useful, I've trained it. Before all this started, I had only ever met one little-boy vampire with a permanently high voice, and he made me uncomfortable. I have always felt that whoever turns anyone less than thirteen needs to be taken sunbathing.

So there I was on her third-floor iron balcony, the smell of the iron making me horny for blood, smiling at her where she peeped around the curtain and saying, "You need to water your coriander," through a cracked pane. She understood the third time and smiled back and absolutely should not have opened the French door but did. I mean, there wasn't a fire escape on that side, how did I get up there?

People don't think when they see something they like.

And we're all hypnotists anyway, vampires I mean. We get what we want.

So she cracked the door of her own free will and that was all the invitation I needed. In came my little white hand, pushing the curtain aside, pushing her back, but playfully. Not really, but it seemed like it to her because I was smiling. Her cat was the smartest thing in the room. He didn't like me. He didn't scream and shit himself like they do sometimes, but he decided now was a great time to go in the closet, up on the towels. Fine by me, kitty. Stay out of my way.

"Do you want tea?" she said. Did I want tea! "It's chamomile. I just put the water on." Trace of an accent, like she came to America when she was eleven or twelve. "Or I've got beer." The thought of beer in my empty, black stomach made my empty, black stomach turn. I hadn't fed in days and it was getting urgent. So I charmed her hard.

"My earlobe tastes like cinnamon."

"*Mentiroso*," she said, glass-eyed, her lips staying open after the final *o*. I always remembered that word. I asked Cvetko about it years later and he said, "That means 'liar,'" which is about what I guessed. Cvetko was Slovenian, spoke like eight languages and read even more, but I'll get to him in a minute.

"You don't have to take my word for it," I said, so she leaned in, openmouthed, and I saw her teeth. Dark fillings in the back ones. And she never had braces; her bottom teeth formed a kind of slack W and she had tiny crooked canines sharper than normal. Not sharp like mine, and certainly not as long, but she couldn't see mine because I was charming her not to. You can't see a vampire's fangs unless he wants you to, or unless something startles him good, but it's got to be something big. Terrifying. Then all those unconscious charms go right out the window and you see him just as he is, which isn't so pretty, especially as we get older. But you know what we don't do unconsciously? Blink. When we're around you guys, we have to remember to blink, another reason we like sunglasses.

The Mexican fox leaned close, first sucking then sharply nibbling my earlobe. She giggled and said, "*Canela*," licking her lips, and now it was my turn. I tasted her earlobes and she shivered. Then she wrinkled her nose. Goddamn it, I had forgotten to breathe on the way here so now my breath smelled like a dead dog in a Dumpster. I poured on the charm.

"My breath smells like cinnamon, too."

She unwrinkled her nose and smiled, nodding in agreement, a little bit of drool falling from the corner of her mouth. I was drooling, too, but not because I'd been charmed slack-jawed. I was getting ravenous. I licked her neck. Just once. It was rank with psilocybin, bitter with patchouli, but the salt shone through it all like a nickel in a mud puddle. I got hard again, glad Robert Plant had nothing to do with it. Her jugular vein pulsed delicately, but I was feeling naughtier than that.

"Take your jeans down," I said.

She raised one eyebrow. I like people who can do that; I taught myself how when I was a kid, before all this.

"Take your jeans and panties down," I commanded. She drooled and complied.

She was hairy, but had shaved her thighs at least. Not that I minded hair. Cvetko hated hair. I'll get to Cvetko.

Now I put my nose in the corner where her leg met her hip, Christ-awfully aware of the mother lode of dark, soupy blood coursing in her femoral artery. I licked there, just at the juncture. She moaned a little, then tried to maneuver my head so I could lick her slit. Normally I might have, but I was too hungry. I scratched her thigh with the pricks of my fangs, noticed her cat looking at me from its perch on the towels. Keeping eye contact with the cat, I jammed my fangs into the femoral. The blood jetted around my teeth, flooded my mouth, hot and ambrosial, and now I moaned. My hand was spidered flat on her belly, the tip of my ring finger in her navel. She squealed and squirmed while I drank. She came, I think. I made myself stop at what felt like a pint, took care not to backwash in her. Not that I thought she was going to die—death plus backwash equals new vampire. A pint isn't going to kill anybody, just ask the Red Cross.

I pulled out. Her body jerked. Her teakettle sang. I pulled off my shoe and sock, stuck the sock on her bite wound, put her hand on top of the bite, then closed her legs around that. She was sleeping already, which was normal. Tomorrow there wouldn't even be any holes, they close up fast if you're healthy, but there would be bruising.

I went into the kitchen, turned the stove off, and moved the kettle. Damn it, I was still hungry. In a spasm of poor timing, the cat hissed at me. Fine. I grabbed the little beast, flipped it over (ignoring its flurry of claws—the scratches were shallow, healed almost as fast as kitty made them), and sank my teeth into its belly, stabbing for the big vein there. Cat blood isn't great, but it does the job. I only meant to take a swallow, but I took more and the cat shuddered and became an ex-cat. "Oh, hell," I said. The girl didn't deserve to wake up to a sore crotch, a hangover, and a dead cat. I kissed her temple, holding the cat behind my back, and was just about to make my way out the French doors. I remembered my shoe, put that on sockless, and jumped down all three floors to the dirty street. Left the doors open to support the runaway cat theory.

I walked all the way to Murray Hill with the cat under my jacket before I broke the window of a Buick Centurion and flung it in the passenger seat. Funny that I remember the car but not her name. Was it Yasmina? Did I fuck her around the hand holding the sock to her bite wound, leaving her full of my lukewarm, dead seed?

You would have sex with me if I weren't charming you, right? You saw me and thought I was sexy, I might have said.

I thought you were sexy, she might have slurred back. Or maybe I'm remembering other girls, other nights. I'm not sure. Probably did get with Yasmina, Violeta, Rosa, whatever her name was. Feeding makes you a little drunk and you forget things.

God, she was pretty. I think of her when I hear Led Zeppelin, her face, yes, but mostly the blood in her thigh. And the high-in-the-nose tang of her sweat.

And the teakettle.

CVETKO

Whatever year the Zeppelin concert was, forget that.

This is about what happened in 1978.

It started on Valentine's Day, a couple of weeks after the blizzard.

It was cold enough to make a polar bear put on wool underwear and Cvetko had red envelopes for his letters. I'll get to the letters in a minute, but now it's time for me to try to describe the charmless but endearing calamity that was Cvetko.

Imagine a friend of your parents, someone you knew as a kid, that person from before you were born who came over sometimes and sat around with your dad and mom drinking a little, not too much, talking about the most boring shit in the world and there's no such thing as a radio or TV yet but you have to sit there and not fidget while he goes on and on laughing at his own lame jokes, pushing his glasses up with the wrong finger, not exactly "old" yet but already has that old-man smell like socks and wood and some shaving cream they don't make anymore. And everybody listens to him because he's actually very nice, would loan you money or help you move before you asked him to, one of those guys, but he just doesn't understand that nobody cares about a picnic he took on a mountain in Yugoslavia in 1925 or whether Father Jumping-Jesus sounded nasal after Mass and we all hope he doesn't catch a cold.

Cvetko was Yugoslavian, but he would point a finger up at the ceiling and tilt his head and insist that he was Slovenian. Not much of an accent; to give the guy credit, he had a gift for languages. Once, when God still rode a tricycle, he taught linguistics in that Yugoslavian city that sounds like "lube job."

He came to the loops only two years before, and Margaret didn't want him at first; Margaret didn't want anybody at first, she was not the trusting type. But this poor schmuck. He'd seen some nasty stuff in World War II, lost his family, two boys and a girl. Fucking Nazis. He wasn't a Jew or anything, he was as Catholic as they came, but he didn't sign on with their program. And he says it wasn't actually the Germans that killed his family, it was the Italians, who were allied with Germany then. Except it wasn't actually the Italians who destroyed his house, though it was their fault. Because it was the guys who fought the Germans but got their ass kicked and came south to fight the Italians instead because Italians were pussies, at least next to the Germans, but these partisan guys had bad information and blew up Cvetko's house because they confused him with another professor who had ratted them out, and they didn't like him anyway because he wasn't a commie like half of them were, though he says he is kind of a socialist.

Who can follow all that shit, right?

Anyway, he ended up coming to America after the war, right here to New York City, but couldn't get a job in a university because, and this is the ironic part, they thought he was a commie. Not commie enough for the freedom fighters of Lube Job, too commie for Columbia University. So he ended up teaching in a

Catholic high school in Park Slope, living in Bedford-Stuyvesant, riding his bicycle back and forth like a schmuck. The vampire who got him knocked him off his bike, got him under an el. Never taught him anything, he had to figure it out. He's smart like that, though.

Figured out he should move away somewhere his nocturnal hours wouldn't raise eyebrows, hole up in a place that had a basement. He picked Bushwick because it was quiet and he could afford it, told people he was working at the navy yard. Then the navy yard closed and it wasn't quiet anymore. Twenty years go by fast when you're dead. Now it was 1975. The neighborhood fell apart around his ears; all the blacks and Puerto Ricans were setting fires, burning down buildings. The white people who owned the buildings were playing with matches, too. No shit. Arson to collect insurance, arson to evict deadbeat tenants *and* collect insurance. Arson as pure mischief when you're a ghetto kid. Low water pressure in the summer because the kids are out opening hydrants to cool off, plus Ford told us to drop dead so we fired half the cops and firemen. In short, lots and lots of arson. One thing vampires don't like is fire. So here came Cvetko, into Manhattan, got himself a shithole in the Bowery, but he was already thinking about moving underground when he saw one of us. Ruth, to be specific. Followed her. Asked about her situation, was told he should talk to Margaret. He did. It went okay. He moved in temporarily at the 18th Street station, which is abandoned. That's where vampires on probation go.

He didn't stay on probation long. Margaret had a soft spot for another former Catholic, plus she rapidly figured out that he was smart, if bland. Really bland. Human oatmeal. I took him on as my neighbor half out of pity. You'd pity him, too.

Here's Cvetko in a Polaroid:

Picture a guy about sixty, wearing a suit. He's one of those squares that's always wearing a suit. A sad little potbelly on him, not a big one, but you feel bad for him carrying that around forever—you're pretty much stuck with what you've got when your clock stops. Mostly gray hair going white at the temples, horn-rimmed glasses on crooked, smiling nervously at you even though you just said something mean to him. Familiar but forgettable face, like you'd seen him before, but then, not five minutes after talking to him, all you remember is that he had boring glasses and he was boring.

"You know what it is, writing letters to people you're going to bite, asking them if it's okay? Retarded, that's what. It's retarded, Cvetko."

In this imaginary Polaroid, he's hunched over a letter he's writing with one of those pens you push down different buttons to make different colors. He's writing in blue. On a tablet with that guide paper behind it so you don't curl up with your sentences at the end, which is what I do. But I write on lined paper when I write, which is never, because typewriters are much more my style.

The tablet's on his lap where he sits Indian-legged, hunched like I said as if he's doing something bad. Which I guess he is. Biting people is bad, right? Even if they're lonely or crazy enough to give you permission, which, believe it or not, some are. He's got three or four letters already in their envelopes, red because it's Valentine's Day, stamped with identical thirteen-cent Washingtons praying at Valley Forge like holy little old men in miniature. Normally he'd only send about four letters out, but he likes Valentine's Day so he'll probably do like ten. Yep, look at all those stamps. He's not fucking around.

Polaroid's over. You get it.

"You speak differently than you used to. This word, *retarded*, I think you say it too much."

"Just write your retarded letters."

"You're always picking up new words and using them too much. I think it is the effect of television."

"What do you know about television?"

"I know that between the ages of five and fifteen—or perhaps it was sixteen—the average American child will witness, on this television you love so much, the killing of thirteen thousand persons."

"Where did you get that BS?"

He put his may-I-bite-you love letter carefully aside, walked on his knees in front of his bowed-in-the-middle bookshelf full of egghead books over to one of his stacks of papers, and shuffled in them until he pulled out a mimeographed copy of something. He held it up for me to squint at.

HEALTH POLICY 1976:
VIOLENCE, TELEVISION, AND AMERICAN YOUTH

"Oooo, that's fun. What are you doing reading stuff like that?"

"I read about such things because I am concerned about your habits."

"What, are you afraid I'll turn violent? Guess what? I already am violent. And so are you."

"You're going to have your brain for a long, long time. I do not think you should rot it with unhealthy habits."

I looked out the door to his room: a big metal door on a wheeled track. I wanted to go get dressed up for the hunt. Actually, I wanted to shut his door real hard and stomp off to show him how boring he was. But I wasn't quite that crappy. And he wasn't done yet.

"You are addicted to the television."

"Bullshit, Cvetko."

"You watch it every night."

"So what?"

"So don't watch it tonight."

"I'll watch if I want to. And I want to."

"It controls you."

"No, I just want to."

"You have no choice."

I really hated it when he started dad-talking me. He was a little older than me—he was born in like 1890-something, turned when Ike was in office, when he was as old as I should have been this particular Valentine's Day. But I had been a vampire longer. Doesn't that count for something?

"Fine. I won't watch television tonight."

"Do you promise?"

"Sure. If you let me read one of these."

I snatched his letter off the floor.

It made him uncomfortable, but he didn't try to stop me.

I held it up and read from it like a beatnik poet.

"'Dear Mrs. Greengrass.'"

(Really?)

"'Although you do not know me, I hope that you will forgive me for saying that I have for some time now been impressed from afar by your charm and bearing. It is evident to me that you emigrated here from the British Isles; I gather this less from your accent (Buckinghamshire?) than from the old-world discipline you show in taking your nightly walks and the grace with which you . . .'"

He just blinked at me, smiling nervously. I could see the tip of one fang.

"So when do you get to the 'would it bother you ever so much, Mrs. Greengrass, if I poked holes in your jugular vein and sucked black heart's blood out?' part? And what is she, like ninety?"

"Eighty-five. And I will not admit to vampirism in the letter; I will only hint at it. I will tell her that if she wants an early-morning visitor, she need only close a handkerchief in her window so it is visible from the sidewalk. We will talk about the world outside her neighborhood, and about times others are too young to remember. The specific language in the letter will make her understand on a subconscious level that this is a supernatural opportunity."

"This is really creepy stuff, Cvets. Like heavy-breather-on-the-telephone stuff. I don't see why any of them do it."

"There comes a time when loneliness is stronger than fear."

"Well, that's depressing."

He nodded.

"Which is why sometimes they let me finish it."

"Even more depressing."

"They ask me to."

Now I nodded. I had had that happen, too.

A kid. Just a sick Greek girl in Astoria whose parents were going to the poorhouse taking care of her. Polio. Wouldn't let me pull my face away from her neck. Held her weak hands on the back of my head, saying, "Take me away, take me out of here."

I took the part of her I could.

Joseph Hiram Peacock, angel of Passover.

We don't kill often. Vampires that do kill we call "peelers." If you peel somebody and it gets in the paper, you get a talking-to. If you do it again, Margaret gets some of us together and comes for your head, or farms it out to the Latin Hearts under Alphabet City. They're all pretty new; Margaret turned one like ten years ago, then he turned his friends and family. The Hearts were a gang before and they stayed a gang. Smart of Margaret; you weren't supposed to go turning more than one every ten years or so, but her one multiplied. Now their leader, Mapache, was loyal to Margaret and they were all loyal to him. Instant muscle. There were less of them than us, like five, but they were good at offing vampires, they had machetes just for that. I think they liked it. But even they didn't fuck with Margaret. She used a shovel. And she had Old Boy. More about him soon.

Peeling was stupid anyway, though. It was better for everybody if we just took what we needed and made them forget. They were cattle, but you took milk, not meat, or the herd might stampede.

Cvetko hated when we did a peeler, which had only been twice for us, and once for the Latins. No, twice for them, too. Killing bothered Cvetko in general, though.

"Promise me you won't watch television tonight."

"Fine," I said, "I promise."

SOAP

meant it when I said it, but not an hour later I broke my word.

"Took my time? I'm standing on a ledge in a rainstorm and I took my time. What was I supposed to do? Jump down thirty-eight floors on a messenger to stop him?"

That was Eunice.

Eunice was indeed standing on a ledge, Eunice and ledge contained in the frame of the luxurious console television that dominated this modern and well-appointed living room.

"My luck, you'd miss," Walter said.

This was on *Soap*, which I love. Nine thirty P.M. every Tuesday, A and the B and the C. If I was really going to break myself from the tube, and I wasn't, it would have to be on some weekday other than a Tuesday.

I was lying back on the couch, holding Mrs. Baker's arm in my lap, a sort of ugly orange-and-brown knitted couch cover under her arm because her wrist was bleeding and I didn't want to get it on my faded bell-bottoms. I held the wrist up every once in a while to drink from it, wiping my lips with a paper towel. I'd had quite a bit from her already; she was looking a little peaked, although everybody looks peaked with that blue television light washing over them. Her head was lolling a bit and she had the drool-strand you always saw on the chins of the heavily charmed. All three of the Bakers were in la-la land, hardly aware of my presence, completely unaware of the context, ready to forget me the second I slipped out their window. At the commercial I'd change seats and start working on Mr. Baker, and when he was good and sponged, I'd bite the fat, surly preteen boy with all the football posters in his room. Even charmed, he was a pain in the ass.

"I wanna go to bed, this show is dumb," he said, even though *Soap* was off and a Fixodent commercial had taken its place.

"Bullshit," I said. "*Soap* is the smartest thing on television right now; soap operas have been begging for satire since they were invented, and *Soap* knocks it out of the park. But that's not good enough for Michael Kiss-My-Fat-Ass Baker, is it? You love, what, *Happy Days*?"

"Yeah," he said thickly, staring at the white paste pouring out of the larger-than-life Fixodent tube on the screen.

"Did you watch it tonight? *Happy Days*?"

"Yeah."

"Well, what happened? Did Fonzie and Richie jerk each other off yet?"

"No. They were singin' love songs. The Cunninghams."

"Right. Valentine's Day. But you love Fonzie, don't you?"

"Heeeyyyyyy," he said.

The hypnotized little dumpling actually said *Heeeyyyyy!* I laughed so hard a little of his mom's blood bubbled out of my nose.

"You know he's a Jew, right?"

He wrinkled his brow; he didn't like this. Oh, this was fun. I stuck a fresh paper towel on his mom's wrist and went over to the kid, plucking his half-eaten Pringles can off his lap and tossing it across the room, then sitting on his lap where he lay poured on the recliner, crossing my legs, feeling like a big, naughty ventriloquist's dummy. I was the same height as him, five foot five, but, he was a chunk and I'm like ninety pounds wet—we're lighter than we look; I'd been slowly losing weight since I turned. Anyway, I know I wasn't crushing his little nuts for him.

I had been about to drain his daddy, but then he had to go and badmouth *Soap*; besides, that doughy white neck looked like it needed biting. As soon as I was done fucking with him.

"That's right. Arthur Fonzarelli likes matzoh balls and bagels."

"Thought he was 'Talian. Like Rocky. The 'Talian Stallion."

"Nope. Sorry to hurt your feelings, but Fonzie's a big fat Jew, just like me. Well, half Jew on my mom's side."

"Are you gonna bite my neck now?"

"You're a smart kid."

I mussed his hair.

"Are you a vampire?"

Still staring at the tube, didn't know what he was saying.

"What? Don't talk crazy. I'm Cupid."

"Oh. That's okay, I guess. But . . . you still gonna bite me?"

"Oh, you know it."

He made an I'm-gonna-cry face and squirmed.

"What'sa matter, Mikey? Does it hurt when I bite you?"

He nodded and made a little whimpering sound, which triggered something in his semisleeping dad. Mr. Baker got up, looking all Korea-vet tough in his tobaccoey Fruit of the Loom T-shirt, turned the corners of his mouth down, started to make a beefy fist.

"Sit down, Victor," I said to him, pointing my index finger at him like a gun and letting a little menace into my voice.

He nodded, smoothed his pants, and sat down in a hurry, looking grateful I had reminded him he was supposed to be sitting down now. He even tilted his head so I could get at his neck when it was his turn. But now I spoke to Mikey.

"When I bite you, it only hurts a little, right?"

"I guess. Like a shot. Then it feels kinda good, but I don't like it that it feels good. Makes me feel like a queer."

"It's like a shot," I said. "Let's go with that."

"Shots are good for you," his mother slurred. She reached for her wine without looking at it, spilled it all over the carpet. Luckily it was white wine, so it wouldn't stain, but her spastic movement started her wrist bleeding again, and she got a smear about the size of a garden slug on the arm of the couch.

The father nodded, agreeing about the virtues of getting a shot. They were all watching the Magnavox, which now showed a rust-bearded Burger King with a rust-colored semi-Afro appearing from behind a magic door. Twin rusty caterpillars over his eyes. They had some dumb little bathtub toy with a rubber-band propeller making a pair of little kids squeal. It was so easy to charm people who had been watching the television—maybe Cvetko was right. Maybe it does rot your brain.

So I poked the chubby kid's sweet, chubby neck and drank and then I stuck my fangs into the hot, flushed neck of the ham-handed dad who smelled (and tasted) like Hai Karate aftershave, and then we all watched the rest of *Soap* together. I cleaned up before I left—picked up the Pringles, scrubbed the blood with Joy so it mostly came off the ivory-colored couch's arm, put the wadded-up, bloody paper towels in my pocket. I even wiped the dad's upper lip, which was coated with nasty little white wings of snot. I hate snot. And it wouldn't do to have them start to figure out something was wrong. I came here maybe twice, three times a month.

Of course I visited other places, I had a kind of routine, but the Bakers had the biggest veins, the weakest minds, and the most comfortable furniture on the East Side. But mainly I picked them for the huge, glorious console television I saw lighting up their window lo these many months ago as I walked on the sidewalk below. Think about that the next time you shop for TVs.

THE GIRL ON THE SUBWAY

I skittered down the fire escape doing my best impression of a monkey, but moving so fast and light anybody who saw me wouldn't know what they saw. The Bakers had good, fatty beef-fed blood, singing with iron, and I felt like a million dollars. I wanted a mirror even though I had already used one in the Bakers' bathroom to tidy up before I left (I helped myself to Dad's cologne, too), but I never got tired of the way I looked after I fed: healthy, strong, just as much color in my face as yours (if you're a Caucasian, that is; I shouldn't make assumptions). My hair always looked dynamite after a good feed, too, like a dog's coat when you feed him an egg every day, although I never tried that even when I had a dog. I think I heard it on TV.

The point is, I had a real spring in my step, which is quite a spring when you're a vampire. I wished it were warmer, I felt like running, but it wasn't running weather. Big heaps of unmelted snow from the blizzard stood packed here and there, forcing what people there were on the streets to bunch up, the long-legged ones in a hurry making grumpy faces behind the old and slow, trying to pass but here comes a dad with tiny kids in parkas, jumping in front of them won't look too cool. Between the packed snow you got an ugly slurry of ice-mush and dirt that a lesser fellow would be prone to slip in and fall. No, really, if you grew up somewhere south and you think all sweetly about snow, or if you only ever saw it on the tops of mountains for Heidi to yodel over or melting down into streams for Bambi to lap up, come to Manhattan in February. New York'll bust your snow cherry fast. You show me a postcard from Lapland with mountains and a reindeer and I'll show you a man-high, snow-capped heap of trash bags and cardboard piled around a tree that probably has tuberculosis, little yellow pockmarks of dog piss at the foot of it, all of it sprinkled with soot, real evenly like it came out of a shaker, and garnished with soda cans, cigarette butts, and, for no good reason, a brand-new left shoe, but just the left one and there's dried blood on it, so who's going to take it?

I was in the mood to hear music and meet a girl or two, so I decided to train my way to the Village. Down I went into the mouth of the subway, hopped the turnstile fast as a squirrel, then just for a laugh I walked in the blind spot of a briefcase-carrying guy who smelled like hooker, real close to him, my toes almost on his heels like something Charlie Chaplin would do. He didn't see me at all, even when he turned around once. There was a girlie in a denim jacket getting on the car past the closest one, so I ditched my first playmate and popped the collar of my shirt over my leather jacket. I had already checked myself postfeeding, but I spat on the back of my hand and wiped my lips and chin just in case; I guess you'd call it a nervous habit. She was dirty blond, taller than me, but that's not unusual; she would have been taller than me even without her platform shoes. Very sexual vibe from that one, automatic, broadcast to mankind in general like Radio Free Europe. Nice hips, and

I liked how shaggy her hair was; she looked tough and pretty at the same time.

She was just about to look at me; I can always tell when you're about to look at me. There came the eyes. Brown eyes. I would have thought blue. I smiled, she smiled. Quick shy looking-away game, but one of us would peek again in ten seconds or so. The only other person on our car was an older Chinese woman reading Danielle Steel, *Passion's Promise*, don't make me laugh.

The third time girlie peeked at me I leaned back and swung around gracefully on the pole, sort of an ironic comment on the awkwardness of flirtation, right up her alley. She laughed. Also, I was charming her a bit so I looked twenty-two-ish, like she was. Maybe more like twenty-five. She looked like she knew what she was doing, and she fit nicely in her jeans.

I remember her down to the button, not because I fed on her or slept with her—I swear, Your Honor, I never touched the lady—but because of what I saw next. You know how that is? Like you remember the book you were reading when somebody told you Elvis Presley died (*Exodus* by Leon Uris, don't be impressed, I never finished it) or what you were wearing the night you lost your virginity (a tweed coat and suspenders, but don't think "how cute"—I was already a vampire so it was weird).

The point is, I remember this girl because I stood with her on the ledge of great and permanent change, though neither one of us knew it, and she would never know it. The ledge was mine only.

I was about to see one of *them*.

But not just yet.

Not until Lexington.

And we were just coming up on 68th.

More people got on, but I wasn't paying attention to them.

"Happy Valentine's Day," I said.

"Yeah?"

"Yeah."

"Why would you say that?"

"Why not?"

"It just seems a funny thing to say before hello or anything."

The train started moving.

"Maybe one day you'll want to remember the first thing I ever said to you. Maybe it should be more interesting than 'Hello.'"

She liked that.

In the next car, past the tangle of unreadable Magic Marker graffiti that had sprouted on every subway car like chest hair on a Greek, through the porthole window and the graffiti on that, too, hooker-smelling briefcase man was writing something down on a little notepad, wrinkling up his mustache; he didn't like whatever he was writing. He was just about to look at me. He looked. First time I saw his bored eyes behind those slightly tinted big brown eyeglasses so much in fashion. My reflection and the girl's swam over him like giant ghosts. A kid behind him, not his, sat alone, and that struck me wrong though I wasn't thinking about it yet because the train was moving from the lit space by the platform into the darker space of the tunnel, my real home, Cvetko's home. And I saw tough girl's reflection turning toward me, her reflection in profile, so I turned also and looked her straight in the nose—I did mention she was tall? She giggled, warm fake-fruit smell of chewing gum riding her out-breath, and I took her chin in my hand to point her mouth down at mine. Her eyes darted at the Chinese woman, but I guess Danielle Steel can write the hell out of a book, because the Chinese woman's face was like eight inches from the page.

My lips brushed the girl's; I put my hand on her backside and she didn't push it away. After a second, though, she pulled back, smiling in that "wait a second, what's going on, wise guy?" way that really means, "We'll be fucking soon but I don't want you to think I do this all the time. Even though I probably do this all the time."

Then the train swung around a curve in the dark and she stumbled on her platform shoes. I caught her; I don't stumble, we're all half cat. Her fingers lingered on my forearms and she looked at me, but I looked away. Something caught my eye in the next car. It was the kid. A little girl. Long black hair like an Oriental, but she was Anglo. Pale skin. Pretty but haunted. She was sitting two seats closer than she had been, though I never saw her move, holding a Raggedy Ann doll she didn't seem interested in. She was looking at briefcase-hooker-notepad guy.

He looked back at her. And stared. It was all wrong.

But here's what else was wrong: She was wearing makeup. Like a lot of makeup. She looked more like a doll than Raggedy Ann did.

My new girlfriend was oblivious, said, "So what's your name?"

"Joey," I said, distracted.

The train swerved again and the lights flickered, but I could still see. The Chinese woman looked up from her book. Something moved on the next train, in the dark.

Now the girl was holding the man's hand, like she was his daughter. But she wasn't! She was charming him. A vampire? That young? She looked seven.

Now she looked at me.

I couldn't remember the last time I had a chill, but I caught one. She looked through me.

Was she a vampire?

I didn't know what she was.

At Grand Central, she got off the train with that guy, just a girl and her dad walking home. He left the briefcase, just left it and looked at it and left it anyway, and that one fact let me know in my black, dead heart that he would never get on another train. I knew it again when two little blond boys joined the girl, one of them taking the man's free hand, one of them skipping alongside. The boys were pale, like her, no makeup, just very pale. The hooker-smelling guy looked stoned, drooled all over himself, but nobody in the subway gave them a second glance. Why would they? This was Grand Central Station; Hare Krishnas were dancing ecstatically near a bag lady with a Burger King crown on, a drunk guy was puking in the trash can but holding up a slice of pizza so he wouldn't get any on it.

And a happy family was going home, only the children weren't children, and Daddy had dying to do.

"Aren't you going to ask me my name?" the girl said.

"No."

PUNK CLUB

I went to the Village as planned, went to the loudest bar I could find—the Ammonia. It wasn't as cool as CBGB's—Chinchilla only went to CBGB's—but I found the girls were consistently hotter at the Ammonia. Like just a little less punk, just a little more hot-poser. Okay by me. I wasn't part of the fucking movement. And the bathroom at the Bowery place was fucking raunchy, even by guy-who-lives-in-the-subway standards.

Anyway, the Ammonia.

Kids jammed up the doorway, fast, blurry guitar licks hammering out the door through the hot jungle of limbs and vinyl, beery musket-puffs of breath billowing up under the streetlight. This under the eyeless gaze of Gilda Radner, a poster for her live comedy album; I say "eyeless" because some less successful comedian had ripped square holes where her mouth and eyes should have been, like the blackout smudges in a porno, only with brick showing through. The doorman, a sort of badly shaven ox-shank in a clownishly small porkpie hat, pushed two fingers into my shoulder as I tried to slither under his gaze.

"How old are you?" he shouted over the exploding guitars.

"Fifty-nine," I shouted back.

"Cute. Get out," he said.

"Be friendly. Buy me a beer," I said.

He blinked twice, the charm hitting him like a baby's fist between the eyes, then he said, "You want a beer?"

"Love one."

Oxbody actually abandoned his post, shoved two girls out of his way, and deposited me at the bar like a cop bringing a collar to his desk. He gestured, the bartender nodded, and soon a frosty Molson Light was fizzing before my eyes. I tipped the bartender a quarter and swigged. I like beer okay, and I can keep it down if I have blood in my stomach. Food's a different story. I won't barf if I've got blood in me, but the food-processing factory isn't what it used to be and just digesting something wears me out. There's more, but you don't want to hear about that. Basically, if I eat food it's just for show, and I'll pay for it later. Drinking anything but blood wakes the pee-works up, and that's no fun, but every once in a while it's nice to feel like you're still a person.

I was glad the music was loud, even though I'm not really a punk fan. According to the posters, we had ourselves a double bill—the band was either the Skullpumps or Miss Katonic, depending on what time it was. Probably the former.

I got no time for
people in the city
I got no time for
people in the country
I got no time to
do my fuckin' laundry
so I hope I smell bad

real bad
I hope I smell real bad!

The lead singer had white, square-looking shoes with no socks, super-tight jeans and white-blond hair teased up into a sort of hurricane of dye and hair spray. Fake fur half-coat over a T-shirt with the nipples cut out, his own nipples taped over with swatches of black electrician's tape. Something about his aesthetic made me think I might have found the culprit in the case of the vandalized Gilda Radner poster. The punked-out crowd was really into these guys. A couple of them held up bicycle pumps, confirming my guess about the name, and up toward the front the dancing was pretty thrashy and violent.

I wouldn't stay here long.

I would just drink my Molson and hopefully the guitars would hammer-wash the image of those creepy children out of my head. I had had a case of the thousand-yard stares since I saw them, had been only marginally aware of the "Happy Valentine's Day, prick" from the girl I had completely ignored after seeing them, this dropped as she popped a stick of Juicy Fruit gum between her lipsticky lips and exited the train one stop after the others did. She had said some other things to me, but I had turned off like a transistor radio, it's a very bad habit of mine. If I'm focused on something, I just shut down to everything around me. It's inexcusably rude, I know it is; she wasn't entirely off base calling me a prick.

I am kind of a prick.

Take what happened next at the Ammonia.

The thrashy dancing had gotten intense—I don't know how bouncers are supposed to tell that kind of horseplay from a fight—and pretty soon a guy with bushy black hair got popped in the face with an elbow so hard he started bleeding down the front of his shirt, kind of a button-down zebra print. He dove onto the stage and scrambled to the drum set, upon the face of which he planted a smeary, bloody kiss, like his big *Happy Valentine's Day, pricks!* to the world. Oxflanks had already been making his way there, and now he grabbed the bleedy kid by the Chuck Taylors and hauled him belly-down off the stage, rolling up his shirt to expose his greyhoundy ribs. I thought he would kick him out, but he contented himself with jabbing a warning finger in the kid's face and heading back to the door. Some freckly, overmascaraed redheaded girl materialized and kissed zebra-shirt's bloody mouth. They frenched for a good five-Mississippi, and she broke away, laughing with her friends, her mouth bloody now. She didn't even know the guy.

Everybody clapped, even the bassist, but nobody notices when the bassist stops playing.

Before I could even think, I was on my feet and had ducked through the bouncy tangle of the crowd. I grabbed her by the hand, spun her around, and went up on tiptoes. Still laughing, she bent halfway down and kissed me, a beery, bloody, hemoglobin kiss, bitter with cheap cigarettes but salty and elegant and perfect for all that. It was his blood, but I wanted hers.

"Come into the alley with me!" I shouted into her ear.

She just laughed at me and sat down, now watching the band.

"No, really, come into the alley with me!" I said, pouring on the charm. She went glass-eyed and drooly, but she got up. The charmed, it might not surprise you to learn, are not known for their physical grace, and we weren't Skynyrd's three steps toward the door before she bumped straight into a mean-mouthed girl, knocking from her hand the three beers she had been finessing back to her table.

An apology would have fixed it, but my new girlfriend was slack-jawed. "Sorry," I said, moving between them, pulling my new friend toward the cold air coming in the front door. A man with a bandana and dogtags around his neck decided he didn't like me, I can't say I blame him, and took a poke at my eye. The Ammonia was kind of a punchy place, if you haven't already gathered that.

He connected, I saw the proverbial stars, but even so I kicked out at him almost simultaneously, heard him yelp. I kick pretty hard. Now I was separated from the girl, but that was just as well. I wasn't starving, just being greedy. Now Oxlungs was blocking my way to outside, he had seen the kick, maybe suspected I had been up to no good with the girl, and he grabbed me by the coat, which I slipped out of quick as an eel. The door was more crowded than the toilets, so I ran back into the bar.

Bandana was limping after me, Oxballs too, so into the filthy-but-better-than-CBGB's little john I went, hoping for a window I thought I remembered. I got one. Painted shut and small. I leapt up on the shoulders of one guy pissing in the trough, but he was high as a kite and just laughed, at least until the counterforce of me wrenching the window open knocked him down. I went with him, paint flakes showering everywhere, but leapt again as soon as I hit concrete.

I don't know what it looked like to the guys coming in, but I got small. That means my body changed shape a bit, just a bit; shoulders came dislocated, ribs flattened out, you get the idea. "Whoa!" somebody said behind me, probably pissing guy. Next thing I knew, I was long-legging it through a dirty heap of leftover blizzard snow, my pants good and ripped, my boots still in the bathroom, my belt off and in one hand, I don't have any idea how that happened. But I saw Oxtongue's oxey head and one arm come out the window behind me. He had that back neck-roll fat tough guys all have. The devil was in me, I guess, because I turned around. Went back up the snow mound. He flailed at me.

"Come here, you little shit!"

"Okay," I said.

I stood up on the snow heap, one foot propped on a Dumpster. He grabbed my shirt but I pried his hand open; that surprised him! I resisted the urge to break his arm, just shoved it down good and hard. I could see he wanted to go back down now; this wasn't going the way he planned, but he was wedged in.

I could not help but see his predicament as a gift from the gods, which must never be scorned.

So I fed. Pretty hard. He made a weird sound, like with his tongue jammed up against the roof of his mouth, his eyes rolling up white in his head. He might have creamed himself, that's not unusual.

Blood and beer, blood and beer, mine was a happy mouth.

I stopped myself at about a pint and a half, he was a big boy, then I delicately plucked his porkpie hat off his head—it seemed a fair trade for my coat—and tramped down the snow heap.

"Come back," he said, more like a lover than an enraged bouncer.

"Sorry. Past my bedtime."

A rat in the Dumpster squeaked and moved up to get a look at me, dislodging a bottle. I tipped my new hat at it and made my way down the street, my breath steaming with borrowed warmth, whisper-singing, "I hope I smell real bad, real bad, I hope I smell real BAD!" which was great for a while. Great until I got back down into the subway and found myself looking everywhere for pale, haunty-eyed children.

"And what do you think these children were?" Margaret said, her Irish brogue still porridge-thick after three-quarters of a century in New York. She wasn't even from Dublin or someplace civilized like that; she was from some turf-cutting wasteland where they pronounce their *B*s like *W*s and only speak English in banks, which they never go into because they're shit broke. She was in her thirties when she was turned, which was not long before I was turned. I'll get to that.

"Vampires?"

"Is it a question you're askin' me, or are you tellin' me your own thoughts?"

"Vampires, I think they were vampires."

I was sitting on the old refrigerator that served me as a coffin, avocado green and covered with magnets. I collect fridge magnets. Snoopy lying on his doghouse is my current favorite. Did I mention I used to have a dog?

Margaret crouched on her heels in that weird third-world way so she looked like a witch in want of a pot, her tangled, ratty, browny-red hair spilling over her shoulders in an open challenge to all combs. On this particular evening she was wearing her second-favorite outfit, a faded, flowered housedress that had clearly been bled on repeatedly, and a pair of thong sandals. Most vampires avoid sandals because our veins are more pronounced, especially in our extremities—our feet aren't that attractive. Margaret just didn't give a shit.

Cvetko was looking at her in that lovelorn way he has of looking at any woman over thirty who talks to him for more than thirty seconds. Margaret looked like a dishrag-pretty thirty-five, sassy in that using-a-rolling-pin-as-a-weapon way, big blue eyes made for being bloodshot, made for anger, the kind of woman who would stab a drunk husband in the gut with a meat fork and never interrupt her lecture. Sorry, did I say "would stab"? Make that "did stab." I think that was in 1930 or so; he survived that but was probably as dead as James Joyce by now.

Margaret charmed better than anyone except maybe me. No, she was better than me. There's a lot of variation with us—some guys can barely do it to a drunk; some, and this is rare, can charm a whole room. Margaret wasn't quite like the last kind, but she could really operate one-on-one. She could tell you to cut your own throat with a soup can lid and you'd do it and hope you hadn't pissed her off by being too slow about it. She was completely brazen. I watched her get into a limo behind a woman in minks, tell the driver to keep it running and roll up the windows. Three minutes later she climbed out still checking her face in her compact and the limo drifted off slowly, hit a cab. The cabbie was screaming at the limo driver, but he just drooled and said he was sorry. Mink woman got out, confused, went to light a Virginia Slim, then barfed on everybody's shoes and sat back down. Margaret must have tapped her for a good quart. Would have joyfully killed her if she'd had more privacy, and if we didn't have rules about killing. I think Margaret bends her own rules sometimes, though. Margaret hates rich people.

Did I mention I used to be a rich person?

I had better do this now.

MARGARET

Margaret McMannis came to work as a cook in my father's house, our narrow, four-storied Greenwich Village town house, in the spring of 1933, when I was fourteen years old. The last cook, Vilma, a chubby Hungarian woman with a birthmark like a sunburn on about a third of her face, had been like an adopted mother to me since my own mother was always busy with shopping, organizing parties, and charity work that involved little charity and even less work. Children were for cooks, teachers, and nannies to worry about. She was the kind of woman who would wear shoes she knew would give her a blister to Central Park just so she could buy shoes that would give her a blister somewhere else and pick up a third pair a block and a half from home. Because she couldn't be bothered to carry two boxes, she would toss the first pair in the trash. The family money was mostly hers, her dad was big in textiles, but still.

Is it any wonder I ended up selfish?

Vilma never thought I was selfish. Vilma taught me spices, tarragon and paprika and rosemary, coriander, too. Vilma let me taste brandy and eau de violette; she made lemon cookies and short-bread and gingerbread men and cupcakes and when I remember the sun I remember it coming in the kitchen window with Vilma bending down to put a wooden spoon slathered in batter to my mouth, calling me Joey-bird.

"You want taste, Joey-bird? You come taste!"

Her English always sucked. I miss Vilma like I miss nobody else in this world and I don't even know what happened to her after what happened with us. I'll get to that.

Dad wasn't bad when he noticed me. Always seemed genuinely interested in what was going on in school, what have you, bought me a Yorkshire terrier over my mother's protests about hair getting on her dresses. Any dad anywhere can get a get-out-of-jail-free card for about three years by buying his kid a dog. The Yorkie's name was Solly, but you don't give a shit. Other people's dogs are boring. Suffice it to say that a dad, a cook, and a dog can just about make up for a mom.

I didn't mean to turn this into a headshrinker's couch or anything, but it feels good to get this stuff about my mother off my chest. It isn't like her family was bad. Her sister Golda had been a nurse in World War I and she came to see me when I had chicken pox and told me stories and I remember praying to God asking why she hadn't married my dad instead. That sounds rotten, and kids can be rotten, but just wait.

My mom, as it turns out, got this idea that my dad was sweet on Vilma. More than just sweet on her. Not the sort of thing you called a family meeting about in 1933, but I heard them fight. I couldn't make out everything through the walls, but I picked out enough to know (a) my mom could have married any one of about ten thousand handsome, successful Ashkenazi in Manhattan, (b) my dad planned to poison Mom, run off with Vilma, and leave little Joseph an orphan, and (c) my mom was nuts. Just fucking nuts.

First off, Vilma wasn't exactly Miss Rheingold; she was chubby and huggy and sweet, yes, but my mom was a svelte, well-put-together woman who looked good in a tweed peacoat, got plenty of looks in the park, blistered feet, crazy eyes, and all. Second of all, my dad, Edwin Davison Peacock, was a rock. Worked all day in a fever of Presbyterian capitalistic mysticism, yes, expected roast beef and mashed potatoes with lots of butter on the table at seven sharp, nothing unusual about that back then. Kept us treading water in the crash of '29 without help from the in-laws because he was sus-picious of the market—that whole buying-on-margin thing smelled like rotten meat to him long before it gave the whole country a bellyache. Pops invested in real estate, sold his Lower East Side pushcarts before La Guardia outlawed them, and modernized his three clothing stores so they looked airy and full of light when everybody else's discount stores looked like you were looting some-body's basement. But having an affair? I'd have been less surprised to hear FDR won a silver medal jumping hurdles.

Then it happened. My dad, respected by employees and feared by competitors, chickened out before his raving wife. He up and fired Vilma. Did it while I was at school so there'd be no tearful good-byes, but there were tears all right. I didn't sleep for a week, just punched my pillow while Solly soldier-crawled on his belly squinting and licking his nose, trying to get close enough to lick the tears off of my cheeks, which I finally let him do. He was good at that. We just don't deserve dogs, do we?

Leah Peacock wasn't about to cook her husband's meals just because that "liver-colored Magyar cow had gone back to Buda-pest," so the cook interviews began immediately. Based on one plate of Salisbury steak, an enthusiastic recommendation from her last employer, her strict Catholic values, and her thin, un-Vilma-like frame, Margaret McMannis won out over the other appli-cants. I think, too, that her Irishness appealed to some charitable

impulse of Leah's without fully rousing her under-the-surface bigotry, as the dark faces of the two colored candidates doubtless
had. The maid, Elise, was colored, but she didn't touch food. Yeah,
racism's like that. It wasn't the bus seats that got all the rednecks
worked up in the '50s. It was the water fountains. As for the situation in the Peacock house, however, Mother actually seemed to
like Margaret Evelyn McMannis.

And for that reason above all others, Joseph Hiram Peacock
decided she had to go.

It really isn't tough for a kid to get a domestic fired, particularly
in a house where the mother thinks of the kid as a swatch of wall-
paper that occasionally needs food and school.

I was too smart to think one theft would do it, and I was too
smart to take something they might think a boy would be interested in. I knew where the money was kept. That was out of the
question.

I started with earrings, a pair of modest pearls. Nothing so
expensive Mom would make Dad call the cops; something small
and losable. Something she wore a lot so she'd notice and it would
bug her and put her on notice that something was wrong. I hit the
bull's-eye.

"Edwin?" she said; it was always *Edwin* when she had a demand
and *Ed* when she wanted to make sweet. "Would you please keep
your eyes open for those pearls I got in Chicago? They seem to have
grown wings."

"They're not in the box?" he said from behind his newspaper. Of
course they weren't in the box, nobody says their earrings are missing if they're in the box. It was a bullshit question so he could snatch
another paragraph off the *New York Times* before he had to pay attention to what she was saying.

"No," she said, more quietly. More quietly meant she was going to handle it herself. Louder would have meant he'd better get in there. She put just enough pout in it so he'd know she knew he was more interested in the paper, but really it was just for herself since he wasn't fucking listening.

It certainly wasn't for me. She didn't know if I was in the house, in the garden, in the park, or at the bottom of the East River. I actually put my hand in my pocket and rolled the earrings in my fingers while she stomped and huffed around upstairs, making the floorboards creak. For a woman with size-six feet she had quite a huffy stomp.

The only person looking at me was the maid, Elise, who was tickling the bookshelf with a feather duster. She caught my eye just then, not that we were chummy, but her look seemed to say she knew something had been set in motion, that she would come under scrutiny, that my words for or against her would be the finger on the scale. She was only four years older than me, but we couldn't have lived in more different worlds. Doing her very best every day, never stealing, never lying, she might or might not be able to keep her reputation intact. I was a rotten little bastard, but because my face was white and my name was Peacock, it would have taken an act of Congress to put me under suspicion.

Another complicating factor was my attraction to Elise. She had the dubious good fortune to live under the same roof with me at the very dawn of my adolescent sexuality. You know what teen-aged boys are famous for doing? Of course you do. I had just discovered that very thing the previous year, while holding a heavy encyclopedia on my lap and simultaneously nervously twitching my leg up and down. Soon I gave up my hunt for John Wilkes Booth and started fanning the pages for anything female, finally settling on Joan of Arc. I imagined her sweating under all that armor, then, God help me, I pictured her in a cell like in a dungeon getting ready to get burned at the stake. This whole thing took like three minutes; I didn't know what dizzying, rapturous thing had happened to me, I had an idea, but I had better sense than to tell my parents about it. I just cleaned myself up and resolved to investigate the situation further. It actually took me a week to figure out a book on my lap wasn't necessary.

But Elise. She went from being sort of an older fellow child from a less fortunate family to being Cleopatra, Bathsheba, Jezebel. I loved watching her polish the silverware, clean the glass, make the beds; I lived for floorboards day. I tried to talk with her a few times, and she was polite without being overly friendly. I think she saw through my interest, understood this was normal for boys and that it was best not to encourage or offend me. I think she was perfectly neutral toward me, no love, no hate, and as guilty as I felt for the unlikely situations I imagined us in together, I was grateful for that neutrality. I expected that neutrality to end any day; any day she would sense the secret and anatomically naïve relationship we were having inside my skull and begin to despise me as a peeper and a sex pervert.

But that's not what happened. If she knew, really knew how much I thought about her, she never let on. And now she would need me.

Help me, Joey, her look said, dust motes in the air lit up by the sun. *You know I'm good.*

I let myself almost smile, which she took to mean yes. She almost smiled, too. This all took less than three seconds. Then Solly started yapping because a key slotted into the front door and it opened, and Margaret came in with her big tatty coat and the paper sacks of groceries she would turn into Saturday dinner. A bunch of cold air came in with her.

She said, "Good afternoon, Joey," to me, but I just looked down.

Rolled the earrings in my fingers.

Tried not to smile.

* * *

Mom did ask Elise about the earrings but seemed mostly to believe her when she said she hadn't seen them. She was on guard, though, and now so was Elise. Runners on first and third. I went for the base hit the following Saturday. Not earrings this time, but a cameo. Valuable, but not send-you-down-the-river valuable. Just pretty, something a woman would love. A white Grecian lady with snaky hair on a coral background the color of good salmon. I had always liked that one, had asked Mom about the pinkish stone when I was a kid, had loved the idea that it came all the way from the sea. *Coral* is still one of my favorite words, even after everything. But I hadn't paid it any mind since I was little; she'd never think I took it.

She'd certainly never think I would put it in the purse of an Irish cook who had done me no harm. The idea was so shitty, so cowardly and rotten as to be beyond belief; her Ashkenazi blood was too noble to produce such corrupt stock, right? But Irish thieves crawled off the bogs in droves and freighted themselves west across the Atlantic; what was Brooklyn, where the McMannises had their hatchery, but a weigh station between Ellis Island and Rikers Island? That cameo would land in Margaret's purse with an audible thud, David's stone hitting Goliath right on the Xs-for-eyes button. Only I was Goliath. I knew I was going to win this one. But how to get it in there? And how to see that it was found?

"Why does the lady have snakes in her hair?" I had asked my mother years before.

"Because the gods were angry at her and turned her into a monster."

"You mean God?"

"No, Joey, back in olden times the ancient Greeks believed in lots of gods. Some were nice and some were mean."

"Like the devil?"

"Something like that."

"Why did they put snakes in her hair?"

"You know, Joey, I forget. Go ask your father."

I don't know if she forgot or she just didn't want to tell me, but I know what the snake lady did. Medusa. She got raped. The god Poseidon went and raped her in the temple of Athena, and Athena was pissed. She couldn't punish Poseidon, her uncle, but Medusa? Just a woman in the wrong place at the wrong time. Just an Irish girl off the bogs.

My plan was to slip the cameo into Margaret's purse and then tell Elise I had seen Margaret take something from my mom's jewelry box. Remove myself one step from the crime, enlist an ally with skin in the game, it was perfect. You see why I'm such a good vampire? We're all lying, devious bastards, not like were- wolves, if there are werewolves, whose MO is, "Hi, I'm a werewolf, surprise! And fuck you!" No, we lurk. We're lurkers. And I was off to a good start.

But not perfect.

I went upstairs to Elise's room. Elise lived with us every day but Sunday when she trained it north to some crumbling shitbox in the 130s where they took her money but no longer had a bed for her; here she slept in a sort of glorified, skylit closet on the top floor. One closet within this closet was where the cook kept her affairs. Margaret went home at night, but worked from six thirty A.M. until eight P.M. six days a week, with a two-hour break in the middle of the day, just enough time for her to get home, slap her children, and clean the whiskey bottles off the stairs, or whatever poor Irish women do in Brooklyn. Anyway, there I was all quiet in my sock feet, opening the cook's closet door with nary a creak. Medusa was in my hand and only inches from slipping into the cheap canvas handbag. And then I stopped. Cold sweat on my temples and upper lip. I know how much this sounds like trying to make myself look better after the fact, but given the other rotten things I have told you, and will tell you, why would I tidy this up? Anyway, whether you believe me or not, I stopped. I was suddenly aware that this was a big moment for me, that who I was as Joseph Hiram Peacock was getting decided exactly then, not in trench warfare, not in some deal with the devil with a fancy contract and an offered pen to dip in my own blood, but right there. On the fourth floor of a narrow town house in Greenwich Village with a stupid little cameo in my hand. I shook my head a little. It was too rotten. I couldn't do it. I started pulling my hand back.

"Mr. Joey," she said. I almost jumped out of my skin. Elise. Only she called me Mr. Joey. She said it breathy, a stage whisper, she knew something bad was happening. I turned around to look at her. All of a sudden I couldn't breathe. I looked at Elise and she at me and just like that I failed. I ran from the trench my buddies ran into. I dipped the pen in the blood and signed, the devil twirling his waxy black mustachio and chuckling at his windfall, or maybe at the irony of all this ceremony for such a wormy little soul.

I held up the cameo on its chain, Medusa spinning in the dim light, my eyes begging Elise to believe me as I said, "I found this. I mean I saw her. Margaret. She put this in her purse, from the dresser." Something very complex but quick happened in Elise's eyes just then, something I only fully understood later: the arithmetic of the real world carried out by a young woman of fragile circumstances, an expert in such calculations.

She didn't believe me any more than the man in the moon. But she knew her best chance of staying on here was to side with me. If she tried to rat me out, I might say she was the thief. Even if they believed her, she'd have a permanent enemy in the house that could never, ever be fired. She knew all this in a second.

"Missus Peacock," she said, tentatively, looking me in the eyes as if asking, *Are you sure? Are you sure this is who you are? Because we* can do it this way if you want, but you're starting on a long road now and you might not like where it goes. Or maybe she was just a scared kid from Harlem learning yet again how bad the world sucks.

I almost nodded at her, the way I had almost smiled before. She almost nodded back, and then she called for my mom again. Louder this time.

"Missus Peacock!"

I looked at Medusa.

Turning on her fine chain, turning.

The next cook was colored. My father overruled my mother on that, stopped her from hiring a mealymouthed sixtyish Russian crone I'm reasonably sure was a witch, and insisted on a cocoa-skinned, smiley Tennessee negro named Susie, though it wasn't a week before we were calling her "Sugar," as she said everybody else did. In addition to the permanent, genuine smile and pearly teeth, the gods had gifted Sugar with perhaps the largest bosom I had ever seen; it made a sort of geological shelf above her small-ish waist. It wasn't a point of sexual interest, not for me anyway, but it was definitely a novelty. Sugar's audition consisted of her cooking us six fried eggs in a row without breaking one yolk, making jokes with my dad the whole time. Mother wasn't hungry, she was never hungry, so Solly got her second egg. It was a good day for Yorkshire terriers. It was even a pretty good day for me, despite my guilt for what I had done to Margaret.

Margaret.

Yeah, let's go back to that Saturday.

I had asked Dad not to call the police, trying to sound persuasive while remaining aloof. My dad was quiet but shrewd, very shrewd. You don't steer a business through the Great Depression by being a sucker.

"Why do you think we should be lenient with this kind of behavior, son?"

"Because. She has a family?"

I made myself look at him. He would notice if I didn't look at him.

"Most people have families, Joseph. And most people don't steal." His eyes were cannons, ready to fire a broadside that would knock my head clean off.

Margaret sat stiffly in a dining room chair, her chin high, her arms folded in a pose of suffering righteousness as old as accusation.

"Call the police if you'd like, Mr. Peacock. I'm an honest woman, and I'd like to see this sorted out as much as you." She looked at Elise then, which was a relief, but then she cut her eyes to me, dragging Elise's gaze my way with her. She knew. She knew, but had no proof, and hoped I would panic.

Yes sirree, she was going to eyeball me straight into a cold sweat.

Those outsized blue gorgon's eyes of hers went through me, her gaze worse than my father's, tempered by neither love nor doubt. Her look was not a question mark, it was the *drip, drip, drop* of Chinese water torture, but I couldn't look away.

Suddenly, my mother walked over and stood between us, standing closer to Margaret.

"I would appreciate it, Mrs. McMannis, if you would stop staring at little Joseph as though it were his fault you're a thief."

"There's a thief in this house, and no question," she said.

"If you've got some ridiculous accusation to make, well, you just go ahead and make it, but I'd think twice if I were you," said my mom.

Now the gorgon's eyes swung up to her.

"I've no interest in seeing you arrested," my mom went on,

"but neither will I stand for your lies. Your position here is terminated—"

"And good riddance."

"Do. Not. Interrupt. Me. Your position here is terminated. I will not call the police, and I know that's a great relief to you whatever you want me to think, but only *if* you admit what you did. I cannot conscience a liar."

My mother was doing the finger-pointy thing that made you want to sock her; I could see Margaret was thinking about it.

"Leah," my father started.

"No, Edwin, I want to hear it from her mouth."

"If I say I stole that thing, I walk out of here and never have to look at any of youse again?"

"Yes," my mother said, using the word like cheese wire.

"Then I stole it," Margaret said, standing up. "I reached my filthy little hand into your drawer . . ."

"You know good and well it wasn't in a drawer."

"No, I don't know that. And you just think on that later. But I reached my filthy little hand into whatever you say, and I slipped that ugly necklace into my handbag. Never mind the diamonds and pearls you own, I wanted that tawdry little pendant, to match the collection of gold and necklaces you always see me wearing. And I lied about it all. And sure an' I'm going to hell if I don't confess it all to a priest before I die."

Now she looked at me again.

"Get out," my mother said.

"Nothing would please me more."

I know she wanted to storm out on that line, but these things never happen cleanly in real life; the dog went to the door with her, overdue as he was to water the flowers on his afternoon constitutional. Slamming the door might well have decapitated Solly, and that would have been a bit much, even for a pissed-off Irish gorgon. So instead of a dramatic "Nothing would please me more," Margaret's last living words in the Peacock house were actually a staccato "Go on, go on now, stay here" while Elise, with difficulty, gathered Solly up in her arms, avoiding contact with Margaret's eyes.

VAMPIRE

Now we go forward two months or so. May in New York City, warm days, cool nights, used to be my favorite month. I liked sleeping with the windows open, I was never bothered by the sounds of traffic or people on the streets, and the bugs weren't bad if you left the light off. I liked being under a blanket in the cool night air. I was a good sleeper.

That's why I was so bleary and confused when I heard the coin land in my room. Followed by another coin. Followed by a third. I sat up in time to see the fourth one coming straight at me. It hit me on the chin, but I caught it before it fell into my lap. A silver dollar, which believe me was worth something back then. I looked at the window, and there was nobody there. And then there was.

Margaret.

Pale and sick-looking, wearing a torn, dirty dress.

"Joseph," she said. "I've got money for you."

She opened her hand and it was true. A whole fistful of silver dollars.

"What are you doing here?" I said, still more confused than frightened. It hadn't yet occurred to me to wonder what she was standing on. "What's the money for?"

"For?" she said. "Why, for all the trouble I caused. For being a thief in your house. May I come in?"

"No," I said.

"Well. That's too bad," she said, letting the money fall from her hand to jingle onto the sidewalk below. It must have been thirty dollars.

And then she was gone.

And as soon as she was gone, I wasn't sure she had ever been there. Except there was a smell in the room. Like something dead in the attic.

I went to the window and shut it. Locked it.

It was a long time before I slept, but I did, at least until I had the nightmare. I dreamed there was a skeleton outside my window, rubbing its bones on the glass. I sat bolt upright, looking at the window, and indeed there was a shape there. I switched on the bedside lamp, almost knocking it over in my haste. You can imagine my relief when I saw that the shape at the window wasn't a skeleton at all. Just Margaret in a torn dress. The sound I had mistaken for bones on the glass was actually coins; she was playing a game where she used the tips of her fingers to slide coins around against the pane.

"Joey!" she said, smiling. "Come open the window and let me in!"

I shook my head. She mocked me shaking my head, like a mother would do to a stubborn child. "What'd'ye mean, shakin' your head at me like that? I thought we were friends?"

I just stared at her. Everything was wrong. What the hell was she standing on? I thought about calling my mom.

"Mommy!" she said, one step ahead of me. "You're a grown man with hair on it and you want your mommy, don't you? Go get your nasty Jew mommy. Tell her I brought money, she'll let me in!"

It was when she said "mommy" that I first saw her long, sharp teeth, white at the tips, a dirty yellow-gray near the gums. You never forget the first time you see a vampire's teeth. I think I pissed myself.

"Go away!" I said.

I heard nails clicking on the wooden floor. Solly heard voices and now he was coming to investigate. People stirring predawn might mean breakfast, or a trip outside, right? He poked his snout around the corner and gave a low, uncertain growl. By the time I looked back, Margaret was gone.

Solly stayed with me till morning. I didn't sleep again.

I sleepwalked through school the next day, unable to focus, unable to stop yawning. I nodded off in American History class, although with Mr. Gunderson's way of stressing seemingly random words when he lectured, this wasn't unusual. They could have hired that man to test coffee.

"Are we *boring* you, *Mr.* Peacock? Would you rather a *nap* than to hear about the exchange of *cannon* fire between the *Monitor* and the *Merrimack* and the end of the era of *sail*-powered warships?"

"I'm sorry, Mr. Gunderson. I was—"

"Dreaming about *Harvard*, or Yale, or Brown? You don't *work* hard enough to go to *those* schools. But, no matter to *me*; I can write a C as *quickly* as an A, and the *world* needs *tailors*, too. Just keep nodding *off*, Mr. Peacock, and sharpen your *shears*."

I had just enough of my mom in me that I wanted to jab my finger at him saying, *Do. Not. Interrupt. Me!* but that would have gone over like a pig stampede at temple. Not that I went to temple. We practiced Dad's religion, which meant twice-yearly trips to church and saying "Amen" after Dad thanked Jesus for the pot roast. The whole thing seemed pretty skinny next to the angry Irish bitch-monster outside my window. That looked real. I was going to need professional help.

"Vampire?" Reverend MacNeil said.

I nodded hesitantly. "Is this some kind of a joke?" I could see in his eyes that mischief or mental illness were the only motives he could imagine for such a question coming from a boy already in high school.

"Did some of the other fellows put you up to this?" he said, rubbing at a pinkish eye under his little round glasses. He was one of those unlucky pale types who always looked allergic to something.

"That's right, Reverend. They did. I'm very sorry."

"Who was it?"

"May I have a cross?"

"I beg your pardon."

"A cross. You know."

"Joey. This just sounds like more horseplay to me. Besides which, the true cross is in our hearts."

Tell Margaret McMannis, I thought, but kept it to myself.

I looked around the church to see if there was something cross-like I could make off with, but nothing looked carryable. I was eyeing a wooden cross on the wall, trying to make out how well attached it was—it looked pretty solid—when Reverend MacNeil said, "Joey?" I had forgotten he was there. So I shook his hand good and hard like my dad taught me and set off for the park. They had branches and stuff in the park, and, with a little bit of kite twine, I could make a cross. Then I remembered that my kite had a frame like a cross, and I could skip the park entirely. Then I remembered the reverend rubbing his eye with the hand I shook, so I wiped it on my pants.

Did I mention I wasn't that smart in 1933? I wasn't. Maybe the only smart thing I did that year was to tell Margaret she couldn't come in through my bedroom window. Weird vampire rule, but it absolutely works. Only with somebody's home, not a business. I've tried to defy this little ordinance, we've all tried, but you just stand at the entrance and can't go through. You can't make yourself do it, like one of those darted lions on *Wild Kingdom* thinking about getting a good chew going on Marlin Perkins's face, but he's paralyzed so he just lies there and pants and looks at him. Last year I conducted a little experiment: I had Cvetko push me into a window I hadn't been invited through, some little old lady Cvetko had bitten already, a house he was welcome in so he could go in and get me if I got in trouble. He said it was "an exercise in ignorance," but he was too curious to refuse outright. Damned if I didn't fall down and scramble back out the window on my hands and knees against my own will.

I didn't know any of that on this particular evening, but I knew good and well what Margaret was. She was a monster. And she had it in for me. She came back.

"Joey," she said, outside my window, just a wick of her brown hair and one hungry eye visible between the curtain and the frame. That eye like a lamp, once blue like the sea but now lighter, luminous. I turned away from it, probably just in time.

Solly was curled up in a ball between my legs. He growled.

It wasn't all that late, and I hadn't quite gotten to sleep yet. The kite-frame cross was leaning up against the wall, behind my nightstand.

"Joey, may I please come in?"

I switched on my table lamp.

I shook my head, said "No," and fumbled the cross awkwardly from behind the nightstand, almost knocking the lamp over. I was having trouble catching my breath, I got light-headed, almost passed out, but I held my bumpkin cross up and tried to think of a picture of Jesus with lambs behind him looking up at the sky. To my surprise, Margaret had a reaction to the cross; she turned away from it, not hissing like in the movies I would see later, but sort of hitching like she was being racked with sobs. Anyway, she moved away from the window. I was tempted to look after her to see if she was gone for real, but I didn't think it was smart to get close to it—I could just imagine her punching a fist through the glass and grabbing my wrist or something.

I sat there, my heart pounding. "You'll stop dirtyin' that cross with your little Jew hand and you'll open this window for me or else," I heard her say. I wasn't sure where she was. "Or else what?" I said, not smarty-pants-like, I really wanted to know what she was going to do to me.

"Or it'll go worse for you."

"Worse than what? What do you want?"

"I just want to hold you in my arms, little Joey. Just to squeeze you tight, wee little prince that you are. And I will. Make no mistake about it. Be it tonight, tomorrow, or next month. I got nothing but time now, thanks to you. Open this window and it'll stop tonight, and it'll stop with you."

I had the urge to call for my dad, but what was I going to say? *An Irish vampire is threatening me outside my window?* No . . . but maybe *an Irish thief* was plausible.

I got up then, made my way to my parents' bedroom, tried the doorknob. Locked. I knocked gently. "Dad?"

"What," he said, almost immediately. They hadn't been sleeping.

"I think there's somebody trying to get into the house."

"What? Are you sure?"

"I think so. An Irishman."

I realized that sounded flimsy the second it stumbled out of my mouth. I bit my lower lip, looked behind me down the hall to make sure Margaret wasn't coming. The floor runner, usually cheerful with its Turkish birds or whatever, looked foreboding, like the carpet they roll out for your murder. It seemed to go forever.

"How do you know he's Irish?"

Good question, Pop.

"Because I think I saw Margaret. I think she wants to get back at us."

My mom mumbled something low and fast and the springs creaked and the floorboards creaked and then the closet door opened, and I knew what that meant. I tried to peek through the keyhole for a minute, but then I heard Solly yapping. Really barking this time. I glanced back down the hall, and there stood Elise. My heart almost hiccupped out of my mouth.

"Elise," I stage-whispered, "make sure the . . ."

Doors are locked, I was going to say, but she interrupted me, speaking in a wet slur. "Forgot something," she said. Was she drunk? Was she drooling?

"Who forgot something?"

"Hurry up, Edwin," I heard my mom say from behind their door. "They're in the cigar box."

Solly stopped barking.

Elise wound up and spoke again, looking toward me rather than at me. "Marg'it. Marg'it forgot. Her necklace."

I heard the sound of a shotgun shell dropping on the hardwood floor, Mom saying, "Edwin!" Then I saw her. She was in the house. Margaret, looming up just behind Elise. Grinning with those awful teeth.

I tried to say "Dad!" but nothing came out. I held up the cross. Margaret looked away, but whispered something Elise heard. Elise blundered forward, her face almost apologetic, and grabbed the kite-frame cross away from me, snapping it over her knee. For as clumsy as she was, she was fast and strong. I couldn't stop her, and we made a ruckus.

The key slotted into the door, turned it so it swung inward, revealing my pajama-legged father holding the short, double-barreled shotgun he shot partridges with.

"What's going on?" my dad said.

Margaret was gone. Just gone. All he saw was a drooly maid with broken sticks in her hand.

"Elise, what is the meaning of this?" my mother said, pushing her back. Elise seemed to come unplugged. She looked at the broken kite frame in her hands as if it had just appeared there. My pop moved past her, drawing back the hammers of the shotgun. He went room to room, clearly meaning to check the whole house.

My mother was running a string of "I want an explanation"s and "Do not ignore me"s at Elise, who seemed completely out of it.

"Be careful," I yelled to my dad, suddenly wondering if his sixteen-gauge full of birdshot would do any good against the ghoul I had seen. My interjection caused Elise to stir. Though still heavily charmed, she now became aware of me, and she considered me with an offended drunkard's dawning contempt.

"You look at me when I'm talking to you," my mother told the back of her head.

That seemed to decide it. Elise, wrinkling up her face like a baby about to have a tantrum, cleared the space between us in two steps and jammed the broken end of the kite into my thigh. Leaned into it. She should have worked the harpoon on a whaling boat. It stuck deep. I leaned against the wall, shocked past speech. My father was downstairs already. My mother, afraid to strike the crazed woman, just stared. As did I. The puncture was only just starting to hurt, and didn't bleed yet—that would come later.

Regaining some composure, Elise stood up straight, said,

"Excuse me," and walked upstairs, locking herself in her room. When the police came, she was already packed and as ready to check into jail or the looney bin as any college freshman was to move into his dorm. Not that I saw this. I was on my way to the hospital.

Everybody decent has a guy like Walther in his life: a guy who comes over when you call in the middle of the night. He's the guy who loans you money and never asks for it back, the guy who tells the cop your kid was with him when he was really getting in trouble; he's the guy who takes your wife and son to the emergency room. Walther ran Dad's flagship store on Broadway; he was a big guy, about fifty, had met Teddy Roosevelt, spoke Spanish 'cause he lived in Cuba for a while, made a hell of a pork roast that tasted like garlic and oranges.

"Take them to St. Vincent's while I wait for the police," Dad said, and that's all he had to say. Walther had his hat on before he hung up his phone. When Uncle Walt, as I knew him, showed up, Dad had already put a tourniquet on my leg. My pants were getting all spotty with blood now. Mom was shrieking through the locked door at Elise with one shoe on and one in her hand.

"Go with Walt, Leah," Dad said, mostly because he didn't want to hear her anymore. Too bad for me and Uncle Walt. Mom put her shoe on. Walt carried me downstairs. On our street, West 11th, a lady in pearls, a fox fur, and iridescent stockings was passing by with her man-friend, but she went white and said, "Oh, my, oh my" when she saw the stick sticking out of me. I remember trying to smile at her, but the man-friend hurried her along. Walther bundled Mom and me in the back of his car, saying, "Don't you worry, kid, they'll fix you right up for Saturday baseball. Wanna stick a' gum?" I shook my head no. "Shouldn'ta said *stick*, huh?" He mussed my hair. Whatever Walt drove, I didn't know cars then, it was a big car that smelled like leather and Cuban *puros*. I remember that.

Then my mom fixed everything.

"Don't take him to St. Vincent's. My family uses Beth Israel."

"Leah, it's farther."

"He's not dying, Walter, and Beth Israel is more sanitary. I read an article."

Thanks to that article, if there was an article, I was driven to the thirteen-story medical wonder near Stuyvesant Park where Beth Israel had relocated in '29. A new, sanitary building with first-rate doctors, shiny bowls to catch the blood in, and freshly painted walls uncluttered with pictures of saints.

And not a mother-loving crucifix in sight.

A word about the cross business: They work on vampires if those vampires believe in them. Margaret, like Cvetko, was Catholic as hell, and a cross will turn and maybe burn either one of them. Me? If I'm coming after you and you pull out your rosary, good luck. I can juggle 'em. But for the newly minted vampire Margaret McMannis, formerly of Connemara, Ireland, where the only comforts were High Mass and killing weevils, St. Vincent's would have been like Fort Knox.

"So, you made a new friend tonight, did you?" the doctor said, looking things over under the bright light while his nurse snipped open my pants leg and dabbed with her swab. It was really starting to hurt and I whimpered. "There, there," he said, his tidy mustache sitting on his upper lip, shaved down so it didn't crowd his nose. A young guy. I thought about him later. I thought they might have shipped him out in the next war where he'd see things that would make him miss his Beth Israel anginas and dog bites and kite sticks in legs.

"That's right, she *stabbed* him," my mother said for the third or fourth time, "like a savage. Just not like a civilized person at *all*."

"Well, I'm sure the police will sort that out, Mrs. Peacock, and, with your permission, I'll sort this out."

She took the hint and sat down.

He sorted me out pretty well, truth be told; it hurt like a bastard, but he was quick and tidy, got the stick out (boy, did it bleed), made sure the puncture was clear of splinters and swabbed out with disinfectant. Talked to me the whole time. I remember being fascinated with the greenish area between his mustache and his nose, thinking it must take a surgeon to shave a line that neat in a space so small, and I was tempted to try to count the little black follicles there; this guy was hairy, could have grown a big King Solomon beard if he tried.

Then I remembered Solly.

"Where's my dog?" I said. The doc was stitching me. "Stop!" I said. "We have to find my dog! She's going to hurt him!"

Then, to my surprise, the doctor stopped. He just stopped, midstitch. I looked at his fingers, holding the needle. Now some clear liquid ran on my leg, right next to the wound. Drool. A long strand of it spilled from his mouth. He swayed, very gently. "Solly," he said, his voice sleep-thick. Now the nurse loomed up. The nurse took the needle from him, stuck it in my thigh. Not like giving me a shot, just stabbed me with it and left it there. I gasped and looked up. Her tall nurse's hat sat crooked, it had been hastily put on. It wasn't a nurse. Of course it wasn't. You know who it was.

Margaret stood towering over me, glorious in victory, her teeth bared. She looked me in the eye, her eyes moons, cat's eyes, each one of them a headlamp in the devil's fastest car. "You won't make a sound," she said, and I felt my muscles go slack, felt myself start to drool. It was kind of a good feeling, getting charmed, like nothing could go wrong because you just weren't in charge anymore.

"But you will have a look around, won't you?" she said. "You'll want to remember this night." She put her hand on my chin and turned my head this way and that so I could see. My mother lay slumped against the wall, charmed, holding up a *Life* magazine that happened to be upside down, examining it like a strange dead bird. The actual nurse lay half-naked on the floor, her mouth opening and closing like a fish's mouth, like she wanted to warn somebody but couldn't. Now Margaret said, "Sit still, my little prince. Watch it all and then it'll be your turn."

My mom started to say "Joey" then, and she kept saying it like a broken record, soft and helpless-like. I think she really did love me in her way, as much as she could love anything. The vampire walked over to her, licked her neck good, then bit. I'll never forget my mom's gloved hands holding the false nurse's back, saying "Joey" the whole time, moaning at the end like she was under my dad. Margaret pulled away, a jet coming from my mother's neck, arcing up and spattering everything. Margaret stuck a sponge in her hand, put that to her neck. The wound was already starting to heal.

I saw Margaret look at the nurse, consider drinking from her, but I now know she needed room in her rotten stomach. Room for my blood. She walked over now, looked at me. Her big light-blue eyes in the yellowish sclera of the new vampire.

"Move aside, Doctor," she said. He moved aside.

With a pale finger, she plucked open the stitch on my leg, pulled the thread out. Lipped the blood off it and tossed it down. I whimpered.

"Shut up."

I shut up.

She bent and put her lips to the puncture, sucked hard. Sucked as much blood from that wound as she could get. But it wasn't enough. So she shifted and slipped a sharp fang under the skin near the crotch, fished around until she found the femoral artery, punched a burning hole in it. Drank. She didn't stop. She arched her back like a cat.

"Joey, Joey, Joey," went my mom, her feet kicking weakly like an infant's feet, letting her magazine drop.

Someone knocked on the door.

"Dr. Goldman?"

"I'm in surgery," the doctor said, staring at nothing, leaning back now so his drool ran on his tie. "Stay out, please."

"Sorry, Doctor."

The room began to go black.

Margaret stopped drinking, let the blood jet from my leg while she said, "And now, you lying little bastard. Now you'll die."

Joey, Joey, Joey.

I heard my pulse in my ears weak and slow.

Then I heard the sound where my pulse should have been.

And I died.

HOW TO BE DEAD

If there's anything as black as the inside of a hospital morgue drawer, I'm not sure what it is. Maybe the middle of a barrel of oil, maybe a mineshaft after a collapse. I returned to something like consciousness aware that it was dark, that I was cold and that my throat, stomach, and ass were raw and burning. Images played in my head, not dreams exactly and not memories, sort of in between, like what you see when you're dozing off. Margaret was at my window, pale and puffy-eyed and dead, she was looming over me in a big nurse's hat, and then I was running from her through a jungle. I came to a big chasm that dropped down a good mile through vines and rocks, but there was a fallen tree across it so I ran for that. A bunch of other guys were running for it, too, but no sooner had we gotten to it than King Kong came around the bend, bigger than life and blacker than hell, beating his chest and roaring. You probably know what happened next; he started rolling the log around and thumping it and guys started dropping off to their deaths, screaming all the way down. That was the scariest scene in that movie, to me at least. This big monkey has you trapped and he knows what he's doing and there's nothing to do but die, it's just a matter of time. I saw it with my folks and Uncle Walt at the premiere—we couldn't get into Radio City Music Hall like we wanted, but we did get seats at the RKO Roxy after a long, cold huddle in line, mostly handled by Dad and Uncle Walt while Mom and I went for doughnuts. Dad made nice with the people behind us by giving them doughnuts. And business cards.

So there I was in my dead-dream, about to get pitched off the log, feeling seasick from all the rolling, and then, as life imitates art, I became aware of actually feeling nauseated. I opened my eyes as hard as I could, I had never been fully certain they were open before, and thought about yelling, but some instinct told me that was a bad idea. I remember my eyes were puffy and sticky and that stuck-together feeling only made my nausea worse. So I barfed. I'll spare you the details, not because I don't remember them, but just, you know. Courtesy. Except one detail's kind of relevant, so you get that one. Sorry. I thought I should turn over to keep from choking, I'd heard that about stew-bums, roll 'em over, but I wasn't choking. Because I hadn't been breathing. I felt scared then, like maybe I should see a doctor about this not-breathing thing, and then I realized my pulse should have been racing. It wasn't even idling. Still. Everything was still in there, except the stomach. I puked again.

That's when I heard voices. I didn't hear them clearly through that drawer, but I heard most of it. Here's how I think it went:

Deep-Voice Guy: *Not in three, three has a resident. Put her in five.*

Really-Yiddish-Sounding Guy: *Who's in three? This must have happened last night.*

DVG: *Yes. Peacock, Joseph. Exsanguination following a stabbing. Date of birth January 9, 1919.*

RYSG: *Just a kid. Bad luck. May I see?*
DVG: *Sure. Three's got a trick door—you have to jog it left first.*
You'd think a door would last four years. I'll get it.

I got this really clear feeling that I should play dead. We're good at that, by the way. Not real fidgety, high pain threshold, room temperature, no breathing or pulse. I lay as still as Abe Lincoln. The door went *shhk-chunk*, deep-voice guy grunted, and then my drawer slid out. I was aware of light on my eyelids. I know I stank and looked a mess. Yiddish-sounding guy said, "Oy." I shit you not, he said, "Oy." How I wanted to peek at him! Was he orthodox?

RYSG: *Aside from the pallor and ejecta, he looks like he's just sleeping.*
DVG: *Here's the wound. Clipped the artery. Doctor removing the foreign body caused him to bleed out. Funny, the wound looked bigger earlier.*
RYSG: *What was it? The foreign body?*
DVG: *A sharp stick.*
RYSG: *Not your night, was it, young man?*

I was scared as hell now. I wanted to move just to prove to myself that I could, that I wasn't just a cold, dead kid getting talked over by doctors, but something told me to stay still, all but *made* me stay still.

DVG: *You never know what you'll see in here.*
RYSG: *Isn't that the truth.*

They slid me back in. I was thinking *Don't shut the door, don't shut the door, don't shut the door,* and they shut the door. They went back to talking about weird deaths they had seen and they put away some other stiff two doors down. Then they left. I had to know if I was really dead, so I moved my hand, or thought I did, then I pinched my own nipple and felt that, or thought I did. I was starting to panic. Then I *did* panic. How would I get out? Where would I go, what would I do, where was my dog, was my dad all right? I wanted to start screaming and kicking the insides of the drawer, that would have made a hell of a racket, but I couldn't. I mean, I could have made myself, I guess, but the urge to bang and yell was less powerful than the need, the *command*, to remain quiet. It was like wanting to get away from bees, only you'd have to jump into a blazing furnace to do it. So I lay there. But the little movements I made in the dark, was I really making them? Was I thinking I had better stay still because the truth was that I couldn't move and never would again? Before long my door went *shhk-chunk* again and a woman cleaned me off with a bleachy towel; soap must have been for the paying customers. She was talking to herself the whole time, half whispering, rehearsing some speech she was going to give her husband when she got home:

"I really don't care *what* your friends think about it I won't have you going to the bar where that tramp works like nothing ever happened between you something most certainly *did* happen even if you think kissing someone isn't a big deal it is to *me* and there comes a time when you've just got to put your foot down so I'm putting my foot down it's a certain kind of woman who works in bars to begin with and what I do may not be glamorous but it's honest not that that cheap piece of goods knows from honest but you should Arthur you really should by the age of thirty-two you're not a kid I won't have it, I won't have it. I won't *have* it."

Every time she said, "I won't *have* it," she gave me an extra hard wipe with the cloth. By the time she was done, I was pretty sure poor Arthur had been stepping out on her. Jesus, who wouldn't? My skin stung from the bleach and she slid me back in.

After she left, I started feeling around for the latch on the inside, but I couldn't find it. Because, of course, there wasn't one. A corpse needs a door handle like a hamburger needs tap shoes. I felt the panic start again, but I fought it down. At least I wasn't covered in puke anymore.

Not long after that, my bowels voided. I thought *no, no, no!* and went to say it, but couldn't do more than move my lips. I had no air in my lungs. I hadn't even noticed. So I just lay in the dark, though it didn't seem *as* dark as it had before, and started having more dead-dreams. The next one was about ants. Everyone in my house was dead, mother, father, dog, Elise, Vilma. We were lying there chopped up like someone had gone at us with a meat cleaver, only there was no blood. Just sugar. Sugar ran out of us like we were burst sacks and countless trains of ants marched from the cabinets and cracks in the walls, little pain-in-the-ass black ants like at picnics. And even though I was lying there on the wooden floor, open-eyed with sugar running out of my mouth and a gash in my neck, I was also standing over me. I started trying to kill the ants, stepping on them with shoes, really nice shoes for some reason, but they wouldn't die. It was like stepping on BBs. But you don't want to hear this, other people's dreams are boring, so who gives a shit?

One more thing, though—I remember ants crawling over my open eyes. I was watching myself not blink while ants crawled on my corneas and through my lashes. And it was just then that my morgue door went *shhk-CHUNK* and opened. I lay still. It was harder this time because my feet wanted to twitch from the memory of killing ants, but I made myself just lie there. My drawer slid out. The lights weren't bright on the insides of my lids this time. This time the lights were out.

"Open your eyes," she said.

Margaret McMannis's voice, emotionless, like she was telling a stranger what time it was.

I wasn't emotionless. I was terrified. I opened my eyes as instructed and tried to give a good yell, but my lungs weren't working. Margaret stood there next to a drooly nurse and an equally charmed young man in shorts and suspenders, his upper lip shiny with snot. Margaret was still wearing her bloody nurse's gear, which she now climbed out of, saying, "You, too," to her hypnotized friends. They both stripped as well.

Even though the lights were out, I could see pretty well. Like everything was gently lit with candlelight though there was no candle. It was kind of pretty, though it would be a while before I learned to appreciate it.

"Get up," she said to me, slithering into the nurse's underthings. I sat up. *Lazarus*, I thought. *This is what it felt like for Lazarus.* I always liked that Bible story in Sunday school. I only actually attended Sunday school about ten times spread out over my whole childhood, but I got the story of Jesus bringing Lazarus back from the dead no fewer than three times. I guess God was giving me a hint. He does that. God or whatever's sitting where God ought to be. I don't think it's what they told us in Sunday school.

I stood up, covering my nakedness as best I could with my hands. When the other boy was naked, she walked over to him and grabbed his chin and the back of his hair. She twisted his head violently, I heard a nauseating crack, and he jerked and went limp. I went to scream again and couldn't. She piled him into my drawer and shut it. The naked nurse moaned a pathetic, helpless moan and drooled. Her glasses were on crooked.

"Look at me," Margaret said. I had been staring at my pale, dead, veiny feet. Now I looked at her. Her eyes, which had looked like lamps to me before, looked more like regular eyes. I was shivering with fear. She slapped me. I stopped.

"No screamin'. No yellin'. I'm gonna give you yer breath back now," she said. And she put her mouth to mine and blew hard. My lungs filled with her lukewarm, stinking air, and I took my first breath as one of the living dead.

"Just so you know, we're even," she said. "You took my life away, and I took yours. Now clean the shite offa yerself, put that kid's clothes on, and let's get out of here. I've got some things to tell you. And more to show you. Smile for me."

I did.

"Yeah, they're comin'," she said. Then she leaned in close and looked at my eyes. "You're gettin' the sight now, too." I made myself breathe in again, then forced the air out past my vocal cords.

"My stomach," I said. "It . . ."

"Yeah, it burns, I know. All right, go bite that tart first and then get dressed."

"What?"

"Don't act innocent. There's nothing innocent about you, and hasn't been for a long time. Put your face near her neck and it'll come to you."

I walked over to the woman. She looked at me, mouth-breathing.

"She's . . . she's too tall."

Margaret laughed a gravelly laugh.

"Look her in the eye and tell her to bend down. She will."

She did.

Her glasses slipped off her head and broke.

I noticed she was sweating. I licked her. I got an erection. The nurse noticed and reflexively reached for it. Margaret slapped her hand away.

"Get on with it, it's almost sunrise," Margaret said. "And if you need to fuck something, you can fuck me. Later. In the dark where I can pretend you're someone else."

That sounded weirdly thrilling.

But not as thrilling as what was coursing through the awkwardly bent-over nurse's neck. I smelled her. Instinct took over. I fed. Salty iron and warm, damp copper rushed into my mouth and I drank hard, grunting with how good it was, arching my back; I came all over myself and the nurse. That's not unusual your first time. The first time's great. And the rest aren't so bad either.

I cleaned up and got dressed.

Just outside the door, Margaret put me in a wheelchair and wheeled me out the front door of Beth Israel and nobody gave us a second glance.

PART 2

F rom the *New York Daily News*, dated February 4, 1978:

CHILD DISAPPEARS FROM MADISON AVENUE HOTEL

A 12-year-old Maryland girl, Renotta Vogel, went missing from a Midtown hotel Thursday afternoon and may have been abducted. The police have no suspects and no motive, but two unidentified children are wanted for questioning.

Mark Vogel, an instructor at the U.S. Naval Academy in Annapolis, brought his family to New York to see their first Broadway play, *St. Joan*. The Vogels report that Renotta befriended a couple of younger children in Central Park and invited them into the lobby of Manhattan's popular Hotel Seville to play.

"I was right there the whole time," said the distraught father. "Monica [Mrs. Vogel] went up to shower, I used the phone in the lobby to call our house sitter about the dog, but I never looked away for more than a minute. One second they were there, the next they were gone. Just gone."

Umberto Pérez, 29, a bellboy at the hotel, remembers seeing the children. "Sweet-faced kids, they both peeked from under a big umbrella. I remember the umbrella because I thought it might snow, but not rain. Too cold for rain."

Despite the freezing weather, both witnesses recall the children were lightly dressed and wore no shoes. "I wasn't going to let them in," said Pérez, "but the older girl [Vogel] said they were friends, and I knew she was a guest. Guest gets what she wants."

Mr. Vogel at first told police that the children, a dark-haired girl and a blond boy, both between seven and nine years of age, never spoke to him, then changed his story. "I have the impression that she was a little foreign girl, maybe British, but I can't base that on a specific memory. I can see her opening her mouth to speak, but when I try to remember what she said, there's no sound there. It's the strangest thing."

Mr. Vogel has offered a $20,000 reward for any information leading to his daughter's safe return. Renotta is five feet tall, has auburn hair, and was last seen wearing a green wool sweater and a white knit cap.

It figures this was one of the few news articles Margaret missed that winter. She was the first generation of her family that could read, so she gobbled up newspapers like she was trying to prove something. She moved her lips, but you wouldn't want to be the one to tell her.

Anyway, she missed that one. We all did.

I don't know that it would have changed anything.

But it might have.

OUR TRIBE

1978
LATE FEBRUARY

Margaret was squatting, looking at me. Cvetko was looking at her, rubbing his hands a little like he was washing them in slow motion. Ruth was standing near her, Old Boy working a toothpick around in his mouth where he would have had a cigarette a few years ago. Smoking's no good for us; all that breathing gives us a headache and the nicotine does nothing because our blood doesn't run much, it mostly just sits there. Most turned smokers try for a month or two, then get tired of it.

Margaret said, "We'll need to call a town meeting. Tomorrow night, an hour past sunset. Tell everyone you can find." And with that, Margaret McMannis strolled off into the tunnel with her escort, the three of them briefly silhouetted by the light of an approaching car. The other two scooted forward into niches for workers, but not Margaret. She kicked her thong sandals off and moved left, fast. By the time the train reached her, she would be up on the roof of the tunnel, hanging over it so the passengers didn't see her; when it was past, she'd drop like a spider and fetch her sandals, Old Boy and Ruth falling into place on her flanks like Thing One and Thing Two.

Cvetko and I retreated back into the darkness that led to our abandoned service rooms, then made our way upstairs. "I'll tell Billy. You tell Luna," I said. Cvetko nodded, said, "Thank you." Luna would be working close to where his latest rash of letters had gone, and, after he found her, he would have time to go socialize with his bridge-club biddies and drink their moldy old geriatric blood.

There were fourteen vampires in our group, all sleeping in little clusters or alone but nobody more than a ten-minute walk. Cvetko and I were in workrooms next to each other; most were in proper rooms a little bigger than mine, quarters for the construction crew when they were building all this.

Margaret, of course, got the sweet spot. The mayor's apartment. Like the governor's mansion or the White House or Buckingham Palace, only under New York City and fitted out for a vampire. Really beautiful place, the cream of nineteenth-century engineering and architecture. Back in the day, they tried out all different kinds of subway cars and tracks before they figured out the system they got now. But instead of getting together and talking it out, all these fat cats just started digging their own tunnels. This one failed experiment was supposed to be high-end, and Margaret's vault was where they were planning to entertain the press and eat caviar with the mayor and all that, only they ran out of money. Of course they ran out of money, tiles from Spain and that green velvet couch and all, a mahogany bar and little statues of angels, I mean Margaret's digs were sweet. Her box was behind the bar, nice and snug, she had it lined with fur. Just on the other side was a fancy door leading to a station platform that never got used except for one demo run by a car that now sat abandoned off its rails (that was where Old Boy lived), and then there was this half mile of tracks before a hole in the wall that opened on a big, deep pit that collected groundwater and stank. We called that Purgatory. That was where we put what was left of people we peeled. There was a rolling cart on the tracks that worked just fine for body dumping.

All of this was on the far side of our little colony, about ten minutes away at a stroll, though I could get there much quicker if I had to. Much quicker.

RUTH AND OLD BOY

Ruth had been friends with Margaret since about 1945, but Ruth was old. Not Clayton or Hessian old, but suffragette old. Born about when Cvetko was (1890?), fifty-five-ish when her clock stopped, square, grim head like a monument, like the Statue of Liberty or Blind Frowning Fucking Justice. Everything on her is square, mannish, solid. Even her fangs are less sharp than most; she has to tear more when she bites, like a dog with a sock. If you think Cvetko's a drag, this woman could have killed the mood on V-J Day. Which was right about the time she got turned—some bughouse-crazy black woman vampire bit her up in Harlem, had the idea she was Margaret Sanger (different Margaret), the woman who opened a colored women's clinic up there fifteen years before. Point of fact, the woman *had* seen Ruth running messages to the clinic, Ruth *did* work for Sanger. Just not real recently. She had been in Harlem that day to visit a woman who used to work there but now had leukemia. The vampire who jumped Ruth told her it was for coming up where she didn't belong trying to get rid of all the black babies. Only Ruth's disappearance made the paper, complete with "her colored assailant seeming to embrace her intimately," and, like I said, our Margaret reads the paper. Scours it for vampire stuff, and this was a bull's-eye. She went up there looking, asking questions, found Ruth. Taught her. Tore the head off the one who turned her. That was the first time she used her shovel, and adopting Ruth was one of the smartest things she ever did. Nobody loves Margaret like Ruth. Ruth doesn't talk much, but she's determined and strong and if Dr. Van Helsing himself were coming for Margaret McMannis, he'd have to get through Ruth first.

Another thing about Ruth. She *looks* dead, even when she just fed. Clayton said older vampires use a constant, automatic low-grade charm that even works on other vampires, even works on themselves, to look the way they did when they were turned. It's the same kind of charm that hides our fangs, only even more automatic; the only thing it doesn't hide so well is the way our eyes shine like cat's eyes when light hits them in the dark. He said it only drops when a vampire is frightened or dying, or when he wants it dropped. He said that he had seen himself and didn't want to again—Clayton was really old. But Ruth, she had learned to relax that. Her skin was greenish-gray and her irises were too light all the time. Except when she hunted. She would charm herself warm-looking like the rest of us to hunt. The thing about Ruth was she hated a liar, which I could understand.

I hate a liar, too.

Old Boy, now here was another beast entirely. Like Baldy, we'll get to Baldy later, Old Boy's name is deceptive. He actually had a boyish face, only got turned in 1972 or so. Wouldn't say who did it, but we all know it was Margaret, she told me. Only Margaret was allowed to turn people whenever she wanted. If one of us wanted to, we could ask, but she almost always said no. She didn't want anybody else having divided loyalties, and a lot of loyalty comes with being turned, even if it's a hostile act. Very conflicting stuff, take my word for it. I *hated* Margaret when she stopped my clock, but I loved her a little bit, too. I couldn't imagine hurting her, and not just because she could kick my ass for twenty years before I got a lick in. There's something instinctual about it. Anyway, Old Boy was a good choice; he was young, but dangerous. He'd been in Vietnam. "Old Boy" was what they called him in his Marine recon unit, and he was really out in the shit, where people took ears and dicks and fingers as trophies. He was good with a knife and stealthy as a mother even before he got turned. Now? Now he was like a breeze you couldn't even feel. He was like a nothing that would kill you before you knew you were in trouble. Big fangs on him, but he used his knife, cut and suck. He watched out for Margaret, sometimes close, sometimes at a distance, and if Ruth would take a bullet for her, figuratively speaking, everybody knew it would be Old Boy who'd get revenge if somebody had two bullets.

He had been working as a security guard at the port. He hated it. He was close to killing himself because he didn't understand life back in the States, preferred moving in the darkness out where you had to machete your way through the mosquitoes and the only friendlies were Hmong and beardy Green Berets who'd half gone native. No, America didn't fit him anymore. Where most guys had nightmares about Nam, he had nightmares about the United States. One of the rare times he talked to me for more than five minutes, he told me he dreamed about having to walk across open places with a tight suit on and everybody looking at him from every window and he couldn't hide anywhere. He'd wake up in a cold sweat dreaming about being drunk in a house full of children, reeling from room to room with tiny children in his way, knowing it was only a matter of time before he hurt one of them and then he'd go to the electric chair. He had Nam dreams, too, but they didn't bother him like that. He woke up from dreams about burning hootches and covering himself in mud to wait in ambush and then he'd wake up and get sad when he realized he was just in his shitty apartment and he had to go out and talk to people he wasn't allowed to punch. He actually spotted Margaret while she was hunting, followed her, kept up with her. That she was able to climb on the sides of buildings didn't surprise him much after the shit he had seen. She didn't even know she had grown a tail. For a while. When she realized a warm body had actually gotten the drop on her, she was intrigued. They sat by the water and talked. She gave him a choice. He took the one that sounded the most like being back in-country.

LUNA AND BILLY BANG

Luna was our closest neighbor. Luna was a prostitute, which, as you can imagine, is a profession that lends itself to vampirism. I'll go out on a limb here and say that as many vampires become prostitutes as prostitutes become vampires, but of course I have only my own bullshit to back this up. Think about it, though. Darkness, privacy, secrecy. It's perfect. They probably start off pretending to be hookers to hunt, but soon they're going through with it because sex and feeding go so well together.

But I don't mean to confuse the issue; Luna was a prostitute first, had a real fucked-up family. Not that all prosties do, that's a cliché. Plenty of them do it just because that's how they're built. But with Luna, the cliché was true. The dad broke the older brother's arm when he found out he was visiting Luna in the basement, but not because it was wrong; because he was jealous. Dad was visiting Luna in the bath. The only people who know where she goes are me and Cvetko; she always lets us know where she's going in case she gets arrested and can't get away. I can't much imagine the scenario in which she wouldn't be able to get away, but the idea of waking up in a cell scares her senseless, so she drops off a piece of wide-ruled notebook paper with the neighborhood she intends to prowl Flair-markered in so we'll know what precinct to bail her out of should she not turn up by four A.M. or so. Of course, this has never happened. The one time she almost got arrested, a john flashed a badge at her and she was so startled she punched him in the mouth rather than charm her way out of it; she hit him so hard she heard one of his teeth hit the window. Backup cop was a lady, pulled a gun. Luna was still freaked-out, showing her fangs, so the cop panicked and shot Luna, shot her right in the forehead. That stunned her, it takes a second to get the brain going again, but lady cop was stunned, too. First time she'd used a gun on something three-dimensional that bled. By the time she stopped making a goldfish mouth and went for the radio, Luna was back in business. She sprained the lady cop's wrist taking the gun from her, threw it in a trash can, and, blinking her own blood out of her eyes, told the cop, "This didn't happen. Go home!" She went home. The male cop was still conscious, so Luna charmed him, too, told him to ram his El Camino into a fire hydrant and forget her face. He did. Case closed.

The notebook paper tonight said,

TIMES ■

I kinda had a crush on Luna when she moved in down the tunnel. Okay, I never completely lost it. Okay, I never lost it at all. She was pretty in that Goldie Hawn way; the other Times Square girls hated her because few of them looked as good as she did when she put on makeup, but they knew better than to fuck with her and so did the pimps. Clayton brought her here from Milwaukee, I don't think she'd been a vampire long, she never said much about that.

He was old, though, like I said. He'd been doing this since Mark Twain was barefoot Sammy chasing Missouri grasshoppers; he got night fever and went sunbathing. More about night fever and Luna later. Luna was Cvetko's business. Billy was mine.

I went up into the tunnel not far from Union Square, waited for a train. I was wearing a black leather jacket, lambskin, really suave, but when the train went by I turned my back, tucked my head, and squared my shoulders. People don't think rectangular shapes are people, it's a ninja trick. Okay, so I had a paisley purple-and-blue scarf on, I loved that scarf, but nobody would know what they were looking at should they see that flamboyant little jab of color, not in the split second they might see me from the train window. I timed it so I turned with the train as it went by me, switching from ninja to torero, letting it glance off me a little and leaping up onto the platform just behind it, turning my landing into a kind of a groovy little dance step. Anybody who caught sight of me would think I had been there all along and they just hadn't noticed; nobody jumps up on a subway platform in midgroove and keeps walking all funky and casual. Nobody but Joey Peacock. That's not ninja stuff, or maybe it is, but I like to think I'm the originator. Did I mention I had numchuks? I was pretty good with them, too. Though that's Korean, I think, not Japanese. Ninjas use *sais* and *shurikens*. That means throwing stars. I had been practicing with those, too.

I made my way through the station, momentarily confused by the blizzard of smells and colors and all the bright light. I kicked a mashed-up half hot dog out of my way, then immediately regretted it because I was wearing my nice zip-up ankle boots. I grabbed a piece of the *New York Post* and wiped off the little bit of mustard and relish, close enough to the 14th Street entrance now to hear Billy. He was playing "Ain't No Sunshine When She's Gone" by Bill Withers. Billy has a taste for the ironic. I like Billy. Even though he got Luna. They were splitsville now, but he definitely got her. You know what I mean when I say got her, right? Yeah, I thought so. Billy *got* everybody.

Anybody else walking up on Billy Bang would have thought he was just a particularly good busker, one of those world-shakers you just know is only stopping underground for a little spare change and a laugh on his way to a recording contract in L.A. or Nashville. Billy was a black guy, mostly, maybe some Puerto Rican. He played his steel guitar like something he stole from angels and he was going to wring one more song out of it before they came to confiscate it. He was a handsome vampire; it was hard not to envy him, twenty-eight forever, wearing only a suede vest on his trunk even in this cold, mirrored sunglasses over his eyes, an ironic cowboy hat on, a foxtail hanging off his fret. Tight jeans and snakeskin cowboy boots. You get the idea. Only Billy wasn't a world-shaker, he was a bloodsucker, and he would never get to Nashville or L.A. because his gig in the tunnels was just too sweet and the blood was too easy to leave behind. Billy was still passionate about music, you could hear it, but it was his second love and always would be.

I walked up to Billy behind a fat lady so he wouldn't see me at first. She bent down to put a quarter in his guitar case and I popped around her side like a tugboat around a freighter, shaking my hand slowly and O'ing my mouth as if to say *Big Spender!* Billy smiled just a little, finishing "Ain't No Sunshine" and tipping his hat for the loose semicircle of listeners, who clapped and came up with another couple of bucks between them before slouching off to their unguessable destinations.

"Joey Peacock! My man!" he said, flashing fangs only I could see, closing his guitar case and giving me some kind of soul handshake I never properly learned my half of. "What's shakin'?"

"Town meeting," I said. I told him when and where.

"What's up her skirt now?"

"Kid vampires."

"Up her skirt?"

"For all I know. But definitely on the cars. Hunting."

I told him what I saw and a big smile crept onto his face. He peeked over the sunglasses, showing his big brown eyes.

"You wouldn't be fuckin' with Billy Bang now, would you?"

"Scout's honor," I said.

He shrugged.

"So, we kick their little asses and make it clear they ain't welcome. Can't be huntin' on the cars where everybody can see. Don't need no new tenants downstairs, neither."

"Makes sense."

"We really havin' a town powwow over this? This sounds like light work."

"Yep. But you didn't see them."

"Well, that's a good thing for them."

Now a slightly chubby part-Asian-looking fellow stood staring at us, holding a Slurpee cup. Denim jacket. Poker visor, don't ask me why.

"What. May I do. For you?" Billy said, putting on his fake-ass cordial DJ voice without actually looking at him.

"Are you done? Your set?"

"Did you see me close my guitar case?"

"Yeah," he said.

"Then, my good sir, I am done. My set."

The guy was shy. This was hard for him and Billy wasn't making it any easier.

"Oh . . . Well . . . I was hoping . . ."

"There's your problem right there. HA-HA!"

"Hoping you might play . . ."

"Get it out, Oddjob." I don't know how he made that sound friendly, but he did.

"Something by the . . ."

It became clear to me that poker visor wasn't just shy—he had something like a stutter. Billy didn't notice or didn't care.

". . . by the Dock of the Bay?"

"No. By the B . . . by the Beatles. 'Hey Jude.'"

"You believe this guy?" he asked me, jabbing a thumb at him and looking at me over his shades. "Man, I ain't got that many na-na-nas in me tonight, cut me some slack."

"Oh," he said, starting to turn away.

"Don't give up so easy, big boy. Just ask for something shorter. Something *civilized*. And feed the crocodile." So saying, he used the toe of his cowboy boot to flip the latch and reopen the guitar case, scooting it around to gape at poker visor, who floated a rumpled dollar into it.

"'Time in a Bottle'?"

"Fuck that. You'll get 'Bad Bad Leroy Brown' and like it. And then we'll go take a walk in the snow."

"Walk in the snow," he said, drooling a little.

"You comin', little man?" he said to me.

"I like the snow," I said, my stomach rumbling.

And then poker visor and me listened to Jim Croce's song about how the big guy doesn't always win.

TOWN MEETING

I won't bore you with the meeting in its entirety. Just the minutes, maybe, would you like that? Members present: thirteen, I won't name them all. Ruth. Old Boy. Me and Cvetko, Billy Bang, Luna, Margaret, Baldy, not really bald, just starting to bald when his clock stopped, but that's got nothing to do with it. His name was Balducci, ex-mob. You know how they say you're never out of the mob? He was out of the mob. And always attached at the hip was Baldy's dago friend Dominic. Dominic was younger, real handsome, a flashy dresser like me. But Brooklyn dumb.

I should tell you about Baldy and Dominic now. Baldy got turned by some hooker (See? Lots of hooker vampires out there, watch yourself!) while he was on business in Philadelphia like eight years ago, came back to New York as soon as he figured out enough to get by. But whoever she was, she didn't stick around to show him anything. Maybe *she* didn't know anything. Dom had been his driver. Dom didn't know why his friend was so sick and pale, had figured he had gotten whacked and was surprised to see him at all, took him home, put him up in the attic. Dom wanted to tell their associates Baldy was okay, things had heated up a little with the Philly people over the disappearance, but Baldy said no, let him lie low for a while. "And stay with me, Dom. Till I feel better." But he wasn't going to feel better till he fed. Which he did, on Dominic, bled him out and backwashed by accident. Bang. New vampire. They knew better than to go to anybody; these dagos aren't big on turning the other cheek but they do call themselves Catholic and know what a vampire is. They knew they were done aboveground. Then they remembered how sometimes the family moved guns and other stuff under the tracks, so they got the bright idea to move in down here. Only they weren't the first vampires to think that. Not by a long shot.

Margaret was in charge then, calling herself the mayor. That she called herself the mayor was kind of a running joke because she had founded this colony, she had charmed the Hunchers into showing her where the best digs were, and she was damned if she was ever moving out of them just because she didn't shake the right hands. She was our chieftess. She was our queen. Our capo. And if anybody understood how those things worked, it should have been a wise guy.

Baldy had never seen the inside of her huge, cush apartment, but he had heard how good it was. The mayor's apartment. He wanted it. It wasn't long before Baldy asked when there was going to be an election. He did it with Dominic standing near him, at a time when Old Boy was away.

Margaret jumped him, dragged him down to the tracks, put his head right by the third rail, and he couldn't do a damned thing. She was stronger. Dominic didn't know what to do; he saw in her eyes she was perfectly ready to fry them both, Dominic too if he touched either one of them, not that Ruth would have let him.

"Let's have an election," Margaret had shouted in his ear. "Right here, right now. I'm running for mayor of the underground, with full and unquestioned authority over every dead person in the tunnels. Will you vote for me, sir?"

He couldn't get any traction. The only thing he could have braced against to try to push back was the rail itself. She was braced against the running rails, and she was just *so much* stronger.

"I said. Do. I. Have. Your vote?"

"Yes."

He never openly bucked her again, but you could see he was waiting. That was Baldy and Dominic.

The rest I'll get to later, too many names at once is a drag, like, how are you supposed to enjoy the party when everyone's rushing up to you with a hand out and saying their name? And you're so busy thinking about how you're going to say your name you miss half of them, even the foxy chick you've already pictured belly-down in a back room getting her bra unsnapped by your fang. Or maybe that's just me. Oh yeah, minutes.

Members' apologies: Sandy. Sandy was only six months into night school, not that there's really a school, that's just a term for it. Being it. Sandy wasn't coping well, prime candidate for sunbathing. We're not even sure who got her, or why—turning somebody is pretty deliberate unless you're new at it and fuck up; spit closes wounds, but if you spit *in* the vein and they die, *shazam*, which is probably how this went. I mean, who'd want to turn a nice mom-looking woman who worked in programming for WNET down in Newark? That's the PBS station. I fucked with her once acting like the Count from *Sesame Street*. "How vell do you see in the dark? How many fingers am I holding up? Vun? Two? Yes! TWO Fingers! HAHAHAHAHA!" I was just trying to cheer her up, but she cried so hard she had a convulsion or something, or thought she was having one, which is what most vampire medical issues are—ghosts of problems we can't actually have anymore. Anyway, Sandy got freaked-out seeing too many of us in one place, so Billy Bang would swing by later and tell her what happened, down where she slept in her cardboard box because she wasn't ready enough to accept her situation to commit to a proper freezer, Dumpster, refrigerator, or coffin. She lived in the most remote part of our loops, under a staircase that led to a walled-up doorway, near Malachi. Malachi had a piano down here, used to teach it before; he kept to himself, but you heard him playing jazz sometimes. You won't hear too much about Malachi, I really didn't know him. Anyway, Sandy. The only reason she was still making it at all was because Billy would take her out and make her hunt, but she had to adopt a whole different persona to do that. Put on a shitload of lipstick and act like some 1940s movie star. Slowly closed her eyelids and opened them again like a lizard before she'd answer you. No, Sandy was a short-timer and we all knew it, even Billy. So no town meeting for her.

Right, minutes.

I forget the date and time, just that it was an hour after sunset and it was cold.

Item #1: There are weird little pale kids who may or may not be vampires charming people on the cars, probably hunting.

Discussion: Baldy pointed out that only I had seen them, but then Luna said she thought she had, too. Another vampire, a light-in-the-loafers, always-overdressed strawberry blond named Edgar, spoke up and said that he had definitely seen two such kids approach, charm, and accompany a woman to the platform and away. Edgar lived with a quiet little vampire named Anthony. Three sightings, all on subway cars of different lines, and that was enough for Margaret.

Action: We would take turns riding the cars in pairs, fanning out to different lines, looking for groups of unescorted children. Upon sighting any, we were to follow them as discreetly as possible so we could see where they were holing up. In the event of trouble, the pair would beat feet back here as soon as they could be sure they weren't followed.

"Everybody pick a partner," Margaret said. I picked Luna, but she picked punked-out Chinchilla, who was turned at eighteen or so. Cvetko picked me, so I picked Cvetko back.

"When do we start, Mama?" Billy said.

"Tomorrow night, Mr. Bang. Two hours of riding, then the rest of the night is yours. And you'll be going with me."

He performed a brief soft-shoe and bow.

"And please knock off that jigaboo shit," she said, smiling inscrutably. He smiled back, just as inscrutably. To this day I don't know much about their relationship, except that I think he *got* her. Billy Bang *got* everybody.

THE SWEETEST GIRL IN NEW YORK

Well, not everybody. He never got Chloë. Chloë was my secret. I went to see her after the meeting. It wasn't so easy to get to Chloë's place; you had to take an abandoned subway tunnel all the way to the Manhattan anchorage of the Brooklyn Bridge. They had all these vaults there, beautiful brick vaults from the 1880s, I swear we forgot how to build nice things. They were nicer than a lot of apartments, only underground, so they were dark and some of them were wet. Hunchers slept in a couple of them; one guy who lived there used his as a carpentry workshop. Made cabinets and tables and stuff; he was the one who made Cvetko's coffin. I liked that guy. I called him Blond Jesus even though his name was George, because he kind of looked like Jesus, except blond and half-blind, had big, thick glasses. A very accepting guy, like you'd expect Jesus to be. Here's an example: This guy really was almost blind; he had to get close enough to his work it looked like he was doing it by smell. No power down there; he lit like twenty oil lamps so his place looked like a cathedral. Used oldey-timey tools. His eyes got a little worse every year. He was thirty now, figured he'd be completely blind by forty, but did he cop an attitude about it? No.

He said his eyesight got him out of the war, and he was really eager to go when the draft board sent for him. Said he was a different person back then, grew up on stories about Mount Curry-botchy or whatever where John Wayne put up the flag on Okinawa. He had been counting the days until he could be a Marine. It broke his heart when the sawbones at the induction station declared him 4-F. He thought he could make it with glasses. His little heart had thrilled every time he saw the evening news and spotted a soldier with glasses, thinking, *That's gonna be me one day!* But his eyes were truly bad—even with glasses, he wouldn't have known Ho Chi Minh from Santa Claus, and Uncle Sam knew it. After he got 4-effed, he was wrecked. But then he had a "holy vision." He understood that he would have "done bad things, really bad things," and I had to wonder what he thought those bad things were. I just couldn't imagine this guy doing stuff Old Boy talked about. I don't think he would have made it out of basic training, he was so high-strung. And gentle. Weirdly, nervously gentle, like couldn't stand the idea of hurting a rat, though everybody underground has to hurt some rats sometimes. In any case, in this "holy vision" he understood that he was supposed to do the work of Jesus on the earth and read about the Buddha, that the only way he could get to heaven or enlightenment, either one was fine by him, was by climbing a tower of cabinets and bookshelves that he built with his own sweat and charged fair prices for. Also, he shouldn't buy the flesh of pigs, though it was all right to eat it if someone gave it to him because it was worse to be rude. Not that people were lining up to hand Blond Jesus pork chops. I know, bugshit crazy, right? But what do you want from a half-blind carpenter who lives in a hobbit hole under the Brooklyn Bridge? You'd have been crazy, too.

Anyway, I tell you about Jesus-George because he was Chloë's closest neighbor. Once you got to George's flickering, lamplit vault and heard him planing away at a long slice of pine, you were almost to Chloë.

Beautiful Chloë.

She had a vault in this same anchorage, only it was set off by itself and hidden. You had to get on your hands and knees and slither through a rusty-ass pipe; seriously, you didn't want to wear nice clothes to see Chloë, but she didn't care about clothes. Once you were through the pipe, you dropped down a crescent-shaped hole into a kind of brick anteroom facing a wall of newer bricks, like somebody had partitioned a bigger room, which they had. There was a place in the wall, about six feet up, where a couple of bricks didn't lie flush, and these were loose, you could see them. If you pulled these out, there was just enough space so a skinny guy could crawl in without getting small.

And that was Chloë's room.

Chloë sat up on a sort of bedrock ledge chest height to me, tucked back in kind of a brick recess. She had a dress on, an old dress from the '30s or '40s, and a bobby pin stuck through her hair; there was still some hair on her, brown and dusty. Though she was mostly a skeleton. Yeah, it's fair to say Chloë was a skeleton. She was small, but not a child, not completely. Maybe a teenager. She huddled against the back of the brick alcove and held her bone knees with bone hands that had the nubs of the fingers worn off. There was dried, old blood on the dress. She was missing teeth, too; she only had a few teeth left in her head.

It seemed to me that Chloë was some kid who got trapped in here and starved. Maybe somebody worked her over at home, maybe her mom found a gentleman friend who knocked her teeth out for her, and she went exploring, found a place to be alone, but couldn't squeeze back out of the hole she had crawled into. Maybe she was too weak. Maybe she was already starving, who knows? Anyway, there were scratch marks on the walls, lots of them. That's what made her fingers shorter. Nasty stuff.

Anyway, I wasn't the first one to find her. Or to take pity on her. She was crowned with dried flowers, had flowers stuffed in the niche behind her, all around her; it was creepy and sad and beautiful. Sometimes I would get flowers for her, too, walk them all the way from Chinatown or Little Italy with old ladies smiling at me like they knew I was on my way to see a dame, and bring them to her. The only bits of real color in Chloë's room were the sunflower I had left behind her and the red roses I had gotten her last Valentine's Day and woven into her head garlands with the drier, brown ones. Mine had dried extra vibrant.

There were other offerings near her, too, cups and saucers with what looked like dried-up wine, coins, a toy horse from way back in the day. Like maybe whoever else found her loved her as much as I did.

This was my favorite room in all of the underground; I came here whenever I was sad or lonely or had to think. There was something so beautiful about the way she sat, sort of defeated and yet like she had kept just enough of her dignity. Something like a kid and a young woman at the same time. When I first found her, her mouth had been frozen open like she had been wailing or sobbing when she died. I remember how carefully I closed it. How tenderly. Like this was the closest I was ever going to come to handling a baby. I wished I had known her. I might have saved her. Might have turned her. She might have been my girlfriend.

Though I never told anyone else about her, I talked to her all the time. About Margaret and about Cvetko, about everything. Even really bad things.

I got the feeling that the real Chloë was a sweet person through and through. I imagined her walking in Central Park back in the day, when we would have both been little kids, back before the crash, before the Hoovervilles, her daddy holding her hand and me walking with my uncle Walt, our two little groups passing on the sidewalk while a guy blew big soap bubbles and somebody in the distance played the clarinet. Both of us young and healthy and full of possibilities, before she was a corpse and I was a monster. I was sure the two of us in that room together was some of kind of mistake. Like she didn't deserve what happened to her, like she was something to blame God with, the patron saint of injustice. Maybe I would have married her. She might have made me a better person. The Chloë I liked to imagine probably wouldn't have wanted me teasing Cvetko. But really I just couldn't help myself.

I SHOT A TIGER IN THE ASS

"I meant to ask you, Cvets, how did the hunting go near Broad-way? Did you ease the melancholy of the postmenopausal? Did you play any exciting games of Hearts or Spades? Did you see Frank Langella?"

This was at the very end of the night, when, above us, all the regular schmucks were fisting the sleep out of their eyes, getting ready to zombie-walk onto their trains and earn their bread.

Cvetko had his big-ass table lamp going; Baldy had run a line down here stealing power off the grid. Cvets didn't need a lamp to see any more than I did, but he said it was easier to read. I read just fine without one, but maybe it's because I got turned younger? Anyway, he was sitting on the floor next to his stack of *National Geographics*. The one he was reading had a freckly redheaded kid on the front, a Mazola corn oil ad on the back. Besides his groaning-ass shelves of actual books, he probably had forty, fifty issues of *National Geographic*, plus *Life*, travel magazines, anything with good photos. I don't think any sad bastard thing Cvetko did broke my heart like watching him thumb through magazines and stare at pictures of sunny places. He waved away my saucy query and pointed at a picture of Arab guys building something, a boat? No, a house like an upside-down boat, made of reeds. Marsh Arabs, three of them smoking, palm trees splayed in the distance against a white-blue sky that stirred fleeting sense-memories of heat and pain.

"Tell me, Joseph Hiram Peacock, about the time you went to Al Kabayish."

"Al Kabeesh my ass, I've barely been out of the boroughs, you know that."

He kept talking, still staring at the picture. "No, Joey, that is not how the game works. I say tell me about the time you went to Al Kabayish, or, if that is too obscure, Egypt. And you entertain me with tales of your adventures there. Perhaps you went to a camel market at the foot of the Great Pyramids and haggled a magnificent bargain."

"Because I'm a Jew?"

"You are, if I remember correctly, half Jewish, raised Presbyterian."

"My mom's a Jew, that's all it takes to get in the club."

"I concede the point, even though it is immaterial. Everyone haggles in Egypt, the Arab as well as the Jew."

"I still think it was a Jew crack. Did you hear Margaret whip out *jigaboo* to Billy?"

He waved that off, never looked up from his magazine, just turned the page. "Or I might say, 'Tell me, Joseph Peacock, about the time you traveled in India.'"

He waited.

"And then you say . . ."

"What?" I said.

"Anything you like. So long as it is entertaining."

"Oh, you want me to lie."

"A mundane lie hiding an exotic truth is deception; an exotic lie hiding a mundane truth is storytelling. Deception may be necessary to preserve life, but storytelling makes life worth living. So make my life worth living."

"I shot a tiger. Like that?"

"Yes," he said, looking at me now, pleased with me. "Exactly like that."

"I shot a tiger in the ass."

"You don't have to be vulgar."

"What?"

"You could shoot the tiger anywhere you wanted to."

"I shot a tiger in the poontang."

"What is *poontang*?"

I smiled a fangy smile at him so he guessed what *poontang* must be. He sighed deep, stale lung air and went back to his *National Geographic*, where, I guess, tigers only get shot in legitimate body parts. He was pissed. I scooted around in front of him, pulled his magazine down with my finger so he was looking me in the eye.

"I shot a tiger straight through the heart. It yawned a big whiskery yawn and stretched and died. It was as long as a small horse, and the raja was happy. He gave me opium to smoke and then the coolies picked up the tiger, only it wasn't really dead, and it clawed a man who died later. Infection. Now everybody shot the tiger. And the raja made the man's family rich beyond their dreams, with rubies and emeralds and pearls and coral. Especially coral."

Cvetko smiled. His eyes twinkled.

"I think there is hope for you. Not much. Just a little. But enough so we may not yet declare you an American savage."

I made like an Indian patting my open mouth and going *woo-woo-woo*.

"It's almost sunrise," he said, a little sadly.

I wasn't sad. I was full of blood, ready to curl up in my fridge like Oscar the Grouch in his can and get some sleep, maybe dead-dream about getting me some little vampire kid scalps on the subway raid.

Cvetko closed his book, crawled into his coffin. For the record, he was the only one of us who slept in an actual wooden coffin, but that's just how he was.

After he tucked in, I picked up his magazine. Wrinkly old Irish fuckers from the Dingle peninsula, a San Antonio colored girl who looked a lot like Elise (only nobody let their nipples show through their dresses back then), and an article about Brazilian killer bees. How they were coming north, all pissed off, how amateur bee-keepers were going to have to find a new hobby. *Nearly identical in appearance to gentler honeybees of European origin, the African bees quickly dominate the hives of the less aggressive strains.* But that's nature, isn't it? Nice guys really do, really always finish last.

We didn't see anything on the subway the next night. Well, no creepy little kids. Just the usual weirdness; punks, dudes with big Afros, women in pantsuits, guys in sideburns, cops. New York cops always impressed me by looking bored and dangerous at the same time, like big, sleepy crocodiles who probably wouldn't notice you, but could really fuck up your evening if they did. Big asshole croc-odiles in their chalky blue shirts and stop-sign black hats, silver badges shining like a lie only kids believed. I always smiled at them, broad enough to show my fangs, confident the constant low-grade charm was humming along, hiding them. One cop, kinda meaty in that used-to-play-football way, woke up a sleeping pot-smelling kid with long hair and a yellow but stained Pittsburgh Steelers T-shirt. He woke him up by poking him with his nightstick. "Hey," he said. "My partner wants to know if you got a joint on you."

"No, man, I'm clean," he said reflexively, rubbing his eyes.

"He's clean," he said to his partner, who barely looked. You could tell he wished he had a different partner. "Too bad. We wanted to party. Anyway, sit up. No sleeping on the cars."

"Okay," he said, and sat up.

But the cop kept looking at him. He wasn't done. "You got your terrible towel on you?"

"Excuse me, sir?" the sleepy kid said. The cop gestured at the T-shirt, so I guessed it was a football thing. Have you noticed that most bullies are boring?

"Oh," he said, getting it. "No."

The cop saw me looking now, looked back. I grinned at him. "How about you, kid, you a Steelers fan?" The train turned, everybody shifted. I let my charm drop for a second, just a split second, giving him a flash of the fangs. He blinked twice. Looked at his partner to see if he saw, but he wasn't paying attention. I kept smiling at him, no fangs. He looked at me, mouth-breathing. The Steeler kid nodded off, started slumping. The train pulled into Penn Station. The cops got off.

Cvetko had watched the whole thing, knew what I had done; I felt him disapprove, but he kept his mouth shut for the moment, went back to reading his book, not a *National Geographic* but some pervert book about naked apes.

I looked at the sleepy kid with his thin, shitty blond mustache, so long it fluttered in his breath. He must have been a mess eating soup. This was a newish style, just the mustache, long hair. I'd seen a lot come and go, hats, no hats, short ties, thin ties, wide ties. I wondered about really old vampires, if they even noticed anymore.

"I want to get really old," I said to Cvetko.

"Why?" he said, without looking up.

"I don't know. I just do."

"You can't bear to think of the world going on without your contributions to it?"

"Ha-ha. I just mean, I'm glad I got bitten, you know? If I hadn't, I might, I mean I *would* . . ."

"Look like me?" Cvetko finished. That caught me up short. He *was* about the age I should have been, after all. Poor Cvets, stuck in that old body. Stronger, more vital, sure, his arthritis went away and all, but he looked old; worse, he *thought* old.

"You know what I mean," I said.

"There are compensations for aging. Children. Grandchildren."

"You didn't have those."

I winced when I said it, I shouldn't have said it like that, but he didn't make a big deal out of it. He was good like that.

"Status in society. Pride in accomplishment. I had those things."

Now three thug-looking teenagers got on the train. They started laughing about Steeler guy, sat around him. One of them reached into his pocket, pulled out his wallet, looking at me and Cvetko with an I-dare-you-to-say-a-word look on his face. Stuck it in his own pocket while his impressed friend stage-whispered, "Oh shit, man, you *didn't*!" Cvetko smiled pleasantly at them, checked his watch. The thief smiled back, mocking, making bug eyes. Cvetko's nostrils flared a little, so I sniffed, too. No beer. He was checking to see if they were drunk or high. He hated biting anyone who was drunk or high.

"Our two hours are nearly up," he said. "Will you finish without me?"

"You bet," I said.

They got off at the next stop, still giggling. Times Square. Cvetko followed them off, keeping a discreet distance. I watched Steeler kid snore his mustache into his mouth, thinking it was quite likely he was going to get his wallet back in the mail.

NIGHT FEVER

Now's a good a time as any to tell you about night fever. You might guess it's kinda like cabin fever, and, yeah, that's close. Night fever is what happens when a vampire can't take being in the dark anymore, but it's more than that. It looks neuro-whatsical, but Cvetko says it's a disease of the soul.

The guy who brought Luna here from Milwaukee, Clayton? Clay, really. He was smooth. He was from Boston, though he'd lost the accent. Born around 1820, turned before the Civil War, traveled around on trains, developed all kinds of tactics for sheltering during the day while on the road; he would do anything, submerge himself in mud bogs, sink himself with a big rock and sleep in a lake, dress as a cop to get himself invited in someplace, then hide in the attic or basement and sleep there. He knew a lot about vampires, kept a book just full of notes describing some of the vampires he met, where he met them. Margaret was keeping it now, had been since Clayton died last summer, we called it *The Codex*, and what sad bookworm bastard do you think came up with that? Cvetko is right, sixty-four dollars to you.

The first symptom of night fever: increased desire for blood. You can't stop drinking. This is dangerous because you end up killing people. Killing people means you risk making more vampires. Clayton made two new vampires, both in '76 when he was starting to slip his chain. Billy Bang is one. The other didn't make it.

Second symptom of night fever: desire for abasement. As opposed to what you get in Kansas when you see a tornado coming, which is the desire for a basement. Don't worry, Cvetko didn't laugh either when I told him that one. But you start feeling dirty, like you're no good, like you don't deserve to drink human blood anymore. Clayton started bringing food down here on purpose, stuff he got out of the trash, but any kind of food is a big no-no in the tunnels because it brings on rats. Lots of them. Carpets of them. But that's what Clayton wanted. We'd find him sleeping outside his box, just surrounded by dead rats like pistachio shells or something, smiling and shaking. If you're in a neighborhood where pets start to go missing, you got either a psychopath working his way up to people or a vampire working his way down from them.

The third symptom is the worst. Tremors. I've seen a vampire pull out of night fever before, but not once they started rocking and rolling. It's like they just can't hold still anymore, not their head, not their limbs, you hear them scraping around in whatever they're sleeping in.

Symptom four? Not really a symptom, more of an event. You go sunbathing. For real. Not just tooling around Washington Square Park when it's raining and the sun won't come out; not getting yourself sick by going out without sunglasses when it's overcast and the bright gray clouds press a headache behind your eyes; I mean stepping right into full-on sunshine naked as a jaybird and dying forever. The newspapers never cover it or, when they do, they make up some normal explanation or call it spontaneous human combustion, which is right except for the "human" part.

Anyway, Clayton. One day I was walking near his and Luna's cavelike place and I heard him moving around, dragging his limbs and whimpering. Luna was outside his box crooning down mother-tones to him even though she was so sleepy she could barely stand from the last two days. He finally convinced her he was all right and she collapsed into her junkyard armoire. I went to my room, but I heard him. He went.

Next night there was a bit in the *Times* about a guy who doused himself in gasoline and jumped off the Brooklyn Bridge. "Fell like a comet," the *Times* said; "Blazing like a star," said the *Post*. Coincidence? I don't think so. They said it was some other guy, a Steven Bergman or something, who also went missing, but newspapers are like cops, they just don't like loose ends.

It had been summer, bright, warm. That matters; what *kind* of sun you get hit with, I mean. Cool winter sun makes you smoke; you can actually get a dose of that and live, if it's hazy or misty at all. Bright summer sun, you catch fire. Takes a couple of seconds. I hear in the desert it's almost instant, you go up like a torch. Not a lot of vampires in the desert. We like it up north.

I had bright winter sun on me once, thank God it was through a window, glass helps just a little. A normal kid I used to hang out with and pretend to smoke cigarettes, his name was Freddie, played a nasty trick on me once. I actually told him what I was, this was like five years ago. He was kind of a nerd, went to Stuyvesant not too far from us. He kept me out after sunrise in his room, had the blinds down. There was a manhole cover just outside his house I figured I could get to when a cloud passed, it was stupid. But the bastard actually lifted the blind on me because he thought I was bullshitting him. "Vampire my ass," he said. I still have the scar from it, a permanent pinkish-gray triangle on my left elbow that's really intense and knotted at the point, then fades out as it goes. It smoked like a bitch, hurt like a bitch. I punched him in the nose and took the blanket off his bed, busted out the window, and went down the manhole. Who was he going to tell? Who would believe him? Fuck Freddie, I never saw him again.

But Clayton, he got the full treatment.

Those Hudson River frogmen weren't going to find a damned thing; when sunlight torches one of the family, it even torches the bones.

Clayton was the second-oldest vampire I knew about in New York.

The oldest was a Hessian. Like, played for the other team in the Revolutionary War. Big bastard, pale as death, never fully lost his German accent. Had a house in Greenwich Village, beautiful place with bars on the windows and a servant; the Hessian is stinking rich and nobody fucks with him. Or at least they didn't for a long time. More about him later, much later.

But enough about night fever and Hessians.

You probably want to hear about the next time I saw those kids.

Okay.

But the story jumps ahead now.

THE RAIN SONG

You know how when you're a kid a rainy day seems like the end of the world? You press your forehead to the window and sigh, fogging the glass, drawing squiggles in the fog with your pudgy little finger or maybe writing the word BORED but not backward so a woman walking by on her way to the bank or somewhere errandy glances at it but doesn't take the time to work it out, just clip-clops along hunched under her umbrella, those perfect, temporary circles pinging in the puddles at her feet. And the sun, fickle in this gray city, always a flight risk, seems gone for good. No note, just went out for cigarettes and never came back. Your dad and mom are seething with some just-under-the-skin fight and they wish you could go play even more than you do, if that's possible, cause they've got awful things to say to each other, things you can plaster over maybe but they're part of the architecture now. And you? You're tired of your toys and nobody will play a game, and you've read everything twice and the dog barely wags at you, barely cocks his eye at you, knows you're dangerous somehow.

That's a rainy day for a kid, a rainy Saturday anyway.

When you're a vampire, a rainy day is a hall pass.

This particular day, a freaky warm Saturday in March, I was sitting just inside the entrance to the subway with my soccer gear on and a transistor radio on my lap, not caring that I was in the way, making the wet, grumpy lava flow of mass transit users even grumpier for having to step around me. One lady actually shook her umbrella out practically on me, said, "Oh, pardon me, I didn't see you." I thought about following her down but didn't want to taste her, thought her blood might be rank with all that sourpuss she was pumping out of her sourpuss gland.

The radio was fuzzy; I twiddled with the antenna.

"Warmer than normal (*pffft*) time of year in the greater New York metropolitan area. Expect light rain (*pffft*) cloud cover for the rest of the day and over . . . (*pffft*) clearing tomorrow morning. The temperature at Central Park is (*pffft*)."

Music to my ears, static and all.

I slipped out of the Columbus Circle entrance and crossed the street to the park's southwestern corner. I stayed away from the carriage horses—one tried to bite me once, made quite a scene—and instead steered toward the guy at the kosher hot dog cart, asked him what time he closed. Six? Perfect. Would he mind holding on to my radio till I got back? Drool and nod, surprisingly feminine way of patting his mouth with the corner of the napkin, I think this guy wore lipstick in his free time. It was already after four; I'd probably forget the radio, but I had six or seven more of them in my room—if shoplifting were an Olympic event, I'd be Mark Spitz.

I tooled around for a while, past the big, useless *Maine* memorial, I mean, the Alamo's a good story, I get that, but the *Maine*? Smelled like an inside job to me. Fuck the *Maine*! I went to Umpire Rock to look at the skyscrapers jutting up past the trees, Essex House blazoning its name in hooker red, much less elegant than the Hampshire House next to it; then past the Carousel, the dilap-idated Dairy, up and patted Balto's head. When I was still a real kid, me and a bunch of other small fry hitched our sled behind the big bronze doggie and Dad's friend Walther took a picture. Must have been 1929, 1930, after the crash because I remember looking at the skyscrapers on Park Avenue, watching for guys jumping. Uncle Walt told me about the jumpers; he was always telling me creepy shit in that matter-of-fact way that made you love him, made you sure everything was all right because all the bad stuff he told you about had to get through him to get to you. I don't know what happened to that Balto picture. I don't know what happened to anything.

I doubled back to the Sheep Meadow; I knew that on this first almost warm day of 1978 I'd see kids playing soccer there, rain or no, and I did, a bunch of them all muddy and swearing and laugh-ing, a few spectators sharing cigarettes on the sidelines. I asked if I could play, and they didn't let me at first, and then a few of the older ones left when some girls came by and I was in.

At first nobody wanted to pass to me, younger as I was and dressed in my really square parochial soccer jersey and all, but a ginger kid got in trouble and booted it sideways to me, so I yo-yoed that ball around like Pelé and scored bigger than hell. I dialed it back after that, let kids take the ball off me half the time, but scored twice more. One of the fullbacks on the other team called me "shrimp," a tall, skinny, bucktoothed kid you just knew would end up in jail. One of my teammates stood up for me, said, "That's *Supershrimp* to you! He fucked you up twice now!" and bucktooth didn't like that. Made a point of tripping me the next time I got near him. I gave him a cleat in the nuts during a big tangle-up later and I could tell he wanted to fight but didn't want to look like the bully he actually was. The rain got heavier then, and most of the kids left. But bucktooth wasn't done with me, nor I with him, so we stayed on to keep playing three on three. A Puerto Rican kid split for dinner, so we were left with five. Soccer was out. Bucktooth suggested Smear the Queer, looking right at me, and I said, "Hell yeah!" in my ten-year-old's falsetto, making the others laugh. One threw me the ball, and off I went, weaving around the dirty, mostly pale legs and twisting out of feeble claw-hands until it began to strain credibility and I let myself get smeared. But something had shifted in the group dynamic; they liked me. I had outmaneuvered seemingly older kids well enough to make them go "Whoa!" and "Damn, Supershrimp!" and then taken my lumps while laughing. They piled on me, sure, but the late knee or elbow from bucktooth never came. Instead, he awkwardly patted my back as I got up. At that moment I decided I wouldn't follow him home after all.

But I had to follow somebody. The hunger was on me. And the place was emptying fast; Central Park wasn't a place where good citizens wanted to get caught after dark.

I left the meadow, looking back over my shoulder as I went. I remembered when that other big, open space, the Great Lawn, was a Hooverville, full of improvised shacks and tents put up by the poorest of the poor during the Depression. Not long after I got turned, I saw a guy cut another guy's ears off with a razor up there, just cut 'em right the fuck off, said what did he need ears for if he wasn't going to listen. Kids then played stickball, kids always play, but when they weren't doing that, they were hunting pigeons and squirrels with slingshots. You know, for dinner. People now bitching about gas rationing and recession have no idea. No fucking idea whatever.

I steered toward the Delacorte, deserted now, but the theater crowd would come in a few months with their rich, winey blood corralling themselves within the limits of the lights, laughing their pretty laughs, the women in their pantsuits, the men in their longish hair and wide ties. But before I could get there, I entered the drip-ping green little forest of the Ramble, an especially bad place to hang out when the light was failing. On a lucky night, you'd trip over gays gaying it up. On a less lucky night, well, let's just say the weath-er's a little muggy. As if to illustrate this, a pair of nearly skeletal black dudes noticed me; one got up from where he had been squat-ting beneath the shelter of a branch-hung garbage bag, burning the edges of a plastic orange Frisbee with a lighter, I can't say why, sometimes there is no why. Sometimes it's just Frisbee-burning time. "Li'l man, li'l man," he chanted in a kind of singsong, motioning me to him for what purpose I did not know, flipping the smoking Fris-bee in his hand, grinning a big alligatory grin. But then the older fellow that he had been squatting near said, "Butterbean, let him be! He one a' them." Butterbean stopped cold and turned around, moved back into the darkness under the bag, saying quietly, I think to me, "I didn't mean nothin'. I wa'n't gonna do nothin'."

One of them? One of them, who? Inquiring minds want to know. I walked toward them.

"Get on outta here!" the older one said. "Go on back to the cas-tle, now, you don't want us. We dirty."

Even as he said that, I heard the crunch of a syringe under my shoe. Dirty indeed, and he was talking about his blood. He knew what I was!

"The rest of us are at the castle? Like, the Belvedere Castle?" I said.

"I dunno, just get on. Please."

"But at the castle?"

"Some nights."

I stopped. They both visibly relaxed. The older one took a hand out of a pocket.

"Th'ow me that Frisbee."

WHAT I FOUND IN THE CASTLE

I walked up the steps to the Belvedere Castle, a nineteenth-century fairy-tale castle overlooking the turtle pond and the Delacorte theater. The fairy tale had turned dark, though; the windows were boarded up with plywood and the stonework and doors were blemished everywhere with shitty graffiti tags. The plywood, too. The only ones I could read were *MASTER* in rain-washed labia pink and *Lucky I* or *1* in Casper-the-Ghost white.

Stay focused, I thought.

Blood.

I smelled blood.

It wasn't dark yet, but it would be within the hour, normally my time, but I found myself feeling nervous. I had only met new vampires a few times, and always vampires like me. Were there other kinds? I had heard rumors. Vampires that fly. Vampires that are really insects. But who knows? My rumor policy is keep an open mind but don't believe until you hear it from somebody who saw firsthand. Someone you trust. Still, I found myself looking up in the sky.

It was raining harder now. I opened my mouth and let the water run in; I blinked my eyes against the drops that fell, watching them make their way down to me from on high. Normally I only saw rain up to streetlight height, but here it came, real and ordinary water falling from higher than I would ever reach.

Stay focused.

I knew what I was doing. I was putting it off. My heart beat once or twice like a rusty old engine trying to turn over, which of course it only really did when I jumper-cabled it to a living heart by feeding.

"Hey, kid."

I turned and saw a husky negro cop. His overlong mustache wasn't even. Probably a bachelor, a wife would have told him.

"Get outta there. It's not safe."

He was genuinely concerned.

"What's in there?" I said in my best ten-year-old kiddie voice, pointing at the castle.

"Nothing for you. Now get on home. This is no place for kids."

Not living kids, I thought.

"Okay," I said. He watched to make sure I went down the steps, then kept walking.

"Thanks," I said, making as if to take Transverse out of the park like a good lad. Once I was out of his sight, though, I pulled off my shoes and socks and plastic shin guards and skinnied up the wall of the castle: bad cat, bad rat, dead kid. Actually slipped once because of the rain but caught myself so fast you wouldn't have noticed if you were watching. I went all the way to the top tower, approached the round window upside down. I peeked in. Just weather equipment, no visible way farther down. I went down a half story to a busted-out slot window, too small for a person but I wasn't exactly a person. I got small, felt my skull squish flat, my vision went screwy until my head formed up on the other side; then I wrestled one shoulder at a time through, mashed my pelvic bones flat, tore up my shorts and soccer jersey real good. But it took less than five seconds and I was in.

Be so quiet.

The landing up top was littered with clothes: a girl's green sweater, torn and bloody; a suede hippie coat with a fringe, likewise bloody; two pairs of prescription glasses, one broken; some poor fucker's fake leg, a purse, two wallets, a Timex, a bloody knit hat, a pack of gum.

Oh fuck, this is for real.

I went down the stairs against the wall, one delicate step at a time.

Easy does it, grasshopper. When you can walk on rice paper and leave no mark, it is time for you to go.

I remembered that Margaret had said we should only report where they were staying so we could come back in force, but I was too damned curious. Plus, I knew I could get back up those stairs and out the window so fast nothing could grab me. None of the other vampires I knew were as fast as me. I would be okay.

Breathing.

I froze. Whoever was breathing was barely breathing, and doing it through his nose. I slid up against the wall and took the rest of the spiral staircase sideways, belly against stone. I took it slow.

When I got to the second floor I saw him. A man, stripped to the waist, bloody to the waist, tied to a metal folding chair, gagged with a knotted bandana. He was barely conscious, heavily charmed and dying. His possessions lay scattered about the room like debris, as if he had exploded: keys, a wallet, a corduroy jacket, broken sunglasses, the other Hush Puppy.

Trace light from the failing day leaked in around the edges of the boards over the windows.

His head lolled.

I debated going over to him, looked at the floor. Stained with blood but not pooled; whatever blood had fallen there had been lapped up. I looked more closely. Bloody footprints, bloody hand-prints. Small ones. Child-sized.

Rather than add mine to them, I crept across the wall, over the boards on the windows.

This poor fucker. I crawled closer. It's hard to stay stuck sideways on a wall with only three limbs, but I reached for his wallet, the contents of which lay pooled half in it as if the wallet had vomited. I saw his driver's license and plucked it up.

Gary Combs.

A much younger, healthier Gary Combs smiled at me from the photo on the plastic. The guy in the chair looked like his dad, pale as a jellyfish, his neck and wrists brutalized with multiple bites that weren't healing; they had made him too weak to heal. He was shivering. His foot twitched and sent a Fanta grape soda can rolling.

Vampires don't drink soda. I noticed other cans, a hamburger wrapper, a plastic bucket that smelled like piss and hamburger puke.

They were trying to keep him alive. How long had he been here?

I looked behind me and listened—nobody coming. I stole closer to him, stepping on the wallet and Hush Puppy so not to add my size-eight footprints to the smaller ones on the floor. What should I do? Let him go? He wasn't going to make it unless he got to a hos-pital right now, and maybe not even then.

Cvetko would let him go, maybe even take him for help. Cvetko didn't believe vampires should kill. And certainly not like this. This was *nasty*. It was like they didn't care what they were doing, or didn't know any better.

I started loosening the knot of the bandana so he could maybe breathe a little. It was soaked with drool. And blood. Out of nowhere I realized I was hungry, ravenous even, but feeding off this guy would put him under.

"Gary," I said.

His eyelids fluttered.

"Mr. Combs."

He looked at me. White guy, a little funky, had a graying goatee. A professor? Bookstore owner? Something smart. I scanned the floor for glasses, didn't see any.

He looked at me now, afraid but charmed enough not to panic.

I poured a little charm into a harmless lie.

"You're going to be okay."

He didn't nod. He just accepted the sentence, too tired to agree or disagree.

"Who did this to you?"

Mild surprise filtered through exhaustion. I should know very well who did this to him, his eyes said.

"You."

"Me?" I said, touching my chest exactly like my mom would have, very Jewish.

"You. Kids. Ghost kids."

"How many of us are there?"

He smiled and shook his head.

"You're. Not so bad. Don't mean it. Can't help it."

"How many?"

He looked sad now. Balled up his face to cry.

"Nobody's . . . feeding."

"It sure looks like somebody's feeding."

He shook his head.

"My bird. Gonzalo."

"What kind of bird is it?"

That sounded stupid as soon as I said it, making small talk with a dying man in a vampire lair.

"Pretty," he said.

He shivered really hard.

"Want. Coke," I heard. I looked around, found a Pepsi can with a little sloshing around in it. I held it to his lips. He shook me off.

"Cold," he said. "Coat."

Duh. That's what he said the first time. Poor bastard's in shock. I went to get his coat, but couldn't pick it up because there was something on it. A foot. Attached to a boy. A very cold, very white little boy, dressed up as if for church but wet, and barefoot. And a little bloody.

He stepped off the coat. I picked it up, my rusty old heart fear-beating now. I draped the coat around Gary Combs, who shivered again, but I kept an eye on the boy.

"Have you come to play?" he asked.

I noticed he was holding a folded-up umbrella.

British? A British kid?

He looked to be about eight years old.

Be friendly. Be sweet. They're dangerous. He won't be alone.

"Is this how you play?" I asked, nodding back at the expiring Mr. Combs.

"No, silly. It's how we eat. We're like you. See?"

He showed me a vicious set of fangs, showed them to me like another kid might show where a grown-up tooth had replaced a baby tooth. Now a little black-haired girl came down the steps behind him, white and quiet as a ghost, her hair wet from the rain.

It was the girl from the subway. Without her makeup.

Get out.

I looked at the boarded-up windows leading to the balcony on this level, assessing whether I could actually bust through the plywood on the first try. I thought maybe I could. The image of Wile

E. Coyote leaving a coyote-shaped hole in the plywood came to me and I almost laughed, but I didn't.

Now she stood a little behind him, taking his hand. Like siblings.

"I can hear your heart," the boy said. "You're affrighted."

"Frightened," I said.

"Yes," he said, smiling a little. "I forgot."

"I think I just want to go."

"Please don't," the girl said, so quietly I barely heard her. "What's your name?"

"Joey," I said, without thinking about it.

"Joey," the boy said in a childish singsong. "I knew a Joey, push-come-shove he ran very slowey."

"If you didn't come to play, what did you come for?"

Gary Combs groaned, pissed himself. The boy said, almost absentmindedly, "You were supposed to ask for the bucket." Then, to me again, "My name's Peter." His little white hand came out. We shook. Two cold boys. He was colder.

"He needs a hospital," I said, indicating the man in the chair.

"What for?" the girl said.

"He'll die without it."

"He's supposed to die," she said, all innocence.

"No," I said. "He's not."

"He's just a poppet. It's what they're for."

"No."

"Why?"

"Because. The police. They'll find out and start looking. Eventually they'll find something."

"Oh," she said.

Peter said, "How do you not kill them?"

"Nobody showed you?"

He shook his head. So did she.

She said something so low I couldn't hear. I leaned closer, still standing awkwardly on shoe and wallet.

"Won't they come looking if we take him to hospital?"

Smart thing, I thought. What was she, seven?

"Maybe," I said. "You've made a huge mess of this."

"Sorry," she said, nudging the boy. "Sorry," he echoed.

Not as sorry as him.

As I went to look at poor Mr. Combs again, I noticed he had a third child in his lap, another boy. This one in dirty jeans and a *Keep on Truckin'* T-shirt. Vaguely Indian looking. The man started muttering to the little creature, and at first I thought he was pleading, but he wasn't. *"I just want you to know it's okay you're just kids someone did this to you and you're just kids just kids pretty kids like Gonzalo pretty bird talks and whistles you'd like my bird."*

The boy petted his hair while he spoke, all the while squirming up his lap, positioning himself closer and closer to the insulted neck. Still petting, he bobbed his head once, gouged his outsized teeth into the man's neck and drank. A weak jet of blood escaped around the boy's teeth, made him squint and grunt, and the girl darted forward, licked the drops from the ground.

The first boy, hopping from foot to foot, opened and closed the umbrella, his mouth open in a dumb, hungry smile that showed off his fangs and let fall a runner of drool.

Jesus, they're animals.

But not as bad as whoever turned them.

That fucker needs to die.

Gary stopped talking. I watched his head drop as slowly as a setting moon, so slowly you almost couldn't see it happening.

Hungry as I was, I didn't feed on him.

Not with them.

Not yet.

GONZALO

"**S**o what's your name, ugly parrot?"

It didn't say anything, just cocked its head and blinked its huge, smart yellow eye at me.

"Say *Gonzalo*," I said. "Gonzalo? Is that you?"

It bobbed its head. Was it nodding? I didn't think so, they just bob their heads sometimes, right? What the hell do I know about parrots? Why was I here? I looked around Gary Combs's Chelsea apartment, which was full of all kinds of Japanese and Chinese stuff and heaping shelves full of books and stacks of records. The dominant feature of the room was the cage. It was a big cage.

"Pretty bird," I said. It scratched its face and stood on one foot.

"I don't know what I'm doing here," I said. "I just, I don't know. Are you hungry? Where's your food?"

It went back and forth on its wooden bar, clicking and whistling now. It knew what was up. I found a bag of sunflower seeds under the sink and poured some into the feeder. I didn't know how much to pour. Whatever, it ate, and, while it did, I peeled a magnet of a cockatoo off the fridge and stuck that in my pocket.

I caught my reflection in a mirror, sort of a big tin square thing from Mexico or somewhere. I grinned at myself, stuck my tongue out. My tongue was still bloody, and I had some around the gums. I hadn't done a great job cleaning myself after biting the man in the park, a big guy I charmed into bending down to hug me. I patted his back in that huggy way while I fed, made sure we were mostly hidden, but just in case I told him, "Sob a little," and he had. Just a kid hugging his dad, maybe getting over some tragedy. People turn away from a man crying. They'll watch a woman, but not a man. He was big enough I knew I could take a pint and a half off him, and he'd been okay. Staggered a little, still sobbing, holding his neck. "Put your hand down, stop sobbing," I had told him, and he had.

"Good-bye," he'd said sweetly, like he missed me already.

"Yeah," I'd said, hating myself and what I was, which was something I didn't feel very often. "Keep walking, go away."

He went away.

I went to the sink now, splashed some water on my tongue. Evidence, shmevidence, the police wouldn't find anything, even our fingerprints disappear. Still, I shouldn't hang out too long.

I looked at the books and records formerly owned by Mr. Combs: science stuff, physics. Some of it in German. Yawnsville. This guy would have gotten along great with Cvetko. Novels, mostly arty-smarty: Günter Grass, Herman Hesse, *The Little Prince*. I liked *The Little Prince*. The music was better. Jazz, mostly—Miles Davis, Charlie Parker. I took the Miles Davis, *Sketches of Spain*, slipped it under my arm. It was a pretty cover.

Of course I went through his drawers and got some cash, a tie pin with a diamond, a silver ring with three pieces of onyx; he wasn't going to need any of that.

I noticed his bed was made. He was a bed-maker. Made sense, the place was cluttered but clean. His mommy taught him right.

I was about to leave. I had fed the bird, filled my pockets, gotten a snootful of a dead man's scent and now I had a bad case of the what's-it-all-fors. My hand was on the knob.

"Want to groove on Miles?" the bird said. Then, more excitedly, "Miles Davis!" And it clicked and whistled its ass off.

One thing about carrying a birdcage on the subway, everybody looks at you. Saturday night, the 6 train. Everybody was on their way out to a movie or a late dinner or just to get good and schnockered at some Midtown watering hole. Too many people to charm more than mildly; hiding my fangs was as good as it was going to get.

"What kinda bird is that?" said a cowboy-looking guy, good and loud and twangy, doing that thing hicks from the sticks do when they want to show they're more sociable than New Yorkers.

"I don't know."

"What do you mean you don't know?"

I shrugged, looking at him.

"Well, what's his name?"

"Why, you want his phone number?"

"Nice kid," he said to everybody and nobody, laughing like, *See, I knew you were all a-holes here.*

Maybe we are.

"Hello?" Mrs. Baker said from inside her apartment.

"It's me," I said, grinning a shit-eating grin at the little round peephole, holding the cage while Gonzalo said, "Are you cold? Do you want the heater? Are you cold?"

I laughed.

The bird laughed, too, but like somebody else, probably his master.

I heard her draw the chain out of the latch and open the door. I stepped in quick. Little Baker was at his post in the recliner, eating a bowl of ice cream with M&M's on top, pouring Coke in. Well, he wasn't keeping that ass on him with baby carrots.

"Who is it, Mom?" he said, sounding annoyed. "The commercial's almost over."

"Just me," I said, and he looked up and started drooling.

"It's an African gray parrot," his mom said absently, also drooling a bit.

"Is it?"

"Yes."

"Well, his name's Gonzalo, and you're all going to be very happy together. He eats this stuff."

I handed over the bag of sunflower seeds plus a box of macaw feed. At the sound of the bag, the bird went back and forth on his bar.

"They like fresh fruit, too. And nuts," she said.

Gonzalo clicked and bobbed his head.

"How do you know this stuff?"

"My sister's ex-husband owned a pet store. He threw himself under a bus. Right in front of her. I didn't care for him."

"That's nice. Where's Pops?"

"Out."

This was a problem. I'd have to charm him, too, or he might dump the bird.

"Out where?"

"Felix's. On the corner. It's the only bar on the block."

Problem solved.

Back in television land, the commercial ended.

"MO-om!" little Baker said.

"MO-om!" the bird said, exactly imitating the kid's bratty, entitled whine.

I laughed and Gonzalo said, "Live from New York, it's Saaaatur-
day night!"

Damned if it wasn't, too.

I loved that bird.

I walked into the corner bar, Felix the Cat's, one of those old-guy
places that smelled like weak beer and Kool cigarettes, a shitty
television over the bar next to a little team of Clydesdales pulling
their beer wagon around in circles under a glass dome. The only guy
in the place with long hair was swearing at that stupid game where
you slide the disc down the plank.

Mr. Baker was bellied up to the bar, watching himself get old
in the long, dirty mirror. He said "Hi" mildly when I slid up next
to him.

"Who's the kid?" the bartender said.

"My son."

"I thought I met your son."

"My other son."

Howard Cosell was talking away on the television. Someone
threw a peanut at him, earning him a finger wag from the barman,
but it was a good throw, would have hit Howard right in the eye,
might have made him jerk his head and knock his lousy toupee
crooked.

I told Mr. Baker that he and his family were the proud owners of
a new bird. "What kind?" he drooled. I mopped his lip with a napkin
before the barman saw.

"African. It's gray."

"A bird? A real, honest-to-goodness *bird*?"

"Well, yeah."

"I always wanted a bird. I have to go meet him! Is it a him?"

"I didn't look. But I think so."

"Him," he said. "I have to! I . . ."

"What?"

His eyes started to moisten. Then he grabbed my shoulder hard.

"Good-bye."

He got up in a spasm.

He was so enthusiastic about his new bird that he stuffed his pockets with peanuts and left immediately, forgetting to pay. The bartender called after him; he held up the I'll-be-back-in-a-minute index finger and kept going, but he wasn't going to be back in a minute. I paid for his three Budweisers. I had already said my good-byes to Gonzalo, but they were really so-longs. I had to find Cvetko and tell him what I saw, but first I had to make sure I got to see that bird again. It was a really cool goddamn bird.

LUCKY LUCKY

"And they just let you go?" Cvetko said. The old woman walked up to me with a tea tray for the third time in ten minutes.

"He does not care for tea," Cvetko said again, but he wasn't particularly good at charming. I was.

"No tea," I said. "Now knit or something." But I shouldn't have said "now" because she dropped the whole tea set with a crash-bang and went hobbling off for her needles and yarn. The whole rest of the talk with Cvetko she just sat there, bleeding and knitting; she must have been on some anticoagulant. Cvetko wiped at her neck with a cloth so she didn't mess up her nightgown. Kind of a saucy nightgown for an old bird, like satin or something; she must have really been looking forward to her visit.

"Of course they let me go, they're just little kids."

"I should loan you a book about 'just little kids' on a desert island."

"Is it like *Gilligan's Island*?" I said, fucking with him.

He sighed.

A little white paw flicked out under the bathroom door. The light was on in there.

I asked Cvetko, "Why do all old ladies have cats?"

"I enjoy cats," the old lady said. "They sit on your lap and purr when it's cold. It's a great relief to loneliness. Do you have any idea what it's like to know that you are unlikely to live more than a decade? To have survived all those who were familiar to you so that everyone is a stranger? To feel that you're tedious to these strangers? But really, it's the nearness of death, especially for a secular person. Cats help with that." She went on smiling, knitting, drooling, bleeding. Cvetko dabbed at her. She mouthed a silent *Thank you*.

"Are you done here?" I said. "Can we go talk somewhere? Maybe Old City Hall?"

In the same way that I had Chloë to go to when I wanted some peace, Cvetko had the Old City Hall station. I'm the one who showed it to him. The first time he saw it I thought he was going to cry at its vaulted ceilings and chandeliers, the beautiful brickwork. He even loved the blacked-out windows on the roof that used to be stained glass, used to let filtered sunlight in. It was magnificent. This was the place they had built to knock the socks off anybody who visited America back in the day, like "we're so rich this is the stuff we stick underground." Only problem was it was too small for how long the new trains were, just like 18th Street, only worse because this was a loop, not a straight line, so it would be impossible to fix. There was no way to let passengers on and off all the cars; some would still be in the tunnel. So this big, beautiful station got closed in '45 and empty trains go through without stopping. Mostly empty. Citizens who want to peek at Old City Hall can still ride the 6 to the end of the line and just not get off before it starts up again. They're not supposed to,

But most people do what they're not supposed to, as long as it's fun, and sometimes even if it isn't.

"This is a good place for conversation," Cvetko said. "The temperature is agreeable and there are no unwanted listeners. Mrs. Dunwitty is an expert at keeping secrets. Do you know, she used to work in a speakeasy frequented by underworld figures. She was in charge of the coat room, and also the firearms of guests."

"I fellated Lucky Luciano!" she said.

"Yeah, she's buttoned up as tight as Fort Knox."

"She won't remember our visit."

"Of course I won't. Are you a vampire like Mr. Štukelj?"

"Yes."

"That's fine. Are you a Jew?"

"Shut up and knit."

"That's fine, too."

She went back to her needles. The cat yowled. Another joined it. She had at least two of them in there.

"So you believe them to be feral?"

"What?"

"Your little associates in the park."

"Oh. Yeah. Wild, untrained."

"Did you ascertain how many there are?"

He said the word *ascertain* like he was smearing butter on fresh bread. He gave it like a gift.

"I saw six. I asked if there were more. They said no."

Cvetko nodded.

"What do you think Margaret's going to do if we tell her?" I said.

"You have known her for longer than I. I turn the question around on you. And please stop agitating your knees in that fashion; it is obvious that you are stimulating yourself."

I hadn't realized I was doing it. I got up, paced around, looking at the pictures on the walls. Guy smiling in a U.S. Army Air Corps cap, black and white and dead, nice chin on him, though. Really old people in sixties shots, young people in really old photos, one of them water-stained, showing a pretty couple, big mustache on him, hats like the Gay Nineties. Three babies, all in dresses, even the boy. Bet one of the girls was her.

Hey, Dad! She's going to blow a gangster! Marry a pilot! End up as a midnight snack for a dead guy from, what, hungry-Austria!

"Joey."

"Huh?"

"Stay with me, please. This is important."

"Oh, Margaret. I don't know."

"Most important is the question of who turned them and then let them go with no knowledge of what they are or how to survive in the world as it is now. This individual is dangerous."

I considered a fern hanging in macramé from a hook on the ceiling. I pushed it, set it swinging. I set another one swinging, too.

"I really don't know what she's liable to do, Cvets."

KILLING MARGARET

Let's go back to 1933.

All those years ago.

Margaret wheeling me through the streets of Manhattan in the Beth Israel wheelchair, my belly full of nurse's blood, the darkness of the morgue drawer still sitting at the center of my mind like a base a runner can't quite steal away from, always back to it and back, *I'm dead I'm dead I'm dead.*

I remember the slow parade of streetlamps over me, the tide of car headlights in the street, brighter now than they had seemed before, the only suns I would ever know.

"I would have left you there," she said. "I wanted to, believe me."

"Why didn't you?" I said.

"I'm responsible for you now. At least until you learn."

"Learn what?"

"Learn how. The how of it. He'll show you."

I started to ask another question and she cuffed my ear, hard.

"Shut up now. I don't like your questions, and neither will he."

"Hey," a woman with a grocery bag said to Margaret. "What kind of nurse are you, smacking that kid like that?"

Margaret ignored her, but the woman trotted up next to her.

"I mean it, what's wrong with you? You don't smack a sick kid."

Never slowing down, Margaret turned her head, looked her in the eye, and the woman stopped and tilted her grocery bag so an apple fell out and rolled, just stood in the sidewalk with her mouth open, making a sound I'll never forget. Almost a cow sound, full of despair, the sound of a woman who hadn't realized that behind every face was a skull and behind every skull, worse than the skull, was nothing. Just nothing. Margaret could show you that in a second.

One thing I need to say about Margaret's family situation is that when she worked for us, I pictured the Irish stereotype, house full of kids, drunk husband, you know. Turns out I didn't know a thing. When she left my house that day, the day of the gorgon, she had gone to her wretched Brooklyn tenement building with few windows and coal soot on the burlap walls, and she had passed the night staring at her son, a pale, freckled boy of six named Liam who had fallen from a snowy rooftop and lost the use of an arm. Worse, Liam was simple now. No school, no work, no wife for him. Ever. She had driven her violent husband off the year before and had leveraged herself as far into debt as she could go before finding the job at my family's house. Things had started to get better. Just the week before the incident, she had paid one dollar fifty cents on the sixteen dollars she owed the grocer, given her sister a dollar against the ten she owed her and gotten her ice skates out of hock. Turns out Margaret in her daylight life wasn't a half-bad skater.

And then?

"I tried being a whore," she told me once. "I went with a fella, but ended up changing my mind about it halfway into the thing. He punched me good a few times and tried to take what he wanted, but I waited until he had his pants down and cut his mickey with a razor in my shoe. Not off. Just nicked it, but you know how they bleed, or maybe you don't, but I do, and he wasn't for fighting anymore after, and wasn't worried about getting his money back neither. Just ran out into the street howling, holding a towel bunched up on it. Still, my eyes swelled up near shut and I knew I wasn't no good for whoring. I didn't know what I was good for."

The food had run out and eviction was looming. They were living on soup kitchen and breadline charity. Margaret's sister, who had five kids of her own, wouldn't take the boy permanently, and neither would the home for boys. Not while Margaret was alive.

"So I did it."

Picture this. You're a vampire. You've bought a tenement building in Brooklyn, some leaning-over piece of shit waiting to collapse or burn to the ground. You've got some schmuck who collects rents and manages things so nobody has to meet you. You live on the top floor with the windows boarded up and a pipe leading down to the ground and into the sewers, and that's how you get out unseen. You make a point not to hunt in your own building, but there's a wrinkle. There's this woman. Irish, like half your tenants, but she doesn't walk around beat-up looking and sad with a scarf around her hair waiting for her teeth to fall out. She's got spirit. Like some old Irish clan chieftess or queen or something, she could walk down the sidewalk naked and never drop her chin. She had a piece-of-shit man who tried working her over with his belt one time too many, meaning once, and he ended up pushed down the stairs with a meat fork in his belly, went septic, almost killed him but he got better. Somebody said he went to Ohio because Pennsylvania was still too close to her. Only she's got a sick kid and a perpetual case of bad luck.

You look in her window sometimes, watch her comb out her reddish-brown hair, you notice that her big blue eyes never look far-off or dreamy but like there's work to be done and she's going to do it. When she goes to bed she doesn't read or pray—just washes up, combs her hair, lies back straight as a board in the middle of the bed (now that she can) and off goes the lightbulb behind its ratty shade. Only you can still see because you're a vampire, and you just watch her in the dark, watch her close her eyes like a dead soldier, watch her chest rise and fall and think about how clean her neck is, how hot her blood is, how good it would be. She's a beautiful woman, but not in the way the girls in the magazines or paintings are. She's beautiful like a horse is beautiful, in her veins and the shape of her head, and her eyes. Especially her eyes. You want her in all the ways you can want a living woman. Only you never do it, any of it. Not here. Not where you live.

Then one day she sends the kid off, borrows a thimbleful of cheap perfume from the young mother two doors down, gets tarted up in torn stockings and shoes you'd never seen her wear. She goes out late. Comes home bruised and bloody. Not her blood. You're intrigued.

A week or so later she sends the kid off again. It's a cool, cloudy night. And the Irish queen who seemed to be made out of stone has a breakdown. She doesn't break with sobbing or hysterics or booze; she starts busting things. Dead-faced, dead-eyed, she breaks her plates and cups and saucers, she takes a soup can to the glass parts of the cabinets and the clock and then chucks the can at the bathroom mirror. The neighbors knock and she tells them not to be concerned, she's cleaning house, and what can they do?

You can't call the cops on a woman for breaking her own shit, and they've got their own lousy lives to worry about.

When she's busted enough bustables, out comes the razor and she starts in shredding the shreddables: bed linens, towels, dishcloths, a picture of FDR, her underthings, her dresses, isn't this fascinating? Then she draws her bath, and you have a good idea what's coming, especially since she's still holding the razor. A woman who cuts up her towels before she gets in the tub probably isn't planning to dry herself off after, right?

She seems to think about it for a long time, though. And that's when she cries. Like how unfair things have been to drive her to this place finally hits her and at last she shows a moment of weakness. It's not like you really know how to love anyone or anything being what you are and all, but whatever affection you felt for her because of her strength doubles now that you see that strength's limit.

How fast she does it surprises you. Just one wrist, hard, more of a gouge than a slash, across the wrist like an amateur. And what does she do? Gets out of the tub and starts trying to bind the cut with the strips of towel.

But you can't help yourself anymore.

Not with all that blood.

"As soon as I clipped myself I saw myself in hell. That's where suicides go, as I'd long been told, and I supposed I believed it, but not really. It had started to seem to me that the Lord actually wanted it of some of us; that he would just keep shoveling out the misery until we got the idea that we wasn't wanted here no more. And if he was going to stick us in a second hell because we were sick of the first one, then he wasn't no better than the worst of us, so what was the point of it? Only, the instant the cold pain of the razor hit me and the blood started fanning out in the water, I saw myself. Jerking like, with my eyes rolled back in my head, in a dark, hot place, my skin as white as ash and burning now, everything burning, and a crowd burning with me. So up I jumped, splashing water everywhere, fetching what was left of a towel and trying to stop it. I started saying *Jesus* then, but Jesus wasn't what come through the window."

So in you go. Nobody's going to pay attention to the sound of something else breaking here, so you go through the glass. She doesn't go to scream, just looks at you like you're something in this life she hadn't imagined and she doesn't know where to put you. Still, you jam your hand over her mouth and start lapping blood from her arm, and oh the salty, frothy, watered-down goodness of it, like the faintest memory of hot broth on a cold day, and now you've thrown down her poor excuse of a bandage and you're nursing straight from her gushing wrist, opening the wound bigger with your big yellow teeth, it's spraying so fast you can't get it all in your mouth, it jets on your chin, up your nostril, and this is bad because you're going to kill her. Or are you?

"Live or die, he said, and I said live, not because I wanted to but because I wasn't ready to go to hell. But he kept taking the blood from me, and I'd been thinking it was the devil, but now I remembered Dracula, and what a silly business that was, or had seemed, but here was one like him. And killing me, too, despite his question. So I made the decision to fight him, but it was too late. I'd no strength left. I clawed at his eye once and he didn't like that, twisted my arm near off and I wanted to yell but couldn't through his hand, which I bit, and hard, but he paid it no mind. Just kept draining the life out of me until the darkness rose up like a buzzing mass of flies and took my sight away, but I heard knocking at the door again, and then I felt him spit something back in my arm. Just for a second I got my vision back, got a good look at him. Jesus, I wished I hadn't. I was hoping that wouldn't be the last thing I saw before I died. But it was. I died just after I felt the air get colder. I died just about the moment I knew he was taking me out the window. Christ, he was hideous."

Oh yeah, I forgot to tell you that part of this little make-believe. You're hideous. Christ, you're hideous.

The vampire who turned Margaret was named John Valentine. Kind of a bad joke, pinning a hearts-and-flowers name like Valentine on a kid after you reached your great Godly scepter down into the womb and gave him a stir. He looked like he'd been squeezed out wrong, one big goldfishy eye, the other one sunk in his head, and what a head. Broad nose and lips on him like he had a little chocolate in the blender somewhere, but his hair was pure dago, black and greasy and not enough of it. He might have had a widow's peak once, but that peninsula had mostly sunk, leaving one sad little island of hair, one stubborn patch of it he grew out long and put a ribbon on sometimes. He was half-mad, which you might have been if you had literally been sold to a circus. But he was brilliant, too. Brilliant enough to talk a vampire into turning him so he could escape the freak show. Brilliant enough to run schemes, steal and extort his way into property ownership and never blow his cover.

He was big and strong, almost as strong as the Hessian.

He was the only vampire I knew that horses and dogs were okay with; I saw him ride a horse once.

And if it weren't for John Valentine, Margaret might have left me in that morgue drawer to figure it all out on my own. But she owed him. He had shipped her kid off to live in a home for people like that and bribed them to favor him. He taught her, and made her teach me, and we stayed together, the three of us, until the bright, sunny day when his building collapsed and his box popped open and mine and Margaret's didn't. Dumb luck. That was in 1942. But nobody cared about collapsing tenements then. There was this war on.

MARGARET KILLING

NOW
1978

stood with Margaret in her vault, the mayor's apartment, surveying the wreckage. Four Hunchers had found their way into the place and it hadn't gone well for them. She was spitting out the last of the blood from her shot mouth and rubbing her hands, which were sore from what she'd just done to the intruders.

"Never call me your mother again," she said.

I held up my hands like *I wouldn't dream of it.*

"Oh, would you look at this, now," she said, pointing at a hole in her sage-green velvet couch. Never mind the brain and hair on it, she could clean those off with a stiff brush. And never mind the point-blank gunshot to the face she'd absorbed. It was the bullet hole in her couch that pissed her off.

One of the Hunchers was still alive; she had broken his back and stuffed a sock in his mouth. Now she pinched his nose until he came to, but then she charmed him. "You won't yell, but you'll listen and you'll answer when I ask you something."

He nodded, his eyes tearing up. He couldn't see us in the dark and his little gang's flashlight was smashed.

"Did nobody upstairs warn you not to come down here?"

He shook his head no and started crying.

"Stop yer blubbin'," she said. He did. I glanced over at one of his friends who had died so fast he fell back on his own legs like a contortionist, his face baggy-looking from the busted skull, one eye bugged, brain in his hair.

"Are you going to kill me?" he asked.

"Course I am. Where did you fine fellas come from?"

"The Bowery," he said in a sleepy voice.

"Anybody else know you're here?"

"No."

"Anybody gonna come lookin' for you?"

"No."

"All right," she said, nodding. And she rolled him over and fed while he moaned. And then I fed, and he died while I did it, his body seeming to deflate. Ridiculously, I thought of a basketball that would never bounce again, but it wasn't funny. He had been full of pot but not smack, so my head just got a little achy. Smack makes me throw up.

I thought about Butterbean and his burned Frisbee in the park, the older one saying, *You don't want us, we dirty.*

I thought about Gary Combs's head dropping like a setting moon as he died.

It's what they're for.

No, it's not.

Margaret sat on the couch, her legs crossed, looking at me.

"What was it you wanted to see me about, Joey?"

I told her.

THE STEEPLE OF HIS HANDS

Me and Cvetko in my room.

This was after the three of us pulled the four Hunchers out of Margaret's apartment and then dragged them down the tracks to Purgatory, a sick rat following us in a woozy S-pattern.

Rats didn't last long in our tunnels because we kept them covered in rat poison. It didn't bother us.

Cvetko had his fingers steepled under his chin, waiting for me to say whatever I had come to tell him.

"Margaret says she's taking the Latins and going to the castle," I said.

He looked bothered, broke the steeple of his hands and touched his face like he does. He hated killing anyone, but the thought of setting that grim bunch of Puerto Rican killers loose on teeny little kid vampires clearly ate him up. Those guys were killers *before* they got turned, which wasn't long ago.

No, Cvetko hated this and I wasn't in love with it myself.

"We should talk to them," he said.

"What, the kids? I already talked to them. They just don't get it."

"The Latins."

"Are you kidding? Margaret will flip her *shit* if we go around her like that."

He looked at me over his glasses, clearly scared but determined.

"They were still people ten years ago, all of them. Their communities live with three generations under one roof; as brutal as they are, they won't like the idea of destroying children any more than you or I do."

"I don't know, Cvets."

"Why do you think, Joseph Peacock, that Margaret decided not to call a town meeting?"

I put my hands behind my head. I was lying on top of my fridge like Snoopy on his doghouse.

"I dunno. Just to get it done."

"Have you been watching television?"

"No," I lied. "Why?"

"Because you are exhibiting signs of mental atrophy."

"The fuck does that mean?"

He took his glasses off and polished them, still looking at me.

"It means you are giving me a lazy answer instead of thinking. Now, *why* does Margaret choose not to bring this up for discussion?"

"Because nobody'll like it."

"Precisely. If we talk to her Puerto Rican friends and harden their hearts against her plan, she will, of necessity, call a meeting in order to gather enough strength to deal with the little ones decisively. But the meeting will not go her way because she is not a diplomat. She will have to bend to the will of the group. Let me ask you another question."

I nodded.

"Rather, why don't you tell me what my next question is and then answer it yourself?"

I rolled off the fridge and paced. I think better when I'm moving. Not that I could pace far in that cell with Cvetko in it.

It hit me and I stopped cold.

"Why did she tell me? What she was going to do, I mean."

He smiled at me in that happy-professor, Joey-isn't-a-retard-after-all way.

"And?"

"And it's because she doesn't really want to do it, either. She wants me to stop it."

He pretended to applaud.

"I would not go so far as to say she actively wants you to stop it. But she does, I believe, want you to share in her guilt by assenting, and she will not retaliate against you even if she reasons out that you betrayed her confidence."

"Why not? She doesn't like me."

"Never forget that you alone remember her when she was a living woman. She has known you longer than any of us. You are no incidental traveler, no Jonah she can cast into the sea for the whale to swallow. Except perhaps for Ruth, you are the closest thing she has to family."

I guess I never thought of it that way.

THE RACCOON AND THE VAN

"**S**he know you're here?"

He met us in an unused subbasement below a *tienda* on Avenue B that sold brooms and mops and cheap cookware, but also candles for different saints. The shopkeepers didn't know it was there, let alone that it was connected by crawl spaces to active subway lines, and abandoned loops to the west, and to wherever these guys lived. I had never been past this sort of cobwebby parlor. It was about the size of the inside of a McDonald's. You called these guys by tapping a pipe with a wrench three times, then counting to five and tapping three more. If it was early evening, before they went out, or early morning before they tucked in, one of them would show up within five or ten minutes.

"No, she does not," Cvetko said.

The other squatted down on his heels, thinking about this. To look at him, he was just a very pale Puerto Rican kid with torn-up jeans and Bruce Lee–looking kung fu shoes, a hooded sweatshirt, navy blue. But his eyes were too dark and small, and he never liked to look at you. If you looked closely at his jeans, you saw that they had been bled on. Plenty. He wasn't much older than me. A mustache had just been coming in when his clock stopped. He wasn't the leader, but he was the little brother. What he thought mattered. I didn't know his name.

He nodded, glanced up at us for a second, then looked at our feet. We should talk now. We did. We wanted to meet with Mapache. His dark eyes went back and forth a couple of times while he thought about it, and I thought maybe Cvetko had been wrong, maybe whatever embers of humanity were left in this kid had just gone cold, we might have missed it by a month. I could only too easily picture him hacking the head off the little British boy or his maybe-sister; he looked closed-off and bitter. I wonder how much choice he had in whether to join his brother underground.

He moved over to the pipe and banged it twice, real gentle. Then once harder. And then he sat really still with his head down like he wasn't even there; I'm sure this kid could disappear like that, just squat in an alley, cold to the touch and motionless so you never knew he was there till you felt his hand over your mouth.

When the kid heard his brother approach, he lit a candle in the corner, a saint candle from the *tienda* but with the saint's face and name spray-painted over. Nobody needed a candle to see, but newer vampires still need a little boost to see well.

Mapache was less creepy than the kid, liked to smile, would actually look at you. The one creepy thing he did was to stand kind of close to you while talking, but I think that was a Hispanic thing in general. He would touch you, too, and vampires don't touch each other much. Mapache had a big fucking mustache and I know he was Puerto Rickie, not Mexican, but I thought Pancho Villa must have been like this. Big mustache, easy to like, but still a killer. And this guy killed vampires, which isn't easy.

After we told him what we had to tell, he said, "I see why you came to me. This needs thinking about. I'll talk to the others, and either way I won't say nothing."

"We are grateful," Cvetko said.

I thought he would go back into the hole now, but he didn't. He stood even a little closer to us.

"Meantime, you wanna hunt?" he said, grinning like a bastard. His eyes caught what little light there was in the room and shone like raccoon eyes. I later learned from Cvetko that's what *mapache* means. Raccoon. At the offer to hunt, Cvetko shifted his weight, which meant he was nervous, but I answered for him before he could cough up some chickenshit excuse.

"Hell yes."

I have to give it up to the Latin Hearts; these guys had fun hunting. You're not going to remember all these names, but there was a husky one who looked older, Gua Gua. I think that means *van*. He wasn't quite van-sized, but he was a little more than person-sized. He was the uncle of the two brothers. Anyway, we went to a little alley not too far off 1st Avenue, between a pizza joint and a pawnshop with a shitty saxophone behind the bars, like even the musical instruments here were felons. Gua Gua was all camped out in a wheelchair, blanket around his legs, Greek fisherman's cap on his head, his greasy hair uncombed. He had a PLEASE HELP BLESS YOU cardboard sign on his lap and a half a milk carton next to it to collect change. Here's the brilliant part: He parked his rig out in the sidewalk, near the street. If you were actually moved enough by the human tragedy of this big coughing slob on wheels to put money in the carton, you were walking closer to him than the alley and you got by safely. If you weren't feeling generous but weren't repelled by him, you walked in the middle of the sidewalk and you got by safely. But. If the phlegmy coughing and the sight of the poor fat fucker drove you far enough away, you walked close to the alley. If Gua Gua sneezed, that meant the coast was clear. And that was bad news for you.

Mapache snatched the first one, an artist-type lady older than she was dressed, wearing a man's hat and a big pair of round earrings like a second pair of eyes. He moved so fast she didn't have time to make much noise, just went *EEP!*, kinda cute actually, but still the younger brother stuffed a pillow over her face, pushed her up against the wall, and went to work on her neck. A little guy they call Bug actually darted up her skirt, sucked her femoral. This whole thing took like forty seconds, during which Gua Gua rolled his chair back against the alley to block the view with his girth. When it was done, he turned around, he was the best at charming, and told her, "Nothing happened to you, lady, just count to five real quiet, then give me your money and go home. Go to bed." She did exactly as she was told, emptied the green, foldy stuff in her purse into the milk carton and stumbled away in a daze, her scarf knotted around her neck, dripping blood from up under her skirts, but that stopped soon.

A couple came down the sidewalk, then a black guy who gave Gua Gua a quarter. It only cost a quarter to get down that street safely.

The next one who came too close to the alley was for Gua Gua. Kind of a badly shaven PLO sympathizer guy with a— What's that word for the Yasser Arafat scarfy thing? I don't know. He looked all hard and flinty, hawk-faced like he practiced it, though I only saw that look for a second before Bug and I caught him and flung him in. Mapache pillowed him, but he was strong, wiry-like, punched me a good one, which started me laughing. Like he finally gets to hit a Jew and this is how it goes for him. Anyway, nobody bit this one. Mapache pulled out a little knife and did his wrist, bled him down into a plastic McDonald's glass with a picture of the Hamburglar on it. Then Gua Gua coughed twice and Bug draped a big garbage bag around us and we lay still. A laughing, carousing bunch went by the alley, somebody saying something Spanish, somebody else belched real loud like on purpose and kicked a bottle. Then three more coughs and we finished with Arafat. Bug licked his bleeding wrist with the flat of his tongue, it's the spit that makes the wound close up, and sure enough the well sputtered and went dry. We stood him up, straightened up his kerchief, and Gua Gua charmed him off home. Then Mapache pulled out a little bottle of rum and poured some in the glass, stirring with a straw. He gave us each a sip—rum and blood is *good*, they called it *ronrico*—then wiped the rim with his shirt and passed it on to Gua Gua. Cvetko and I fed next, then we moved on to another ambush site, splitting up on the way there, moving in ones and twos. Always Mapache and his brother.

Oh, I forgot to tell you, Mapache walked with a cane. Made him look a little like a dirty, smiley pimp. I really liked these guys and their system; getting into somebody's house was safer, but this was downright fun, like trick-or-treating. Give the fat man a quarter or else! Even Cvetko seemed amused by it.

Until they peeled a guy.

I didn't like that either.

They jumped a very brown, white-haired man on his way home from working at a taquería or some beaner place, he smelled like beef fat and beans and olive oil, he must have been fifty. Too old for a job like that. But he was alone and more interested in his beer in a paper bag than in his surroundings, so they flipped him up into a Dumpster next to an old broken couch and started drilling him to make more *ronrico*. But he was a little drunk and stubborn, wasn't taking well to the charm, even when Gua Gua tried it—sleepy drunk is good for charming, angry drunk is not. He yelled a lot, he wouldn't shut up, and now people were coming. Mapache full-on cut his throat. Just cut it. We put him in the old couch, which had about a thousand mice in it, we had to shake the mice out, and dumped him in the river. When it was done, Cvetko made that uncomfortable face he makes where really he's just not sure what to do, but it looks like maybe he smelled a fart, and it's easy to take it the wrong way. Mapache was a guy who took things the wrong way.

"What?" he said.

"We aren't supposed to kill them."

"No, *viejo*, we aren't supposed to kill them and get *caught*."

Cvetko should have shut up then, but he was so smart he was dumb, one of these guys who couldn't let something go if he knew he was right. And mostly he was right.

"Not to differ, but we need not get caught for the body to be discovered. If a great many bodies are discovered, the police will increase their scrutiny of this area."

Cvetko really should have shut up.

"Hey! I don't know where the fuck you're from, but I'm from *here*. People *die* here. Every day. As long as they're poor or brown, and that guy was both, the cops could give a shit. That poor motherfucker couldn't get in the newspaper if he flew to the moon."

Shut up Cvetko shut up.

But he was going to say something else. I knew he was.

"Still," he said. Just that one word, but one too many.

Mapache walked over, stood real close like he does, making Cvets pull up his lip in that uncomfortable, fang-showing sneer like a dog waiting to get hit with a rolled-up magazine.

"What the fuck are you makin' that face for, man? And talkin' that talk? *Police will increase their SCREW-TIN-KNEE.* Fuck you, man. This is how it is, and you know it even if you wanna act like a priest, fuckin' *maricon* vampire priest. What, you never peel nobody? It was a *accident*!"

Cvetko just sneered, actually closed his eyes like maybe his aggressor would just go away if he ostriched.

"Mapache, please, he doesn't mean it," I said.

Gua Gua walked over, said something in Spanish, put his huge, white hand on Mapache's shoulder. Mapache relaxed a little, started to turn around, then fucking face-touching, fucking autistic Cvetko had to burp out some more wisdom, eyes still closed, one hand held halfway up as if to stop a smack.

"We have to work together, we have to try to agree on common governance . . ."

Mapache, quick as hell, and I mean this guy moved more like a panther than a raccoon, grabbed the machete off his brother's belt and came at Cvets. I stood in his way but he pushed me aside, grabbing Cvetko's hand with his free one and then swinging the machete down. He lopped Cvetko's hand off, lopped it right the fuck *off*. Tossed it in the water.

Cvetko and me just stood there.

"It'll grow back, man," Mapache said, a scrawny olive branch if ever I heard one, and the four of them walked away. I wanted to kill that fucker but knew I couldn't, not him. Not now.

Cvets just stood there bleeding, his hand already re-forming off the bone, the severed one down in the river doubtless dissolving, unmaking itself. A regular hand, crabs would already be fighting over that, but not one of ours. Animals don't eat us. I used to cut my fingers off and throw them at track-rabbits to see if they'd eat them; they never did, the fingers just bubbled away like butter in a hot pan at the same rate the new ones grew in.

Cvetko was already wriggling the new hand, touching his thumb to the new fingers.

What kind of bully do you have to be to hurt a guy like Cvetko? But some vampires were like that, hated weakness. Hell, a lot of people were like that, too.

"You okay?" I said, a stupid question but I couldn't think of anything else.

"As they say, nothing hurt but my pride," he said, trying to smile, but it was so pathetic I was almost glad when he gave up and let himself look real sad.

"My ring," he said.

I never noticed one on him. I mean, I knew he had one, on his pinky, gold, but I never really looked at it.

I guess I wasn't much of a friend.

"My wife gave it to me."

THE GARGOYLE

When we got back to our tunnels, Margaret was waiting for us. She perched up in a brick niche like a gargoyle, holding her shovel. Her head-taking-off shovel.

"Did . . . Did you want to speak to us?" Cvetko asked. She just squatted up there in her shitty bathrobe with her fangs showing, her shovel idly scraping the wall, staring at us. I opened my mouth to speak but then shut it again. That was the thing with Margaret, you always felt she was looking right through you.

"Just get into your boxes and shut them real tight," she said. "There's a meeting tomorrow night, Eighteenth Street station, early, and then we're going on a little walk in the park. All of us."

She watched us go to our cells. She waited. It was a while before I slept, knowing she was out there, but I dead-dreamed her sitting there in her niche until she turned into an actual gargoyle, opening her mouth so blood came out of it, and out of her eyes, like rainwater, filling the tracks until they flooded and I knew she was going to flood the city that way.

* * *

There's a boulder in Central Park, I'm not telling you where, but it's a boulder that a pack of vampires can lift. Barely. So they did lift it. This pack of vampires rolled a shopping cart up and the weakest of them, that would be me, dumped the cart while the rest of them grunted, holding up the boulder, and then they let it down so heavy the earth moved under their feet. There's three stiffs under that boulder, but nobody's ever going to find them. They're as flat as stingrays now. They're part of the park and that's all they are.

I'll back up a bit.

Turns out not all of us went to Belvedere Castle, but most of us. Ten. We approached the building from all sides, probably nine o'clock or so, didn't bother going up to the top windows, just peeled the boards off one big window and walked into the first floor like we owned the place.

"Fuckin' animals," Baldy said.

The elementary class of night school had been busy.

A bigger woman, bag lady type, lay spread-eagled like the X on a landing pad for a helicopter, all chewed up, dead about a day, her raw-sausage-looking ankles stuffed into too-small sneakers with the backs cut off. She was staring at the ceiling with her lips pursed together, like her last out-breath had been a horsy noise. Less fresh than her was Mr. Combs, crumpled in a corner starting to look black, his eyes dusty and sunken. He had worms.

Want to groove on Miles?

How had nobody smelled this place? Were people so used to how rotten the park was that they didn't even care anymore? Had no cops come by? The flies were thick in here.

I led the way up the stairs, knowing as I went the kids wouldn't be there. They had cleared out. But I smelled something familiar, something that filled me with dread. I knew what it was even as I poked my head around and looked.

The Negro cop. Handcuffed to the chair, his head twisted all the way around, his sad-bastard, uneven mustache an upside-down horseshoe that caught no luck. He was missing teeth. This was bad. This was going to bring SCREW-TIN-KNEE. I felt his cheek. Warm as hell.

They saw us coming, popped his neck, got out without us seeing. The cop's mouth was still drooling bloody drool.

"Well," Margaret said, addressing mostly Billy Bang and myself. We were the two loudest ones arguing not to hurt the small fry. She said it again.

"Just, well."

After we cleaned up the mess, we all fanned out across the park in twos. Cvetko and me headed southeast; I picked the direction.

"You seem to have a hunch, Joseph," Cvets said.

"Yeah," I said.

We were supposed to get one of them, any one of them, and bring it back to our loops so Margaret could talk to it and find out where it came from, besides England. Did I mention Margaret didn't like England much? Cvetko had objected, pointing out that they might all be together, that it might be dangerous. "If two of youse can't handle a pack of little children who don't know nothing yet besides peelin' bums, then you deserve what you get." Me and Cvets felt dubious about this, but we saluted and marched like good soldiers.

Really, we all but sprinted because of my hunch, and then I caught their scent. I was right.

"Brilliant," he whispered when he saw where I was taking us. He patted my shoulder.

The children's zoo.

Whatever else they were, they were children, and children love a zoo.

IN THE BELLY OF THE WHALE

"**Y**ou have come to play, you have!" Peter squealed, smiling so I got another good look in his mouth; something I haven't mentioned yet is that Peter had been about eight when his clock stopped, so now he was stuck with this cluster of gaps and mismatched teeth around the very sharp, yellowy fangs in his mouth. Now he was smiling this mess at me in pure, innocent joy, sitting huddled with the others. Five others, just as he said. Six dead children in the belly of Whaley the whale, who served as the entrance to the children's zoo they put in like ten or fifteen years before. There used to be aquariums and all in the whale's mouth, but these were empty now and the place was graffitied and trashed like most of the rest of the city.

"Gimme that," I said, scared of them, but not too scared to snatch the cop's hat off Peter's head.

He made a pouty face and grabbed my nose, hard. Like he was going to rip it off for me. I twisted out of it and he laughed, grabbed the little girl's nose instead.

I put the cop's hat under my jacket.

"We were playing at jacks," he said, and a little ginger boy held up a red rubber ball. I smiled. Then I saw what they were using as jacks and I stopped smiling.

"Look," I said, "I need one of you to come back home with me. Would you like to see where I live?"

"Where *do* you live?" Peter said, the look on his face suggesting this had best not be boring. I had the idea they were still trying to work out if I was a kid like them, thus worth associating with, or a square like Cvetko, who they pretty much ignored. Cvetko was hunkered down next to me, looking like a teacher in his suit, looking like someone to be disobeyed, mocked, run in circles around.

"Someplace cool," I said. "But first I got a better idea."

"What, what?" said the ginger boy.

"What?" said the little dark-haired girl, almost too softly to hear.

"Yes, what?" Cvetko said, cocking an eyebrow at me.

The smaller little blond boy, who had ignored everything else as he tried to bend a penny with a pair of pliers, now looked up.

"Let's go see a movie!"

Clearly Cvetko didn't want to go see a movie. Neither did I, if the truth be told, but I needed time to think.

Want to know what they were using as jacks? A couple of jacks, sure. But also bullets, six of them.

And teeth.

I knew as soon as the epic symphony music banged up and the little ones all jumped that *Star Wars* was the right movie to keep them still for at least half an hour while Cvetko and I thought about what to do with them. The Astor Plaza Theater in Times Square was the last one in Manhattan still showing *Star Wars*, and only for late-night screenings. Peter had wanted to go see another movie, *A Hard Knight's Night*, because there was a knight on the poster and he liked knights, but that was at another kind of theater altogether, the kind where middle-aged guys sat by themselves in raincoats.

Thank God for *Star Wars*. What else were we going to watch, *The Bad News Bears Go to Japan*? Sure it had kids in it, but it sucked, and sucked big. *Corvette Summer*? They weren't going to sit still for that. Not a bad film for what it was, though. I had jerked off at least twice about Annie Potts. I'd love to meet Annie Potts. Still, you almost felt bad for Mark Hamill trying to be somebody besides Luke Skywalker. Fucking *Star Wars*.

Funny the power of that film—everybody clapped when it started, they often clapped. The little ones were staring at it open-mouthed, whispering among themselves, pointing. At one point during the fight on the Death Star, the littlest one crawled into Cvetko's lap and hugged his neck like he was Grandpa, which seemed to really embarrass him, so the girl pulled the kid off. Point is, they loved it. Hell, I loved it. I had seen it nine times already and I never got tired of it.

I was so into it that I almost felt bothered by Cvetko asking me, "What do you think our next step is?" I was holding a bag of popcorn just for appearances, no butter, it's not really butter anyway and it smells like shit. Darth Vader was holding up the rebel guy by the neck, smoke everywhere, and Princess Leia was about to get caught.

"I dunno," I said.

He went quiet then, thinking, didn't say anything else until the stormtroopers stopped the speeder with Obi-Wan and Luke.

He said, "Let's take them back home. All of them."

A guy behind us shushed him, and I did something just to show off—I turned around and said, "Move along," charming the guy. Not a second later, Obi-Wan charmed the stormtrooper, saying "Move along," and the stormtrooper said it back twice, *Move along, move along.* The kids loved this! The guy I charmed stumbled all over everybody's feet moving along like I told him to, I don't know where to. His woman friend said his name after him.

"Yeah," I said. "Home. But after the movie."

Turns out we didn't go home right away.

When the movie was done they were hungry, really hungry, despite having fed so recently.

I guessed I was, too.

And I knew just the place.

I hailed a cab.

Poor Mrs. Baker.

Can you imagine? There you are, suffering insomnia or whatever, three pillows behind you, reading *The Thorn Birds* with a penlight while your man snores beery snores and then you look up and I'm walking up on your bed as quiet as death by carbon monoxide, all shiny-eyed with six shiny-eyed little children behind me.

She jumped and went to shout, her arm knocking over the lamp, but I stuck my hand in her mouth and killed the shout and the red-haired boy caught the lamp. Fast little thing, they all were. Mr. Baker made that can't-breathe, snoring-gag sound drunk sleepers make and lifted his head, but no sooner had he done that than the Indian boy, Peter, and two others were on him, Peter lying across his nose and mouth and hugging his head, all but smothering him while the others latched onto his neck and wrists. The quiet little girl had gone into the other bedroom to tap the boy. I heard a brief struggle and then soothing words from Cvetko. I charmed Mrs. Baker and then Mr. Baker and they settled back, let us feed. I could hear Gonzalo in the other room, moving back and forth on his wooden bar.

Peter stopped drinking first, looked for a second like he was going to retch, but shook it off. The others kept going, hunched like nursing piglets.

"Okay," I said. The Indian boy stopped, looked up smiling, bloody.

"Stop now," I said, and all but the redhead stopped.

The red-haired boy wasn't about to stop; he was gorging himself on Mrs. Baker so fast I was getting worried about her.

"C'mon," I said. "Enough's enough. Save some for the fishes."

Mrs. Baker started breathing hard, trying feebly to push him away, aware even in her charmed state that she was in danger.

"Knock it *off*," I said, pinching ginger's nose and pulling him off her neck. I put the dish towel I had in my back pocket on the neck and put her hand on it, said, "Press that." She did. But ginger was fuming at me. He slapped me. Not hard. Before I could slap him back, Peter lunged and poked the kid in the eye with his finger. Hard.

"OW!"

"Don't hit our friend," Peter said.

The ginger looked even angrier for a second, his eye tearing up, then Peter said, "Caught a fart in your eye, didn't you? Didn't you just?" The kind of thing that's only funny to kids, but boy was it funny to Peter and carrot-top. Whose name was really Sammy. I learned all their names that night. Sammy was British, too. The boys giggled.

In the other room I heard Cvetko saying, "Good girl. You took just enough. Now let him sleep."

I heard the Baker kid groan.

I realized I hadn't even fed yet, but I dared not; they really chewed on the Bakers good.

Whatever was up with these kids, they were ravenous.

I had my first moment of doubt, wondering if maybe Margaret had the right idea.

Then I heard the girl in the living room.

"Pretty bird," she said softly.

"Pretty bird," Gonzalo agreed. "*Happy Days*, time for *Happy Days*."

Then he made the sound of a doorbell.

All the kids went to him now. It was hard getting them away from the gray bastard. Gary Combs had been right; they *did* like his bird.

PENNY DREADFULS

"**S**o what are your names?" Margaret said. She had them lined up on the platform at the deserted 18th Street station. A jungle of graffiti stood behind her on the tiles; vines of it climbed up the posts. All of us were there, except Sandy. Even the Latins. Even Old Boy.

"You first, blondie. Who are you?"

"Peter," said Peter, puffing out his bony chest as if for military inspection. His bloody shirt was off soaking in a bucket.

She pointed at the rest in turn.

The girl mumbled something.

"Speak up," Margaret said. "Was that *Carmilla*?"

"*Camilla*. No *r*. I don't like the *r*."

"Sammy," said the redhead.

"Manu," said the Indian boy.

"Alfie," said the smaller blond lad.

"Duncan," said the smallest of all, a brown-haired boy, all smiles. It was hard not to smile back at Duncan, but Margaret managed.

She was still thinking about taking their little heads off, I could see it in the narrowing of her eyes and the set of her lips. The shovel wasn't far off.

The little girl was fidgeting.

"Camilla," Margaret said. "Who turned you into what you are? You know what you are, right?"

She nodded.

"So who turned you?"

She looked down at the floor.

Margaret pulled off a sandal and slapped her with it.

"Easy, baby," Billy Bang said.

The girl looked at Billy Bang.

Margaret did, too, with hard, don't-fuck-with-me eyes, but she spoke to the child.

"Answer me."

"Varney," Peter said. "His name is Varney."

Before Margaret could say anything else, Cvetko caught her eye and said, "Varney was the name of a fictional vampire in the mid-nineteenth century. It was a penny dreadful."

"What?"

"The book was called a penny dreadful."

"That's what he called us, too. His penny dreadfuls," said Duncan. Duncan looked like the youngest, maybe six. Really infectious smile on that kid, he could have done commercials.

"He turned us all into little boys who would stay little boys," Peter said. "He only likes little boys."

"And one girl," Camilla said low, "as long as she stays quiet."

Were they saying what I thought they were saying? Oh, this was nasty.

"Where is this fine gentleman now?" Margaret said, cutting her eyes to her shovel.

Nobody spoke, they all looked down. Margaret was out of the child-slapping mood, though, so she just said, almost gently, "Tell me where he is."

Peter met her eyes.

"Looking for us."

There was more, lots more. Margaret kept them up past sunrise, with the light filtering through the dirty ground-level windows of the abandoned station, not enough to hurt us beyond making us a little headachey and queasy if we looked directly at it. They were saying they wanted to go to sleep, but she kept on them, trying to wring the names of their parents out of them, how they got over here from England, if they were English. They were. They flew over on a plane, Eastern Airlines; the Indian boy even had a piece of his ticket. She tried to get them to talk about their parents, but they just cried. She looked like she was going to start working them over with her Sandal of Slappery, but Billy Bang was giving her the stink-eye; he wasn't into how mean she was to them.

Cvetko said quietly, to me and Margaret, "I wonder if these tears are genuine," then, more loudly, "Why will none of you tell us anything about your mothers and fathers? I find this very odd. I'll tell you about my parents."

"They really will go to sleep," I said, and Baldy laughed; Margaret almost smiled.

"You," Cvetko said to the quiet girl, "tell me your papa's name."

She scrunched up her face and made with the waterworks.

Margaret aimed those big blue gorgon lamps of hers at the girl and said, "Stop yer cryin', you're not a baby, are you? Tell the man about your father."

She cried harder.

Cvetko squatted down in front of her; she turned her face away.

"Leave her alone," Peter said.

"Yes," Alfie said, "Let her be. She's our sister."

"Now we're getting somewhere," Cvetko said, looking at Alfie. He pushed his old-man glasses up his nose, then asked Alfie, "When your father went to work, did he wear a tie?"

Alfie put his balled-up fists over his eyes, shook his head miserably.

Luna said, "Hey, why don't we lay off them for a while? Let them rest."

Margaret said, "Nobody comes to live with us until we know who they are and where they come from, not even children. Those are the rules and we all agreed. Didn't we?"

Luna looked away, nodded.

"Does your father wear a tie to work?" Cvetko said again.

"He's dead!" Peter blurted out, angry now. He pulled Cvetko's glasses off his nose and threw them on the tracks. Margaret smacked his hand hard with the sandal. He showed his fangs but wisely didn't bite. Cvetko leapt down on the tracks, fetched up his glasses.

The little girl said something quietly.

"What?" Margaret said. "Say it again."

"He was a king."

"A king, my arse. King of what, Piccadilly Circus?"

"And Mother was a queen."

Everyone was quiet for a minute.

Then Cvetko, standing on the tracks and peeking up over the platform, said, "Well, we don't know how old these children are."

"What?" Margaret said. "This is horseshit."

"What's your mother the queen of?" Cvetko said.

"Of a castle. With a dragon under it. She's dead," she said quietly.

"We can't rule anything out," Cvets offered.

"I can rule out a fuckin' dragon," Baldy said, getting a laugh from the Latins.

Baldy and Dominic hadn't said anything through all of this, just watched quietly, but you could see Baldy's wheels turning. Whatever happened with these munchkins was going to be a big change, and change is good when you're in second place. He wanted that apartment of Margaret's and, while he never did anything that would give her reason to move against him, you know he never forgot his humiliation by her.

"Mr. Štukelj, you're not really askin' me to entertain the notion that this ragamuffin's some kind of ancient vampire princess."

"Don't forget the dragon," said Dominic.

I felt bad for Cvetko, so I said, "He's just saying we don't know. That's all he's saying."

Luna spoke up now.

"If this Varney motherfucker did my parents and turned me into a rape puppet I might tell you stories about being a princess, too."

Cvetko looked down, touching his face. He had his glasses now, but just held them. He looked like a dog in the doghouse standing down there.

"Besides which," Margaret said, "they flew across the Atlantic on an airplane. Have you forgotten that little detail? What's that, eight hours now? I'm thinkin' they'd have got some daylight on them if they were already *family*."

Now the air changed. A light shone down the tracks, a train was rumbling down from 23rd on its way to 14th. Cvetko leapt up to the platform.

Normally it would be too dark for anyone to see us, but there was just enough light, so we all slipped behind posts, got small. All but the children. They didn't know how. Margaret yelled over the growing rumble, "Lie down and hide your eyes! Hide your eyes from the train!"

That was one thing that stuck out in the dark, our reflective eyes. They did as they were told.

When the train was gone, Peter walked up to Margaret with his little fists balled.

"Our father wore a tie," he said, still crying. "All right?"

Then he stomped back to his sister and hugged her. The others joined them, all of them sobbing and hugging her, forming like a protective circle around her. It was sad and sweet. I was starting to like these little shits, and I wasn't the only one.

Billy Bang started playing "While My Guitar Gently Weeps."

Margaret pretended not to hear him, talked over him like he wasn't even playing.

"All right. Until we get some answers out of them, they don't come live with us. They stay right here. And someone stays with them to teach them."

"I'll do it," Luna said.

"Someone older, and more than one, in case this Mr. Varney shows up."

"We'll do it," Baldy said. Dominic gave him a look like *Oh, will we?*

"Thank you for your team spirit, Mr. Balducci, but I think not. Mr. Peacock and Mr. Štukelj, are you up for it?"

"Oh shit," I said.

"I'll take that as a yes."

A few words might be in order concerning the 18th Street station, which was going to be my temporary home while we sorted out the kids. Just like Old City Hall, they decommissioned it in 1948 because the trains got longer; it was either shut it down or make it bigger, and after the war there weren't exactly bathtubs full of money floating around for public works. We were too busy paying to rebuild German towns we just paid to knock down; I never get politics. I don't vote. Anyway, I'm glad they shut so many stations down. This is prime real estate for vampires, what with no sun, easy transportation, an endless sea of humanity to hide among. Notice I didn't say *feed on*; we aren't supposed to feed down here just so we don't get anybody wise to us. Commuters, I mean. Hunchers are fair game, if you can stand the drugs and booze in their blood. They don't exist.

Oh, but the station. It's small, typical. We had to chase a few Hunchers out when we annexed it—that's a Cvetko word, by the way, *annexed*. I like it. Makes it sound official, more like a real estate deal and less like we just took it. Here's how we do it. Say you're a bum—or "homeless person" if you're all sweet about it—and you're hunching down here with eleven others, an even dozen. One morning, this voice comes out of the blackness of the tunnel saying, "Get out of this station. This is your only warning. If twelve of you sleep here tonight, eleven will wake up tomorrow." And that's it. What do you do? If you're new to the loops, you might tough up and decide to post watches, dig your heels in. But that's not you. You actually *have* been around, living underground, going to soup kitchens, scoring smack or drinking yourself slobbery, but you've heard about the "tunnel talker." He always keeps his promises. You heard about a group of seven that got the same rap at the Worth Street station, some voice in the tunnel told the seven of them to pack up or they'd wake up with six, but they sat tough. Or tried to. The guy they posted to watch fell asleep, and in the morning, they woke up to squealing brakes and sparks and feathers all over the place because a train popped the guy and dragged him, goose down vest and all, halfway to the next station. Then the transit police came and moved them all out anyway, and they didn't come back. And you, do you really want to stay now that the tunnel talker has paid *you* a visit?

Hell. No. Not even in the winter. And this was spring. Better to take your chances in a cardboard condo.

So it's just that easy.

Cvetko and I stole a set of lockers out of a shitty gym on 14th Street, moved them through the tunnels wearing our stolen transit authority uniforms, set the kids up in those. Vampires don't actually need coffins, we just *like* them. It's instinct. Plus, it's good hygiene, what with bugs and all crawling all over the place. I mean, you could get perfectly used to sleeping on the floor, but why would you? Beds are nicer. Same thing.

Before we left to get the lockers, we had a chat with the kids.

I did the talking; I related better to them.

"It's like this," I said. "You need to learn some things about being what you are now."

"Dead!" Duncan offered, smiling.

"Yeah, dead. Undead. But you need to learn how to keep from peeling people. Otherwise you're going to blow it for all of us, get it?"

They said they got it. I wasn't sure they got it.

"Let me put this another way. You have to stay here while we're gone, okay? If you leave, Margaret . . ."

"The scary lady," Camilla whispered.

"Yes. The very scary lady will come get you. But if you stay here, she'll be your friend. Like me and Cvetko."

"Friends," Peter said. "I like having lots of friends."

"Right. You're going to learn a lot of neato things from me and Cvets, and we're all going to be fwiends." I said that last bit like Elmer Fudd.

The kids giggled at that. And they did stay put. Or at least I thought they did.

When we got the lockers in, I went back to our loops under Chelsea and got some clothes for me and Cvets, as well as my numchuks and a bunch of his travel magazines. *That* was a fun trip, carrying all that shit alone. But the alternative was for both of us to go again, or for me to trust Cvets to get the clothes I told him I wanted, and that wasn't going to happen.

The sun hadn't been down too long, so I went up to a corner market I knew that had a rack of six coin-operated toy dispensers. I traded a shiny new bicentennial quarter for a little plastic bubble containing a brand-new superball and stuck that in my pocket before hefting my box of stuff again. I thought about getting a Spaldeen, but those weren't fast enough. Not for vampires.

Before we started playing games, I had to establish rule number one, what Captain Kirk would call the Prime Directive. I caught a rat and threw it against the third rail. *Pop-ka-BANG!*

They got the message. Now the fun could start, and what fun! A superball in the subway is a riot. The kids *loved* it, and I loved watching them chase it. Fast little bastards, so fast, and I'm no slouch. I chased it, they chased it, they threw it at me so I could swat it with my numchuks like a baseball. We practiced getting small between the running rails and letting the trains go by over us, getting small behind posts, climbing sideways and upside down. They were naturals.

Cvetko sat on his ass with a *Time* magazine and read about Kampuchea or somewhere.

Then they dropped the bomb. It never ceases to amaze me how kids can just forget to tell you something important, even something you asked them about before.

I said, "Varney'll never catch you guys now. Or are all English vampires this fast?"

"Oh, Varney's not English," Peter said.

"No? Is he a Yankee-Doodle Dandy like me?"

"No."

"What is he?"

"A henchman!" Duncan said.

"Whose henchman?" I asked.

Cvetko was paying attention now, to hell with Kampuchea.

"No," Camilla said. "Not a henchman."

My heart turned over and scraped out a beat. I knew what she was going to say before she said it.

"A *Hessian*."

THE HESSIAN

Wilhelm Ulrich Messer, I wasn't allowed to call him Willy, was, as far as I know, the oldest New Yorker, maybe the oldest American, which was kind of ironic because he spent a few months trying to kick Americans out of New York. He came over from Germany when it wasn't Germany yet and fought for the British in the war of 1776, in a couple of places your war buff types would know, but the only one I remember is Saratoga because he claims he shot Benedict Arnold's horse there, and I don't care for horses. Or Benedict Arnold. Traitors chafe my ass. So Wilhelm Messer was all right in my book, even if he was mental, but maybe that's not his fault. He was old-ass-old. Got turned in his forties, after he had settled down and married, like 1800 or so.

First thing I want to say about old vampires is that they *all* get weird. I don't know how he was back when he was wearing a pigtail under that pointy brass hat he showed me and shooting traitors in the horse, but now? Like an old dragon sitting on money. They say Jews are stingy, but this guy wouldn't accept a collect call from Jesus on Easter morning. He was friends with John Valentine, which might have been the last time he was friends with anybody. His relationship with my old mentor was the only reason I ever saw inside his tall, narrow brick house in Greenwich Village, and that was in 1940 or so. He's still in the same house, which is only maybe four blocks from my old house, how's that for creepy? Moldy old vampire in the neighborhood where I grew up, I probably sang Christmas carols outside his door. Big shade trees in front of that house, servants upstairs, nobody on the ground floor, and he had the coolest basement you ever saw. Had a basement *under* the basement nobody got to see and that's where he coffined up and kept his treasure. I think he had tunnels going out under the village.

After Valentine cooked, Messer didn't have any use for me and that was okay by me. When Margaret decided to go underground like fifteen years ago, she found me in the Warehouse District basement apartment I was renting and we told him, asked him to join us. He said no. We were sitting in the basement library on a couch almost as nice as Margaret's, surrounded by swords and pole-arms and oldey-timey maps on the walls, this guy loved a map. His tall brass hat and Prussian-blue uniform hung in a glass case, all lit from below like in a museum. The uniform really brought home how big the guy was. It was jarring that he had been so massive even at twenty years old, even back when everybody had little tiny shoes and chairs like for dolls, when a shrimp like me was average-sized. No wonder he didn't want to go into the tunnels. I wondered if he even could get small. Probably not very.

He said, "It is undignified to live in the sewers and unsafe to live under the trains."

Did I mention this guy had a mustache? Huge fucking mustache on him, like Burt Reynolds, only sandy-red. Probably used to twirl it on the ends back in the day.

"What do you mean, *unsafe*?" Margaret asked.

"Mrs. McMannis, I mean that it is not *safe*," he said, a little crazy in the eyes. "Vampires have disappeared down there, many vampires, as anyone of a certain age can tell you. Your youth and enthusiasm are attractive"—it sounded like *attractiff*—"but tunnels are for vermin."

An awkward moment passed. "Is there any other way in which I might assist you?" he said, leaning forward and putting his hands on his seat like it was time for us all to stand up now.

"No," she said, a little pissed. Truth was, he didn't need us. He had been doing just fine for a very long time, and if Margaret thought organizing underground was smart, she could hardly say his way was dumb.

Oldest, richest monster in a city of monsters, and as big as Mean Joe Green to boot.

"Then it is my pleasure to wish you both a good evening," he said, just like Dracula, if Dracula were a kraut. The new servant opened a white-gloved hand and gestured at the stairs. His old servant, back in 1940, had been a light-skinned colored that could have been mute for all I knew; this 1960s servant was a young German-sounding guy, though he didn't talk much either. If listening to a clock tick was your idea of a good time, this was the house for you. Anyway, quiet young German guy showed us up and out, opening a door for us with another "Good evening." Handsome guy, kind of Luftwaffe-looking. Both of the servants had been real handsome. I think maybe Wilhelm the subway-hating Hessian swung AC/DC, just a feeling I got.

But kids?

I never saw him being into kids.

HUNGRY

"Those kids know how to *eat*," Billy said. Luna, Billy, and me were sitting in the Empire Diner in Chelsea drinking coffee just before tucking in. There was already light in the sky, just that little bit so you can't call it blue yet, just like dark with a glow to it. No sweat, though, there was a manhole cover just outside and the traffic wasn't bad. I had money and tip lying on the ticket. We could be underground within sixty seconds; by the time somebody notices one of us slipping under, all three of us are under, and what are you going to do? Call the cops?

The waitress came by; she hadn't come by for a while and Luna said it was because I hadn't been remembering to blink, only now I think I was doing it too much, but still she came and poured a little more thick black coffee in my cup. We were all filling our bellies with warm java so we could sleep better. We were all hungry. I was so tired I just watched the steam rise from my cup and said, "Yeah. That they do."

Watching the six of them nearly peel the Bakers the other night had convinced me we needed to split them up, so Luna had taken

Camilla, Cvetko had taken Duncan and Alfie, and Billy had taken Manu and Peter. I got stuck with Sammy.

Cvetko was with the kids already, getting them squared away in their little metal bunks.

Billy said, "Manu ain't too bad, but my man Pete? He starts bitching and moaning after an hour or two. He don't take much, but he takes *often*."

Luna nodded. "The girl's the same. We almost got caught because she bit a guy on the subway, said she couldn't wait. I charmed three people who got on while she was doing it. But, no, she doesn't take much."

I was thinking about Sammy. Little redheaded Sammy with a belly like a camel. He didn't need to feed all the time like Peter and Camilla, but getting him off somebody before he drained them was hard; he'd fight you, try to take a quart.

"We hit three cabdrivers, two around here, one down by the Brooklyn Bridge. The third time I said, 'Lay off, it's my turn,' but Sammy jabbed him anyway, latched onto his wrist while I was on his neck and sucked so hard the guy arched his back and rolled his eyes back in his head, so I stopped. The meter was running the whole time. I didn't pay."

The waitress passed by again and I waited till she was out of earshot.

"What do you think it is? Because they're kids?"

"Maybe," Billy said. "Maybe not."

"Well, what else?"

Billy grimaced and washed down the last of his coffee. He made sure nobody was listening.

"What if they're another kind of vampire?"

"What, like a different species or something?"

"Yeah," Billy said, standing up and hefting his guitar case, "just like that."

* * *

They were snoozing in their lockers. Cvetko had taken to sleeping in a big blanket by the turnstiles; he wasn't about to drag his coffin out here any more than I was about to move my fridge. He just wrapped himself up good and tight so no light got in, making kind of a turban around his head. But he wasn't out yet, just sitting up Indian-style, looking for all the world like a guy who smoked. I wondered if he used to smoke.

"Did you use to smoke, Cvetko?"

"Yes," he said. "But only socially, never as a habit."

"You wanna walk with me?"

He nodded, got up.

Someone kicked inside one of the lockers.

Someone kicked back twice.

"Settle yourselves and go to sleep," he said. A halfhearted kick followed like a mild act of rebellion, but then they fell silent.

We hopped down onto the tracks and into the darkness of the tunnel.

"Billy said they might be another species of vampire," I said.

"What are your thoughts on the subject?"

"I don't have any. It's why I'm asking you."

He walked, his hands in his pockets.

"Mr. Bang is an intelligent man. It is possible that there are different strains of vampirism, though it must not be thought of as a disease."

"You've said before you think it's a curse. Magic."

"Yes."

"What is magic, anyway?"

"In my opinion, it is simply a series of phenomena or forces that science cannot now explain and might never be able to explain.

Phenomena that are not subject to rules as we understand them, that may, in fact, change the rules we pretend to understand. *Pretend* in the French sense, as in *to claim*."

"Why not just say *claim*?"

"*Pretend* is a more elegant word, as there is a sort of elegance in the best science. A child watches his parents dance a complicated waltz. The mechanics are beyond his power and will be for many years. But he may sketch a few steps of it, his head erect, his arms almost in the right position. He says, 'I am dancing!' One may say that he claims to dance, but really he *pretends*."

"You think too much."

"As you *pretend* not to understand the concepts I challenge you with. You do not believe the myth of your own ignorance. But you perpetuate it out of habit, out of a desire to align with the ideals of American pop culture. Charisma, action, dumb luck. You will not learn chess because you are too vain to imagine yourself bent over a board with dull old men or with the hucksters in Washington Square Park. You enjoy poker because it is an American game, the game of saloons and broad smiles. A game where luck or sudden violence may yet save the unprepared."

"Train," I said.

We took a niche, got small and flat, him higher, me lower, our backs to the tunnel. None of the sleepy fuckers goldfished behind the windows of the morning 5 train would know what they saw.

"So, magic," I said.

"Do you remember the man you called the Pied Piper?"

Of course I remembered; it was one of the weirdest things I ever saw, which is saying something. There had been this guy, shabby-looking guy, I thought he was a Huncher. He walked through the sewers on his way uptown, a mob of rats around him. He was pointing at the biggest rats like a stickball captain picking teams, and damn if they weren't following him. He must have had forty, fifty trailing behind him like a bride's dress, all as big as cats or beagles.

"You said don't fuck with him because you thought he was a wizard."

"I said, *Do not disturb him.*"

"You said he was on his way to kill somebody."

"I believe so, yes."

"With rats. And he saw us."

"He was aware of us."

"What's this got to do with the kids?"

"If magic is a current or river, perhaps some manipulate it, as that man with his rats. And perhaps others are caught in it. Those who are accursed."

"Us," I said.

"And them. Perhaps there are different streams in this river. Perhaps slight alterations in the nature of this curse result in something like speciation. Vampires like us, but not like us. This may account for their increased appetite. Or . . ."

"Or what?"

"Or anything. This is only one possibility among countless possibilities."

"Like what else?"

He stopped on the tracks, picked up a coin. Looked like a buffalo nickel, I wasn't sure.

"I am officially on strike. I refuse to do any further thinking for you until you offer me your own theories."

"Maybe," I started.

"Not now. You are tired and hungry. Watch them. Think. Avoid television. Tell me your theories this time tomorrow."

"Okay."

We walked on for a moment.

I could feel him looking at me.

"Do you think the Hessian is like us? The same species?"

He didn't ask why I said that. He didn't have to, a guy like Cvetko.

He just drew in a little breath and said, "Ah."

That *ah* was the start of the third part of all this.

Or the end of the second.

PART 3

SCHISM

The Latins went after the Hessian three days later. Don't go thinking this was all about holy morals and the despoiling of children, though that was how it got dressed up. Wars are never officially about taking shit away from somebody else, be it oil or land or money; officially they're always about liberty or God or saving somebody. Avenging some wrong works pretty well. So the Latins said they were going to Greenwich Village to avenge a great wrong.

"And get your hands on his money," Margaret said. It was a hell of a fight. Margaret was dead set against peeling him until we talked to him, but they said talking to him would just warn him and he would button up or run.

"He won't run," Margaret said, but she didn't like the idea of attacking him, as disgusted as she was by what he stood accused of. Attacking a beast like that seemed like too much risk for too little gain. But then, she was already in the mayor's apartment and likely to stay there. With the Hessian's money, the Puerto Rican guys could set themselves up in some nice, basemented fortress like the Hessian had, get out of the tunnels, pay guys to watch over them by day, roam rich neighborhoods by night, unsuspected because of their fine clothes. Rich vampires definitely had it better.

"But he will fight. Have you perchance noticed how you've gotten just a little stronger every year? Do you know how old he is, and how well dug in? This'll be no easy matter. We talk to him first."

"We don't fucking *need* to talk to him, *Puta Madre*, what's he gonna say? 'Yeah I did it, *¡cortame la cabeza!* Now cut me my fucking head off please'?"

"He's too dangerous."

Old Boy got up from his leisurely squat and walked around to flank the Latins, standing now about ten yards behind them and to their right. He let them see where he was putting himself. He was a guy who spoke with gestures and motion.

Mapache flicked his eyes at Old Boy, but then settled them back on Margaret. He wasn't giving up.

"So what? So, you're dangerous, you get to turn six children, *six*, and fuck them, too?"

"Are you suggesting, sir, that we should police every vampire on this island? Or just the very rich ones?"

"You disappoint me. I thought you were in *charge*, man."

His men were on edge. They hadn't anticipated things going south with Margaret, they were always cool with Margaret.

"When it comes to these tunnels, I *am* in charge, Mr. Ramirez, and you would do well to remember it."

"Or what?" he said, getting much closer to her than she liked. "You gonna *talk* to me?"

Old Boy gritted a boot on the concrete to let them know he was now five yards away. Margaret, never taking her eyes off Mapache, held a hand up to her pet ghost, as a master might to a dog. *Not yet, boy. But maybe soon.*

"If you don't take one step back," she told Mapache, growling a little in her throat and speaking slowly—it was always bad when she spoke slowly—"We'll talk, just you and me. And much will be said between us in a very short time."

Margaret didn't bluff.

Ruth was already standing next to her, frowning her Statue of Liberty frown.

I moved closer to Margaret and Ruth, looking at Mapache, which didn't impress him. Billy Bang stepped up, too, though. On Mapache's side, Bug and Gua Gua got closer. *Damn*, Gua Gua was big. Dominic was about to step up next to Margaret, but Baldy hung back so he did, too. This could be bad.

Nobody said anything for about five seconds, but it felt like an hour.

Mapache stepped back, but he did it slowly, sarcastically, like *Okay, but fuck you.*

Margaret took it because everyone knew he still backed up. We were on uncharted waters now. I knew it. Baldy knew it so well it was all he could do not to smile, not to show the tip of a fang which is like the bird finger from a vampire. If this didn't get fixed, Margaret's biggest counterweight to the Italians was gone. And they weren't the rookies they were before, they knew what they were doing now. They might move on her when Old Boy was on one of his walkabouts. They just might.

And she knew it.

"You want it done?" she said.

"We want it done."

"Fine," she said. "Then you'll do it on your own."

Let's back up.

The night before this went down, Margaret came to the 18th Street station to check on things, and Cvetko told her what had been said. The kids wouldn't utter a peep to Margaret, though; they didn't like Margaret. She wasn't exactly child-friendly. She wouldn't have lasted long on *Sesame Street*.

But then the weirdest thing happened.

The little one, Duncan, said something in German. To Cvetko. Like he had heard Cvetko's accent and decided it was close enough to German that he would try it out. He popped an eye over to Margaret to see if she understood.

She didn't.

But Cvetko did. Cvetko's dead fluent in German, just like Russian, French, English, Spanish, Latin, even Hungarian. Who the fuck speaks Hungarian? Cvetko, that's who. But German.

When they had gone back and forth for a good while, Cvetko sent them off to play on the tracks, they liked the tracks, and took Margaret and me aside to tell us what they said.

"This boy, Duncan, speaks German because his mother is from East Berlin. These are all the children of British diplomats or translators. They went missing some time ago, perhaps last year, perhaps several years ago; Duncan doesn't understand time very well and the others will not discuss these matters. They were all charmed away en masse from where they played in Stuyvesant Park, herded into our very old friend's van, and turned in his basement. They lived with him in captivity until the winter, I assume this winter, when Peter decided he wasn't going to take it anymore."

"Take *what* anymore?" Margaret had said.

"Must I say it?"

"Don't be squeamish. If something's to be done, it won't be done on hints and rumors."

He said it.

I'll spare you the details, but games were played. You know, those games that aren't really games, but the grown-up puts child-friendly names on them. Margaret's fangs were showing completely by the time Cvets finished that part, and it looked like it took some effort for her to drape her lip back over them and put them away.

"I'll have to speak to him first. I'll see it in his eyes if it's true. I just can't seem to make myself believe it," she said, drooling and wiping it off with the sleeve of her bathrobe. People drool when they're charmed. Vampires drool when they want to bite.

"We often live next to monsters unawares," Cvetko said. "Look at us, carrying on our business below the feet of stockbrokers and secretaries; their shadows pass over our grates by day and we crawl into their windows by night."

"You and your fucking philosophy," Margaret said.

"The Son of Sam," I chimed in. I had followed that with interest. She waved my comment away.

"How did they bust out?"

"As Odysseus escaped the cave of the Cyclops," Cvetko said.

"I must have missed my lesson that day. And how was that?"

"Sammy blinded him with a pencil."

Peter liked the Rolling Stones. He must have seen Mick Jagger on TV because he actually did a little imitation of him, dancing and shaking his ass, hands on his hips, pouting out lips still bloody from the hunt. Watching him wiggle around like that was a little ooky after learning what had happened to him, but I put that out of my mind. He was just a kid. This was our third time playing "Gimme Shelter" on my hi-fi set and he was lip-syncing almost the whole thing. I boogied with him, tried to get Cvetko to join in but that was like trying to make a turtle play basketball. Manu danced with us, though. This was taking place in the common area outside our rooms, mine and Cvetko's, I mean. We had abandoned their lockers and stolen new ones, easier than humping theirs all the way here, and Peter's had been just a little small for him anyway. This time we got individual lockers, put them in their individual cells. These cells were honeycombed back here.

The transit police had come by the 18th Street station, like a dozen of them with lights and guns. We heard them a mile off, got clear fast, hiding our most important shit behind a false panel of loose tiles we hoped they still didn't know about, came back for it later. This was nothing unusual, they did it from time to time, but it meant we should leave it alone for a while. That station was too close to the surface to be good long-term digs.

Probably some observant conductor caught sight of one of us, saw the lockers, who knows. Whatever the reason for the lame little raid, I asked Margaret if we could move back into our regular place and move the kids in with us. I could tell she wasn't thinking about peeling them anymore. She was on their side now.

It had been a tense night. Hunting had gone okay, even though we had to feed Peter four times. The kids were happy, but the rest of us were on edge. We knew the Latins were going to peel the Hessian tonight; they had been casing his place and had a plan. I, for one, didn't have a lot of faith in that plan. But I have to admit, I was curious to know what he was sitting on. Gold doubloons?

"What do you think the Hessian's sitting on?" I asked Cvets. "Underground, I mean. What do you think he has?"

"Besides a room that locks from the outside for the imprisonment of children?"

"Don't be a grump. You know what I mean. Treasure-wise."

"Perhaps the lost gold of the Knights Templar."

Always some obscure shit with him.

"No, really," I said.

"Why didn't you go on the expedition with our Hispanic friends? You might have seen for yourself."

"I don't think it's going to go well for them," I said.

"No," he said.

"What should be done, then? About this kid business?"

He looked at me.

"Must something always be done?"

"Everybody knows you don't turn kids. Let alone all that other stuff. Are you saying we ought to let that slide?"

"I am playing devil's advocate. Indulge me."

"It's not right."

"Neither was the suppression of Hungary by the Soviets. Or the invasion of Tibet by the Chinese."

"Yeah, I remember people saying something about Tibet. The Dalai Lama, right?"

"Yet both acts went unpunished. Why?"

"What's that got to do with anything? I'm talking about our neighborhood."

"It is only a question of scale. Why did not the brave American army march into Budapest and save the Hungarian resistance who begged Mr. Eisenhower, in the name of democracy and free-dom, to take their side? Why did we sit by while the Soviet tanks rolled in and hammered the beautiful old city?"

"That happened?"

"You have just written the epitaph of America. Yes, that hap-pened. Twenty-two years ago. It was on the radio. It was in the newspapers. What were you doing, watching the Looney Tunes? Sitting in Battery Park with Emma Wilson?"

"Shut up."

He knew better than to talk about Emma Wilson.

But I saw what he was getting at. He spelled it out anyway.

"The application of justice is a by-product of power. We look to leaders to protect us. We organize for collective defense. Or collective acquisition. Why do we submit to Margaret's governance?"

"She's tough and she knows her shit."

"Precisely. But is she tough enough to impose her ethics, such as they are, on other groups not under her direct supervision? Should vampires in Brooklyn refrain from feeding under Borough Hall or Court Street because she has decided it is verboten for us?"

"The feeding thing is about protecting your turf. Let them do what they want."

"Might not the discovery of murders underground in Brooklyn lead to sweeps of the tunnels in all of the boroughs? The transit police are not parochial."

"Sure. But we can't make Brooklyn guys do what we say."

"Can we not? I doubt there is a larger enclave than ours in Brooklyn. We could give them an ultimatum."

"Yeah, but that's a big fight if they say no. What's it win us?"

"Now you are thinking like President Eisenhower. And like Margaret."

"The kid thing is different," I said, not feeling so sure. Cvetko always made you feel like you were on thin ice.

"Not feeding in the subways is a matter of survival. Not matriculating children is a matter of taste."

"*And* survival," I said. "They don't know what they're doing."

"They can be taught. My point is that your disgust at the actions of the Hessian, while understandable, is not necessarily sufficient motivation to attack a creature of his age and tactical knowledge."

"He gets away with it because he's strong."

"This is the story of mankind."

"I thought you were going to be a priest at one point."

"Yes. But then I read the newspaper."

EMMA WILSON

Emma Wilson was my girlfriend for the summer and fall of 1955 or '56, I don't remember. I think '56 because of what Cvetko said, but I don't know if I ever told him a year. I never bit her. I never told her I was actually dead. I think I loved her, if it's possible to love somebody without liking her that much. I think it is. She was pretty like some Dutch porcelain thing; she had a closet full of angora sweaters and a neck like a swan's. We used to sit on benches and make out; I liked the innocence of it so I never pushed her, I let myself forget what I was when I was with her. She thought I was a student at Columbia; I even charmed a professor into bumping into me at a late-night diner and acting like I was the smartest guy since Einstein. I ate hamburgers and French fries looking into her big baby blues even though I knew the food was going to twist around in my rotten old guts and come out practically the same way it went in, and that that was going to hurt. It was worth it for her to look at me like a real boy, I felt like fucking Pinocchio with her. Did I charm her a little? Yeah, not to the point of drooling, but you would have, too, I don't care who you are. I really don't. She was just that pretty, Grace Kelly pretty, blond Adele Mara pretty, and I think of her when I smell certain flowers, I don't know their names. Her in her painted-on capri pants, tiny veins almost invisible on the tops of her feet in their white slippers. She gave me her virginity. She did that, even said it like that. "Joey, I want to give you my virginity." I got us a room at the Astor hotel and everything, this after I sucked it up and took her to see *My Fair Lady*, which looked like only girls would ever like it but turned out not to be so bad. She had told her dad she was sleeping over with a girlfriend, so I had the whole night with her, and that was the only time she didn't have to cut it short. It was me stealing away before morning, though, rushing out of the Astor and down into the subway to run back to the draped-off, bars-on-the-windows, triple-locked apartment I rented off Bleecker Street, sure I was going to burn. It was the longest and shortest night of my life. The seconds were pouring through my fingers like sand and I could watch them go but I couldn't stop them. I remember every minute of it. We made love three times. In between, we ordered drinks and room service; we talked about *Forbidden Planet*, which was the first movie we saw together; we talked about London and put on Cockney accents. We ran the halls and ballrooms, trying to see every inch of this glorious hotel, and I mean this thing was magnificent. Coral Room, Rose Room. A section of the bar just for the gays. They had this garden on the roof; we walked around up there and the moon was out, not full but big. It's all gone now, the Astor. I was hoping it would be cloudy when they knocked it down, I wanted to come outside and see. But it wasn't. And I didn't.

Emma Wilson.

You'll never guess what broke us up, and, if you do, you're such a cynic I feel a little bad for you.

I was so busy keeping the fact that I was a vampire hidden that I let slip the fact my mother was Jewish. And once I said it, I couldn't charm the knowledge back out of her, her bigotry was that deep. "It changes the way you smell to me," she had said, making a face like she knew what an asshole she was but that she couldn't help it. "I'm going away to college anyway," she said. "Winter session." That's when it dawned on me she wasn't a nice person, and that I had never really liked her beyond the way she curled up on a sofa like a cat or the way the light looked in her eyes, or those almost-invisible veins at the tops of her Grace Kelly feet. I was in love with a doll. And when she spoke, when she spoke from her soul, she came out with that anti-Semitic horseshit. After all her pretending to be worried about children starving in Communist China.

"It changes the way you smell." Can you believe that? I breathed the stale air out of me for half an hour before I saw her, I practically drank mouthwash, I charmed her, but now I smelled "Jewish." Here I was crawling in windows, drinking blood, she never saw me in the daytime, but never mind that; she would never get past the idea that my mother ate matzoh.

Maybe it was in 1956.

Maybe she did say something about Hungary.

It was a long time ago.

THE VELVET ROPE

Back here in 1978, I needed some time to myself.

Away from Cvetko, away from Margaret and the kids, all of it. I was sick of politics and everybody getting all wound up. I wanted to dress up and look good, maybe get some action, feed on new people without the hungry little brood tugging at my shirt wanting their turn again and again.

I wanted loud music to make me feel sexy, young, and powerful.

The Ammonia was great for that, but I was feeling more disco than punk, and, besides that, I had an odd craving.

I wanted to bite somebody famous.

I knew just the place.

"What about me?" I said. I was on the wrong side of the velvet rope at Studio 54 and the little dago-looking tyrant who decided who got in was lording it over the crowd.

I was dressed to the nines, putting out a low-grade charm so I looked twenty-twoish, but never mind all that, he looked straight over my head.

"Okay, you with the poodle-fur vest or whatever, you can come in. And you, geisha lady, I like the way you dance."

"Hey," said a man with a fedora and a pin-striped coat.

"I told you not to wear a hat, nobody wears hats in here." The loser threw the hat away like a Frisbee but it was too late, he had lost any hint of cool he might have had.

Limos, cars honking, somebody yelling farther up 8th Avenue.

Grace Jones poured herself out of a limo. We parted like water around Moses. Of course Mussolini let her in without her asking, she just said, "Hello," and slid past the rope on her mile-long legs, so tall and black and elegant she was like another species, a better one.

"What about me?" I said again.

"What *about* you?" said the frowny-faced guy next to me with tangled-up gold chains nesting in his chest hair and a collar so wide I thought he might fly. He'd already been waved off but wasn't giving up, was ready to stand there for hours if he had to, and he resented the fact that I just walked right up with attitude like I knew I was getting in. Fact is, I knew I was getting in. All I had to do was catch Little Italy's eye, but that wasn't easy. He purposely wasn't looking at me because I was short. I hate that. He wasn't so tall himself.

So I took out the greasy red firecracker I brought for exactly this purpose and lit it with the Zippo I took off the dead Hunchers. People stepped back from me, called me names while it sizzled, and I flicked it down right in front of my boots, BANG! A lady who had been too busy tripping balls to hear the hiss went "AAH!" and waved her hands like she was trying to dry her nails.

"You!" the dago said, pointing at me. "Don't do that, it doesn't help."

He looked me in the eye.

Gotcha!

You don't need eye contact to charm, but the subject needs to know it's him you're talking to. And eye contact definitely makes it take better.

"It helps plenty," I said, "but I won't be a bad boy once I'm in."

I kept his eyes nailed to mine; he wouldn't have looked away if a golden unicorn walked up waving a big boner. Which could have happened there.

"No?" he said, starting to drool a little.

"Of course not. So point at me and tell me to go in."

He did exactly that.

General groans erupted from the others.

"No fuckin' way," somebody said, as outraged as if St. Peter had waved a known pervert into heaven. Somebody else said, "I'm bringin' a cherry bomb tomorrow." The balls-trippy lady, in a spasm of druggy clarity, even said, "He hypnotized him! I watched him do it!"

But fuck them, I was in.

I walked through a sea of half-dressed and freaky partiers; man, this was the place to be. Here was a woman all in blue body paint with seashells on her tits, and what tits, and there went a super-buff Asian guy wearing zebra-skin pants and cowboy boots, a cowboy hat, no shirt, a monkey on his shoulder. At first I thought it was weird that they let monkeys in, but I had heard about a horse getting in with Bianca Jagger riding it, so what's a monkey? But then I realized the monkey was stuffed. It wore a little cowboy hat, too. Funny a monkey and a buff Oriental could wear hats, but not that schmuck outside. Asian guy smiled at me. I had heard this place was a circus, and boy that was no lie. A big crescent moon hung over the dance floor with a light-up coke spoon under his nose, the busboys ran around in short-shorts and bow ties like Christmas presents, everybody's hand on their asses or thighs, people were actually screwing on the balcony, and there were gays *everywhere*. This was like the Indianapolis 500 of gays, all souped-up and rolling around in circles, happy as hell, and why shouldn't they be? Nobody was going to curb-stomp them in here, nobody was going to judge them. And, let's be clear, I wasn't judging them. I just didn't want them, you know, touching me. Not even the guy who looked like Freddie Mercury. I mean, I thought he looked like Freddie Mercury. Turns out it fucking *was* Freddie Mercury.

Who else did I make that night besides Grace and Freddie? Andy Warhol for sure, you can't miss that wig. Captain Kirk from *Star Trek*. Billy Joel. One of the chicks from *Charlie's Angels*, not Farrah (I wish!) but one of the brunettes, her brunette locks tumbling all down her bare back. I wanted to bite her, but she was going to be hard to get away from her table. I didn't recognize anyone else at her table, but they were attractive and intense and at least two of them were coking it up. Cocaine people don't charm easy; what you want is a drunk or a pothead.

Then I saw her.

The prettiest girl in the place, and that was no easy feat here.

I couldn't remember her name, but it was that girl from the remake of *King Kong*, her character name had been Dwan. She was prettier than Fay Wray had been, sort of all-American wholesome but smart in the eyes. I mostly didn't care for the remake, but I saw it twice just because of Dwan. She was out on the floor dancing, really graceful, simple black dress. I think they were playing Earth, Wind and Fire. I watched her for a minute, then I went out on the floor, too. I had to duck the flailing arms of a highly energetic pantsless fireman on roller skates; earlier he'd been letting people pull him around by his cock, and I stopped to boogie with a cute little lady like eighty years old, what the hell was she doing here? But then somebody picked her up and the whole crowd passed her overhead as carefully as they might pass a baby while she giggled and spread her arms and legs wide. I worked my way closer to Dwan. She smelled like the best perfume, just undercut with sweat; I was starting to get a little bit aroused. I looked at her face while I danced, waiting for her to notice me staring at her and then look down at me so I could get my hooks in her, tell her to follow me outside or to a booth; I was actually hot enough and hungry enough to risk biting her in a booth in here. Anything could happen in here. People who saw would probably ask me to do them next. Anyway, Dwan turned her face to me and I caught her eyes and held them. But before I could say anything, I got bumped into. Hard. I looked over and saw this very tall, incredibly sexy brunette in a black choker and a black sequined flapperlike dress with tassels. She was staring down at me.

"Sorry," she said, like really she wasn't.

Was this how she flirted?

The girl from *King Kong* danced away.

Now the Fifty-Foot Woman grabbed my hand, danced me off the floor, danced me almost into one of the short-shorts-wearing busboys holding a tub over his head, danced me up against the wall. Don't get me wrong, I like a woman who knows what she wants, but I really had a crush on what's-her-name, so I craned my neck around trying to keep a bead on where she went. She was at the bar, doing that incredibly sexy thing where she lifts up one foot and lets the shoe dangle off her toes. I wanted to bite her ankle, her heel, I was drooling.

The tall woman grabbed my cheeks in her hand and pointed my face toward hers. Her face looked young, vaguely Liza Minnelli, but she didn't smell young. I caught a whiff of her breath. It smelled like a dead dog in a Dumpster.

"Jessica Lange wouldn't give you the time of day unless you

charmed her," she said. Her voice was lower than I would have thought. "And I'm not having that. Not here."

She lifted her lip in a brief snarl, gave me the fang-tip *fuck you*.

"Holy shit," I said.

"That's right."

Now she took my hand and put it palm-down on the front of her dress. There was a rather large dick there.

"Holy shit," I said.

"That's right, too. Now run back home before you get stepped on, little cockroach. You're dirty, you smell like trains, and you don't belong here."

She/he (I'll stick with *she* for simplicity's sake) stepped back and gestured at the door.

"But," I said, just about to protest that all I wanted to do was dance, but I didn't get past *but* before she grabbed my hand again, her grip as hard as pliers.

"Wrong answer," she said. Out came the fangs and she *bit me*. Fucking *hard*.

All the way through the bones of my hand.

My eyes teared up from pain, not from wanting to actually cry or anything. The dead shouldn't cry, not even the lesser dead, which I clearly was next to her.

She was stronger, older, and it was her place. His place, whatever.

I grabbed my hand to keep from bleeding all over myself, licked it so I would heal faster.

And I left.

DOWN THE RABBIT HOLE

A lot happened while I was gone.

Nobody had heard from the Latins, for one thing, but I'll get to that.

The first thing I saw when I got back was Peter and Alfie sitting back against the rock wall looking sleepy, holding hands. Camilla had already gone to her locker; she was singing a song, but too softly for me to understand any of the words. It sounded like a lullaby.

"You guys all right?" I asked.

"Yes, Joey," Peter said, but it looked like he was having trouble keeping his head up. It was still a good hour till sunrise.

"Hey, Cvets," I called into Cvetko's room, "did these kids eat?" Cvets wasn't there.

"Joey," Peter said, sounding almost as quiet as his sister.

"Yeah, kid?"

I walked closer, noticed that they smelled bad, like sewage, and their pants were wet at the bottoms.

"What have you guys been doing, playing in the toilets?"

The ghost of a smile crossed Alfie's lips.

"We've been talking about you," Peter said.

Alfie nodded gravely.

"All of us."

"Is that so?"

"Yes," Peter said.

Alfie whispered, "We even asked the god of small places."

"Who's that?"

"It's the god we talk to since Yayzu doesn't want us."

Yayzu?

"It's really just pretend," Peter said, "there are no gods."

"You'll make him mad!" Alfie said.

"Let him get mad," Peter said, looking at me. "The point is, we were all talking about Joey."

This *god of small places* shit creeped me out. I changed the subject.

"Well, what did you say? About me, I mean. Nice things, I hope."

"We've decided that we quite like you."

"That's good," I said.

"It is," he agreed in that serious way kids have.

"You sure you're okay? You look wiped out. Did you eat?"

He nodded, then stuck out his tongue to show me the back was still bloody.

"As much as I could," he said.

What the hell did that mean?

"Would you hold my hand, please?" he said, holding his small, white hand up. There wasn't a lot of light down here, just Cvetko's lamp, which was always on, but that was far away so everything had that pretty cat's-eye candlelit look. It would have looked solid black to you, assuming you're alive.

"Please," he said again. "I'm cold." I realized I had just been looking at him. I wasn't much of a hand-holder, but he seemed so sad.

And so small. They were all so small. It seemed like a miracle they'd made it as long as they did.

"Yeah," I said, and slipped my bigger hand around his. His *was* cold. Colder than mine, anyway. Vampires normally only get that cold when they're starving.

"We've decided," Peter said, with some effort.

"All of us," Alfie interrupted.

"Yes. All of us have decided . . ."

"Except half of Sammy."

"But mostly Sammy, too."

Alfie considered this, then said, "Maybe mostly Sammy, he did say yes."

"We've decided that we want you to be one of us."

"That's funny," I said. "I thought you guys were becoming part of us."

"Yes, of course we are," said a very sleepy Camilla, holding a Raggedy Ann doll. This was her third or fourth one since they came to live with us; she stole them whenever she could. No one ever saw her take them. She was standing right behind me; I hadn't even noticed her song had stopped. I hadn't heard her walk up. "But while we're all joining your group, you should be joining ours, too."

"But only you," Alfie said.

"Yes," Peter said, his eyes closing like he was in his mother's lap trying to make it through the late show, my hand still holding his up. Like a little dead fish out of a lake.

"Only you," Camilla said.

"Why," I said, "something wrong with Cvetko?"

"He's old," she said, wrinkling her nose.

She hugged me.

Then she helped her brothers to bed.

* * *

I went to ask Luna if she knew where Cvetko was, but he was already there; I heard them talking but they were talking so low I didn't understand them till I climbed up. There was no ladder or stairs; you had to be a vampire or a rat to get up to Luna's cell, and rats weren't interested. Luna's room was really like a half-cave with wires dangling out of the roof, I have no idea what it was for, and lots of movie posters. Luna liked movies almost as much as I did, especially movies with Paul Newman. *You never met a pair like Butch and The Kid*, one poster said, Paul Newman and Robert Redford running and shooting in that browny oldey-timey color. Other posters crowded that one, lapped over it where she'd glued them onto the rock: *A Streetcar Named Desire, Super Fly, The Life and Times of Judge Roy Bean*. That one I saw with Luna; we used to crack each other up saying, all serious and proud, "I am a Bean," like his daughter does in the film. Maybe you had to be there. The walls were swimming with band posters, too, but nobody you've heard of. The Boats, Pissnuts, Jesus and the Iguanas; she saved any flyer any tight-pants kid handed her on the street, and she hadn't gotten around to gluing them all up. Her place was full of papers like a loose carpet that stuck to her bare feet and came away with charcoal footprints because she never wore shoes in the tunnels. Not the best housekeeper, Luna, especially after she lost Clayton. The cleanest spot was where his box used to be.

Her box was an old hutch lying on its back with a dirty green sleeping bag tucked sloppily into it, and she had a yellowish pillow crammed into a too-small flowered pillowcase that had been bled on and washed a dozen times, but you could see where the blood had been. There was a metal folding chair, we all had those, we had pinched a bunch of them from a Universalist Unitarian church on East 35th Street, but nobody was using it. Cvetko stood while she squatted. She was crying.

"Don't you get it?" she said. "They're still doing it."

She shut up when she saw that I had crawled up her wall.

They both trusted me enough to keep talking, which made me feel good.

"How many?" Cvetko said.

"I don't know. Maybe six," she said, wiping runny mascara with the backs of her hands. She sniffled a wet one and said, "She's gonna kill them, isn't she?"

Cvetko didn't say anything.

"Isn't she?"

"Tell me exactly where it is."

The Balworth Theater was a little black box in Chelsea that couldn't make its rent and ended up closed. Nothing unusual about that. What *was* unusual was that its basement had a tiny half door that opened on a crawl space down with iron rungs drilled into it, and this crawl space led to a section of sewer that led to a boiler room that led to a length of active subway line that, in turn, led to the inactive subway lines, experimental subway lines, and defunct underground workspaces where we lived. The shinbone's connected to the collarbone, you know? The whole underground's like that; you can get anywhere in New York without seeing daylight if you're willing to get dirty. This particular crawl space looked like Prohibition stuff to me, like maybe the building with the theater had been a speakeasy and the customers needed a back door out when the cops came knocking.

We had to wade through some ankle-deep unmentionable stuff in the sewer part, and I remembered Peter and Alfie's pants cuffs. I opened up the door, Cvets was right behind me, and I crawled in like a cat through a cat door. I remember having this fear like a guillotine blade was going to pop down and cut my head off. But of course it didn't.

The first thing I saw was the puppet, like a big papier-mâché Humpty Dumpty figure. A couple of painted wooden spears and swords, too, a rack of wigs and shoes. Prop room. Then I realized it wasn't Humpty Dumpty at all, it was Tweedledum, and there was Tweedledee behind and next to it. A huge Queen of Hearts crown and gown hung up on the wall, too, the wig under the crown all done up like Marie Antoinette. A pair of red ladies' pumps sat in the middle of the floor, one turned on its side. I could almost hear the actress, one of these waitresses who can't get commercials and only does plays with five-dollar tickets, plays only other actors go to, yelling *Off with her head!* to an audience of ten, eight of them friends of the cast. So the last thing they did was *Alice in Wonderland*. But they left half their shit here. A folding table, a heater, a makeup box. Maybe somebody died? Maybe the place got foreclosed on? Could be that nobody wanted these costumes; they were kind of high-school looking.

Then I saw the writing.

Not very big. Waist high, on a wall that might have once been light brown but had faded to the color of a tobacco stain.

The writing was so small I almost missed it.

I DO NOT LIKE THE WAY HE LOOKS AT ME
nor I
SHALL WE MAKE A RABBIT OF HIM?
Yes a blind rabbit
YES!

Small fingers had painted those letters on the wall. You know what they used for paint. Sure you do. On the wall nearby, dozens of round blotches like polka dots, browny-red but fading, some of them barely there. Like the wall had the measles.

Now Cvetko was in, too. We hadn't brought Luna or anybody else, just us. A fly, a fat one, drowsy with the cold, came through the open door at the top of the stairs and buzzed around the room making lazy circles. He landed on the letter Y in WAY, his little mouth dabbing down on it like the sucker end of a kid's toy arrow. Neither one of us said anything. We went up the stairs.

The body sat in in the front row, as if watching a play. Fit young guy, or had been fit, but now he was bled out white, almost as white as the rabbit's ears that sat on top of his head, though the tip of one of those was bloody. The man's eyes were gone, just two holes, and it looked weird, looked wrong that he had eyebrows over the holes. His mouth had been stuffed with socks. Vicious little bites cratered his neck, wrists, and inner thighs. Two seats away from him, a bucket. A trail of blood led from the floor in front of him up the raw concrete stairs toward the sound and light room. A bloody handprint on the glass. Grown-up-sized; a crack webbing out from it made me think of Spider-Man.

"Spider-Man," I said before I could stop myself. It sounded stupid in that room. Cvetko didn't say anything, just walked up the stairs and looked into the booth. I went behind him. Five more bodies lay in there, half-undressed, but only to get at their arteries. These had their eyes, though. They were stacked. The one on top, an Asian woman, had her eyes open and cut to the door like she'd been waiting for us, like maybe we'd set her loose and tell her she could tidy up and go back out shopping for lychee nuts or whatever she was doing when they got her. And how did they do it? When it was just them? Charm them off a train like the guy on the 6, *Come and help us find our mommies? Leave your briefcase, you won't need it.*

Cvetko bent over and picked something up. It was my superball, sticky from the puddle of blood it had been sitting in. Now I understood the blotches on the wall of the prop basement; I closed my eyes and heard the ball thump-thump-thumping, saw Peter and Sammy taking turns catching it, Camilla clomping around in the Queen of Hearts' shoes, *Off with their heads, out with their eyes, make him a rabbit!*

"This is bad, Cvetko."

"Do you think so?" he said, with that tired sarcasm he uses when I say something obvious.

"What do you think?"

"I think we must tell our esteemed mayor that the children are incorrigible, and that they are going to get us found out. And I think we must burn this place."

I pictured Margaret like the real Queen of Hearts, rather the Queen of Spades, coming down the tunnel with the shovel over her shoulder. Would she do it one at a time, in separate places? Or all lined up, with us holding them down? Old Boy and Ruth would be on board, maybe Cvetko now that he'd seen this. But Luna? Forget it. Billy, too. Baldy and Dominic would say no just to make trouble, take advantage of the rift. And me. Could I do it? I pictured sleepy little Peter, holding up his white hand. Camilla clutching Raggedy Ann and crying. But sleepy Peter. It was like he was sick.

"Cvets, I think something's wrong with those kids. The way they eat. How hungry they are."

He looked at me like *go on*.

"I mean, what if it wasn't their fault?"

"Intent doesn't matter when the results carry consequence."

"Yeah, but what if we could fix it?"

"I am skeptical."

"But you can't rule it out. Night fever is a vampire disease. What if there are more of them? A disease might be fixable."

He considered this. A fly lit briefly on his head, then decided it didn't like him and flew away. He absentmindedly touched the spot where the fly had been.

"It is possible that some of them are starving despite their feeding, which would explain their carelessness and excess. It is possible such a condition could be reversed. Your argument is sound," he said. In Cvetko's world, there was no higher praise. "But, as you noted, we need more information."

"That book," I said, "the one Clayton made."

"*The Codex*," he said, "may or may not contain answers to this problem."

"We'll ask Margaret for it."

He scoffed.

"This is important, Cvets. She might."

"She trusts no one with that book."

"Then we should borrow it."

"Are you talking about theft?" he said.

"Theft's when you don't give it back."

He nodded slowly.

"Even so, we must burn this place."

"Yeah," I said. "I guess so."

I didn't like fire so much. None of us did. We made our way out of the theater, back down to the basement.

Shall we make a rabbit of him?

"And we must remove the door to the sewer, brick up the wall."

"I don't know shit about laying bricks."

"I was, for a short time, a gardener."

"Figures," I said.

"I think this place will keep one more day. Tomorrow night. Tonight we get the bricks and mortar."

"Tonight hell, it's almost morning."

"I will place the masonry, you will only be in my way. I can set the fire without assistance, too."

Fine by me.

"Yeah, but how will you get the bricks? In the daytime?"

"You're wasting time. Go home. Make sure they're all there. Make sure they don't leave."

"And if they get hungry?"

"Feed them. Or else they will feed themselves."

THE DEVIL'S DICE

was dreaming about a game I was playing with the devil. This was your typical red devil with goat feet, horns, big backward-curving horns like on one of those African antelope things, but not an antelope. I don't know what the point of the game was; it was like dominoes, which I never played, because we each had stacks of little stones or pieces of ivory, or tiles, definitely square. He had a big pile and I had a little one. He kept rolling dice and every time he rolled, he did something different with his other hand, made some sort of Freemason sign or something. It was fascinating. Only while I looked, with his dice hand he'd steal away another couple of tiles from my pile, then roll again. I realized I wasn't ever going to get a turn at this rate. *Hey!* I said, but when I said it, it wasn't the devil, it was the Hessian. Bigger than death and all dressed up in his Prussian blues. He rolled the dice again, a twelve, then did the thing with his hand and I looked, like a dog at a treat, and there went more of my tiles. *I don't want to play this anymore,* I said, and it was the devil again. This pissed him off, so he turned over the table and the tiles poured on me like an avalanche. Only now I was lying next to Margaret in a bed, which was creepy by itself. She looked dead, like Ruth, gray and clammy. I said, "Today's your death-day," and I don't think I told you about that. That's the day you figure you would have died. I picked January 9, 1999; I would have been eighty, and that's how long my grandpa Peacock lived. But she said, "You're coming with me." And she took a soda straw and shot something up my nose; I thought it was a BB. It hurt. It went up into my sinus, like above my eye.

"Ow," I said, only now I was really saying it. I was awake. Only it wasn't night yet, or I don't think so. I felt something moving in my head. Above my eye.

"Ow," I said again, reaching up for the door of the refrigerator by habit, only it wasn't closed. I sat up. Whatever it was, was wriggling and I knew; I had bugs in there. "Goddamn it," I said, pressing one nostril shut and blowing. Three or four roaches skittered out; I slapped them off me, but there was another one in there, and he went into a panic.

"Ow, *fuck*!"

Took me two or three snotty honks before I shot this one into my lap and then I picked him up, clapped and smashed him. Sometimes bugs crawl into us because, if we've fed, we're a little warmer than the rocks, and a nostril or an ear is a very tempting hidey-hole. We mostly don't sleep naked, you can figure that one out for yourself.

But who opened my door? That's what let the little bastard in. Now I saw him. Sammy. He was squatting down on his haunches against the wall.

"Did you open my door?"

"No," he said, but defiantly, meaning *yes*.

"Well, don't."

Nothing.

His eyes shone in the darkness.

We want you to be one of us.

Except half of Sammy.

"What do you want?"

He didn't talk for a second or two, like he was weighing me.

"Peter hurts. He needs you."

A flame flared up as Sammy lit a lighter. Closed the lid on it. Opened it and lit it again.

"That's my Zippo!" I said.

The sneaky little fucker.

He considered it, placed it carefully, maybe sarcastically, on the floor like a little tombstone, then walked out, looking after me to see if I was coming.

I got up, thought about waking Cvetko, didn't. I followed Sammy into the little honeycomb of rooms where we'd put them and saw that Peter was sitting up in his locker, watching for me.

"He's hungry," Alfie said. Alfie stood nearby, just next to Camilla. "Me, too," she peeped.

"It's going to be night soon," I said.

"I can't wait," Peter whimpered. He really did sound pitiful. Tears streaked his cheeks. Hunger for a vampire is an awful thing, worse than it ever gets for a boy—*at least an American boy*, I can hear Cvetko saying. Blood hunger sits in your guts like a rock. Then after a day or two that rock heats up and your limbs get cold and they hurt. If people talk to you, they just sound like insects buzzing or dogs barking because all you can focus on is that coal burning in the middle of you; you have to put it out. And every living neck is a fire extinguisher. If you let it get to that point, you just drink and drink and you don't care about peeling people, you'd peel them all to close that smoldering hole in you. I could see in Peter's eyes that was where he was. And he'd fed, they'd all fed. They confessed to the killings in the theater, told me they would

sneak down there in the middle of the day to fill up again, like raid-
ing the fridge when everyone else was asleep. I didn't bother lectur-
ing them or warning them; it was clear they couldn't help it.

"Where are the others? Manu and Duncan?" I said.

"Sleeping," Alfie said. "They don't eat so much."

"And you," I said to Sammy, "are you hungry, too?"

"Not like them. But yes."

Not like them. *Them* meaning Alfie and Peter and Camilla. The
siblings. I could almost hear Cvetko telling me to think; I was
tempted to wake him up, but he would want me to work this out on
my own. Was it hereditary? *Your argument is sound,* I could hear the
old egghead saying. But hereditary would mean unfixable, which
would mean *Off with their heads!*

"Have you always been like this?" I asked.

Peter shook his head.

"How long?"

"I don't want to talk. I want to go to the theater," he said.

"But they're all gone," Alfie said. "Dry-dry-dried up."

"Even the rabbit," said Camilla.

"Because *you* took his eyes," said Peter.

"It was only a game," she said.

Alfie said, "Anyway the rabbit was already dead."

"Poor rabbit," Camilla agreed. "But I don't want to talk anymore,
either."

Now her belly hitched and she held it and sat down, a tear spilling down her cheek.

"May I . . ." Peter started.

"What?"

But I knew what he was going to say.

"May I bite you, Joey? Only a little?"

"No!" I said while he was still saying *little.*

That was absolutely against the rules. Margaret laid down the law on that at our very first town meeting and said it again every time somebody new came in. Her rap went something like this:

"This colony is *hunt or die*. Nobody asks to feed off another, nobody lets anyone feed off 'em. I hear about anybody doing that, they're out. I'll have no dependents and no weaklings here. And don't go cryin' charity; all charity died with the hope of heaven."

That bit about dependents and weaklings rang false with me; what happened between two of us wasn't any of her beeswax as far as I could see.

I figured out the real reason later. When I broke down. Of course I broke down. The hope of heaven may have died (like when I was nine), but I still couldn't listen to a kid whimper in pain like that when I might do something to help him. Or her. But I wasn't stupid about it, at least not completely. I wasn't going to make myself that vulnerable with half-of-Sammy watching. I went to Luna. She was a softie like me. I told her what was happening, what I was going to do, asked her to watch and make sure I didn't get in trouble.

"How long do we carry them?" she said.

We.

Just that fast, she was on board, too.

"I don't know," I said. She nodded. We went. So now I was protecting peelers, hiding their crimes from Margaret and letting them feed from me.

She had plenty of reason to kill me if she found out.

And that was before I stole her book.

THE THING IN THE TUNNEL

etting that *Codex* from Margaret wasn't going to be easy; she never left anybody alone in her place and she kept irregular hours. She was funny about her stuff, too, like with that couch of hers. I had the feeling she would know where everything was, would smell where your fingers had touched her things. The only thing I had going for me was that she had just torn the joint up killing the Hunchers; she might not have everything in its place in her mind, you know? She might not think twice about my scent because I had been down there, too. Now what I needed was an opportunity.

Be careful what you ask for, right?

Gua Gua came back. He was the only one of the Latins who came back.

It was daytime when he found us; he woke us up. He was yelling.

"I smell you, you whore! You're going to look at me before you kill me. Do you hear me, *puta madre, te voy a mostrar mi cara.*"

"Joey?" one of the kids said from a locker, I'm not sure which one.

I heard Cvetko getting up; I always forgot how fast he could move when he had to.

I went out to the tunnel, followed it around to where the noise was coming from. Gua Gua was in the tunnel not far from us, down in the trough of an unused section of track not far from Luna's cave.

It had taken him days to get back to us because he did it blind, feeling his way along the tunnels and following scent. He was blind because he'd been burned. Missing an ear, half his scalp, both eyes. Old Boy said everything above the nose got fucked-up because somebody shorter was standing in front of him. Old Boy said it was Willy Pete, white phosphorus, a kind of grenade they used to kill VC in tunnels. Supremely nasty stuff, it would stick to you and just keep burning.

The Hessian.

This is what happens when you fuck with the Hessian.

Old Boy was stalking the Puerto Rican, just walking behind him barefoot with his knife out. How long had he been following him? I almost said *it*. Gua Gua was an *it* now. This was one of the worst things I'd ever seen; this guy should have been dead, he should have been dead twice, but here he was moving around, all pink and black and puckered. Coming for Margaret. Coming for us.

"You told him," he shouted. "You *told* him we were coming. He was *ready!* You're up there laughing at us, but you'll get yours, too. I don't know how, you bitch, but you will. And the last thing you'll think of is my face."

I was hypnotized, everyone was. The whole neighborhood crowded on the rise above the tracks, looking down at the shouting thing with three-quarters of a head. But that's when it hit me. *Everybody* was here: Ruth, Old Boy, Margaret. This was my chance, but who knew for how long?

Gua Gua was getting close now, feeling his way along and yelling himself hoarse.

Margaret nodded at Old Boy, and Old Boy moved fast. I didn't watch. I hightailed it back to Margaret's place; it only took me a few minutes. I flew like the shadow of an airplane; my feet barely touched the ground.

The chain was the first problem; Margaret was strong enough to pull her trapdoor up with a little effort. Me? It took a lot of effort. I wasn't sure I was going to be able to do it, but I got the image of her finding me here and my heart beat once or twice and I pulled that chain with all I had. Up it came with a groan and a shudder; I hooked the chain so it would stay open. Down I went.

I had never been in here alone before. It struck me again how well put together this vault was. If the Big One fell, it might just be Margaret crawling out of the rubble like a big angry cockroach in a bathrobe. I knew she had other clothes, but she rarely wore them. Where did she even keep her clothes? Probably in the big armoire. It had never occurred to me to wonder what she had stuffed in the cabinets behind the bar or in the honeycombed wine shelves or in the big steamer trunk. The trunk had a lock on it. Was *The Codex* in there? Or was it near her fur-lined sleeping box behind the bar? I didn't know how big the book was, I had never seen it. The chest made more sense. But I would need the key.

Just leave, forget it.

Let her kill the kids, they're sick anyway.

I hated that last thought. I closed my eyes for a second and saw Peter crying, heard him whimpering. The reason Margaret didn't want us feeding off each other was that it made you care about the one you gave your blood to. It was that simple. Margaret didn't think it was going to make us weak, she thought it would make us love each other more than her. She was right. I had held Peter's little white hand while he fed from my wrist and I had done the same for Camilla. Luna did it for Alfie, let him take from her neck while she cradled his head like a mother. Now both of us were in their corner. I wanted to help those kids, and any chance I had of doing that was in that book.

Hurry.

It occurred to me to break the lock, but that was stupid, I couldn't cover that up. Was it even in the chest? Cvetko would have said to look everywhere else first, or would he? No time. Best guess and go for it. Back to the chest I had no key for.

Margaret had the key.

But Margaret left in a hurry.

The key's in here!

It sure was. On a ring of three keys hanging on a nail on the wall, next to the narrow door she actually used to get in and out, though nobody but her knew where it led. The trapdoor was just for moving stuff through.

Three keys. I knelt down in front of the cedar chest.

I tried one, too big, it didn't work.

Hurry.

I tried the second one. Little key.

It worked.

I lifted up the lid.

THE VAMPIRE'S TRUNK

arn? Are you kidding me? I've never seen her knit, not once, what does she wear, socks? I guess I have seen her with a scarf once or twice.

Margaret McMannis, the queen of the underworld, at least our mile or two of it, knitted socks. And scarves. Yarn in brown, gray, and blue lay rolled in balls on one end of the upper tray of the trunk, along with a collection of knitting needles, two of them crossed midknit and capped off with pencil erasers. The other end of that tray was filled with money, mostly American fives and ones, but a few pounds, Deutschmarks, and Canadian dollars lay stacked in small but tidy bundles. Coins in a jam jar. A little Japanese figure, like a frog or a dog, I can never tell with that Asian stuff. Rings and earrings stood in tiny rows like Cvetko's chess pieces, grouped by size and type. I had a moment of confusion where it seemed like I was back in my house in 1933, standing near Margaret's purse, looking at the gorgon cameo I was about to plant her with to get her canned, starting all of this business for me in the first place. Here I was again, violating her personal property for the second time ever, and if she caught me the consequences would be just as dire. *Here's to Joey Peacock, the boy so nice I killed him twice.*

I pulled out that tray (carefully, so carefully) and what do you know, more money. Twenties this time, she must have had fifteen, twenty thousand dollars bricked up with dry, yellowing rubber bands about the same color as her fangs. Her murderous, sharp panther-fangs. I picked up a couple of thin little books, like sketchbooks, and looked under them; a nickel-plated revolver and a box of bullets, another couple of boxes, one locked, but too small for the Bible-sized leather book I was imagining. A crucifix sawn in half, that was weird. Seashells. Seriously, seashells? Did she go down to Coney Island at night and wade out in the water?

Wait a minute, I thought.

I took another look at the sketchbooks, opened the top one up. A watercolor painting, not bad, showed some kind of mountain with a couple of shacks just at sunset, a rusty pickup truck. Really spiky cursive script in pencil next to it, Clayton's writing; I recognized it because he had left me notes.

Ozarks. 1953. November

Milo and his brother sleep in basements by day beneath the houses of their mother and aunt, who know what they are. The brothers drive by night into Eureka Springs (?) and feed on women they pay for the privilege. "Blood whores" they call them, and at least one of these women also helps them fence stolen jewelry. They make most of their money through theft, as neither of them is particularly good at charming. How much easier their lives would be if they could simply convince people to give them what they wanted, as I am

*blessed to do. I never would have met them but
that I sighted on one of their women. They were
too bewildered at meeting another vampire to take*

The page after that was missing.

Hurry!

I shut that book and opened another; more paintings, more writing, all Clayton's. A swamp with a man holding a pot to collect blood from a mule's neck; six figures standing around, looking down into a hole; an old man in a chair, his pants almost up to his tits and a fedora on his head—I couldn't see his fangs, but knew he was one of us by the light in his eyes. The writing on that one said:

*Arthur. 1922. I should like to know how old Arthur
really is, but he will not say. If only I could
see him under a strong light; you can tell much
from a shadow.*

I cracked the third book, carefully, this one was older, and saw a moonlit field of dead and dying men, belly-shot horses all unstrung, a woman bending down to bite the neck of a fellow in a dark blue uniform against a tree. This painting bothered me. There was one word next to it, an Indian-sounding word that started with *Chick*, like *Chicken-sausage*, but that wasn't it. The woman was biting the man but looking at you, as if out through time, through the paper *at* you. His hand was tangled in her black hair; her free hand cupped his chin like he was her lover. Like she was showing Clayton what she could do. His lover? A woman who picked over battlefields.

A ghoul, that's the word for it.

We're ghouls.

* * *

What the fuck was I doing, I had no time to read! I snapped that book shut, put it and the other two under my arm, caught sight of Margaret's shovel leaning against the wall.

Exactly, now get the fuck out.

The problem of how to get back in here and return the books was one I would have to solve later; now I had another nut to crack. Go out the way I came or take my chances with the narrow door? I might run into her, face-to-face; I might get lost. But I would know how to get back in without pulling up the trap. I would learn something about how Margaret moves around so fast down here. That was something. That was worth the risk. But how to close the trap and still get out? Drop it and jump? Was I fast enough? If I wasn't, I might get my legs pinched by that monster of a door. I might get pinched in the middle, stuck dying but unable to die until Margaret came home and found me there.

"I am that fast," I told Margaret's room. "I am."

So I put *The Codex*(es) on the bar and got a good running jump that let me skinny up out of the hole. I looked at the chain on its wall hook, going up to its pulley. How like the mouth of a giant, biting clam the door looked. Fuck it. Two steps and a belly-dive. I could do this.

I grunted and strained as I unhooked the chain and the weight of the door immediately yanked it out of my hands. I moved faster than I ever had before. I moved like the shadow of a plane on the ground. I felt the door nip at the heel of my boot as it closed and I just missed flattening Margaret's couch as I hit the floor, coming face-to-face with the faded bloodstain from the black Huncher Margaret had brained.

Go, now!

I grabbed the sketchbooks and slipped into the slot of darkness in Margaret's wall, having no idea where I would come out. There was a story, another Greek story, about a guy in a cave maze with a ball of yarn, looking for a monster with a bull's head. These guys in stories, running in looking for monsters. I *was* a monster, but I knew when I was outgunned. If I still did anything like praying, I would have prayed to the god of small places not to meet Margaret McMannis in that tunnel.

"Did you?" Cvetko asked.

"What?" I said, looking at a picture of a dog. It was a German shepherd, watercolored in, sitting on the trunk of a big 1950s car with fins on the back. His tongue hung down like a piece of ham at the deli. This picture was unusual because it was full of daylight. "How did he do this?" I said. "The dog's not growling or anything, and the sun's out."

Cvetko pointed at a faint crease on the opposite page.

"What?"

"Paper clip," he said. "Photograph." That kind of deflated me. First, because I had liked the idea of Clayton breaking the rules, walking in the afternoon, making eye contact with a dog without it going apeshit. I always liked dogs, hated having to cross the street to avoid them, hated their barking and trying to bite me as much because I felt rejected by an old friend as by the unwanted attention it always brought. *Daisy's such a nice girl, but she wanted to kill that kid. Must be some kind of creep for sweet little Daisy to act like that.* But I also felt deflated because I should have known better. Suns and friendly dogs only existed in photographs, of course that's how he did this. I wondered if the pooch was on the trunk or if Clayton stuck it there, if there were separate photographs of dog and car. Only one crease. Clayton could work from life, too. It suddenly struck me as unfair that I'd never know if that dog actually sat on that trunk or if it was just something Clayton made up.

Now the kids stole up, all of them like a little pack. All of them but Peter. They gathered around Cvetko like he was Grandpa showing vacation pictures. Which I guess these were. They sure as hell weren't the medical encyclopedia about being a vampire I'd hoped to find. What was more, and Cvetko didn't say it, there were pages missing. Lots of them, I think. Did Clayton tear out paintings he wasn't happy with? Did somebody get to these first and yank out the good stuff?

"I like the look of that dog," Alfie said. "That's a good-dog, guard-dog, keep-you-safe."

"Not me," said Duncan, shrinking away from *The Codex* as though even a picture of such a dog might bite, hiding his little hands in the blanket he had taken to carrying even on the hunt. It wasn't the cleanest blanket in the world.

"You ignored my question," Cvetko said.

"Which one?"

"The one about our esteemed leader bumping into you in the tunnel. Did she?"

"Oh," I said, "no."

"No, I don't imagine that would have gone well."

"Turns out her tunnel splits into three. The way I took dumped me out in an air shaft near Penn Station."

Cvetko looked at the children.

"If I promise to show you some of the pictures in these books later, will you all leave us alone for a little while?"

"If you show us properly," Sammy said, bending and unbending his small toes against the concrete beneath him. "And not just for a moment to send us away again."

"I will show you properly, and answer whatever questions I can about them. But first I must speak to Joseph Hiram Peacock."

Sammy kept looking at him.

"Alone," Cvetko said.

The little girl walked away, and the rest did, too, Sammy last, looking again over his shoulder, but more at me than Cvetko. I'd have paid ten bucks to know what that little shit was thinking. If he hadn't gotten his clock stopped, he would have grown up mean and clever. He would have made a good criminal.

"These paintings are quite expressive," Cvetko said. "I think our Clayton would have been remembered as a notable, if minor, early American painter had he not had the sun stolen from him."

"Yeah," I said, "they're great. But what's wrong with these kids?"

"I share your disappointment. I was hoping for more insight into our condition. But, really, these are quite pleasant. There was a painter, a countryman of mine, Anton Ažbe, who had the ability to put the soul of the subject into the eyes. His painting of a Negress still haunts me, her gravitas, her eyes. Ažbe knew eyes. I wish I had met him but he died in Munich. This painting, of Clayton's, *Arthur 1922*"—he traded books and flipped until he found what he wanted—"has much of the same power. Don't you agree? You don't know Ažbe, of course; Clayton had none of his training or photographic mastery of detail, but the sense of weariness is perfectly communicated. I suspect our Arthur did not survive long after this was painted."

"Are you really going on about creaky old commie painters? What are we going to do?"

Now Duncan was at the door.

"Peter needs a bath," he said. "He *needs* one."

"No," Camilla said, coming up behind him and snatching his hand, hard, making him show his fangs at her.

"But he *does*," Duncan said.

"You're the stinky one," she said, and pulled him away, his blanket dragging behind him. I watched them go.

236 | CHRISTOPHER BUEHLMAN

"You're feeding them, aren't you?" Cvetko said.

I trust Cvetko, I do. But I was so scared of Margaret finding out I just lied.

"No."

He looked me in the eyes, tilted down his glasses to do it, smiled at me like my uncle Walt used to. Like he knew I was naughty but it was okay.

"Interesting."

WAYCHEE ROO

The next night I woke up starving.

Feeding the munchkins really wore me out. I had to bleed somebody, and I remembered it was Tuesday night. *Soap!* Gonzalo! I schlepped through the tunnels till I got to the 23rd Street platform and took it north all the way to the Bakers' stop. It was beginning to feel like work, keeping up with them, keeping blood in my stomach. All those paintings of Clayton's had really gotten my wheels turning. Manhattan wasn't the only place to be a vampire. What was it like out in the Ozarks, wherever those were? Down in Florida? Nah, too sunny. But Vermont, up in the mountains? Virginia? This had possibilities. Not too many people around, just you in a cave or a snowy cabin, creeping down at night to terrorize the villagers like Dracula. That sounded like the life. Except, where would I go to see a movie? What if the girls nearby were ugly, like with moles and country accents? Country accents drive me nuts; so does the music, I can't even listen to it. Want to chase me out of a room, don't bother with garlic or a cross, just put some George Jones or Conway Twitty on the jukebox. Not that "Have You Never Been Mellow" is musical genius, but Olivia Newton John (a) is foxy and (b) doesn't twang. No, I keep an eye out for Kenny Rogers down in the tunnels, I'd love to decorate *his* life.

I checked my watch. 9:12. Plenty of time. Two kids on their way home from karate class sat in sweat-stained white uniforms, a green belt and a yellow belt. They babysat a rumpled gym bag between them, one foam shin and foot pad trying to peek out of the zipper like a tongue out of a mouth.

"What style do you kids take?" I said.

They looked at me, not sure if they should trust me, and then the bigger one said, "Waychee Roo." I knew about Tae Kwon Do and the great Bruce Lee's Wing Chun Kung Fu. I'd heard of Dim Mak, the Death Touch; all the comics had ads for that. I had been about to send away for the Black Dragon Society book, but Cvets had pointed out that secrets for sale aren't secrets and that any vampire, even puny little me, could wipe up the floor with Count Danté, however much of a badass he looked like with his 'fro and his snarling and making his hands into claws like he was a big funky wizard about to cast a spell of whoop-ass.

But I didn't know Waychee Roo from a poke in the eye with a stick.

"What's that?" I said.

"It's Okinawan."

"You guys use numchuks?"

He shook his head sadly, like if he'd been a slightly luckier child he could have joined a dojo where they used numchuks.

"I have a pair," I said.

"You mean nunchaku?"

"Yeah, numchuks."

"Are you a black belt?"

"Yeah," I said. Maybe not, but I could kick a black belt's ass, that had to count for something. I noticed how tan these lads looked, which was not really tan at all, but after hanging out with pale, cold Peter and the rest, these warm-body blond kids looked almost like Arabs.

"Cool," the small one said.

"Show us something!" said the brother.

I looked around at the dozen or so other people on the car. Nobody was paying much attention, so I grabbed a pole and extended my body straight out, held it just for a second, pointing my toes.

"Cool!" said the small one.

"My uncle can do that," said the older one. "He's a gymnast. He almost went to Munich, but Dad says it's good he didn't."

"Bad guys," the little one said.

"Yeah? Well, I'll show you something even cooler when the train stops again."

They leaned forward, all eyes.

When we pulled into the Lexington station, I waited till just the last second, waited until the leavers had left and the getters-on had gotten on, then I jumped up and karate-chopped the pole with my forearm, not snapping the pole cleanly like I thought, but denting it good and knocking it loose at the top. It was loud. Everybody looked. I had broken my arm. I made a little squealy sound without meaning to.

The big one said, "Kee-YA!"

"Cool!" said the little one, but a big black guy in a striped tie looked angry, said, "Why'd you do that, man? People *ride* this thing."

I laughed and ran, just beating the shutting doors, cradling the busted arm, which was even now resetting and knitting itself whole.

The Bakers' place was all wrong.

First of all, nobody came to the door when I rang so I had to go back outside the building and climb around to the balcony window, which was locked. I tried to peek in but the drapes were drawn. Had they gone on vacation? I went back around through the front lobby, took the stairs two at a time, rang the doorbell again. Nothing. I put my ear to the door and thought I heard talking. I knocked. Nothing. I was about to pull out Gary Combs's American Express card and jimmy the lock when I heard the elevator ding, so I waited. A lady with curlers under a head scarf came out with a bag of corner-store groceries, the neck of a wine bottle sticking up like a periscope. I know I looked bad leaning against the wall looking at the ugly hallway carpeting, and she slowed up, her hand fishing in her purse for her keys. Her elbow vised down on her purse a little. She came a step closer, pulled her keys out. Jesus, she lived in the apartment next door.

"Can I help you?" she said, scared, but more that I'd try to take her purse or, God forbid, her wine than that I'd hurt her. I wasn't exactly intimidating.

"Everything's cool," I said, using my little-boy voice. Then I got a good look at her. Pretty in a washed-out, Katharine-Ross-with-crow's-feet kind of way. I switched to my sexy James Dean voice and poured on the charm, made myself look older. "Is anybody home now at your place?"

"No," she said, saliva running out of her mouth and into her grocery bag.

"Expecting anybody?"

She shook her head no.

"Do you have a television?"

She nodded. Then she dropped her keys and unbuttoned her coat, rubbing herself in the zipper area, still holding her groceries, which I took from her.

"Jesus, not here. Pick up your keys and ask me in."

She did.

* * *

For an older broad, like thirty-five, she had a good body. It was sitting naked on the couch next to me, a brown couch, thank God, because she was kind of a bleeder. I had tasted the bitter, high-in-the-nose notes of aspirin as I sucked from her thigh and went back for seconds on her wrist. My timing was perfect, too. The naughty stuff was over and now *Soap* was on. Dinner and a show is my favorite. I confess I wasn't paying much attention, though; Jody, the gay one, was ranting about something, but I was in my head, still worrying about how I was going to replace Margaret's books and find out what was wrong with Peter and the others. The sound from the neighbor lady's Magnavox was weird, like it had an echo. That was when I realized the same show was on next door. Somebody was watching *Soap* at the Bakers'. They must have had the volume up to three-quarters. What the fuck? They didn't like that show, not without me there.

Something banged against the wall. Once. Twice. Three times.

"Coming," my companion said, like it was the door, and stood up, a fresh runner of blood going down her leg.

"No," I said. "Go get dressed."

She stopped and swayed, then walked down the hallway bare-assed, one curler loose and bobbing as she went. Bloody footprints on the carpet; the carpet wasn't that dark, I was making a mess here. I *hate* aspirin.

I was thinking it was time to get going when the phone rang.

"I'll get it," she sang out from the bedroom. I couldn't hear what she said to the caller over the TV, but then she said, "Joey? Is that your name? It's for you."

My heart beat once.

"Tell them I'm not here and hang up."

Mumbles from the bedroom. She came out. I stood up to go. The phone rang again. I picked it up.

"Curler residence," I said, trying to make a joke, but I said it flat because I was scared.

"Joey."

A kid's voice.

American.

"Joey."

"Who's this?"

"It's Mikey."

"Mikey who?" I said, though I knew good and goddamned well who.

"From next door."

My heart beat again.

The televisions blared their nonsense.

"You know," he said. "The fat kid you bite and take blood from and laugh at. Why aren't you watching TV with me? Do you like Ms. Kemp better?"

I didn't say anything, I didn't know what to say. I was trying to think but couldn't. He kept talking.

"Are you putting your penis in her vagina? My daddy wants to do that to Ms. Kemp. He told his friend at the bar. He doesn't put it in Mommy's anymore, she says it hurts her now since she's got lady problems."

I made a fish mouth. Nothing came out.

"I'd like to put my penis in Ms. Kemp, too. Maybe I will. I'll be right there."

Oh shit oh shit oh shit.

I had never charmed anyone over the phone before; I didn't know if it would work, but I thought so.

"Stay there," I said. "Unlock your door, sit down, and don't move again till I come over."

He didn't say anything. I started to repeat myself, but he interrupted me.

"Stay there, unlock—"

"I know what you're trying to do," he said. "But it doesn't work on me anymore because I'm like you now."

My heart beat twice.

I wanted to run but knew I couldn't just leave a mess like this. Not unless I ran and kept running, ran to the Ozarks, ran to wherever that long-ago dog was sitting on the trunk of the car.

"I'm hungry," he said. And hung up.

That broke the spell. I looked at Ms. Kemp. "Stay here, lock it behind me, don't let anyone in!"

I heard the Bakers' door unlatch, swing open. I leapt for Ms. Kemp's door, opened that. We met in the hallway.

He looked bad. He stank. Blood bibbed the front of his yellow Izod polo shirt. He looked dead. He showed me his fangs like he was proud of them, little nubby new fangs in his very red mouth. He was about to say something. I heard the door across the hall start to unlatch. I grabbed his chin, shut his mouth, and shoved him back in his doorway, shutting his door just as the one across the hall was starting to open.

Oh shit oh shit oh shit.

"Don't push me," he said, pushing me back, hard. I rolled with it, rolled back to the television, which I turned up all the way, though momentum made me break the volume knob off when I did it.

"Hey, you want to keep it down over there?" a deep voice said from the hall. I clobbered the Baker kid so hard I broke his jaw; he squealed and sat down. I opened the door, looked at the big dago-looking guy standing there, told him and his huge mustache, "Mind your own business! Turn your TV on," saw his eyes go blank, and then I shut the door. Heard him shut his. I turned around just in time to see the coffee table coming at my head, ducked in time so it was a glancing blow, but it still sent me tumbling. Only now did I notice what a wreck the rest of the place was: broken glass everywhere, the refrigerator standing open, one shelf collapsed so the food was on the kitchen floor, the Miracle Whip jar broken with Miracle Whip blobbed out everywhere.

I turned around; here came the coffee table again. I got under the table, slid like I was sliding into third, kicked his legs out from under him. He fell hard. On top of me. The table hit a shelf full of tchotchkes, made an awful noise.

Now he grabbed my neck, choking me. Lot of good that would do, I don't breathe much, but it did hurt. He saw that wasn't working, fishhooked a thumb into my mouth, tore my mouth open all the way to the cheek, and that hurt like blazing hell. It wasn't fair he got to be so strong so young! I remembered a move I saw in a karate magazine, snaked my left arm over his right arm, under the elbow of his left, and slapped up under his elbow, hard. It rolled him, but then he just rolled me over again, straight on top of the Miracle Whip jar and all the other broken glass, I was cut to *shit*.

"OW, *fuck!*" I said, but his knee slid in the mess on the linoleum and he was off-balance enough for me to roll him the rest of the way over. He flopped on his stomach and said, "Mom!"

The telephone rang.

I pulled the open refrigerator over on top of him; the milk broke, tomatoes rolled everywhere, then I slipped in gravy or maybe it was blood. There was an awful lot of blood in this place.

"Mom!" he said again.

The telephone kept ringing.

I had never peeled a vampire before, I didn't want to. But what else? Take him with me? No time to think.

He started wriggling out from under the fridge, so I stomped on his neck and broke it.

Somebody knocked on the door.

Somebody across the room said, "MO-om!" and I realized it was

Gonzalo exactly imitating the way the kid sounded when he was watching TV. Poor bird had no idea, he was running back and forth on his little wooden bar.

"Mr. Baker?" a woman said, her voice muffled through the wood, but I could tell it wasn't my new friend next door.

The kid's neck righted itself with a sound like tearing off a cold turkey wing; it was even worse than the sound it had made breaking. He started doing a push-up, trying to get the fridge off.

I had to peel him.

I saw a block of knives, pulled out the big one, the one for turkeys.

I jumped on top of the fridge and stomped, flattening him out again under it.

The phone rang, the door knocked.

"No, don't! No, don't!" the bird said. I thought it was talking to me, then realized it was repeating somebody else's words. Probably their last words.

Now the little chunk was pushing me *and* the fridge up; a jar of pickles slipped out and went rolling.

"Whatever is going on in there, I want you to know I've called the police," the woman at the door said.

The phone stopped ringing.

I struck, jamming the knife down as far as I could into the kid's skull, which was pretty much all the way to my fist, then pulled out halfway and stirred the point. He went flat, but it wouldn't last. There was only one way.

I pulled the knife out.

"No, don't! MO-om!" Gonzalo said.

I put the knife, edge up, under the kid's neck.

"Sorry, Mikey. I'm so sorry."

Hey, Mikey! He likes it!

Then I did it.

It's not an easy thing. I don't know what you've seen in the movies, but it's not like that. It's awful.

His brain started working again before I got through the bone and he tried to fight, jerking himself back and forth like a giant windshield wiper in all the mess beneath him, wheezing air through his cut pipes, bucking the refrigerator and spilling out more little bottles and fruit.

But I held on and did it.

I got it off.

Just as the police arrived.

This is how it looked on the cover of the *New York Post*:

SATANISTS
STRIKE
YORKVILLE

I won't force their whole shitty article on you, but the short version is this: Police responded to calls about a disturbance at a fifth-floor apartment in the Upper East Side neighborhood of Yorkville. Several commands to open up were ignored, forcing officers to bust in. Officers on the scene claimed to have seen someone holding, and I quote, "a kitchen knife and a head"; they recalled firing on this individual. None of them could supply a description except to say that he or she "wasn't very tall" and "moved with surprising speed." The suspect is believed to have escaped out the living room window despite the lack of a fire escape from that balcony. The headless body of twelve-year-old Michael Baker was found in the kitchen. The brutally stabbed bodies of his parents were found in the bathtub, along with child-sized hand and foot marks, though no readable fingerprints were discovered. Disturbing satanic messages and images had been painted on the wall in blood, including references to the punk band the Ramones and the notorious club CBGB. While the NYPD officially expressed confidence about catching the perpetrators, one unnamed source reported that evidence had been tampered with and that the crime scene had been "heinously mistreated." The family pet, believed to be a parrot, also appeared to have been stolen.

Here's how it looked from my end:

"OPEN UP!" he said. "POLICE!"

I was standing on the back of a refrigerator, holding poor Mikey's head. I knew they couldn't catch me, but they were going to find bodies. I just had to make sure they wouldn't find anything vampirey. Luckily, the bar was low because people generally didn't believe in us, but some of this evidence would be tough to ignore.

Four hard knocks rattled the door. These were pretty good doors, but nothing a determined person couldn't get through.

Think!

First, the head. Mikey's little fangs had to go—I set the head on the counter, knocked the canines out with the butt of the knife, and stuck these in my pocket. My face was itching terribly where my torn cheek healed itself.

"OPEN UP OR WE'LL BREAK IT DOWN!"

Where were the Baker mom and dad? Bedroom? No. Bathroom. Stacked up the way the kids liked to do it. Completely drained, fish-belly white, brutalized necks and wrists, blood all down the front of Dad's boxers where somebody got his femoral. From the stains on Mikey's shirt, one had to guess that he had taken part as well, too scared to leave, not knowing how to hunt. By the time I came around he was so hungry he got brave. But who turned him, and why? An accident? Maybe. No time to think.

Three more hard knocks.

The Bakers' holes would play funny at the coroner's, and there was no time to burn them.

Shit shit shit.

There was nothing for it. I stabbed and cut the fuck out of both of them, doing my best to slash up the bite marks, stabbing them in random places, too, just to confuse things. She belched and he farted a big one while I did it; you know how stiffs are. This wasn't the best way I could think of to spend an evening.

I stepped out into the living room and picked up the kid's head, meaning to hide it, I don't know where, just as the door went *bang!* and the biggest cop I ever saw, a huge Polish-looking guy with no neck, walked in behind his service .38.

"DROP THE KNIFE!" he said, and I did.

"Drop the fucking head! Do it now!"

I did.

Two more cops came in, also drawn and ready to shoot, one with the shotgun that had blown the door.

"Now drop *your* guns," I said.

Two of them did, but the little Hispanic guy in the back was tougher; he only lowered his .38 a bit, then raised it. I was about to tell him to do it again when I felt my back push out a piece of the jar I fell on and I jerked. Hispanic guy shot. He was a good shot. It tore through my chest, clipped my heart, and put a hole right through my lung. He probably would have shot me again, but he saw I was unarmed.

"Lay down on the floor!" he said, moving closer and reaching for his cuffs, perplexed at the inaction of his friends. "You guys want to help me, or what?"

I fixed his eyes and went to give him a counterorder, but my lung wasn't quite healed and I only managed to bend over and cough blood.

He slipped the cuff on one hand and turned me, kicked the back of my knee to make me kneel.

"Seriously, a little help?" he said, grabbing my wrist and darting his eye back at his drooling friends. I yanked my hand free, grabbed his gun hand, and jerked that up in the air as he shot again.

"Stop," I wheezed, looking him in the eye again, really pouring it on. He relaxed, went slack-jawed.

"Holster your gun."

He did.

I peeked out the window. Two cop cars, one cop down at the cars watching the front, talking into the radio. I had a minute.

"You three, listen. I want you to make it look like punks or satanists did this, got it? Get sponges, whatever, paint weird shit on the walls. Stop before your buddies get here. Block the door so they can't get in for a minute."

"What about you?" said the little Hispanic guy, sounding genuinely concerned about me.

I went and grabbed Gonzalo out of his cage. He crawled onto my shoulder.

"Me?" I said, rubbing the already closed gunshot wound on my chest. I made my hand small and shook off the cuff. "I'll be just fine," and I went out the window.

I climbed up to the roof, then climbed down once I got to the other side, the side away from the street. Two more cop cars and an ambulance were just pulling up.

I grabbed the bird's feet so he wouldn't fall off while I ran, and run I did.

Like the shadow of an airplane on the ground.

HOLLOW BE THY NAME

Before I went anywhere, I went to see Chloë. She always calmed me down, lifted my spirits. Poor, beat-up, runaway Chloë, was I the only person who understood her?

I knew I'd probably be waking Blond Jesus up, so I brought him a meatball sandwich, the smell of which turned my stomach a little, what with all that greasy tinfoil with cheese stuck to it. Everything reminded me of carnage now: the Hunchers' brains down in Margaret's apartment, the stuff that came out of the Baker kid. But Blond Jesus loved that goddamned meatball sandwich, ate it with big, grateful bites and chewed with his mouth open. He wanted to talk, but I wanted the company of the dead. After the pandemonium of telephones, gunshots, screams, squawks, and a kitchen being trashed, I needed somebody who knew how to shut up.

"Watch my bird," I said, leaving Gonzalo there. "Make a stand for it or something, would ya? Nothing fancy. I'll give you five bucks."

"Sure thing," he said, showing me a big, steamy mouthful of food, steaming up his own glasses.

I put my hand over my mouth and lit out of there. When I got to the pipe, I threw away my ruined shirt and pants and squeezed through in my skivvies. It felt kind of improper, but never mind. It wasn't like that with Chloë, she was just a kid. I slipped through the hole and into Chloë's cave. I was safe there. I let myself just say whatever I wanted. Or maybe I just thought it, I don't even remember. It was something like praying, something like beatnik poetry I'd heard down in the Village. I just poured out words.

Our Chloë, who art in cavern, hollow be thy name. Thy cavern come, here I come, I played my drum for him, pa-rum-pum-pum-pum. Chloë, I'm feeling bad about the things I've done, the things I have to keep doing just to keep, what is it, living? I'm not saying I've got it rougher than you, your days were few, and very blue. I'm going to stop rhyming now because it sounds stupid. I just think about you, whoever beat your face in. How could they do that? Everything seems set up so you've got to hurt someone all the time, no matter what. I cut a guy's head off today, a kid, I mean I really cut it off. He was a vampire, I probably did him a favor. Maybe somebody should do that to me, I don't like myself very much right now. Probably you don't like me either, bothering you all the time like I do, you probably wish I'd just go away, but I'm selfish and I think I need to talk to you more than you need me to leave you alone. But you don't need that, do you? You don't need anything anymore and never will again. People bring you things, like I bring you flowers sometimes, and would have tonight but I had to get a guy a sandwich for watching my bird so my hands were full, but you don't care. You're like, It's nice that you brought me things, but I'm dead, I don't need anything, I don't want anything, I'm complete. *Maybe that's what you're here for, as an example. Maybe you're my god of small places. You teach me things. Through you I see maybe only the dead are perfect. Maybe only the dead are gentle.*

Something moved on the other side of the wall.

"Hello?" I said.

No answer.

Fuck it, what was I afraid of after the night I'd had?

I went back to communing with Chloë.

Anyway, kid, I thought I should tell you that I'm thinking about leaving. The tunnels, but maybe even New York. Sorry if calling you kid *offends you, I don't mean any disrespect, you're probably the same age as me. What I mean is, we both died at the same time, only you did it right. Not that I really want to die, at least I don't think so. But I've got to get out of here. At least for a while. Not that I know what I'd do out in the boondocks, out in the wilds of Philadelphia or Hoboken, or Milwaukee. Can you imagine? Me out in Milwaukee with Lenny and Squiggy and the Big Ragu? Not that you watch TV, that's* Laverne and Shirley, *it's all right. But what do you think about all this? Stay or go? Let's play a game. If I should go, just be really quiet.*

She didn't say anything.

All right. But that's not fair, is it, because I think I really want to go and I rigged things, and what are you going to do, talk? Let's be fair. If I should stay, just be really quiet again.

She didn't say anything.

But someone else did.

"Town meeting."

I looked up at the missing bricks and saw Old Boy's dully glowing eyes peering in at me.

"How'd you find me?" I said.

"Your bird smells."

"I left the bird."

"I know. But you still smell like him."

"Hey, I heard you," I said. "How come? I heard your foot on gravel. You're normally so quiet."

"Shut up," he said, but not unfriendly. "Town meeting is at dawn. At the water pipe. Margaret's pissed."

"When is she not?"

He smiled and went away.

"What the fuck is that?" Margaret said.

"It's an African gray parrot."

"I can see what color it is."

"That's part of its name."

"Just keep it quiet."

"*Quiet!*" Gonzalo said.

She narrowed her eyes.

"Get it out of here before I kill it."

"*Quiet!*"

"Have I got time? Before you start the meeting?"

"No, you trivial little man, you haven't, but run."

She didn't look at me. I didn't like that.

I ran the bird back to my room, put a shoestring around his leg, and tied him to the stand. He said something to me in German. Something like *Lext Un-Fayger* only the *x* was more like the *ch* in *L'chaim*. I thought that was weird, I didn't see the Bakers popping out any foreign languages, and then I remembered Gary Combs was kind of an egghead, had some foreign-language books.

"Want to groove on Miles?" I asked him, but he didn't, just bobbed his head at me, and off I ran to the meeting, afraid I was going to be found out for any number of things that would cost me my life.

TRUST

"Some of you's been feedin' 'em, and there's more than one. Don't act like you don't know what I'm talkin' about, neither."

More than a few of us got really uncomfortable just then. All of us were there except the kids. Ruth had them at the 18th Street station, no doubt boring them stupid, frowning them into lassitude. She was old and strong enough to keep them in line and loyal enough to Margaret not to need a pep rally.

"I don't want to go callin' out individuals by name because, to be plain, there's too many of ya. You know who you are. But it stops now. Either they hunt on their own without makin' a mess or they die. It's brutal, but that's how it has to be."

I pictured the Bakers in the bathtub. I pictured the Asian lady on top of the stack at the theater. I pictured the blind rabbit. Cvetko and I exchanged a look. Cvets smelled like smoke and mortar.

"We got it too good down here to have the law comin' down with thirty fuckers and a dozen dogs, cleanin' us out, wallin' off tunnels, makin' patrols in force. Which is exactly what'll happen if people up there start dyin' and they figure out where it's comin' from. It was hard enough last year with that crazy kike shootin' people cause his dog told him so, and the cops all jumpy and nobody goin' about alone no more."

"Last year wasn't all bad," Billy Bang said. "The blackout was fun." That got a laugh. He and Luna and I went out on a spree that first night the power went out, just biting the fuck out of everybody like it was Halloween. All the cops were cracking skulls in Brooklyn, so there we were climbing through open windows in the Upper East Side, knocking dead electric fans out of the way and bleeding the wealthy, tasting their fear and their salt, the veal in their blood, enjoying how inconvenienced they were by it all, how embarrassed to be caught with messy hair, sweating through tank tops just like their employees in Astoria and the Bronx.

"That's as may be," Margaret said. "But I want to hear from each of you that you understand me."

"I understand," that Edgar fellow said.

"I got it," Billy said.

Then she stopped.

I swear she tilted her head like a dog hearing a silent whistle, like she couldn't believe what she was seeing.

"And who the *fuck* is this?"

Baldy was standing near an actual bald guy. A very Italian-looking bald guy, clearly a fresh vampire, lots of scars. Shoulder muscles like he juggled engine blocks. Clearly good at getting places without being noticed; even Old Boy had missed him. Dominic stood on the other side. All of them had visible guns, one in a belt, two under the arm in shoulder holsters.

Balducci said, "I figured the meeting was a good time to introduce my friend Paulie."

The Paulie guy nodded, barely. It's the way you nod at somebody you're probably going to try to kill later. Margaret just stood there for another second looking so outraged she was almost amused.

Before I tell you what happened, I'm going to tell you what I think Baldy was thinking. The hardass on his left was none other than Paulo "The Screw" Milanese, a hit man with thirty jobs under his belt. His calling card was to twist a corkscrew into your head, what was left of it, you get the idea. This guy was in the papers. An FBI sting had busted six other guys in his immediate circle, but the Screw shot his way out and went to a safe house, Balducci figured out where. Gave him a proposition. This sounded like a good way to avoid prison and put off hell. Baldy kept him in hiding above-ground, taught him a thing or two, then figured he'd introduce him when Margaret was in trouble. Figured he was a good counterbalance to Old Boy, who wasn't on top of his game just lately because he was letting the kids feed off him too much. He figured Margaret wouldn't go to the mat with the odds evened up and the group divided.

He figured wrong.

Margaret pulled the gun out of the Screw's holster and shot Baldy in the head. Fast. While he was stunned and the Screw was gunless, she grabbed her shovel. Dominic ran. Old Boy's knife was out and he went to work on Milanese; they rolled into the water-pipe area, slammed against the moldy wall right next to where it said RUST. Before Baldy could recover, Margaret shot twice more and scrambled his brains again. She dropped the gun and launched herself. Her approach with the shovel was almost like ballet. Leap, leap, half leap, crouch, uppercut.

Baldy was dead so fast his body took two steps and fell.

Old Boy finished with his man, flung the hacked-off head against the wall. It was still trying to talk.

I had never actually seen anybody get their head taken off before, now it was three in two days. I had to get out of the tunnels. Everything was going to hell.

If you're not a vampire yourself, or have never seen one move for real, you're thinking, *What was everybody doing standing around?* If your experience is a little broader, however, you know how fast these things go down. As fast as two *BOMP-BOMP-Shh*s in Queen's "We Will Rock You." As fast as a car wreck.

But I'm getting to that.

Something else had happened.

When Old Boy and Milanese went thumping up against the wall, they scraped a bunch of mold off it. It turns out some long-ago wall-scrawler had not written **RUST** near the busted pipe that served as our fountain. There was another letter there. Luna scraped more mold away to reveal a **T**.

TRUST

"Look there," Billy Bang said, pointing where the Screw's head had bounced off the wall at another point just to the right of **TRUST**. A tennis ball's width of white paint shone through the caked-on greenish-black carpet of schmutz.

Baldy's dead hand was waving in the air, like *Help me I'm headless*, but everybody was more interested in the wall. Like we knew it was significant. Billy stepped forward, took the bloody shovel from Margaret, started scraping mold away.

THE appeared.

He went to the right of that.

C

"Cops!" the normally almost catatonic Sandy yelled, like she was playing *Wheel of Fortune*. Billy kept scraping. I stole a glance at Cvetko, saw his wheels turning.

CHILD

Billy stopped.

"Keep going," Luna said.

He did.

CHILDREN

"Trust the Children," Billy said. "I think they wrote that they own selves."

Most of them laughed. Not Cvetko. And not Margaret.

Billy rested on his shovel.

"Are ye an idiot?" Margaret said.

Sounded like *eedjeet*.

She took the shovel from Billy and walked to the left of the word TRUST. Scraped. The next word appeared and the whole message stood before us.

DON'T TRUST THE CHILDREN

Everyone gasped in chorus. Cvetko, too.

Then he said something I didn't understand.

It sounded like *Many, many tickle a parson*.

But it wasn't in English.

"I'm sick of shit I don't understand," I said, and walked away.

I spent a long time packing my suitcase; it was one of those 1940s ones with the delicate little latches, but real solid otherwise. Nothing a gorilla could jump up and down on, but classy, kind of an orangey color between a brick and a pumpkin, not that that's important, I just like that color. I stuffed it as full as I could, even sat on it to press it down. I had no idea where I was going to end up, but doubted anybody sold nice vests and coats out in dog-on-a-trunk land with corn and *Hee Haw* and guys that stuck a piece of grass in their mouth while they talked to you. Margaret, Cvetko, and Billy had been talking about who wrote DON'T TRUST THE CHILDREN, but the crux of it was that Margaret was going to kill them tomorrow night, even though none of them could quite convince themselves the wall was talking about these children. That was like twenty years' worth of mold we scraped off. Still, it seemed to superstitious Margaret like a sign, and she was all *Off with their heads!* Old Boy and Chinchilla would come with her, and she even had Billy halfway convinced. Cvetko wasn't saying much about it, taking it all in and pondering. I just wanted to leave. The first time I walked out, though, Margaret stopped me, told me she wanted me to go tell Ruth what was up and that she should keep them there.

I knew better than to buck a direct order, but I must have looked like I just got told to shovel out a Dumpster full of horse apples, because Cvetko spoke up and volunteered to go instead of me. I could have kissed him. Actually I did kiss him, right on the forehead, because I realized it might be my last chance. I gave him a look that I hoped let him know this was it. This was good-bye. I think he already knew. He patted my shoulder and gave my arm a hard squeeze. Margaret waved me off and I went to pack. There was no rule against anybody leaving, but I didn't want to risk pissing her off so I didn't announce my plans. I figured I'd send Cvets a postcard at his dummy address once I got to Peoria or wherever.

I had it all planned out, as far as a guy like me plans anything. I would charm somebody with a car, get them to drive me out of the city, ditch them, get a hotel. Maybe Pennsylvania. I heard it was pretty. I could come back to the city or find another city, maybe Philly, when I ran out of dough. Anyway, I just couldn't take any more peeling. Biting people was one thing, but I was going to feel the knife going through that kid's neck bone for the rest of my nights. I knew I had to get a few hours' sleep, it was already like ten A.M., but I had no idea how I was going to be able to stop thinking about it. Turns out it wasn't so hard after all. I was exhausted. Only I didn't get to sleep too long.

* * *

Cvetko came back with the news about three P.M.: Ruth was gone. The kids were gone. The platform at the 18th Street station was awash in vampire blood. Margaret woke the rest of us up. She's not a gentle waker-upper, either; she banged on my fridge door with her sandal and said, "Rise and shine." When I sat up, she cut her eyes to my suitcase and said, "Where d'ya think you're goin'?" Before I could answer, and I didn't really have an answer, she said, "I'll tell you where. You're comin' with us to find those little monsters and shorten 'em all a head."

Gonzalo flapped his wings real big; I don't think he liked Margaret. I don't think he liked living underground. I caught him pulling feathers out of his own chest; he was working on a little bald spot there.

"I can't, Margaret. I just can't."

That was a mistake, but what do you want, I was sleepy. Next thing I knew she had me by both ears like she really wouldn't mind ripping them off. "You can and you will. You're the one brought those false, murderin' little devils among us, and you'll help us sort 'em out. Then you can go wherever you care to go, if you think anyone else'll have you."

She kicked my suitcase over, making Gonzalo squawk, and left. And then she came back, still pissed. "I've known you forty years now, Joseph Peacock, and I'll tell you somethin' about yourself, whether you want to hear it or not. You start real strong but you finish like a runt. You're forever getting yourself into messes you haven't got the britches to get yourself out of, or else letting people walk on you. That little girlie that left you cold for bein' a Jew-boy? I'd have peeled her."

"But you said . . ."

"The devil with what I said. Do you think anything in this world would have tasted as good as her princess blood pourin' hot down your throat? No matter who her fuckin' daddy was? But you didn't have the stones for it. And that boy, Freddie."

"I know," I said.

"You were stupid enough to tell him what you were, so what did he do?"

"He didn't believe me."

"Tried to let the blind up on you, put sunshine to you. Damn near did it, too, and that would have been the end of you."

I looked at the scar on my elbow.

"He just didn't believe. He wanted to see what would happen."

"He saw, all right. Did you ever wonder what happened to him?"

"No. I never went around him anymore."

"Well, I went around him. I did him. I drank him dead on a tugboat while he begged me not to and I threw what was left of him in the East River."

I just blinked at her.

She smiled an ugly smile.

"Laws are for the stupid. That's what I learned all them years ago, swimmin' as hard as I could and still sinkin'. I never told you this, but there was just a little part of me that admired what you did to me, putting that necklace on me. Not at first, of course, I was for killin' you, and I did. But later, on thinkin' about it, I understood it better. Oh, it was a wretched bit of business, a spoiled child's petty revenge. But here's the thing. You wanted me out of the house and you got me out because you were willing to get dirty to do it. And that's how the world is."

"I'm sorry for what I did, though. I was wrong."

She slapped me.

She actually *slapped* me.

"No, you weren't. You were God's instrument. I failed at everything but this. You *made* me this." She squatted down close to me now, said the next bit practically into my ear.

"Now, I don't know if you've worked this out in your fond brain or not, but them children are no children, so don't you be squeamish about hurtin' 'em. They want what we have. This place. And they mean to take it. They fooled us all because they were willin' to get dirty, and if we don't get dirtier, they'll kill us. All of us."

We spent hours and hours combing the tunnels, all of us together, moving fast and quiet. Margaret with her shovel, Old Boy just out front, running point. We scared the shit out of the Hunchers we ran across, asked them about the kids, charmed them to forget they saw us. Long story short, we didn't find them. Not that day. Not that night.

We went as a group to the 18th Street station and the first thing we found was a bunch of new trespassing notices and rat poison warnings the MTA had stuck on the posts. Then we found the blood. A big pond of it near the edge of the platform, not fresh but not old, like half a day old. Still sticky in places. Margaret squatted down and tasted it. Then she did something I had never seen her do.

She screamed.

She found a small, bloody footprint.

She spat on it like a crazy person and screamed something in Irish. She loved Ruth, or came as close to loving as any of us could.

I couldn't feel bad for the kids anymore, but I certainly didn't envy them. I'd had Margaret come looking for me before, and I can tell you it wasn't a situation you wanted to be in.

Ever.

* * *

We got back from our fool's errand at four A.M. or so, all of us tired.
It had been a grim night, except for one moment. We found some
Hunchers sleeping in a boiler room under Grand Central, four of
them, just runaway kids, and we fed on them all together, taking
turns keeping watch. They'd been drinking, so we all knew we'd
have a little misery when the alcohol came out of us later, but we
needed our strength. Anyway, after we all slaked our thirst, Billy
said, "Shit, man, the first time the whole family eats together and
nobody says grace."

When we got back to the common area near the pipes, we saw it.

A Raggedy Ann doll.

One of Camilla's, clearly.

It lay in front of a worktable we used for folding laundry and
counting out stolen money.

"They've been here," said Chinchilla.

"Someone give Mr. Chinchilla a gold star," Margaret said
wearily.

Luna went to pick the doll up, but Old Boy stole up behind her
fast, pulled her away by the belt. Motioned all of us back. Way
back. Picked up a couple of poisoned rats from a stack of them
Ruth had broomed together. Threw the first one at the doll and
missed. The second one bumped it. It popped, yeah, but then it
flared up so bright it hurt our eyes, hissed awfully, like a dragon.
Filled the whole place with smoke, so much smoke. He saved Luna,
maybe more of us, all because he knew about booby traps. Could
smell one. The table was fucked, bright holes burning in it. White
phosphorus doesn't stop till it stops, water doesn't help. Just burns
right through everything. Sure, vampires are bad, but let's not forget it was ordinary people who came up with the pure evil that was

an incendiary grenade. I didn't think it was possible to feel worse for Gua Gua, but now that I'd seen what got him, felt the heat on my face at even a good distance, I did. Him and the rest of the Latins. What a miserable way to go. Even the smoke smelled like poison and death.

Had the Hessian really killed Mapache and the others? Or was it the kids? Maybe someone we hadn't even seen yet? Margaret was probably right, their story was bullshit. The Hessian might never have touched them, might have had nothing to do with this.

But a guy like that would have had the money and connections to get illegal grenades. Then, so would Baldy and his mob friends. Where was Dominic?

Old Boy probably knew where to get this stuff, too. I looked at him, how pale and tired he was from feeding them, and it still surprised me that he had done something so . . . *soft*. He was always off alone. Had *he* killed the Latins? No, I could almost hear Cvetko saying *think*—if he was in with the kids, why would he save us from the grenade?

Was something truly fucked-up going on here?

I had the deep-in-my-bones feeling that I just didn't have a clue about what was really happening.

"Good ole Willy Pete," Old Boy said, smiling a little. "I don't think we've seen the last of him."

Jesus, he liked this stuff. Booby traps, grenades, having an enemy.

I decided I was leaving the tunnels after all.

After I got Gonzalo out of this mess.

And got some sleep.

Did you know parrots don't fly that well? It's because people clip their wings. Makes sense, especially up in an apartment; you don't want to open up a window to get a breath of fresh air and there goes your parrot saying, "So long, sucker!" all the way back to Africa or Central Park or wherever. Central Park was the first thing I thought, lots of trees and nuts, and maybe somebody would say, "Look, that's a valuable parrot," and come and get him out of the tree. I don't know what with. Maybe just coax him down with egghead German and a bag of pistachios. Stupid idea, but remember I hadn't slept and that messes with our heads as much as with yours.

So I took him to Central Park in a taxi. The cabbie didn't like much about it, any of it, but he needed the fare. These weren't great times in the city for most people, if you hadn't noticed.

"Shouldn't he be in a cage?"

The cabbie was an Indian fellow with horn-rimmed glasses and a fixed harelip.

"Yeah, but I lost it," I said.

"Will he be making a mess in my taxi?"

Gonzalo just bobbed his head, his new bald spot standing out on his chest like a sheriff's badge.

"No promises," I said, and handed the cabbie a five-spot.

We didn't talk anymore until he dropped me off.

I found some nice trees just off Fifth Avenue, across from the Plaza Hotel, and remembered it was supposed to be some kind of bird sanctuary anyway. I told the cabbie to keep the meter running, this shouldn't take long, but I did want to say good-bye.

I walked Gonzalo up to the pond there and set him on my hand, tried to get him to look at me.

He did for a second, cocking his head, then said that German phrase again and nubbed out his tongue a couple of times.

"Listen, Gonz, this is serious. This is good-bye. I thought I'd be able to take care of you, but the tunnels are no place for a guy like you, and even if they were, I have to split. I'm sorry about your old master, he was better for you. Maybe you'll get lucky and get somebody like that again. Funny how everything affects everything. If there were no vampires, you'd still be good and cozy and I'd be old somewhere. Maybe I'd have a parrot, turns out I like you guys. Maybe I would have beat Gary Combs to the bird store that day and you would have been my bird. Anyway, good luck to you and good luck to me."

I tossed him up in the air, toward the trees, but he just flapped like hell and landed slowly, like a guy coming down in a parachute. I had never seen him do more than that, I just sort of assumed he could fly when he wanted to, but he was mostly in a cage. Then I remembered the expression "clipping your wings" and figured that was what happened to Gonzalo.

He walked around on the ground.

I picked him back up.

The cabdriver must have been watching me talk to the bird; he drove away. At least that's what I thought just then, but I looked down at my shirt and saw how dirty it was, noticed a few drops of blood on my shirt from where we bled the runaways in the boiler room. It had been such a long night that it seemed like the night before. I spit-cleaned the bloody part of the shirt, got another cab, and had him take me to a pet store. I bet nobody ever broke into a pet store to leave a pet there. Or maybe they did. Either way, I left a note.

> My name is Gonzalo. My wings have been clipped but you probably know that. I like pistachios. I'm your's for free. I hope I'm worth more than your window.

I got underground just before sunup.

I got some sleep.

I dreamed I had wings.

MICHELANGELO

I made sure not to pass anybody on my way out; I felt like a quitter. Making a stealthy escape was even tougher because I was carrying a suitcase; I could make myself small, but the size of the luggage was not negotiable. A plastic bag would have been smarter than the case, I guess, but it was a hell of a nice suitcase, and if I was going to pare my possessions down to so very few, they should at least be things worth having.

Turns out in order to get out with the suitcase I had to bust an extra brick or two out of the bricked-over basement window in Chelsea, which I did by holding on to a pipe in the ceiling and donkey-kicking with my heels. It was just after sunset; there was still a little red in the sky. The first order of business was to feed, so I charmed a guy with a suit and tie and good, high hair down to the basement I had just crawled out of. He also had a suitcase. Two guys with suitcases, like we were going to have a little business meeting down there with the spiders and that moldy basement smell. After I bit him, and his blood was bitter with nicotine—he must have smoked two and a half packs a day—I told him to open his suitcase and he did. Hair care products, like hair spray and gel and shampoo and shit. A whole box of business cards, one of which I plucked out. It just read *John M. Murray*, gave his 212 phone number.

"What do you, go door to door?" I asked.

"I'm a rep," he said, drooling all over his very wide, white shirt collar. "I call on people who own beauty shops and salons."

His neck was still trying to bleed, so I licked it again to close it up. He *did* smell good, and he could have been a TV anchorman with that head of feathered hair on him. It kind of crunched a little when you touched it, but it looked good.

"What do you use?" I asked him, touching his hair.

"Apollonis," he said, pointing at a bottle of hair spray with a picture of a Greek god on it. I took it out, looked at my own suitcase, but decided I didn't want to risk opening it for fear I might not get it closed again. I stuck the hair spray in my coat pocket.

"There good money in selling this shit?"

"Not bad," he said.

"Show me your money."

He took out his wallet and peeled it open for inspection. I removed the two twenties, the ten, and the five he had in there.

"You got your car around here?"

He shook his head no. I gave him back the ten, told him to close his suitcase, climb out the window, and take a cab west to the Empire Diner. I said he should get himself a chili sundae, I heard they were good, and forget about what happened here. Out he went; I had to give him a boost to reach the window. He was heavier than he looked, kind of a muscular guy, must have played football in college or maybe he was one of these gym guys. Anyway, off he went to the diner, or so I thought. I'd been to the Empire and seen that chili sundae, it was clever. Sour cream at the top like ice cream, little tomato for a cherry. Stuff like that made me almost wish I could eat without, shall we say, consequences.

I sprayed a *SHHT* of that Apollonis on myself just for the smell and went out.

I could still see my guy; he tried to hail a cab but it was too close to rush hour still and every cab had a head or two heads in the back, already on their way somewhere. The charm mostly wore off him, I saw it happen, and he looked puzzled for a minute, then kept walking, still going west toward the Hudson. Looked right at me, didn't register who I was; I smiled a little, that always amuses me.

Now I was looking for somebody with a car, somebody alone.

I stood at an intersection with long red lights, checking out traffic, looking for a nice car with nobody in the passenger seat and the lock tab up. Somebody who looked not too bright, easy to manipulate. I saw my guy again, he passed me, and goddamn if he didn't turn the corner and come up to a big brick-red sedan parked three cars down and fish out his keys. He got in, threw his suit-case in the passenger seat, and started it. I almost yelled *HEY* but instead I went over and tapped on the glass. When he caught my eyes, I poured it on again.

"May I sit down?" I yelled over the honking and traffic.

I saw him mouth *sure* but I had to point at the passenger door lock, which was still down. He leaned over far—it was a big-ass car, like an LTD—and opened up. I tossed his case full of hair shit in the back and got in with my bag.

"Hey, I thought you said you didn't have a car near here?"

"Girlfriend's," he said. "Her name's—"

"I don't care, I'm sure she's a whore. Start the car."

He did.

"Drive us to Pennsylvania," I said.

"Penn Station?"

"No, fucking Pennsylvania with cows and the Amish, let's go," but I charmed him too much. His mouth just hung open, saliva pouring out of him like he was Niagara Falls; he couldn't even figure out the gears. You got to charm a guy just enough if you want him to be able to do complicated stuff.

I had last tried to drive while Eisenhower was president, but time goes fast for us and it didn't seem so long at the moment. Anyway, I didn't need Slobbery McGoodhair gumming up the works all the way out to Injun Hole, Pennsylvania, or wherever.

"Get out," I said.

He got out, reflexively reached for his suitcase, shut the door.

I forgot to say, "Watch out for traffic."

It's the little things.

Just as I was sliding over, the poor guy was hit, luckily just by a bicycle, but it hit him pretty hard, throwing him, the bicyclist, and the bike down in the street. The guy driving in that lane had great reflexes, screeched to a stop before he hit either one of them, but the Apollonis guy's suitcase flew up and got whomped by a fast-moving van two lanes over, shampoo bottles and conditioner and other glop flying all over the place. I panicked, jammed down on the gas, I guess it was a V8 cause it really had some horses under the hood. I slammed into the VW Bug parked in front of me, knocked it forward; there were sparks, I'm not sure what from. I cut out left now and mashed the gas again, managed not to hit the guys in the street, taking advantage of the lane they were now blocking, saying *shit shit shit* all the while. I tried to keep the nose of the thing in just the one lane, but it was too long—who makes cars with mile-long hoods anyway? The fucking thing was like an aircraft carrier—and I got clipped by a taxi, which knocked me back into the Bug, and I bounced off that and into the taxi again, saw some chubby lady's face yelling in the back, she looked like Bella Abzug, could have been for all I know. A bottle of shampoo, which must have sailed up two stories, came down and exploded in pinkish-red glory all over my windshield; this was going to be the best-smelling accident ever. Smash, crunch, smash, everybody honking, everybody yelling. I grabbed my suitcase and tried to get out the passenger door, but it was junked shut for good. A very angry taxi driver with a cut over his eye and half a pair of glasses was shouting in Greek or something into the driver's-side window. I heard a cop blowing his whistle. Here he came on a horse, too. All the cars were crunched up together now, there was a huge pile-up, the final spasm of which was a delivery truck clipping a tree, the goddamned tree falling down in a grand, slow-motion shower of leaves and almost taking a traffic light with it.

"What the fucks is wrong with you?" Greek half-glasses taxi guy was yelling, having switched to English now. The bicyclist was behind me, his arm probably broken, trying to stop the Apollonis guy where he was limping around in shock picking up unopened bottles of conditioner and business cards and the cigarettes that got knocked out of his shirt pocket. The traffic light up ahead wagged crazily, like a signalman on cocaine trying to stop a train. The cop on the horse loomed up over the cars, motioning with his free hand for everyone to stay calm, his horse skidding for a second in oil or hair gel or God knows what. A woman screamed, "Michelangelo!" and a Chihuahua with a green and red sweater on went running down the sidewalk. I swear this all happened in five seconds.

I opened the driver's-side door, motioning angry hurt Greek guy back, but he saw I had the suitcase, correctly guessed I meant to make a run for it, tried to stop me from opening the door, but I gave it a good shove and knocked him on his ass. Bella Abzug tried to get out of the taxi, too, but I kicked her door shut. Here came the Goodhair guy, coming to his senses, slurring, "That's my car!" through broken teeth. Here came the bicyclist with him, chickenwinging his hurt arm, trying to get a good look at my face. Here came the cop on the horse, the horse making crazy eyes at me; I knew it wanted to bite me or step on me, both at the same time if it could manage it.

"Fuck this."

I hugged my suitcase and jumped up high, my butt on the roof of the car, and I rolled backward. This was ninja shit. I hit the sidewalk on my feet just as somebody yelled, "That's the kid, grab him!" and somebody else yelled, "He tried to steal that car!" Michelangelo was way ahead, running in his out-of-season Christmas sweater, dragging his leash, and I ran that way, too. Up ahead, a crowd had gathered to see why the tree had fallen; I couldn't run as fast as I wanted to, two Good Samaritans had almost caught me. This is New York, where a guy can stab a girl to death in front of thirty people, but let a harmless-looking kid try to steal something, ten guys form a posse. People want their name in the paper, but not if they're going to get hurt.

I passed a telephone booth, heard the driver of the delivery truck saying, ". . . hit a tree, I'm okay, cops are on their—" and then he yelled, "HEY!" because I was turning him and his phone booth over to block the guys running after me. One stopped, knew a kid shouldn't have been able to do that, but the other guy meant business, skip-stepped around Michelangelo, who had stopped to eat a French fry, hopped the booth, planting his size-twelve work boot right on the glass over the hysterical face of the horizontal truck driver. The guy was coming right at me in his brownish 'fro and sunglasses. He looked like a white Reggie Jackson, but that's what happens when you watch too much TV, everybody looks like someone famous. I turned the corner; this sidewalk wasn't crowded, I would turn on the jets now and burn this guy, but damn if my suitcase didn't clip a trash can and pop open, all my best shirts and pants popping out and raining down. I stopped and grabbed some; I wanted my numchuks, but they had rolled out into the middle of the street and here came the lunkhead do-gooder. I smelled something shit-like but had no time to find out why. I tore down the sidewalk, vaulted over a bum, slapped a slice of folded pizza and its greasy paper plate out of a pimply teenaged guy's hand just for the sheer *fuck you* of it—I mean my *numchuks* were gone—then I skittered up a ten-foot-high fence using just my feet and one hand. I left the Good Samaritan guy in the dust. I started to laugh, and then I realized that my clothes had fallen in shit with pieces of straw in it, probably that cop's horse's shit, and now I had it on the shirt I was wearing, too, because I had grabbed it all against my chest.

"Motherfucker," I said, in my fouled shirt and my good-smelling hair.

So much for Pennsylvania.

I went down into the subway at 23rd and Avenue of the Americas, walked the tracks until I came to the service shaft leading down to a tunnel that led to our loops. I wanted to wash what remained of my laundry, talk to Cvetko, and think about what to do next. I didn't really trust anybody but him, and Margaret. I guess I trusted Margaret. And Luna. Okay, and Billy Bang. Maybe I could get Cvetko and the rest to come away with me somewhere; Cvetko was better at planning things and Luna kept her cool better than I did. Billy just made me laugh. The four of us would get along okay, I thought. Hell, maybe even Margaret was ready to give the loops a rest and try something else. That grenade had really put the fear of Jesus in me, not really Jesus, but you know what I'm saying. That thing would melt your *face* off, just two bright seconds between undead and dead-dead. I could still hear Gua Gua yelling.

But I knew better. Margaret never had anything of her own in life and damned if she was letting anyone take this place from her. Her kingdom. Her loops.

A train rumbled overhead, shaking the walls. That was when I heard it. A kid laughed.

I never found out which kid.

I probably should have looked for him, or her, but I ran.

PART 4

CHEWED UP BY A GIANT MOUTH

"**H**ey, short stuff!" somebody stage-whispered above me.

I looked up and saw Billy Bang spidered against the roof, looking down at me. "Anybody following you?" he said.

"Maybe."

He dropped down, took a good long look down the tunnel behind me. Then he got close enough for me to smell the fear under his aftershave, whispered into my ear. "Margaret's looking for you. She wants all hands on deck, keeping lookout at choke points. She's got Old Boy combing the tunnels in a loop; whoever finds them bangs on pipes: Bang in threes means we all go there, fast. Just keep banging means they're coming and we should play defense. No fuckin' around this time, she says. We got to peel 'em. You ready to do that?"

"Yeah," I said.

"Yeah," he said, "well, that's my official story, too. But all this war shit? Man, I just bite necks and play guitar. Billy Bang might not be around much after this."

"She home?"

"Far as I know."

"Better go see what she wants me to do."

He gave me an ironic salute.

"And hey," he said. I turned around. "Watch yourself. We found Ruth. I found her. She was fucked-up, man."

"Fucked-up how?"

"Let's just leave it at fucked-up."

Being afraid isn't all bad. It wakes you up. You notice things. I saw Sammy from a long way off, his red bob of hair standing out against the darker walls behind him. He was walking the tracks between stations, just above where you go down to get to Margaret's loops. As far away as he was, though, he knew I was behind him. I think he had been waiting for me to catch up. I thought about trying to find a pipe to bang on, but it was just him. I could handle just him.

"Sammy," I said, walking faster. "Come here."

He stopped. He turned around to face me. His clothes were bloody as hell, and he had tacky, half-dried blood smeared around his mouth, like a kid in Central Park in the summer with a Kool-Aid face. Was eating all they did? It was . . . animalistic. At just that moment I was sure I wasn't like them, that they were a different kind of vampire altogether. A worse kind.

"What are you going to do, Joey?" he said, smiling a little. "Are you going to kill me now for being bad?" He let me walk right up on him. I didn't like this. "At least do it quickly," he said. "I shall be very brave."

He closed his eyes now, or pretended to, keeping one slitted open as though he were cheating saying grace. The wind kicked up in the tunnel; a train was coming, I could see its light. I put my hand on his chin and grabbed the back of his hair with the other. One good twist with all I had, and even if I couldn't uncrown him,

I might fuck him up enough to lay him down in front of the train. I might even be able to throw him on the third rail.

Maybe he can do those same things to you.

I gave his head a little jerk, like a dry run. He was trying not to giggle. He was drooling a little, too.

"Are you going to treat me like you did fat Mikey?" he said, giggling and drooling on my wrist. "Go ahead!" he said, and now his hands were on my wrists, gently spasming as though encouraging me to twist his head. "When I count three, you twist as hard as you can and *pop* goes my head, isn't that how it works?"

The conductor saw us now, started blaring his horn, but he would never have time to stop.

"One!"

I tried to let go, meaning to jump clear and find a niche to flatten out in, but he had my wrists in his hands, his hands like little pliers.

He's stronger than me!

"Two!" he said. I tried picking him up, but I couldn't; he had his feet tangled up in the running rails.

Oh fuck it's coming and if my head comes off I'm dead and if I hit the third rail I'm dead and even if not it's going to hurt like a cunt let go let go LET GO.

"THREE!"

The light on the train was as big as a sun, the horn blew up my ears, the face of the conductor was a Halloween mask of disbelief and horror. It all became unreal to me, like it didn't matter, the sun of the train's light a sun over Tatooine. This letting go at the last second, this was how people died. And deer, I guess. Only I snapped to. Almost in time. I saw Sammy go flat, squeeze himself down between the tracks, taking the only place I knew to go. I remember one of his disjointed eyes looking up at me like a flounder's eye. I took my chances and jumped up, jumped hard and tried to grab on to the roof of the tunnel, only I couldn't get purchase. Worse, I had jumped so hard I bounced, spun in the air, and my legs swung down, breaking my heels on the windshield and knocking my shoes off. Did you ever break your heel? I don't recommend it. I tried to get small, cling to the top of the train, but it was too late, I couldn't get small enough not to take the worst beating of my life between the train and the tunnel's ceiling. I screamed like a girl. I remember seeing a flash of a red letter, like a *P*, where some tagger had climbed the train in the yard. It was like being chewed up in a giant mouth, but *fast*; I broke my teeth, I broke my shoulders and ribs, my *sock* came off, I was half-scalped, the fucking can of hair spray dislocated my hip and tore the bejesus out of my coat pocket but somehow didn't pop and got so twisted up in my shirt it didn't come loose.

I hit the tracks blind in one eye, my nose about an inch from the third rail. I literally peeled myself up enough to roll away from it. The most solid thing on my person was the hair spray can, and I was so dazed I stuck that can down the front of my pants like I was shoplifting it. I tried to stand up but my broken legs wouldn't hold me. Everything hurt and itched at once as my insulted bones already tried knitting themselves together. I heard a *plap* as the skin of my scalp stuck itself back to the top of my skull. Sammy had gathered himself now, and he ambled over, laughing.

Then he *licked* me. No shit, he licked my face and scalp, not like a pervert, but like a dog licking a bone. He was tasting my blood. I tried to push him away, only my arm wasn't ready for pushes and I rebroke it.

"Oooo, that was nasty," I heard another one saying. Manu. No trace of sarcasm like Sammy might have delivered; he said it like he really felt bad for me. No surprise there, *I* felt bad for me, I might have felt bad for Manson watching him take the up-against-the-tunnel-roof train-grind. Duncan lurked behind Manu holding an adult's bloody sweater against his cheek as if for comfort. I thought of Linus in *Peanuts*. I tried to stand but still wasn't up for it. Sammy straddled me and licked me again.

"Knock it off," I tried to say, but the sound I made was all vowels. He understood anyway.

"Or what?" he said, and I didn't have a good answer.

"Leave him be," said Manu.

"I'm older, I don't have to listen to you," the smaller Sammy said.

That was when it hit me. Margaret was right. These kids weren't kids at all. And I was completely at their mercy.

My mouth had formed up enough to speak.

"What now?" I said.

"Perhaps you'd like to hit your pipe so the others will come. We'd very much like the others to come," Sammy said, showing fangs and drooling. Remember, vampires drool when they want to bite, which means when they want to attack. I imagined Billy Bang walking up on them, or Luna. I shook my head.

"Good," said Manu. "The First Three want to see you."

The First Three.

My legs were strong enough for me to stand. I could see out of my left eye again and my headache was getting better.

Just as I began to contemplate making a run for it, bastard Sammy picked up a brick and broke my legs again. He took a pencil out of his pocket and blinded me. I screamed, so he jammed gravel in my mouth.

The two of them picked me up and ran off with me.

Fast.

A THRONE ROOM IN HELL

Everything in me hurt when they set me down.

I didn't know where I was, but it stank like hell. Maybe it *was* hell. Except it was cold.

I felt something crawl over my face.

"Joey-Joey-Joey!" I heard. Peter.

"Joey," a little mouse-voice echoed. Camilla.

"He still can't see," Duncan said. "But look, the right one's almost whole."

"That's the left," Camilla said.

"Oh, right. The left, then. He'll be able to see us in no time at all. When his peepers heal."

"Had you to hurt him so badly?" Camilla mewed.

"He tried to twist my head off."

"I want to twist your head off sometimes, Sammy," Peter said.

Manu said, "You should have seen it! It was brilliant! That was the worst I've seen someone hurt who still lived after."

"You're forgetting the British officer and the elephant."

"It was very much the same sort of thing, only topsy-turvy.

Instead of an elephant mushing him groundwise, the train mushed him roofwise. Anyway, that officer never lived."

"Did so! My pretend-father spoke to him after, they joked about the fat in the bullets."

"Anyway, he never got out of bed."

"That's true."

"And they shouldn't have made them bite the bullets."

"That's also true."

"Shh, he's about to see us."

I became aware of music in the background: Gerry Rafferty's "Baker Street."

My left eye fuzzed in, everything bleary. The room around me was unfamiliar. I heard someone blowing bubbles, like in the bath, but it was thick and sloppy-sounding. Duncan was closest, inches from me, looking down at me like I was a schoolyard bug dying in an interesting way. His big, blue eyes shone faintly in the dim light, somehow innocent. Sammy behind him, not innocent at all. Manu passive, observing. I heard the bubbling again. I looked over and saw a big, industrial trash barrel with two little heads poking out of it. Make it three. Alfie surfaced now, blowing out horsy-lips and spraying a fine mist. You know what the trash barrel was full of. Sure you do. If you don't, allow me to point out the meat hook hanging still but wicked about six feet over the barrel, the rusty old chain leading up from it, the anchor hook someone nailed into the concrete roof and the little brown hand- and foot-prints up there, the stack of naked dead in the corner with their throats cut and their feet bound together with straps. The three kids in the trash barrel had their hair slicked back with it, they were slathered in it, they all looked like they had just been born.

Sammy came up to the trash barrel, cupped his hand, and slurped from it. Peter, a very healthy and robust Peter, splashed at him, laughing.

"Have a care!" Manu said, suddenly animated. "You'll ruin the radio!"

"It's a cassette player," Alfie corrected, now splashing Manu.

"Anyway, stupid to ruin it."

My other eye fuzzed in.

Sammy said, "Manu's just mad because in India a radio costs a prick. I read it in the *Mirror*. There were too many golliwogs, so Gandhi-girl was giving golliwogs little radios just to snip their pricks off."

"Shut your hole," Manu said.

"What do you fancy they do with all them pricks? The wogs, I mean? Woglet-woglings wear them for earrings? Kali got a girdle of them, Kali-wolly-oxenfree!"

"Goolies for your golliwogs," Manu said, grabbing Sammy's hair and kicking him between the legs so hard he lifted him off the ground; it looked like he dislocated his foot doing it. Sammy retched and went down, but sprang up grimacing, hitting Manu in the jaw, clearly breaking it. Manu, now sporting an unhealthy underbite, scrambled to the stack of dead, picked up a head that had been sitting loose, and flung it, missing Sammy but clipping Duncan, who blinked and held up a soft little hand, *Please don't*. Then he went on all fours to a fresh puddle of blood and lapped at it like a tame little lapdog at a table spill.

Sammy balled up his fists.

Manu's jaw reset itself and he crouched, preparing for a spring.

Both of them were smiling.

"Stop it," Camilla whispered.

"Stop it!" Peter said, more loudly.

Then Camilla spoke again.

"You'll wear yourselves out for the hunt."

She slipped under again. My hip settled back into place, more like *wrenched* itself back into place.

The hunt.

I didn't have to think too hard to figure out what that was going to mean. Cvetko, Margaret, Luna. I wanted out, but I had no idea where I was, or how to get past these little fuckers. Sammy was strong, so very strong, though he just looked like an eight-year-old kid with skinny arms. Camilla could probably kick my ass. Maybe even Duncan. Old Boy could maybe handle these little things, but Cvets?

I looked at the dead-pile. The lower ones weren't so new, had bloated bellies, were starting to juice and get sticky. Slow, fat flies circled like jets in a holding pattern over La Guardia. There were baby flies, too. There's another word for them, but you might be overdosing on the filth and carnage of this room, so let's stick with *baby flies.*

"Look, he's whole again!" Duncan said, pointing at me. I sat up; the spray can I had stashed in my pants was uncomfortable, so I took it out, rolled it against the wall. I cut my eyes at Sammy, ready to scrap if the little fucker reached for a brick. He didn't. They were all looking at me now. Camilla whispered in Peter's ear.

"Joey," Peter said, "I just want you to know . . . we want you to know, that you are one of us. If you want to be."

"You're young!" Duncan said. "Say your name like a little boy. He said you could."

That struck me funny.

"*He* who?" I said.

They all laughed. I didn't like that laugh.

"Now say your name like you're little," Peter said, meaning it.

"Joey Peacock," I said in my falsetto. Peter's brow unknit itself and he smiled again like the moon coming from behind a cloud.

"Good enough for me. There's still boy in you, so you're in."

Camilla said something that sounded a lot like that German-ish thing Gonzalo had said. Now I said it, too, just like Gonzalo had.

Lext Un-Fayger, the *x* like *L'chaim.*

"*Yea!*" Camilla said, more loudly, excited, "*Leoht Unfaeger!*"

She said more words like that. Peter and Alfie both answered her; Peter looked at me, shook his head.

"He doesn't speak it," Peter said to his brother and sister, "only we do." Then, to me, he said, "Horrid light. You've got a horrid light in your eyes like us."

"What is that, German?" I said.

Camilla laughed.

"No, silly," she said. "It's English."

"Bullshit," I said, "I speak English."

"Before it changed," said Alfie.

Manu chimed in. "I hate it when they speak all that."

"That's because it's not for wogs!" said Sammy. Manu pushed his face openhanded, something less than a slap but a little less than friendly, and Sammy did it back.

"You don't speak it either," Manu said.

"I know! And who says I want to?"

"Be quiet, both of you!" Peter said, and they obeyed. "Of course, you'd be bottom of the chain. It goes by how old you are."

"And how old are you?"

"Old."

"Yeah, but how old?"

"Second oldest."

"After me," Camilla said, getting out of her gruesome bath now, walking over to a second barrel, and pouring a bucket of water over herself. Duncan retreated from the little wave on the concrete like a kid at the beach. A bunch of roaches retreated, too. Camilla emptied the bucket over her head again, now using a sponge, then dried herself off as best she could with a pair of filthy blue jeans.

"But you're . . . smaller," I said. "Aren't you brothers and sisters?"

"She got the *Leoht Unfaeger* first," Alfie said. "We were babies then."

"*You* were a baby," said Peter. "I was a little boy already. She was older-sister-gone-three-winters."

Camilla held up three fingers.

"But she came back for us."

He didn't actually say *she*, he said her real name, and it wasn't Camilla. Elf-something. I'll just keep calling her Camilla.

Whatever her name was, she sat down cross-legged and Manu, without being told to, found a comb and started combing out her wet hair. He got snagged up in a tangle, pulled at the comb; she grimaced and hit him *hard* in the leg.

"Ow," he said mildly, not worried about it, combing away.

Where the hell were we, anyway? This brick-and-concrete space was new to me. Something about it made me think of movies I had seen with kings and queens, how they would receive hoity-toities while they sat up on their thrones. That's what this place was like, a throne room, with the royal family bobbing around in a plastic trash bin.

I didn't know when I'd get the chance to ask again, so I asked.

"What's with the blood? In the barrel, I mean. I understand drinking it, I do that, we all do that, but why . . . *swim* in it?"

A snatch of DJ blather played from the cassette deck; somebody must have been taping off the radio. Did someone make this tape *for* them or was it just lifted off one of the dead? I felt paralyzed, like I was standing in front of this canyon of how little I knew about them.

"Feeding's not enough now," Alfie said.

"Our stomachs are smaller than they were," said Peter.

"It happens when you're old."

"And they leak," Peter said, making a face.

Camilla said, "Don't tell him everything."

"I'll tell him if I want, he fed us," Peter said. "Baths help us move again. When we don't have enough blood, we get slow with arms and legs like sticks. Baths help us save up. The more we soak, the longer we can go."

"It's like batteries," Alfie said. "You know what batteries are?"

"Course he does," Camilla peeped. "He's new and lives in a city. Now shut up."

"Easy when you're new," Manu said. "You can last for nights without eating. You can sleep in the woods, sleep near little villages or in a temple, come in from time to time like a tiger, at your ease. But these geezers? They need a city. Lots of poppets. Every four hours or so they got to swig or they stiff up. Sometimes they stiff up anyway, but after a bath year, they got a few years. Like they soaked their bones new again."

A bath year!

How many people were they planning to peel, Brooklyn?

"It's why we need the Tube," Alfie said.

"Subway," Peter corrected.

"Right, subway."

America's "Ventura Highway" came on, with its high, pretty strings and beautiful images describing a sunlit California that was as far away from this place as heaven.

In case I had any doubts I was actually in hell, bored, shitty Sammy went to the dead-pile and kicked a young woman the color of a cod belly, causing a pile of beetles to tumble out of the gash in her throat and a hole under one of her deflated breasts.

"Stop messing about with the poppets," Peter said.

"Now make him drink," Camilla said.

"I'll make him!" said Sammy, bounding over.

"No," Camilla said. "Peter will."

"Peter will," Duncan said, looking up at me hopefully. "And Joey will take Millie's place."

"Millie died the death in Wessex," Alfie said.

"*Hampshire*," Camilla corrected. "Joey won't know Wessex."

"I liked Millie," Duncan said, suddenly very sad.

My eyes were sharp again now; I got a better look past Duncan at the head Sammy had thrown. It hadn't decayed like some of the others, though it didn't look fresh either. That's because it was a vampire's head, and we don't rot, we burn or dry up. I saw the mustache riding over the huge fangs, the face frozen in a sneer of pain or defiance, the empty sockets where its eyes should be.

SHALL WE MAKE A RABBIT OF HIM?

Yes a blind rabbit.

It was Mapache. My heart turned over and beat twice, three times, then stopped again. With or without Wilhelm Messer, the *kids* had killed the Latins, right under our noses, too. How truly fucked I was hit me then, and you know what? It was almost a relief.

"Come on," Manu said, pulling me over to the barrel where Peter waited patiently, his hands cupped and full of blood.

"What about Varney?" I said. "The Hessian? You said he turned the bunch of you. You said he did other things to you, not nice things."

Alfie and Sammy giggled now.

"You mean that he *diddled* us," Camilla said. "*Fucked* us in our mouths and holes."

The others giggled at her swearing. She laughed a little, too, then turned serious.

"It makes me sad," she said.

"What does?"

"How easy it is to lie to you."

The little monsters. All that filth they said was just one big lie. I *knew* Messer wasn't into that shit. I was really starting to hate them.

"First say after me," Peter said. Then he pronounced some words in their language, English-before-it-changed. I said the words after him. They broke it up real small; I clearly wasn't the first to say them. I saw Manu and Duncan mouth the words with me. I almost recognized the words, they *were* kind of like English. I think I promised to be with them forever and to share what was mine with them, including my blood. I drank the blood from Peter's hands, then Alfie's, then Camilla's. Then, in what could only have been a fuck-you to baptism, Sammy ducked my head in the blood barrel three times.

I know what you're thinking, that I sold my soul, only I didn't have one to sell anymore. You're thinking I sold out my friends. But I didn't. I said the words, whatever they meant, but who cares? They were just words. And as far as I saw, these little monsters didn't have any monopoly on lying. If I could keep Margaret and Cvetko and Luna out of the dead-pile, I would do anything I had to.

Or so I thought.

Have you ever been argued about while you were sitting right there? That happened next.

"We should take him on the hunt," Sammy said.

"He won't want to hunt for his friends, he can go on the next hunt."

"He's *our* friend now, not theirs, he said the words."

(quietly) "Did he mean them?"

"If not, worse for him."

"Stay with him, Sammy."

"I will *not* miss the hunt."

"You never miss one, I've missed three."

"Wogs miss hunts sometimes."

"Stop calling me that."

"Stop being one."

"I did stop, I'm one of you, and for a long time now."

"Not as long as me."

"And you not as long as them, but they're not garlic-in-ass-boys to me like you."

(quietly) "Stop it."

"Stop it, both of you."

(quietly) "Stay with him, Sammy."

"Yes, Sammy, you watch him."

The two blond boys and the dark-haired girl were all out of the bath now and as clean as they were going to get. Still, cold-drowsy flies that didn't want to fight for space on the ripe ones in the pile lit on them to taste their ears and hair, simply after the blood, not even aware of the unnatural things that blood was on; we were just furniture to bugs. And they didn't seem to notice the bugs, either.

"But Sammy wants to uncrown him," Duncan said.

"Not unless he shows false."

"He *won't*," Duncan whined. "But you'll say he did because you want to uncrown him. Because you're nasty."

"I *am* nasty, booger, and you're a load of cold bogie. I'm *not* missing this hunt."

(quietly) "You'll miss what we say you'll miss."

Sammy went to talk back but didn't. I looked at Camilla again. Sammy was scared of her. Just how strong were they?

"Go and get the pomegranates while we think about it," Camilla all but whispered.

Sammy left.

"We might need Sammy," Manu said, as though he hated saying it. "He's quite strong. There are a lot of them."

"Lots of bugs, too!" Duncan said, rolling Mapache's head over a parade of roaches.

"We could crucify Joey," Manu said, "so no one has to watch him."

Oh shit!

Duncan said, "Someone else must fetch the spikes this time. It hurts my hands to pull the spikes from the tracks."

"That's only good for poppets. He'll pull himself free."

"Wait!" I said. "Why all this 'hunt' business? The underground is huge, goes all the way up to Harlem, all the way out to Queens. Why not share? Pick a spot for yourselves and stay there? I could show you places."

Camilla looked at me as though I'd just suggested she should eat lightbulbs and drink gasoline.

"We don't share."

"Then let them run away. Tell them to go, they'll go."

"Not the queen."

"Who?"

"Your queen. The Celt."

Margaret.

She had that right. Margaret doesn't run. I felt exasperated, afraid, yes, but just overwhelmed by the unfairness of it, how they had tricked us, everything. What I said next was really childish, I know; you won't sympathize much. And neither did Camilla.

"But the subway . . . it's *ours*. We were here *first*."

She walked very close to me and put her little finger in my face; this was the first time I had seen her mad. But still she was quiet, which was worse. Honestly, I wish she had yelled it.

"No," she said. "You were *not*."

Right.

DON'T TRUST THE CHILDREN.
These children.

The mood in the throne room changed quickly when Sammy came back from the shaft they were using as storage.

"The pomegranates are *gone!* Someone *took* them! *You* know, don't you?" he said, pushing me down like I was nothing and looming over me, his white face an angry moon, his coppery hair a fire. I guessed he was talking about grenades.

"I've been here the whole time, I don't know a thing," I said. Scary eyes on that kid.

"It was the quiet one," Camilla said, drooling while she said it.

"Old Boy," said Peter, also drooling. They wanted to bite and bite and bite.

"Where is he?" Sammy asked me, barely able to talk for the spit welling up in his mouth, shaking with the desire to twist my head. "You'd better tell."

"How would I know?" I said. I wanted to say *How would I know, stupid?* but I left the *stupid* off. I might as well have said it for the way he reacted.

He bit my nose off. Just bit it right the fuck off, one of his fangs punching a hole in my upper lip while he did it. I screamed, my eyes tearing up, and I punched him in the throat. It would have killed a regular kid, but he just backed up and crouched to spring, spat my nose onto the dead-pile with the beetles. I stood up. Next thing I knew, Peter had one of my arms in a hard grip. Manu was only too happy to grab Sammy.

That was when the can rolled in, a little gray can with a yellow band around it. Peter knew what it was; he let go of me. Duncan didn't know what it was; he reached for it. Camilla knew what it was; she grabbed Duncan away. Manu knew. He jumped behind the blood barrel. Alfie's the one who saved them. He threw a fattish, bald dead guy on it. Fast. The "pomegranate" went off just as it was being covered, flared so bright and hot it hurt our eyes; a hissing dragon was loose in the room, a piece of a star landed on my foot, burned through my sock to the bone, I would have that scar for keeps. I yelled. Alfie yelled; he caught some on the foot, too. This all happened in two heartbeats.

And I'll never forget what I saw when the grenade went off. It scared them, you see. Just for that second. They dropped their charm and I saw them as they were.

Duncan looked paler, not completely different, but clearly dead. Manu was long dead, gray-brown and dry, but still recognizably human. Sammy, too. But what really burned itself into my eyes was the brothers and their sister. Did you ever see a mummy? Not like King Tut all gold in his death mask out in Los Angeles, and not like a guy wrapped in bandages in the movies, but the little blackened, shriveled children they pulled up out of tombs in South America, in the desert, their heads packed with dried mud, little wigs of hair nailed or stitched to their dried-gourd skulls. Peter, Alfie, and Camilla were like that: their lips dried back from their mouths so their awful, outsized fangs showed, their arms no thicker than broomsticks, ending in curled little fists with fingers missing here and there. Their sunken eyes looked dry and blind. Their ribs bore stains from where their stomachs no longer held blood without spilling it. They were decrepit. I would have time to think about what that meant later, what that meant for any vampire, what happened to us when we got older. I would have time to dwell at great length on the cost of the magic or curse or whatever unnatural law kept these little things going centuries after they should have crumbled away. This was why they needed a waterfall of blood gushing through them. They were like jet engines, brutally strong but unimaginably hungry.

I saw these things in a flash. I made a noise, like "Ahh!" And then it was over. They were pale, handsome children again, scared children, reacting to an oversized flare of white flame just yards away from them. Flame was, of course, one of the few things that could actually harm them for good and ever.

They leapt back.

The dead man was on fire; smoke poured out from under him and filled the room, but I had the impression smoke was pouring out of his mouth, the gash in his throat, his ass. It probably stank. My nose was gone.

The Devil. It's the Devil, here with his angels to collect us all because we're his.

I ran.

Just outside the door, a hand grabbed a fistful of my hair, the edge of a knife tickled my throat, we spun. Just for a second. Then we both ran, ran hard, ran for our lives.

Old Boy barefoot.

Me in one smoking sock and chewed-up clothes.

A star of pain in my foot.

I snatched up a rusty iron bar with a dab of concrete attached to it.

He used the butt of his knife.

We banged every pipe we could find.

THE WATERS OF BABYLON

"Do you know where we are?"

Old Boy shook his head no.

Pipes banged somewhere, distant, impossible to figure out where.

We had just concluded a furious sprint, ducking under trains and splashing through sewers, we hoped in the direction of our loops, but even hard-ass Old Boy was panicked. My heart was beating, actually beating. This was the most afraid I'd been since I was first turned. We stood knee-deep in shitty water. A ladder led up to a manhole, trash collected on that ladder streaming like jellyfish in the current of filth.

He pointed up with his knife.

"Go find out," he said.

"Have I got a whole nose?" I said. It felt like it had grown back, but I didn't want to pop up in public looking like a leper.

He nodded, let himself smile, barely, at the ridiculousness of the question, and I skinnied up the ladder. I felt better turning away from the darkness of the tunnel knowing he had my back. I popped my head up on 4th Street near one of the newer peep shows; since about, what, 1970, sex shops had been metastasizing east from Times Square with no sign of going into remission. This one was called the Owl and Pussycat, get it? The word *Pussy*'s in there.

Anyway, we weren't too far from the bricked-up window I used as a front door. We ran. He hid the knife, clutched the remaining grenades under his arm. People turned after us or held their noses, enchanted, no doubt, by our bouquet of smoke and human waste. The manhole covers and sidewalk grates steamed, neon signs flashed, a lady in a white coat hid her purse from us, another lady in a hideous plaid pantsuit said to her friend, "Did you see that kid? The teeth he had?" I had let my charm drop; I was too scared to bring it back up, I just kept my mouth closed.

A cop's German shepherd barked at me like I was a bag of cats. "Hey," the cop said to us, "slow down!" You could see he half wanted to chase us but knew he'd never catch us; we weren't slowing down for anybody.

We ducked back underground, started making our way to the loops. As fast as we went, I knew in my bones we were too late. They knew the tunnels better than we did. The hunt was on.

Smoke.

We ran from the unused tracks and leapt through the passageway that led to the common room. DON'T TRUST THE CHILDREN. Right. Got it. Luna's mattress was on fire; that was where the smoke was coming from. Someone had thrown it from Luna's high cave, perhaps Luna trying to defend herself. Her movie posters littered the floor everywhere. I saw a pair of shoes sticking out from behind the burned-up table where we used to fold clothes. Edgar. His head lay thirty yards away, near a broken television, holes where his eyes should have been. Sandy, farther off, had been burned, was in fact still on fire, though less furiously so than

Luna's mattress. I only knew her by the platinum blond wig she wore to pretend she was Lana Turner when she worked up the courage to bite people. Farther off, the sounds of fighting.

"CVETKO?" I yelled. "BILLY?"

Old Boy hit me, slashed a finger over his lips.

We moved fast and quiet after that, following those shouts, screams, and bangs. We passed ruined vampires as we went down the tunnel; lanky piano-playing Malachi frozen in a grotesque backbend, the fingers that pounded out his last "Tiger Rag" clutching at his shirt and tie as if he had been trying to get some air, a small, sooty handprint on his sleeve, a shaft of wood sticking out of his chest, his eyes rolled back in his head. Staked. I had never seen a vampire staked. Edgar's lover, Anthony, lay headless a hundred yards down, the head nowhere to be seen. Then we saw her.

Luna.

We were moving through active tunnels, heading for Union Square station; it wasn't far off now.

We found Luna stumbling along the wall, her hair singed, her hands cupped over her eyes. She wasn't sobbing or anything, she was past that.

"Luna," I said.

She said my name.

"What happened?"

"They killed everyone. Or did you mean to me? Oh. Yes, of course to me."

Old Boy grabbed her elbow so she knew he was there.

"Um. Fire. Sammy had a spray can and a lighter. He held me down. Would have killed me, but they needed him. To fight Margaret. She was clobbering them, she and Billy. But she must be tired by now. Yes. I don't think my eyes are coming back, are they? No, of course not."

Old Boy whispered, "Get her off the live track." And he sprinted after the awful sounds farther down. I tried to pick her up, but that was when she lost her shit.

"WHAT ARE YOU DOING DON'T TOUCH ME! FOLLOW HIM KILL THEM GET THEM, JOEY, GET THEM!"

I tried to drag her but she flung herself down, groped till she had purchase on the track, held on.

"Let me get you out of here!" I said, yanking around her hips, crying.

"No," she said, clutching the rails tighter, shaking now, keeping what was left of her face from me.

I let go of her hips.

"Go, Joey. Get them."

I turned away from her, my wrist over my mouth.

"Protect your eyes," she said, almost calmly. "They go after the eyes."

I ran.

"They work together."

That was the last thing I heard her say.

One backward glance showed me she was doing what I like to think I would have done. She was putting her neck on the running rails.

They were killing Chinchilla just as we got there. Manu and Alfie, I mean. Manu was on the ground, on his back, had Chinchilla's arms cinched under his own armpits, kept a foot in Chinchilla's chest, propping him up and anchoring him while Alfie twisted his head in violent spasms.

Old Boy ran at them. Past this, another fight, the four remaining kids were wearing down Margaret and Billy Bang, driving them back toward the light of the Union Square station.

All six of them? Had we lost so many without killing even one?

Chinchilla's head came off in a spray of black blood. Alfie threw it at Old Boy's feet and broke right fast as Old Boy dove for him; Old Boy stumbled, his knife gouged only air.

Yes. We lost so many without killing even one.

Hopelessness tried to wash over me but there was no time. Old Boy had caught Alfie but Alfie curled into a ball, protecting his neck with his arms. None of the truly awful things Old Boy did to him with that knife were enough to get through his arms or make him let go of the back of his own neck where his little fingers interlaced. Then here came Manu, straight for Old Boy's eyes, gouging with his fingers. Old Boy had to cover up; he cut Manu now, flung him against the wall. I whaled on the side of Alfie's head; he kicked me backward, broke a rib doing it, then Old Boy was on him again with that knife. I grabbed Alfie's hands, tried to pry his arms down from around his neck so Old Boy could get at his head, but I wasn't strong enough; it was like trying to pry a statue apart. Out of the corner of my eye, I glimpsed the fight at the tunnel's mouth. Margaret and Billy were in trouble. They had put their backs against the wall so they couldn't be surrounded. Margaret was working that shovel, had half decapitated Camilla, but only half; she was already healing, bent over in a caricature of someone with a migraine, using her little hands to fix her head in place. Meanwhile, Sammy flailed at Margaret's eyes with his pencil, trying to clutch on the sleeve of her robe for purchase. No sooner had she swatted him away than here came Duncan, pitching a fistful of gravel at her eyes. Peter had broken Billy's legs and now hacked at him with a machete; it was all Billy could do to protect his neck. One of Old Boy's grenades fell near me; I leapt away from it, but then snatched it up and pocketed it when I saw it had the pin in it. I ran toward Margaret and Billy, keeping low and quiet.

I pulled the pin.

The children didn't see me coming, had no wall at their backs.

Margaret's shovel dug a groove in Sammy's face, pushed him back toward me. There was no time for the words to form in my mind, but I was glad it was Sammy. I was so fucking glad it was nasty, blood-guzzling, eye-burning Sammy. I grabbed his waistband, jammed the grenade down the back of his pants, then pitched him toward the third rail like a bouncer evicting a drunk. He missed the rail, the bad part of it anyway, bounced off the wood covering on top. Landed on his feet like a cat. Drew his lips back and showed his fangs, blood from his shoveled-in but healing nose and cheek running into his mouth. Then he realized what was in his pants. He yelled, *"NOT ME NOT ME!!!!"* like he'd been chosen as "it" and might change the chooser's mind. He reached down his trousers, but it was too late. It popped and the pain hit him, made him shriek; he ran at me but desperately, like he wanted help as he grew a tail of fire that quickly ate him. He screamed. Came at me like a torch, showering painful sparks and giving off vicious heat. Everyone jumped away from him.

He folded in half and burned like the dry, old thing he was. In a heap. By the wall.

He died.

Still burning, smoke gouting from him.

The fighting had stopped for a second, everybody getting an eyeful of Sammy's big finish and a snootful of smoke, then Margaret punted Duncan's head, I mean she was going for the goalposts, and the fight was on again. She drove her shovel into Peter, breaking an arm. I turned back to see if I could help Old Boy, but Manu jumped out of the smoke and clotheslined me, knocked me ass over tits.

Alfie stomped my spine on his way past; they were both fleeing Old Boy. Camilla was up now. She gasped at the ruin of Sammy and ran toward the light of Union Square station. The rest of the children followed. Margaret stopped to help the wreck that was Billy to its feet.

We chased them.

I admit it was good to see them running.

From us.

Behind us, a light. A train was coming.

Luna.

I heard the squeal of its brakes, knew the driver saw her, would try to stop even though he knew he couldn't, not in time.

Luna!

The train ground behind us slower, slower, raining sparks. People on board were yelling, they had seen the fire, might even have recognized that its fuel was boy-shaped. With the train and the fire blocking things up, we couldn't go back in the tunnel if we wanted to. Whatever happened next was going to happen by the platform in Union Square station, out in the open, under the lights. With an audience.

They turned. The children. They might have kept running, they ran like greyhounds, they could have left us farther and farther behind them until they dropped out of sight. They might have slipped like ghosts into one of the side paths or crawlways about which they seemed to have encyclopedic knowledge, but flight was not their goal. They were just regrouping, choosing their ground. They wanted us gone, all of us, the strong ones dead, the weak ones so badly frightened we'd never dream about returning, except perhaps years later, after they were gone again, to write a warning on the wall. NO, REALLY, DON'T TRUST THE CHILDREN.

So they turned.

Imagine you were on the platform that March night in 1978. Cold outside, so you were wearing a scarf, a jacket. If you're a girl you probably had on tall boots, they were really in, maybe hair feathered back like Kristy McNichol or a Bee Gee. An older, heavy-set guy with an unfeatherable comb-over blew sax, really good sax, but the crowd was cheap that night. Nobody wanted to take off their gloves or take their hands out of their pockets. He had a few crumpled dollars in his beret from the people who got on the last several trains, he had a few quarters and nickels, a strange abundance of dimes, but this particular crowd just wasn't playing ball. Not the student-looking kid with the pile of Art-Garfunkel-kinky red hair, the big Adam's apple, and the glasses that covered half his face. Not the blond guy in the powder-blue suit with his pants too short, showing just a little too much of the argyle socks that didn't quite match the rest of him. Not the old lady clutching the purse with the strap like the St. Louis Arch against her stomach as if to stop someone from punching her there, and what was she doing out this late anyway? Not the black woman with the Dutch Chocolate lipstick and the opaque leopard-print scarf that looked too fragile to have ever been near a leopard. The guy on the horn wasn't playing anything in particular, just letting it caterwaul like the soundtrack to some detective show. Over the horn, you heard something else, was it yelling? Next came the unmistakable squeal of a train's brakes, and yes, definitely yelling. The sax stopped. Some looky-loos were actually crowding *closer* to the platform, stepping all over the beret full of dimes.

"Look there," someone said from the platform. Another one shrieked; there were several shouts of "Get a cop," "Call an ambulance," and the like. A quintet of bloody children spilled out of the tunnel, their clothes in tatters.

"There's been an accident!"

"Oh my God!"

A brutalized teenager and three equally bloody adults, one of them a savage woman with a shovel, followed after the children. Now smoke poured out of the tunnel, smoke that stank of chemicals. People started going for the stairs, tentatively at first, then like they meant it. Behind the smoke, the nose of a train slowing to full stop, like a snake that poked its snoot into a rabbit hole and decided to park there.

What *was* this?

Nobody bombed New York, but this looked like IRA shit, PLO, Red Brigade. Could it have come here, that foreign germ of violence as food for newspapers? No. This was something new. Or perhaps something so old and awful it had been forgotten on purpose. Because now four of the bleeding children (and they weren't really children, were they? Had their eyes not shone in the tunnel?) turned around to face the bleeding adults running at them. They curled into balls like kids in a duck-and-cover drill from the fifties, their hands clasped behind their necks, their heads tucked between their knees. The madwoman with the shovel stood over the dark-haired little girl and rose up like King Arthur about to drive Excalibur into its stone; she was on her tiptoes, almost on pointe. "Stop!" a hysterical cop next to you yelled, his revolver almost next to your ear. He was going to shoot. Thank God you got your hand over your ear in time. Not because your partial deafness would have been such a big deal in the grand scheme of things, what with so many people about to die so strangely, but had you been deafened, you might not have heard the sweet boy who would speak in a moment—but not yet, he was just making his way to the platform.

Now the cop shot at just the instant the lunatic drove down with her shovel. The shot caught her in the hip, turned her just a little, but she caught the kid in the knee, clipped the leg off, and even sparked the running rail beneath, but the kid didn't scream. The woman screamed. You couldn't know, of course, that she screamed not because she was shot but because she missed the child's neck. That her aim was decapitation. That the child had gambled that even this brutal, crazed woman wouldn't be strong enough to cut her head off with her limbs protecting it, not with one blow, but that the little girl who was so rarely wrong had made a millennial mistake. The woman *was* that strong. *Would* have taken the girl's head and arm clean off, drawing a very long, sad story to its end.

Only she missed.

And she wouldn't get another chance, even though she raised her bloody shovel once again. The cop must have put his time in at the range; even jacked up at what he was seeing, his second shot was better, took part of shovel-woman's head off, but she didn't fall. She just looked momentarily confused, like she was struggling to say a word she had forgotten. She looked at the blade of her shovel as though it might be written there. The other adults were doing violence to the other children. People were yelling at them to stop.

Now the sweet boy climbed onto the platform and held his hands up. Everyone looked, you looked, too. He left small, bloody footprints behind him. You wouldn't remember his face, it would blur in your memory, but you remember that his face was sweet, as was his voice.

"Everyone! Listen! Help us! The grown-ups are hurting us! You must pull their heads off! You must hold them down and shock them on the bad rail!"

Yes, we will!

Such a sweet boy, who could want to hurt an angel of his rank?

"Do not let them speak!" he said, and you resolved to keep them silent. Your eyes spilled over, tears streamed down your cheeks with the pathos of it, your mouth opened and you drooled on your shirt or sweater or tie, your saliva ran like you were starving and someone had tucked grains of salt under your tongue. No time for salt, though. You *had* to save these angels from the murderers on the tracks.

Was that how it happened? Was that why you did it? I'm only guessing here. I only know what I saw.

What you saw, I think, was a triumph of mankind, of Manhattan, manna from above, the end of bystanderism forever, I am my brother's keeper, we are, all of us, *going down onto those tracks*. And you did. One big wave of you in your sport coats and London Fogs and turtlenecks; in your saris and jumpsuits and Grateful Dead T-shirts under peacoats and down vests and leather, in your wool caps, deerstalkers, and babushkas, smelling of Old Spice and Marlboros and sub-polyester sweat, you poured over the lip of that platform, elbowing each other out of the way for the privilege of tearing the killers apart, especially the one with the shovel. The mad are supposed to have inhuman strength, and these were no exception. The wild black man in the funky vest tore a man's arm off trying to save the woman. The very pale one in the olive jacket used his knife, tried to cut his way through the crowd and save the woman. But there was no saving her, you were all over her, a swarm of you. She brained the first ones, busted teeth and jaws, she swore and bit in a fury with teeth that belonged on a tiger, she *was* a tiger, but you bore her down, those of you up front, took her shovel from her, stuffed your hands and arms in her mouth though she bit and bit deep. You turned for a moment to see those in the back handing up the children, and a miracle happened, didn't it? These bloody things who seemed too hurt to live were healing before your eyes. The little girl got passed backward over heads; nobody could find the leg that had been cut from her, but that's because it was on again! Now you turned front and the vile tiger-woman-thing was closer to the rail. It was as slow as tug-of-war, moving her there. A POP! and sizzle as a woman in a fox-trimmed coat touched the rail, jerked, and smoked, her fox smoking, too. A man in a security-guard outfit made contact next, jostled into it by the crowd, his life ending in a violent spasm that curled him so the back of his head almost touched his heels. And then it was her turn. You saw her face before she went, her skin the color of ash, her gorgon's eyes, her mouth open in a snarl. Her teeth like a tiger's. A vampire? Why not? Who else would want to hurt that honeyed boy?

"Die, you fucking monster!" you yelled, though you don't normally swear.

And die she did.

The saxophonist, grunting and drooling, wrestled her foot into the lethal rail. Her hand had been gripping the running rail, so the current went fully through her, exploded her hands, popped off her head, set her hair stinkingly ablaze.

A common noise went up of gagged cries and shouts; all those train-moving amps and volts were hungry, they didn't stop with her. The saxophonist jerked and burned as well, his ridiculous comb-over standing on end. The guy in the powder-blue suit caught fire; he kicked his loafers off and wiggled his argyle-besocked feet almost comically. Several others who had been wrestling her died, though none so spectacularly. A good dozen, maybe a score were injured.

You were not among these; you had not been strong or early enough to get to the front. But here came the teenaged boy, the dirty one, spared because the sweet boy had said *the grown-ups are hurting us*, and, whatever he was, this one was no grown-up. He looked you in the eye.

I looked at you, I don't know which one you were, I looked at so many. I saw Margaret burning. I saw Old Boy down, his hands on a grenade, half a dozen hands on his, holding them together, holding the pin in, and here came the college boy with the mane of frizzy red hair and the shovel. I tensed to spring down but saw that I was too late. The shovel fell. Old Boy died the death, the college boy holding up his trophy while the tongue in it moved in and out, as though the last taste in its mouth were unpleasant. The boy yelled a nasal, unlikely war whoop, then stood slack.

Billy Bang had disappeared.

Good for him. I mean that. Good for him.

The crowd seethed, unsure what to do now. Some began to snap out of it. A woman screamed, the old woman with the huge purse, but she seemed less like an old woman than like a child who had gotten separated from its parents in a room full of monsters.

"Forget what you saw here," Peter shouted, his voice carrying throughout the station. All heads turned to him.

"Tell them you just don't remember what you saw."

Alfie took Old Boy's head away from his killer, tore the fangs out with pliers and kept them.

Of course. However the authorities explained this clusterfuck, the explanation was *not* going to involve vampires.

Camilla told the policeman to shoot himself. He put his gun in his mouth, but hesitated, crying. She stomped his foot and told him to again. He did. His hat flew off. Peter picked it up and put it on.

Duncan saw me now, and said, "Grab him! Bring him here!"

He was drooling, showing me fangs no one else could see.

I ran, up the stairs, over people, out of hell.

He didn't chase me.

A COIN WITH THREE SIDES

Joseph Hiram Peacock had never been to a foreign city, but that's what New York looked like to me as I sprinted through her streets. I ran in no particular direction, through the East Village, past the tattoo parlors and record shops in St. Mark's Place, past seedy bars and into Tompkins Park, then down through Little Italy and into Chinatown where I thought about slipping underground into the tightly packed labyrinth of tunnels used by the Tongs, but Margaret kept us out of those because the Chinese mob still used them, and I kept out of them now because underground didn't sound so good. So I ran west through Tribeca, then into the warehouses and art lofts of SoHo; I knocked people down, ran over the hoods of taxis, jumped into Dumpsters and hid; I had to keep moving or hide till I found new clothes, I was a mess. But I had an even more pressing need. When I realized I was in SoHo, all the exertion caught up with me and my limbs went cold, the hot hole framed with burning coals opened in my gut; I needed blood. When people get tired, they pant and sweat, they need water and sleep. We need only one thing; all our strength comes from that one thing. Cvetko said it was the life force in blood, the *magic* in it that kept us alive, since we didn't have moving parts inside anymore, no circulation, no metabolism, no need to breathe. And where *was* Cvetko? I immediately felt guilt for leaving him down there, with them. I had the impulse to turn around and look for him; I pictured him hiding underground, touching his face somewhere in total darkness, hoping he wouldn't see the lights of their awful little eyes coming for him. Probably just like in the war, hiding from Germans, or Italians. Maybe he knew how to survive from the war. But there was nothing practical or savvy about Cvets; I was just making excuses because I was scared. He needed someone to tell him the party was over, help him out of there. You should have seen the state of him when he first came to us from Bushwick because the neighborhood had gone to hell; he was helpless. Like one of those special kids who gets a routine and you'd better not deviate from it. Now the neighborhood had gone to hell for real and everything, but everything had to change.

Whether I was going to find the balls to help Cvets was a problem I would have to work out after I fed. I scanned the windows for one with a light on, found it. It even had a fire escape, not normally a factor, but in my weakened state, sticking to walls wasn't going to be a picnic. Up I went, using the stairs like a citizen, still cat-quiet. The balcony faced the street, too, so I was going to have to be quick about getting in. I kept my eyes peeled open because when I shut them I saw bad things on the insides of my eyelids. Margaret, Luna, Old Boy. Fuck this whole circus.

It was a war.

We didn't know it was one until it was too late.

And we lost.

I shook that off, I was starving. I peeped in the window. A woman in an orange raincoat painted a huge, abstract cat in purple oil, a window behind it open on the moon, in the painting I

mean, and the yellow on that moon was beautiful. I had seen the
real moon through a telescope once, rising, after I was turned so it
was very bright to me even though it was still low and yellow, and
it was one of the prettiest things I ever saw. This woman, she had
the cat, and a table and a teacup, and in the cup, in the tea, the
moon shone there, too. It was definitely abstract, definitely what
you would call modern art, but it was actually good. Who was this
broad, was she in the Guggenheim? Why the raincoat? Was she
cold? I touched the glass, felt no warmth in it. I noticed she had
rumpled jeans on under the raincoat; I thought maybe she had
two pairs on, tucked into the tops of those yellow work boots with
the rawhide laces people who like John Denver wear. She breathed
out; she had been holding it in, using a tiny brush to put moon-
light on a whisker, and I saw her breath puff out. No heat. She was
poor. No Guggenheim for her.

She turned around and looked at me then; I think she saw my
reflection in the windows opposite. She was maybe fifty, mouse-
brown hair, pretty once was my first thought, then I realized she
was still pretty. I had just seen such ugly things that this cold loft
with its naked brick and bare lightbulbs and a mattress on the
floor with a pile of books for a nightstand was beautiful, and she was
beautiful for making it that way and keeping it as nice as she could
and for not having the heart to throw away the Gerber daisy wilt-
ing, already dropping petals from its place in the Coke bottle on
the counter by the stove. And she was beautiful for wearing a raincoat with a sweater under it because that was all she had. I didn't
even know I was touching the glass. I didn't know I was sobbing,
either, until she looked at me and I was embarrassed. I was ready
to jump because I knew how I looked, that my skin was waxy and
dead from hunger and that my hair was dry and dull, that my
clothes were bloody, burned, and filthy, hanging off me like I was
an accident victim, a bum, and a war refugee rolled into one, which,

at this point, I was. I was sure she was going to call the cops, if she even had a phone in this joint. She saw me and froze. Scared, but not for herself, I think. She patted the air twice with her hand like *stay there* and wiped her brush off, put it in a little jar of cloudy liquid full of brushes. She came over, the light from the bulbs flashing once on glasses that made her look like an owl.

She opened the window.

"Come in," she said. I hadn't charmed her, nothing. She just saw me and asked me in. I was still sobbing, so hard I thought I might retch.

"What happened, do you need an ambulance? I don't have a phone, but my neighbor does, I just heard his door, he'll be awake."

I shook my head no. She looked at me more closely. Held the side of her glasses like that was going to help her see some microscopic something she was searching for on my face. Her eyes traveled all over my face. I just sat there, the sobs slowing down. But I couldn't move. It was like she had charmed me. She put the back of her hand against my cheek, felt how cold I was, then put that same hand under my armpit to make sure. Then she said, "Oh." She put a finger near my mouth. "May I?" she said, and I didn't say anything, just sat there. She put her finger under my lip and felt my fangs, like the Wild Kingdom guy feeling around in the mouth of a drugged cat.

"You're not just cold. You're starving," she said.

I nodded my head. I didn't care that she knew what I was, I wasn't concerned about *how* she knew. It was so good to feel safe. But she told me anyway.

"I grew up in Brooklyn," she said. "I knew one of you when I was a teenager. He would visit me. He was . . . kind. At a time when no one else was."

"He have a big ugly head?" I said, so quietly she must have barely heard me.

Off with her head!

She nodded, barely, not wanting to call him ugly. John Valentine. The one who turned Margaret, the one who burned up when his building fell down. The one who could ride a horse. The fact that he turned Margaret made him my grandfather, in a way. Now here was someone who knew family. This was Margaret's wake, in a way, the only one she would get.

"I lost someone tonight," I said.

"I'm sorry. Who?"

Never call me your mother again.

"My mother."

She took my hand in hers and the warmth coming from her almost burned me.

"Your real mother?"

"Real as I got."

She nodded.

"You have to eat. Don't you?"

I looked at my feet. My ugly, veiny, pale feet. My sprint through Manhattan had abused them. New York is not made for bare feet; I had felt the dig of broken glass and the sting of pop tops, I had scraped their tops on curbs, even paused to unsheathe a hypodermic needle from my heel near Tompkins Park. This had all gone away almost as quickly as it had happened. But the worst thing was that I had tracked dog shit into her loft. Of all the things, just dog shit. She noticed, but didn't care.

This woman, and I never found out her name, pulled her scarf away from her neck, pulled down her sweater.

"You have to promise," she said.

"What?"

"You know what. Not too much."

I didn't say anything.

"Don't make me . . . like you are. I don't want that."

I didn't say anything.

"Go on," she said.

I sat there, a drugged cat.

"Go on."

She got the shakes after I fed, but they went away when she smoked a tight little joint; she really knew her way around rolling paper. Neither one of us talked much. I think she was wrestling with whether to ask me to stay, but I didn't want to. Her huge windows faced east anyway, and the filmy March sun was going to come looking in every corner of that place. There was a bathroom, but it had a window, too, and no tub. The shower was just a hose and a hole. The toilet ran all the time. She gave me a pair of jeans that sagged in the butt and a shirt, I won't call it a blouse, with tiny flowers on it like cute, curly weeds, fake pearl snaps for buttons. It was nothing Charles Bronson would wear, but it was better than the shredded, blood-stiff rags I had worn through her window. Clothes were the least of my worries. She went to get me a scarf, too, but I took off out the window while she fished in the closet. I suck at good-byes.

As I walked fast away from there, I stuck my hands in the pockets of my new droopy-ass jeans, felt paper. Three dollars. She must have got them off the dirty pile.

It was three A.M. or so; I didn't have long to find a hidey-hole. The thought that I could die that way, just crisped by the sun, seemed tiresome to me after all I'd just been through, like somebody should have given me a pass just this once. I needed sleep, but I knew what I would dream about so the thought of closing my eyes made me shudder.

My feet took me home. Not to the subways, not down a manhole, but *home*. Before I even knew what I was doing, I was standing in front of the place I grew up, looking up at my old window as Margaret once had, throwing coins up at me. The streetlight was still there. I hadn't been by in a good decade, and not at all before that. When you're dead, you don't want to see your folks. Somebody in my family might have still been there ten years ago when I had walked by as if on a dare, with a fedora on and my head down, but not now. They had changed the place into a café. Stubbed-out cigarette butts, all of them smoked to the filter, a few of them lipsticky, lay on the street and sidewalk; I could almost hear some long-haired schmuck playing guitar surrounded by NYU chicks in thrift-store leather coats. All of them eyeless, all of them blind rabbits, while above them a gorgon in the upstairs window was waiting for me to look at her, ready to turn me to stone. Or maybe I was waiting up there, fourteen years old again, no, more innocent, make it six years old, and if I just looked up and met my own gaze I would magically go back into my body. 1925. The stock market humming along on phantom cash, Vilma making *paprikash* or marzipan. It's magic for me to walk around without a heartbeat, right? It's magic for little kids to live hundreds of years and kill stacks of people, right? Why not something *good* for a change? Why not let me go?

"I'm sorry for what I did to Margaret," I said, closing my eyes hard. "I'm sorry I was such a rotten kid. I'll do better. I swear. Just take it all back, okay?" I turned my head up and looked. No little Joey. Just black windows on the face of that house, one with a crack in it. The blindest of blind rabbits. I didn't know who I was praying to, anyway. I was the property of the god of small places, and that god was deaf to everything said aboveground.

"What am I going to do?" I said.

Go back for Cvetko.

Run away.

Sit on a bench at Battery Park and wait for the sun.

Damned shame coins didn't have three sides.

I didn't feel like I had a whole lot to lose when I knocked at the Hessian's door. I didn't even know I was going there until I found myself looking up at the huge oak door with the carved acorns and oak leaves, little squirrels in the corners. Big mean old bastard like that and he had squirrels on his door. The knocker was more his speed, a big brass bear's head, the coolest knocker I ever saw. I didn't know what I was going to say until just before I knocked. I just grabbed the ring in the bear's mouth like I was holding a sub-way strap and I hung there until I heard the words in my head: *Hello, Mr. Messer. I know I haven't seen you in a long time, it's Joey Peacock, this isn't my shirt, but I was wondering if you would be willing to help me. I want to get rid of these vampires that look like children, but they're not children. They're evil, but the big kind of evil, not like us. They told dirty lies about you and killed my friends. You're reasonable, right? Margaret said you were a mercenary, which means you fight for money, no offense, or at least you did. I could pay you. Not a lot right now, but I could owe you. I'm a really good thief and I don't mind try-ing something big. It would have to be big, like diamonds or a bank, because this won't be easy. They're dangerous. Really, really dangerous. And I don't know what else to do.*

Hopeless, right? But what the fuck.

Really, what the fuck.

I knocked.

The Luftwaffe-looking doorman must have known I was stand-ing there rehearsing what I was going to say; I got the idea that they didn't miss a lot in that house. Maybe they had cameras, but I didn't see one. The door swung open quietly; you expect a creak out of a door like that.

"May I help you?" he said, looking at me in no particular way. Hard to tell if he remembered me. Servants always act like they don't remember you.

"Do you remember me?" I said.

He blinked once, slowly, like a lizard, if they blink.

"Would it please you if I remembered you?"

"Sure. I guess."

"Then of course I remember you."

He was still standing half behind the door, making no move to open it wider or invite me in.

Damn, he was handsome. He wasn't young anymore, but he had one of those faces. Weird watching people get old; you have to be old yourself to get it. I don't like suddenly seeing regular people again after fifteen, twenty years, it's depressing. He still looked good, but for how long? He was the night shift guy; you'd think Messer would have turned him.

"Is your . . . boss home?"

"I don't think so."

Still had that German accent, sounded like he was on *Hogan's Heroes*.

We just stood there for a second. I looked at the bear on the door, then back at him.

"May I come in?"

Slow blink.

"I don't think so."

"Who is it?" a voice said behind him. Not Messer.

"A boy."

"What boy?"

The voice sounded familiar, but I couldn't tell if it was a guy or a girl.

"A boy I remember," he said.

"Show me!" the voice said.

He opened the door a little more, stepped back, not to let me in but just so I would be visible to the owner of the voice. We saw each other. Christ, this was not my night. A tall woman with a cock. The one from Studio 54 that said I smelled like trains.

She laughed.

She kept laughing, covered her mouth with her hand.

The doorman didn't even permit himself a smirk. Damn, he was good. He closed the door with the squirrels and the bear and the acorns at just the right speed. Not insultingly fast. Not awkwardly slow. Just right.

So here's the part where it's four A.M. and I charm some schmuck to let me into his nice, dark apartment and I feed on him and tie him up or peel him and sleep in his bathtub, get a fresh start tomorrow night, right? I *did* peek in several apartments, but every place I looked in, I came up with a reason why I shouldn't bother the people there. Truth is, I did feed one more time; I had to. I couldn't take all I needed from she-who-paints-cats without killing her. So I started scoping, thinking I should choose well in case it was my last meal. I hadn't entirely ruled out greeting the sunrise at Battery Park. The only guy on Christopher Street flagged down the only cab on Christopher Street, and I walked up just as the cabbie asked him where he was going. He hadn't stopped yet, just slowed down and asked through the window so the guy couldn't open the door in case he failed the audition.

I walked up, poured on some charm, said through the cracked window,

You must pull their heads off!

"We're going to Idlewild."

"You mean the airport? JFK?"

I think he was a Sikh, he had the turban. When he said *airport* he pushed his eyebrows together over his nose like affectionate caterpillars.

"I'm not with him! I'm going to . . ."

"Shut up, Dad," I said, and he shut up.

I said,

You must hold them down and shock them on the bad rail!

"Yeah, JFK, I forgot, the airport."

The Sikh rolled off to "seek" another passenger. I knew from the way he asked the guy he was only looking for Manhattan fares.

The Dad guy glared at me angrily but wouldn't speak because I had commanded him to shut up. I told him to come in the alley with me and I would give him a dollar. Turned out I lied. I didn't give him a dollar. But I did have a secret to tell him, if he'd lean down close. And I did take the money out of his wallet just in case I decided against sunbathing.

Cvetko

First I ran away from my problem, headed west. By four thirty A.M. I had made it up by the old dockyards, the crumbling piers where the gays sunbathed in the summer, whole packs of them. Nobody was around now. Too dark, too cold, unless maybe people came here to hook up in hidden places. There were lots of hidden places in this rusted-out set of piers. As long as I looked out for Coney Island Whitefish, I could maybe stay here, cover up in a trash bag, tuck myself into a rusted cargo container. But no. I might surprise some gays, I didn't want to see any of that. Or maybe I did, just a little bit, which was why I kept drifting near places like this. Maybe I didn't want to suck a guy off or anything but I wanted to watch somebody else do that, maybe I secretly liked it when queers hit on me so I could feel attractive but also act superior, like, "Thanks anyway, gay guy, but I'm *normal*." Normal, right. I like pussy. I'm a Capricorn. Oh, and I drink blood and don't get older. Why was I thinking about this now? Maybe it was easier to think uncomfortable thoughts than horrifying, bewildering ones.

Maybe you want to know who you are before you die.

I stood near the water, looking west, where night was running away from me. It was windy, blowing my hair around. A seagull did that thing where he flew against a draft and hovered in one place, he was looking at me like maybe he hadn't smelled me and was surprised to find one of us bread-and-sometimes-Alka-Seltzer-throwers so close to him suddenly. I swear this bird was looking me right in the face. He called out twice.

"Cvetko! Cvetko!" I said back to him, imitating him. He flew off. "Yeah, I know."

I went east.

I went back underground.

THE GOD OF SMALL PLACES

I meant to look for Cvets immediately, but I was so exhausted I sleepwalked into the growing crowd of predawn commuters making their way through Grand Central Station; I went through a door I know that led down. Then I went through a couple of doors and a passageway I *didn't* know until I ended up in an unfamiliar service tunnel, where I wedged myself up high between a pipe and the roof. A lot of bugs crawled around; there must have been food nearby. I plugged my nostrils with dollar bills and went to sleep. Once I heard transit cops walk under me, saw their flashlights bobbing. I guessed it was going to get hot for a while because of Union Square station, however they put it together. But these guys weren't serious. They weren't talking about accidents or bombings. They were talking about Leon Spinks.

I went back to sleep.

I woke up to find that one of my nose dollars had fallen out and sure enough I now had a snootful of bugs, small ones; goddamn, I hated sleeping without a box. I blew them out without much trouble. I knew in my bones that it was sunset. I remembered where I was, in a service tunnel under Grand Central.

I took the 6 down; they had just gotten it running again, it was packed. We didn't stop at Union Square. The station was closed for repairs. I didn't look out the window when we passed, but everyone around me put down their papers, papers with headlines like *4 TRAIN DERAILS!* and, you gotta love the *Post*, *GOOD SAMARITANS FRIED!* I plugged my ears because I didn't want to hear people talking about it like it was theirs, like they had a right to it. Instead I got a dumbshow of craning necks, ladies putting hands over mouths, one guy taking a picture like he came this way on purpose. It seemed like everybody around me had to stick an elbow in my cheek or an ass in my face while I sat with my hands over my ears, not looking through the permanent marker squiggles on the glass to see how the cleanup was going. I didn't look because I didn't want to see where my friends died. But I also didn't look because I was still scared.

I had to find Cvets.

We had to get out of here.

I had a hunch about where he might be.

I didn't find Cvetko in the beautiful old abandoned City Hall station. But I did find a note from him. He had stuck it in one of his hooker-red envelopes from Valentine's Day and put it through the bars of an old ticket window. The outside said *Joseph H. Peacock*. How do you like that? Even with the apocalypse upon us this guy took time to write out my whole name, except for the *Hiram*.

The envelope was heavy.

When I opened it, I saw why.

I pulled on a tiny gold chain to reveal the piece of jewelry attached to it. I found myself staring straight at the coral pendant I slipped into Margaret's purse all those years ago. Medusa stared back at me.

Then I read the note.

Dearest Joseph,

I am writing this letter in some haste, so please forgive me if it is difficult to read. I have deduced the nature of our small friends and I believe our situation is hopeless. Peter, Alfred, and Camilla are quite old, and quite vicious, and they are working with outside assistance. They are coming for us and they mean to kill us and claim these tunnels as their own. I have tried to convince Margaret to flee, but there is more of Boudica than Moses about her, which is to say that she would rather die in her chariot than wander in the wilderness. I have determined to leave these tunnels and would like it very much if you and I should travel together; provided, of course, that your previous statements about finding my company tedious were, as I dearly hope, meant in jest.

I shall return here at midnight for the next three evenings, tonight being 24 March. If you come too late, do not seek me in Manhattan, but let us resolve to enquire after one another wherever we may go. I suggest Boston. If I do not come to meet you here, it means I have died the death.

In that event, please know that I have great affection for you, and that I have tried to serve you in some small way as I would have served my own child had I been blessed with one. I think the closest any of us may come to lasting happiness is in seeing to the needs of others; I think the same may be true for those who go in sunlight, though their lives are so short that many will not discover this in time.

Meet me here, Joey, and I shall take you to my wife.

*I have left your fine clothes and your dirty magazines
with the girlfriend you thought I never knew about.*

*I enclose a small gift so you will know my heart in this
matter.*

> Yours sincerely,
> C.S.

All right, I wasn't the shiniest knife in the drawer, I knew that.
I would never be some super-genius egghead like Cvetko; I sucked
at crossword puzzles and would have sucked worse at chess,
which is why I never bothered. But hanging out with him had
rubbed off on me a little bit—I could almost hear him whispering
in my ear, *Think, Joey, think—what does this mean?*

His wife was dead. She died in the war, killed by mixed-up
guerrillas who thought he was ratting them out to Italians who
were like pint-sized Germans you could actually beat sometimes.
Anyway, she was dead. *Meet me here and I shall take you to my wife*
meant I would *die.* He was telling me to get the hell out of here!

I looked at the white cameo standing out against her coral
backdrop. Medusa. I'd put it in Margaret's purse to get her
canned from her job at my house forty-five years before. And
she'd kept it, maybe to remind herself of something; not to be in
the wrong place, not to trust Jews, who knew? I had no idea how
Cvetko got it, maybe he poked around her apartment after she
was dead. Anyway, he knew what it meant.

"You're a poison pill, aren't you?" I asked it. It didn't say anything back, just turned and turned, this way, that way.

The walk back to Chloë's place was one sad-bastard march of doom.
I took back alleys and little streets, wending my way toward the

anchorage under the Brooklyn Bridge, my head full of grief and shame. They got Cvetko. They got him and tried to use him to get me, but he outsmarted them and warned me, which meant, in a way, that I outsmarted them, too. But they got him. He was probably already finished, and, if not, he would be soon. *Do not seek me in Man-hattan* meant don't look for him. I looked at how he signed it, noticed he didn't capitalize the *sincerely* after *Yours*. He was serving me as he would his own child. He couldn't get out, but he bought my ticket out for me. Right under their noses. I could picture Manu reading it out loud for the others, laughing with them while Cvets hung from a pulley waiting for the little asshole queen to whisper *Off with his head!*

I was still crying when I got to Blond Jesus's place.

He was pretty nocturnal. I expected to see his lamps blazing, but they were out. Could he have been off getting himself a beer? He liked beer okay, but he did that in the afternoons if at all. It hurts me to confess this, but I did bite him a couple of times, and he wasn't what you'd call boozy; he didn't see well enough at night to go too far, either, so his being out would have been weird.

I listened hard, trying to hear sawing or planing or hammering or any other carpenter stuff, but his little brick workshop was all quiet, all still. Too still. All I heard was the endless dragon-hiss of cars on the bridge above.

Why aren't you working, George?

I stopped.

I looked at the entrance to the pipe that led down to Chloë's place. If Cvetko and Old Boy had figured out I went there, maybe they had, too. Maybe they were waiting for me. My head told me I was being paranoid. But when I tried to move my feet toward the pipe, they wouldn't go. What was down there, anyway? A bag of clothes? One last look at my girlfriend? This didn't feel right, not by half. I walked away, backward, slow and quiet, still keeping an eye on the pipe. Now I turned and started off. Then I heard it.

A little huff of disappointment and impatience. The sound a whiny kid makes when he's told he has to do his homework before he gets to listen to the radio.

"*Nff.*"

My head snapped back and I looked at the pipe.

Peter's little blond crown rose out of it.

His eyes shining like cat's eyes.

I ran.

I'm a good runner, that's my biggest strength. Unfortunately, they were damned good runners, too. They kept up with me, sometimes gained on me; I made myself go faster, regained what I had lost, but still I couldn't pull away. It was anybody's race—if I stumbled, I was theirs; if they lost sight of me for even thirty seconds, I was gone forever. My instinct for the last fifteen years had been to slip underground when threatened, but underground was where they wanted me, so I ran past the manhole covers and ignored the grates, drains, and dark stone mouths that used to mean sanctuary. I ran up 1st Avenue, made my way to St. Mark's Place hoping to lose myself there, hoping there would be a crowd. There wasn't, not much of one anyway, just a couple of punkish guys smoking outside a dive whose name I couldn't see. They both watched me sprint by; I'm pretty sure my fangs were showing but I was too freaked-out even to close my mouth. I was halfway to 2nd Avenue when I let myself look behind me, and it must have been some instinct that made me turn my head just then, because here they came. Three of them, anyway. *Oh shit, they're trying to circle me, the other two are going to head me off at the intersection.* Now I risked a glance forward. Sure enough, Manu and Duncan turned right onto St. Mark's, boxing me in. I looked behind me again and saw that the three had slowed down, spreading out now so Camilla was in the middle of the street and one boy was on each sidewalk. Alfie was skipping. Fucking *skipping*.

I realized the only way out was up or down. Down sounded bad. Down sounded like getting penned in where nobody could see what they did to me, not that that mattered. Witnesses certainly hadn't helped anything at Union Square station.

Anyway, I jumped. I jumped straight up, grabbed the bottom of an iron balcony, and swung myself up like I was doing a sawhorse routine in the urban Olympics. I skittered up the side of the wall, broke through an apartment window, blundered through dark rooms while a woman screamed, knocked a hatstand full of hats out of my way, and went out the back window. Behind me, barely audible, I heard a child coo something comforting and the screaming stopped. I had no time to use the fire escape so I leapt again, back-down to save my legs, hit the hood of a cab, felt the skin over my spine split and a rib or two break, but I got lucky and the spine stayed whole; the cabbie jammed the brakes, so I spun off, found my footing, and sprinted toward 2nd again, blinking away the memory of the cabbie's startled jellyfish face bluish behind the windshield. No Manu in front of me, he must have gone for the building, but Duncan came running, his mouth open like a kid running giddy down a hill in high summer or sledding through trees in the snow with a belly full of hot cocoa. He *loved* this. The hunt. I ran at him, took a swimmer's eyeful behind me, saw Camilla pointing, the crazy-fast scramble of Alfie turning on the gas, but Peter was bent over, holding his stomach. *He's starving. So soon.* I slammed into Duncan, grabbed him around the shoulders, went to chuck him out of my way, but he dug his little hands into my forearms. Someone said, "Stop that. You!" and I couldn't look but knew by his voice it was a cop. I spun with the kid, tried to chuck him, but he held on, almost pulled me down to the ground. "I said *stop!*" I got an arm away from Duncan just as Alfie and the cop arrived. Duncan now wrapped both arms around my one arm, became deadweight. The cop grabbed my free wrist. I knew what I had to do. I jerked the cop closer; he was a sturdy guy with bushy eyebrows and salt-and-pepper hair cut short. I remember his surprised eyes when he found he couldn't stop me from bending him down to me. He smelled like English Leather aftershave and licorice, or booze that smelled like licorice. I saw Alfie's drooling, hungry face loom up, saw his hand flick as he motioned Manu to go farther up the sidewalk and close off 2nd. Duncan now had his legs wrapped around my thigh as if he were climbing a jungle gym; he sank his teeth into my forearm, hooking them behind the bone. Just like they taught him. *Christ* it hurt. He wasn't much good as a fighter, not on his own, but he made a hell of an anchor.

The cop's head was in front of me; I had him by the nape now, I butted off his cap. "Sorry," I said, and used my left tooth like a letter opener, cutting him from forehead to temple. He put his hands on my face, tried to push me away, but now Alfie was on him, unable to control himself as the curtain of blood washed down the man's face. He licked him with the flat of his tongue, licked his face like a dog lapping up gravy. Duncan, unsure of what to do, let go of me and joined Alfie. I pulled the nightstick out of the cop's belt and launched myself backward, nearly falling on my ass. Manu went to grab me, but I wasn't about to let him. He was clearly used to getting help from his older, stronger playmates, but all three of them were too busy dragging the cop into the alley so they could poke fresh holes in him, peel him, get their strength back while less-hungry Duncan played monkey-see, monkey-do.

It was just me and Manu; he was stronger, but I was bigger and I was fighting for my life. Plus, I had a nightstick. I gave it to him, too; I beat him for all I was worth.

"Ah," Manu said, and "Ow," and, incredibly, "Please," and I would have said, *Did you go easy when Chinchilla said please, or Edgar, or*

Malachi? but I was too busy swinging like John Henry, breaking his arms, busting the teeth out of his face. "Hey!" somebody yelled at me from a window, "Hey," and a beer bottle broke on the street near me. I broke the wooden nightstick on the ground now, made a jagged point, braced myself to drive it into Manu's chest, but he took a step back from me, tried to protect his chest with his wrecked arms, like a praying mantis I had seen in a picture. A van was coming up the street, one headlight out. I moved toward Manu, knocked one of his arms out of my way, but before I could strike he leapt back into the path of the van, on purpose. It hit him with a sick noise, turned him end over end. The driver got out immediately, left his door swinging open. A bottle hit my head. Somebody said, "Get that kid," and for a split second I thought they meant Manu, that they knew what a vicious little killer he was, but then I felt a hand on my shoulder. I punched somebody's beery gut and he went *Whooof!* and I ran into the blackest alley I could find. I easily outran the citizens, windmilling my limbs, getting tired now, the Johnny Horton song about the British fleeing the battle of New Orleans looping in my head with an idiot's voice, over and over again. I could outrun people all night long. But I knew that if the kids spotted me it was all over; they were freshly fed, mighty little engines banging away with all pistons. I, on the other hand, was running out of gas almost as fast as I was running out of luck.

That's why I went down the cellar doors.

There they were, right on 2nd Avenue, under some kind of Russian or Ukrainian diner advertising *FRESH-SQUEEZE O. JUICE*. I popped the rusty, brown chain and opened the rusty, brown doors, shutting them behind me. I found myself crawling between cardboard boxes, cans of tomatoes, mesh sacks of potatoes, and more mesh sacks of small brown oranges. I hadn't used my lungs in a while, so I sniffed. I picked up the floor's bouquet of bleach undercut with recently swabbed-up rat shit. Just a hint of live rat, too. I followed that smell on my hands and knees, hoping to find a way out, even if it led back underground. I moved a dead mini-refrigerator aside and found a panel that didn't match the rest of the wall. Hiding place or crawl space? Only one way to find out. At just that moment, I heard the cellar door swing open.

Oh shit oh shit oh shit.

I fumbled around at the edges of the panel.

"Hullo?" a British voice asked playfully.

I found purchase, pulled the panel out, smelled a wash of fresher rat shit, saw a hiding space, crawled in, replaced the panel, all as quietly as I could manage. I crawled toward the back of the space, saw the round, black mouth of a pipe.

"Jo-eeey?" Manu said. "Our game was not finished. You played rough and didn't give me my turn."

I reached into the pipe, felt stacks of paper. Figures, the one day in my life I found a jackpot and it was just in the way. I pulled out the rubber-banded bricks of hundreds and fifties as fast as I could.

A little hand knocked at the other side of the panel. Someone giggled.

I took off the shirt, the droopy-ass jeans. The panel came off. I jumped into the pipe, getting small. *They're smaller,* I thought, *I'm done,* but still I slithered and grunted and made my way through. I was maybe ten feet in when the pipe opened up into a larger space. I poked my head through, got one arm in. That was when I felt the hand on my ankle.

"Whither runst thou?" Camilla whispered. "Becalm thee."

I pulled with the arm that was through, but I couldn't break her grip. She pulled, too, but couldn't yank me free. This went on for I don't know how long. It felt like an hour. I grunted, I yelled, I snorted. "Shhhh," she said. She said something in French, I think. Behind her, Peter laughed.

We fell into a kind of truce where I didn't pull forward and she didn't pull back. Time wasn't on her side, though, not with that appetite. She let go. I scrambled forward, into the larger space, and here she came after. Her arm came out first. I kicked at it, wrenched it, broke it, but more of her just kept coming out. I lay on my back and stamped with both feet like a donkey, but her second arm was out now and her first arm had already healed and she caught my foot and twisted. I pulled my foot away and yelled.

The horrible mouth in the pipe hissed again.

Shhhlshhhl

I crawled on my hands and knees now; I was in a sort of natural fissure or something in the rock. It was getting smaller. Becoming a dead end.

I heard her come out of the pipe and start crawling behind me.

I ran out of crawl space. It just ended in a sort of wedge. I backed into it, crying, trying to kick at her. She got on top of my legs, wrestled my arms down. She had gotten small around me, flowed into the space with me.

"Please don't," I said.

I saw one eye, shut as tight as a puppy's, I saw her roll her football-shaped head, felt a tooth drag my skin. She was working her way toward my neck. I breathed in, puffed up, tried to fill the space and keep her out of it, but she slipped her arms around me, squeezed me down, pushed the air out of my lungs. Got a little farther. I tried with all my might to push her down, but couldn't budge her. When I rested from this exertion, she wriggled a little farther up, and then we did it all again. This went on for five minutes, ten, till she had folded my arms all the way down, filled the space around my neck. I know this sounds weird, but I smelled how old she was, smelled time pouring out of her like a bag of moths. I heard the sucking sound of her forming and re-forming her mouth around her teeth, felt her cold lips probing my neck, trying to get the right angle.

There came a point when I realized it was hopeless and relaxed. Let her do it. You would have, too. A long time before I did. She fed in hungry, spastic gulps. I could hear my blood trickling out of her; she wasn't even trying to hold it in. She couldn't feed efficiently like this. But she could bleed me out. I caved in like a jellyfish. I couldn't see or hear anything anymore. I don't think I dreamed.

When I came to, I was sitting on a ledge in a bricked-up room I recognized only too well, except that it was brighter than normal. Chloë sat to my right, holding fresh flowers in one skeletal hand. The other hand was in mine, our fingers interlaced, our hands bound together with human hair.

Margaret's hair.

More flowers, mostly red roses, had been laid around us in a circle. Teacups and plastic Slurpee cups full of what looked like red wine sat among a riot of mismatched candles, all burning. My mouth hung open. It hurt. I couldn't move even my tongue, but I was pretty sure my fangs had been taken out. They wouldn't grow back unless I got blood, but I wasn't ever going to get blood again.

A fly flew into my mouth, back out again, landed on my eye.

I couldn't blink. I wished for it to fly away and, in its own good time, it did.

The kids sat at the bottom of the room, as I had sat so many times communing with Chloë. They sat like a class on a field trip, arranged in a loose horseshoe.

"Are you happy, god of small places?" Peter asked.

"We know Joey isn't happy, poor Joey, but god-inside-Joey, are *you* happy?" said Camilla.

"If you're happy and you know it, clap your hands," Alfie said, quite solemnly, and they all clapped three times hard.

CLAP!

CLAP!

CLAP!

Camilla raised her hands, palms open like a tiny priestess, and said, "Blessed be the tunnels and the staircases going down and the trains that bring us life. Blessed be the mothers and fathers diddling each other so babies might be born and grow and give us life. Blessed be the god of small places."

CLAP!

CLAP!

CLAP!

"Blessed be Millie, who died the death in Wessex. Blessed be Sammy, who died the death in Manahatta."

Duncan sobbed at this. Camilla walked over and pinched his cheek so hard she tore it a little, said, "No crying here. Not here."

"Sorry," Duncan peeped. She took her place again.

"Blessed be the god of small places."

CLAP!

CLAP!

CLAP!

Now they all rose at once. Alfie beat a drum and Manu played a little horn and they danced together, wildly, as kids dance, until they got bored with that.

"Now the kiss," Camilla said. Each of them kissed the others chastely on the lips, little hands holding little cheeks. Then they each, in turn, came up to where we sat.

"Good-bye, Mary," Camilla said. "Give the god to Joey now."

"Still funny he calls her Chloë. Joey and Chloë! Ha ha ha!"

That was Manu.

"Not here," Camilla said, shooting him a look that killed his laughter.

"Good-bye, Joey," she said, and kissed my cheek tenderly, so tenderly.

They each did this in turn.

My mouth hung open.

Manu took out a Polaroid camera and took a picture of me. The flash blinded me for a moment, but I heard the sound of the camera spitting out my photograph. I heard the *flap-flap-flap* of Manu shaking it.

"It's going to be a good one," he said.

In my head I was screaming *DON'T GO DON'T GO DON'T GO* but go they did, slipping out of the hole left by the missing bricks in the wall opposite.

NO!

Then I heard a sound that would have made my heart beat if I had enough blood left in me for that. Scraping, but not just any scraping. The scraping of a trowel with wet mortar on bricks. I saw the trowel flashing, saw each brick settle into place. And then they were gone. They left the candles burning. It took about six hours for the last one to burn down. That's a guess. Without blood, we don't see in the dark so well anymore.

I had forgotten what real dark looked like.

If you're the kind of person who believes things are as they seem, and who doesn't buy it when good things happen at the last minute, then you should stop reading now. It makes sense that I should kick off here, and if you can figure out how I still wrote all this down, or if you don't really give a shit because you think this is all bullshit anyway, then, yes, stop here.

Everything sucks just as bad as it seems to, no more, no less.

I died slowly, in the dark that has no end, thinking at great length about what a poor show I'd made of my one-song life and its ten-song encore.

Final stop.

Everybody off the train.

This is the real world, right?

DISNEYLAND

Still here, are you?

All right, you sap, let's go.

So there I was in the dark that had no end, like I said, only it had an end after all. But before the darkness cracked, something metal *chip-chip-chipped* a chink in the silence and also in the brick wall facing me, and I heard low voices. The smallest bit of light came in then, light from a small flame I think, but whether it was a candle or an oil lamp I couldn't say. My eyes had dried out enough so everything was blurry; my eyes felt like two blisters. Starving to death is probably never a great way to go, but it *really* hurts as a vampire.

More bricks came out. A face filled the hole in the masonry, a face bedecked with blind-as-a-mole glasses. George the Jesus-looking carpenter came in and I would have laughed if I could have done anything but stare straight ahead with my matchbook-dry kisser hanging open, I would have laughed myself into a belly-ache saying, *Hey guys! Jesus saves! No shit, he really saves!*

George climbed down with some difficulty, really it was more of a scarcely controlled fall; he was strong in the arms and shoulders but not much in the legs department. After him, I saw the sweetest sight I ever saw—a chump in a suit slipping through the hole, never a guy I thought of as graceful until I saw him follow Blond Jesus's scuffing, elbow-skinning example.

Cvetko.

No, let me say it more like it sounded in my head:

CVETKO!!!!!!

"Hurry," he said to himself more than to George, who was slobbering all over himself, and he climbed the wall under me and made his way to the nook I shared with Chloë. He lifted the flowers off me, he undid my hand of cold flesh from hers of cool bone, bit through the twine. He might as well have been lifting a wooden sculpture when he lifted me from the ledge, but he moved my stiff limbs so my arms hooked around him, my face buried in his neck, I was like Pinocchio. He leapt with me, caught us on his strong legs. He was standing with my arms around him, like I was his drunk friend; he bit George and filled his mouth, shotgunning the blood into mine. He did this again and again until George began to wilt, then set us both down and continued. My tongue began to wiggle a little in its bath of warm liquid, my eyes lubricated, I made myself blink a dry, painful blink, and then a smoother one. A tear rolled down my cheek, whether from sheer joy or my eye healing itself I couldn't say.

When Cvetko thought George couldn't take any more, he bit his own wrist and drew hard, filling his cheeks again so he looked like a giant chipmunk. He squirted this into my mouth and now I closed my lips, actually swallowed, moved my head a little. You get the idea. He brought me back. Cvetko came back for me and he gave me back my life on a silver platter. He didn't even kill Blond Jesus doing it, though I think he maybe came close.

I ran my tongue over the sockets where my fangs used to be. Felt little points coming in. I didn't mean to smile, but I did. Life as a vampire is pretty awful, but it still seems to beat the alternative. For now, at least. I think we all get night fever eventually. Except the kids. Those kids stay kids, keep a sense of wonder and re-invent themselves every day, even if their wonder feeds on cruelty and they reinvent themselves into different kinds of viciousness. That's what Cvetko thinks, anyway, and Cvetko's pretty smart.

We talked it all out later, of course. Here's a snatch of that:

"How did you do it? Save me, I mean."

"I knew they would take you. I guessed that they would make a little god of you, that they would bleed you and leave you there. It is possible they do that everywhere they go, make sacrifices in thanks for the hunt, make shrines enclosing defeated rivals. I saw photographs among Manu's things, vampires bedecked with flow-ers and wearing expressions of bewilderment; vampires who did not appear to have been beheaded or burned or staked with wood; vampires who appeared to have been exsanguinated, which is not a swift death and one which best preserves our remains. I deduced from the ages of the vampires in the photographs that the children preferred their godlings to be pubescent, something between chil-dren and adults. Perhaps they imagine you as gateways or con-duits to the godhead, as they perceive it. I had seen the remains of the girl you call Chloë and connected her with them, realized they had killed her, taken her fangs, deified her. It seemed likely that they would do the same to you, and, when they turned their atten-tion back to the business of meeting their massive need for blood, I might have a chance to reclaim you."

"How old are they, Cvets? Really?"

"From what you've told me, perhaps a thousand years, perhaps twelve hundred. The siblings, that is to say. They are the oldest. They may be among the oldest living beings outside the plant kingdom. I believe them to be Saxons. I once caught them talking privately, thought I heard Old English, the language of *Beowulf*, but I simply couldn't believe that. I convinced myself I had heard a German dialect and they were careful never to speak their true language in my presence again. Had I only let myself believe it sooner, I might have known how lethal they were."

I asked him how he stayed hidden from them, yet close enough to come find me when the time was right. He showed me his hand. I didn't get it. He sighed and pointed at the ring on his pinky, the ring his wife gave him. I got it then, and I was proud of myself for getting it. He fetched it out of the East River. He hid down there. Just like Clayton had said vampires could, even though we don't like the water. He hid in a sunken car, not breathing, safe from sunlight, getting fucked with by eels. You can't sleep like that, but you can sure as hell hide until sunset and get a fresh start.

"And that's where I figured out how they crossed," he said.

"Crossed?"

"The Atlantic."

"They flew."

"Do you really imagine creatures so old and canny would suffer the risks of discovery and exposure inherent in a transatlantic flight? Even on the Concorde, they could not be guaranteed to avoid delay, emergency landing, the possibility of being expected to cross a sunlit tarmac."

"They had a ticket! I saw it."

"You saw the corner of a ticket. Did you read it?"

"Oh," I said.

"Exactly. Neither did I."

"But what boat?"

* * *

Now you have to read a little bit of a *Post* article.

I apologize.

It's from February 1978, just about the time all of this started.

HELL YACHT BURNS NEAR MANHATTAN

The hulk of a luxury yacht suspected of shuttling sex slaves from Europe or North Africa to the United States was pulled from the Lower Bay on Monday.

The *Étoile Mordante*, a 120-foot luxury yacht registered in Antibes, France, had recently arrived in New Jersey following a journey across the Atlantic from Plymouth, UK, via the Azores and Bermuda.

The yacht, a multimillion-dollar dream ship outfitted with a Jacuzzi and capable of sleeping 15 passengers, had been transformed into a hellish seagoing dungeon, complete with restraints, padlocked doors, and buckets full of human waste. After mooring at the Sandy Hook Yacht Club for several weeks, the *Étoile Mordante* made its final voyage in the wee hours of the morning, where it was burned and scuttled, apparently by members of its own crew, sinking in minutes. The remains of nine individuals have been recovered, including five of the original seven crew members, two missing residents of Bermuda, and a Canadian commercial actress who disappeared while vacationing in the city of Hamilton on Bermuda's main island.

One of the *Étoile*'s two dinghies was recovered at Battery Park, and a search is under way. The two missing crew members, James Kant, 28, and William Mc-

Whirter, 40, are wanted in the investigation, although neither individual has a criminal history and no motive seems apparent.

The superyacht's owner, children's clothing magnate Henri Marceau, 49, was last seen in Plymouth and remains unaccounted for. Authorities will not comment on the possibility that other perpetrators may have been involved, but an unnamed source with experience in modern piracy speculates that the *Étoile Mordante* may have run afoul of baddies based in the troubled nation of Mauritania, where slavery remains legal. Increasingly daring groups have been operating near the Canary Islands and striking as far north as the Azores.

Why seagoing criminals might come to our shores cannot be known, but some theorize that increasing lawlessness and the growth of the Manhattan sex trade could be providing opportunities for foreign traffickers who may not have been so bold in better times.

Mayor Koch, in a public statement issued yesterday, said, "No effort will be spared to locate the individuals responsible for the brutalities committed on this unfortunate vessel." But with the hiring freeze stripping officers from all five boroughs, many believe that the arrival of this gruesome ship is only a sign of things to come.

Continued on page 3

So they started in England. And now they were here.

"We have to tell somebody."

Cvetko just looked at me.

"What are we going to do about them?" I said.

He didn't speak.

He said nothing because *nothing* was the answer.

Nothing was all we were holding, and that was exactly what we did.

There's no point in rolling out the rest of the story in detail because it got easier, and easy is boring. I went with Cvetko to Boston, where we met a new group of vampires; they owned apartments in Brookline, actually rented to vampires specifically. Regular people, too, but there were secret tunnels between rooms and in the walls so those regular people had regular visitors of the nocturnal variety. Visitors who owned the place and didn't have to be invited in. Everyone in that building looked a little peaked, if you know what I'm saying, but rent was cheap. We stayed there for six months or so, long enough, as it turned out, for God to kill a couple of popes, and you should have seen once-was-Catholic Cvetko hunched over the radio, grinning like a baby over the new pope's speeches from the Vatican, except when he grimaced because he wasn't satisfied with the translations.

We went our separate ways in the spring; it's okay, I know where he lives, he even has a phone now. But I had to leave.

Because I met somebody.

And by somebody I mean a vampire. Her name doesn't matter. Her specific looks are unimportant but she should be beautiful in your mind's-eye pinup. She should look as good in a summer dress as in a man's button-down shirt, she should know how to take off a tie, and she should look fucking adorable trying to put one on. She might not look so good in a bikini, not in strong light, but you never see her in strong light. As to her actual age, let's make her old enough to know how to get by but not some ancient thing that looks at even other vampires as house pets. Roughly my age, in other words. Let's turn her someplace interesting, maybe in Oklahoma during the Dust Bowl, let's put her on a bus with her mean-ass mama praying next to her while red sand blows against the window. Let's have that bus stop and pick somebody up at night, a guy who wears his hat brim down.

Wherever it happened, she was turned young like me, like Chloë; adolescent, mature enough to express sexuality, but not so mature that you should dwell on that if you're not adolescent yourself. With just a thimbleful of charm she could pass for ten or twenty-two. And she had a car, let's make it a 1974 Buick Centurion, big enough for two people who aren't afraid of small places to sleep in the trunk. Small is all right. I had been the *god* of small places, after all, if only for a night and a day. It was easy to get across the country in a car like that, with a girl like that. Nobody suspects couples. And she taught me things. I learned to drive without running over people, for example. I learned to look down and to the right when headlights came, blinding as they were to us. I learned how to feed on the road. It was easy to follow a guy up to the restroom of a gas station, getting as close to him as his shadow, laying your hand over his while he turns the key on the end of its log or soup ladle or whatever, enthralling him Venus-flytrap fast when he turns surprised eyes on you. It was easy to hunt in motels on Route 66 with bugs circling the outside lights and clerks drowsing before black-and-white countertop televisions, bored teenagers kicking their feet in the shallow end of the pool in the last hour before they switch the pool light off. Turns out I like pool lights.

Turns out I like California.

Are you ready?

Here comes your happy ending.

Mostly happy, anyway. Not so happy for New York City, which we left in the custody of monsters, but I'm not even sure they were the worst monsters in that city. Either way, the suffering of others is easy enough to endure when it happens in the rearview mirror. If you're like most Americans, the kind of person who likes to believe in the world as it should be, in redemption and the triumph of the familiar over that which is strange or foreign, then put this story down after you read the rest of this page. Watch a game show, watch screaming women with wide eyes and huge smiles bear-hug Bob Barker in thanks for appliances and money. If you don't understand why women in old German pictures look at Hitler with game-show eyes, if you think Disneyland is possible without Auschwitz sitting at the other end of the seesaw, or if the assassination of President Kennedy slides around in your guts like a dead crab because you hate it when bad things happen and the answers don't add up, stop reading as soon as you see *The End*.

Things *can* end happily, as much as anything ends at all. We went to the moon after Dallas, right? Just like Kennedy said. So get the echo of those three shots out of your ears and look at that. The moon, I mean. Imagine me with my girl, pick whatever hair color you like for her, pick any town in California, so long as it's on the coast. Wait, I know exactly the town!

Here's your last image:

Night swimming, Oceano, California, 1979. Two very pale teenagers rise out of the water dripping, giggling, licking salt off each other's temples, teasingly dragging kitten-sharp fangs nobody else can see across each other's necks. These kids like each other, and they like swimming, they can hold their breath a long time.

The boy from New York takes the beautiful Okie girl by the hand and leads her into a draped and triple-locked seaside cottage while first light threatens and the powder-orange full moon sets over the Pacific. Let's have the young lovers cross in front of a balding man with bifocals and a hump in his neck walking the beach beside a formless grandmother with a waterfall of varicose veins; if you're a philosophical person, you might guess both couples are roughly the same age.

As the live ones walk inexorably north, the dead ones cross lengthwise, unlock their door, and head for the shower, where they will wash the sand and salt from their lukewarm bodies before settling into the plush and bugless shared box in which they will make love and sleep the day away. Outside, a German shepherd gets away from his master, jumps between the bougainvillea bush and the mailboxes, sniffs at the wet footprints on the walk, goes to bark at the strange and unpleasant scent he finds there, but instead climbs up on the trunk of the car and bays at the moon until it sinks. He sits there, wagging, until the leash goes on and he's led away.

A convertible drives by, a coked-up young woman on her way home from a party smiles at the man and the dog, Led Zeppelin's "Fool in the Rain" pouring from her speakers.

I'm going to type *The End* now, and that's it.

The End

Please put the goddamned book down.

So.

    You're here.

How unfortunate.

I assume you are the sort of person who would go backstage after the opera in hopes of hearing the prima donna crying on the telephone, or walking in on the baritone fellating the basso buffo. I respect that—I was always the same way myself—though I suspect you are not very happy. Happiness is the province of those who ask few questions. I remember, even before *this* was visited upon me, how I envied those who eagerly did what they were told: those who married without complaint at father's behest; those who looked up rather than sideways in church; those, in short, who honestly believed in God, good kings, and righteous wars.

Envy and respect are not the same things, however.

Before I endow you with respect, I should find out whether your curiosity is intellectual or merely morbid. Not that those who gawk at train derailments are so very different from those who conduct autopsies; both want, at some level, to know what has happened, and, by extension, what *will* happen. Did the liver fail because of the decedent's alcoholism or was some toxin administered? If toxin, who delivered it? If the deliverer is found, he or she may be imprisoned or, in more honest times, hanged, and thus pose no further threat. Or, for the gawker at the accident, espying loose parts not unlike his or her own parts strewn amid wreckage may lead to a sense of awe at death's power, or horror at life's fragility, either of which may be instructive in any number of ways. I am a great believer in the tonic effect of a timely *memento mori*.

Forgive me if the image of the train derailment seems repetitive after the carnage at Union Square; I spend a good deal of time around trains. I have always enjoyed them.

No sense delaying this any further. Whatever your species of curiosity, you've come this far expressly to have your heart broken, as you were promised from the start.

As *I* promised you, even if I am not who you think I am.

I am not Joseph Hiram Peacock, although a boy by that name did exist, was made a vampire in the early 1930s, and did, in fact, live in the tunnels and warrens beneath the sidewalks of Manhattan from roughly 1965 until he was entombed alive in the first part of 1978. Like you and me, he was inquisitive, though he was simple enough to maintain a species of happiness. This happiness chiefly fed itself on fashion, pop culture, and semiconsensual interaction with the opposite sex. He kept an asymmetrically detailed journal that I have taken the liberty of editing and presenting in a more palatable fashion, framing only the months in which the most dramatic events unfolded, his last months in the tunnels. Unless you, too, are an oversexed media-addicted adolescent, you will thank me to have removed lengthy descriptions of coats and blue jeans, sophomoric movie reviews, and meticulous, homogeneously graphic accounts of interactions with scores of young women. Admittedly, the cultural commentaries may have interested those unfamiliar with vampirism. Since Joseph became undead (Stoker's preferred term) at fourteen, he *remained* fourteen thereafter, becoming enslaved to each new fashion and music trend as it appeared. I present, for your consideration, an excerpt from one journal, dated November 1965:

> Rainy day, the good kind with no sun and no chance of sun. Woke up early like 3pm and got my hair cut, but I won't go back to that place, the barber was kind of a square. I told him specificly [sic] to keep it longer like the Beatles and it wasn't like he hadn't seen them, he had Oct. Tiger Beat right on the table, I even pointed at Paul McCartney and said like that. He said yeah, yeah, but just did what he wanted, anything not a crew cut was probably long to this guy, so I charmed him a little and found out where he lived, but I was not waiting around there & DEFINITELY not taking a train out to Queens later just to stick him. I don't even know if he knew how badly messed up his so-called haircut was.

And another, on a similar theme, from 1957:

> I knew I looked good, had just gotten all Elvissed up with my hair swept up and pomped, Sweet Georgia Brown'll never let you down, and little sideburns. Not big wolfman ones, just little. I think if I'd finished growing I might have looked a little like Elvis, him or James Dean. Anyway, I met Darla, an Irish-Italian girl from

Hell's Kitchen, in front of the Landmark tavern.
Kind of a rough neighborhood, she said, she was
impressed that I didn't care. Said her brother
was in The Nordics, some hard-ass gang that
liked to rumble like some kids play stickball. I
bit her, had a beer with her, and bit her again,
she didn't know anything about it. Felt her up a
little, but that's it. I stupidly agreed to meet
her brother, pure greaser, had a studded belt he
broke a kid's nose with and wanted you to know
it. But Darla she had breasts like you just can't
think of anything else, you can't wait to get
them out from behind that big wired bra like
their [sic] in jail and you're their lawyer.

You can see that the mortician's art has made of Joseph a smarter, prettier thing than he was. The other children in this story are real and very much undead, or are as I write these words, even Sammy. His death was a little white lie; a gift to you, the reader, who needed something uplifting in the narrative. It would have been more credible to have the soldier, Old Boy (a formidable warrior despite his youth; he did several of the children great if impermanent harm before succumbing to the charmed mob of commuters), kill him, but you needed something more from your protagonist than he was really able to give. Also, it was Manu who beat *him* in St. Mark's Place; *he* was saved when the van struck Manu. Joseph was no fighter. His one true virtue was loyalty, a virtue I understand well, though my practice of that virtue is, of necessity, selective. He loved his fellows and, in the end, died for them. I think he might have done so knowingly.

I doubt that I would knowingly die for the children, but I certainly take risks on their account. It is difficult to keep them alive, ravenous as their old age makes them (their apple-sized, leaky stomachs, their great, gas-guzzling strength), although I do not imagine they are the only ones to have run such a long race; one suspects the ironically named Countess of Bathory where she lounges in her tub, turning her lovely white limbs (perhaps not so lovely if you startle her) incarnadine; one wonders if Rome's Mithric cult with its bull's-blood shower was not a way for one or several to hide in plain sight. But the children, as I have said, require looking after. Certain among us have done so for innumerable years. Do not imagine some secret, cultish brotherhood worshipping them with robes and signet rings, although, come to think of it, Camilla *did* give me a ring the first year I knew her, a heart-shaped ring of beaten gold that only fits my pinky. Rather, imagine them playing their way through life, picking up strays. Making themselves beloved to more mature, organized individuals, becoming emotionally necessary to those individuals; in many cases, I imagine, taking the place of children left behind in the daylight.

Of course, I can only speak with certainty about myself, and I choose to leave my personal history obscure.

Suffice it to say that I keep them alive because I love them, inasmuch as I love. And also because caring for them preserves me. In seeing to their needs I have a sense of purpose where I would otherwise be subject to the grinding mental claustrophobia that kills so many of my tribe. To care for children who are perpetually children makes a mule of me, and mules do not wither away in existential misery. They do not look behind them. Mules pull.

And how does this mule pull?

I arrange the labyrinthine details of travel for creatures that need blood and may not encounter sunlight, whether they go by train, trawler, truck, or yacht. I act as liaison with adults, playing the role of father, teacher, even priest (crosses only harm former believers; I never thought of the wafer as more than bread). Most importantly, I scout the nests of the lesser dead that inevitably drain from a city's streets to the low places beneath them, the places *we* covet for their darkness, their privacy, their access to prey.

I infiltrate those nests and earn the trust of the fledglings therein, learning their weaknesses, their strengths, their politics. And, when the time comes, I facilitate their demise. The last time we came to Manhattan—1940, you will easily guess the reason we left Paris—we contented ourselves with killing a few of those we found here, "Chloë" among them, and frightening off the rest. One of these, I am not sure which, returned after we left and scrawled several warnings, notably DON'T TRUST THE CHILDREN. He or she also wrote JOHN IS FALSE, such being my alias at the time, and drew a rather credible image of small, fanged children beheading kneeling, fanged adults. These last two went unnoticed by the group, graffiti artists having largely covered the text (TABBY KAT WUZ HERE) and profaned the mural, predictably affixing self-congratulatory male genitalia on the standing figures, summoning detached phalli to float behind the bottoms of the kneelers, threatening penetrations that will, of course, never occur. No further clemency will be given those who might warn future colonies—our migratory pattern has tightened as the children's need for blood has grown. The busker known as Billy Bang will be inquired after and, unless he had the good sense to quit the city entirely, found.

This denouement must be terribly disappointing for you, like watching treasured pets dragged off by anonymous coyotes, their carefully selected collars found in heaps of fur, bones, and similar collars. But this is the way of nature. I tried to warn you here and there, but these warnings were admittedly subtle, easy to willfully ignore.

You have known all along that something in this story wasn't right, that your true narrator was someone other than he claimed to be. Perhaps this knowledge was subconscious. Perhaps, even now, you will feign ignorance, attempt to deny your complicity in the construction of this lie. Even if it strains credibility that a creature as averse to reading as Joseph Hiram Peacock should construct a sentence like the one you are reading now, with its "five-dollar words" and its gentle nod to the subjunctive, let us suppose that some undocumented muse of vocabulary whispered in our simple friend's ear when he wrote of his "anatomically naïve" fantasies about the colored servant Elise. If you venture to imagine Elise for yourself, try not to confuse her piercing, world-weary eyes with those of Ažbe's painted Negress where she hangs in her Yugoslavian gallery; such an overlay might suggest an inability in the narrator to truly see those of different races except through the lens of a fellow central European. If you remember that Ažbe was Slovenian, you might begin to suspect Cvetko. But where does suspicion end? If his story about living in Bushwick and fleeing a plague of arson is false, you might begin to doubt everything about him, from the prescription in his ubiquitous glasses to his apparent age to his nationality. Is it possible that an experienced vampire might have learned to manipulate the charm that projects his appearance? Which of Joey's young, ignorant clan would have been qualified to diagnose a false Slovenian accent, to differentiate it from one fostered in Hungary, Poland, Russia, or (if we wax *romantic*) even Romania?

Romania!

Now, *that* opens up possibilities. If you are an American, with your limited awareness of events outside your own nation and your fawning love of celebrity, perhaps you will go too far, unable to imagine that any Romanian vampire might exist besides a certain count whose story was fabulized by a certain Irishman. Perhaps you will place this count in London at the end of the last century, as in Stoker's tedious fairy tale, the children under his care tucked away underground as he frolicked with Mina and Lucy. If you go as far as that, you may allow for another unlikely collision with fame: What if the children loved Kensington Gardens as they love Central Park and ran across one J. M. Barrie taking the night air? He was, it seems, ever one to seek out children, particularly those of a haunting or *fée* nature. Could our little Dark-Ages Peter have been the actual progenitor of Peter Pan? God knows he and his siblings have made enough *lost boys* in their time; I have kept track of those they mention and my best guess is seventy. Most die the death or fade away after a decade or two. The smart ones flee when it dawns on them that they are tertiary, that they are less the playmates of the Saxons and more servants or *huscarls*, expected to throw themselves on enemy spears to save Kings Peter and Alfred and especially Queen Aelfgifu (or Camilla, if you prefer her borrowed name).

Perhaps these suggestions of Peter Pan and Dracula are too much even for you. You want answers that make sense, but they must be *plausible*; if you can't have justice (and you can't) you crave at least a pleasing, believable symmetry.

I suggest you accustom yourself to seeing things through a warped glass. I have remained vague about everything, from the entrances to the tunnels leading underground and the layout of those tunnels (try to draw a map from this narrative, I dare you) to my original identity and the patterns of my travel with the children. Even if you worked up the courage to brave Manhattan's underground, you would, if you were lucky, come during one of our generational absences. If you were unlucky enough to visit while we were there, you would only end up on the end of a pulley awaiting the knife. And you would have to come alone, or nearly so; the mad run in small packs. Nobody sane will believe a word of this narrative to be anything other than fiction, no matter how many disappear.

After all this, you still know nothing of me.

You do not know who I am, when I started, where I come from.

Under every face lies a skull, under the skull, nothing.

All you need to know is that you cannot trust me.

I am only too happy to smile at you, talk philosophy with you, show you my *National Geographics*, all the while knowing I'll be the one to place the last brick in your tomb.

I am pulling off one mask and putting on another.

Ready?

Here goes!

(Farewell, central European dialect.)

In the next city, I'll be a stylish young man from New York, mad for pussy and always game to watch television.

My accent and word choice'll be perfect, I just wrote a whole fucking book to get this shit down, and, let me tell you, it's going to be a lot more fun than playing that old-fart, lapsed-Catholic disgrace-to-vampirism Slovenian I peeled in London. I hated pushing my belly out. I hated having to act reluctant to kill. Truth is, I kinda like peeling fuckers. But, hey, you do what you gotta do when you play a long game, and the new Joseph Hiram Peacock plays a *very* long game.

I can hear the kids playing in their bath, tossing something, I don't know what, back and forth between them. I'm going to bury this now, it'll be fun to read again one day. If you do dig it out, or if some schmuck publishes it, God knows where I'll be by then, or who.

You might even know me.

ACKNOWLEDGMENTS

Thanks, as always, to my ever-charming agent, Michelle Brower, and to my stalwart editor, Tom Colgan, for their unwavering support in this and previous endeavors. A writer is nothing without readers, and the first to read this manuscript helped it tremendously: Jennifer Schlitt, Naomi Kashinsky, Kelly Cochrane Davis, Chris Holcom, Noelle Burk, Ciara Carinci, Cyrus Rua, and Allison Williams, I am grateful. My old friend Jeff Schiemann deserves a nod for his support, as does Sejal Mehta for an entertaining travel story that made me think more creatively about the troubled relationship between vampires and insects. Thanks also to the MTA's helpful and personable Carey Stumm, who rewarded my trip to Brooklyn with boxes of archived subway photos and some very practical observations about navigating the tunnels on foot (which, for most of us, is neither legal nor recommended). If you will indulge me a moment more, I would like to name a few of the booksellers who have been especially kind over the last two and a half years: Joe at Austin's BookPeople, Dan and Stacie at Milwaukee's Boswell Book Company, John and McKenna at Houston's Murder by the

Book, Ted at Garden District Book Shop in New Orleans, and Bill at the River's End Bookstore in Oswego, New York, have all made me feel welcome in their stores and have kept my novels running across their shelves. Finally, I want to thank Judy Lagerman at Penguin Random House for the magnificently ghoulish cover design that graces *The Lesser Dead*. Brava!